"What's the trouble this time, Mrs Carmichael?"

(Emphasis on 'this' to inform me of my status as a persistent offender.) Alie lowered her eyes and spoke softly. "I know you'll find this hard to believe, doctor, but I don't seem to be on . . . I seem to operate on a different time-scale to everbody else. . . "

"Eh, what's that? What do you mean?"

"I mean, well, . . . I seem to have lived into the future for a while, and then again . . . "

"Are the tablets not strong enough? Is that what you're saying?"

# EVERWINDING TIMES

# EVERWINDING TIMES

## Mary McCabe

Published 1994
Argyll Publishing
Glendaruel
Argyll
PA22 3AE

The publisher acknowledges subsidy from the
Scottish Arts Council towards the publication
of this volume.

**British Library Cataloguing-in-
Publication Data.**
**A catalogue record for this book is
available from the British Library.**

ISBN 1 874640 55 6

Typeset and origination by
Cordfall Ltd, Civic Street,
Glasgow G4 9RH
Printed by
Cromwell Press, Broughton Gifford,
Melksham, Wiltshire SN12 8PH

To Colin and Eilidh
who shed new perspective on time

# 1

WHEN DOES IT BEGIN, and where? Should it start with the lips, the promises, the bristles, the wild wind, the warm arms, the talk of rings and veils, the night of the First Giant Leap? When here was there, and now was then.

As good a place to start as any. The night of the First Giant Leap.

Steve's bristles, sandpaper against her chin.

Steve's lips, bruising hers with male passion.

The wind, howling through the closes. Sliding roofslates, shaking trees.

"That's some gale."

"Mmmmm. . . Ailie, my wee warm sheep."

"You notice, we always get big winds in January?"

"Uhuh."

"You mind the awful storm, last year?"

"Aye. That's what took me into surveying."

"Well, even before that I'd been noticing. They're always in January."

"Ailie. I love you."

"Must be Scotland's version of the mistral."

"My Ailie. My very own Ailie." Another kiss, and a sharp pain in the oily crease between her nose and her cheek. A spot starting. Could he see it? Which way was the close light beaming?

"Want to come up for tea?"

"No, better not." He detached himself, turned his collar up and himself into a lookalike for Ilya Kuryakin. "You're right about the gale. I'll away if I've to get home the night."

Jojo was slumped before the telly. Tanks, soldiers. "What a state of affairs!"

Ailie rushed to the mirror. There it was, rosy volcano, yellow crater.

"I often wonder about that student who burnt himself to death."

"I know. It was terrible." Should she try squeezing it? All the books said you should leave well alone, but unsqueezed they lasted so long.

"Can you imagine his thoughts just before he did it? I mean, ordinary suicide is one thing, when you're depressed. Everybody considers that from time to time"

"Do you?"

"Well, of course! Frequently, in the past. But to kill yourself for a point of principle, and in such a way."

"Sandy's speaking in a debate in the Men's Union next week about it. Czechoslovakia, I mean."

Jojo switched off the television.

"Okay, so you're not into world affairs. Was it a good film?"

"James Bond thing. Steve said it was one of the better ones."

"Steve said?"

"I don't want to talk about films." Ailie plumped down beside Jojo on the couch. "Listen, Jojo – we're getting engaged."

"Well, well. Congratulations. When's the happy day?"

"We haven't decided yet. We're picking the ring on

Saturday. Jojo, you must be my best maid."

"Thanks for the honour. Mind you, I don't think pastel shades suit me."

"Then wear flamenco red." Ailie flung her arm around Jojo's shoulder. "Look, I know you don't approve. . . "

"It's your decision." Jojo met her look. "I just never pictured you . . . How will you feel being a member of the older generation at nineteen? A granny at thirty-five?"

"Don't be daft. We won't have a family right away."

"Surely you know it's better to travel hopefully than to arrive? To flirt, and date, run about in a gang, fall in love and be fallen in love with . . . why do young girls want to be publicly tied to one man, for heaven's sake?"

"I never had all that. Nobody flirted with me. Steve's the first."

"So it's just starting to happen. Why nip it in the bud?"

"You'd think I was fourteen, or something. Lots of folk wed at nineteen."

"More fool them. Reckon because Steve's the first, you're scared he'll be the last. It doesn't necessarily work that way."

"It does if you're wee and scrawny and the boys all think you're a bit creepy, to boot."

"But good old perspicacious Steve sees through to the real you."

"I don't know why he fancied me. I've wondered that a hundred times. And himself so good-looking!"

"Ailie. Don't undersell yourself." She smiled. "Even your looks. It's trendy to be skinny."

"It's trendy to be a beanpole, like Twiggy and Jean Shrimpton. You try being five foot-nothing, with a body like a ten-year-old's."

"Are you fond of him?"

"He treats me like a real woman!"

Jojo laughed. "So he hasn't discovered that you're actually

a bug-eyed monster. What'll you pay me to keep quiet?"

"Don't joke about it, Jojo. You take pride in being a rebel. Me, my goal through life is to be normal."

Jojo lost her smile. "That's not much of an ambition."

"It's enough for me."

"Look at Sandy, joining the French Revolution. That's what you should do with your late adolescence."

"The way Paris looked last summer, he was lucky to come home alive." Ailie rose, went to the kitchen, put on the kettle and mixed up cocoa. When she returned Jojo was still sitting on the sofa, hands clasped behind her head. Ailie knelt in front of her and rested her head on Jojo's lap.

"I'm remembering," said Jojo, "the night you came to stay here. It was just as wild a night as this. I found you crying in the dunny."

"I wasn't in the dunny. I was in the close."

"How would you know?"

"That's how you always described it. In the close. I was in a state and didn't want to go home to Mummy and Roddy."

"It was after your interview for nursing."

"I did want very much to be a nurse," said Ailie wistfully.

"Never mind. It brought you to stay here. All's well that ends well."

"I'm very grateful you took me in."

"That's what sisters are for. I'm grateful you came to stay."

"But you can cope on your own. I can't."

"It's surprising what you can do," remarked Jojo, "when you have to."

The kettle whistled. Ailie scurried through, poured out her cocoa, brought it through. She snuggled up to Jojo and put her arm through the crook of her sister's elbow.

"About Steve. . . "

Jojo closed her eyes. "Do we have to discuss him?"

"Honestly, Jojo, I'm not giving anything up. It's not as if I had a talent, or a vocation. Piffling wee job in an office. I might as well rejoin the bourgeoisie and be a surveyor's wife."

"Have you told him about yourself?"

"Told him what?"

"You know."

Ailie withdrew her arm. "I haven't had an attack in years."

"Thanks to the medication. The very mention of it stopped you getting into nursing."

"So you say."

"That's really what I meant. The other bits. The blanks."

"Jojo." She stroked Jojo's hand. "I know what's bothering you. Of course we'll miss each other. If you ever feel lonely you can spend a few weeks with us."

Jojo stood up. "No thanks."

"I mean it. I'd be glad of the help, once the kids arrive. Steve wouldn't mind. He thinks you're funny."

"The thought is not reciprocal. Anyway, I've always been alone, one way or another." She faced the fireplace and stretched. "I function best that way."

Ailie shook her head. "Nobody should be alone. You're bound to meet a nice young man soon."

"Somebody as special as Steve?" Jojo turned and grinned. "Ailie, you look awfully flushed. If I were you I'd take a double dose tonight. You don't want any wee accidents in the bed."

"Do you know what you are? A pin running about jagging other peoples' bubbles."

"So what's new?"

"Please don't be bitter."

"I meant it about the tablets. For your own good."

"I know. I'll take them. Good night, Jojo."

The landlady provided only lino. Shag mat, candlewick bedspread, furry hot bottle. Years (or whatever) later, Ailie was never sure whether the neighbour through the wall really was playing the hit record *Out of Time*.

> *You're out of touch, my baby,*
> *My poor old-fashioned baby. . .*

What tricks the imagination plays on the memory.

(Soon Steve and I will go all the way! Steve, in rapture. Steve caressing me, kissing my breasts. Steve, finding my body voluptuous! . . . Our first house, before the children come. A three apartment, somewhere in Hillhead, maybe, with a cheap mortgage from Steve's firm. An old tenement, with tiled close, stained glass landing windows, picture lights in the doors, carved centre roses, bow windows. Like this one, in fact. . . Our eventual house. Two public rooms downstairs, three bedrooms upstairs. A study each for Steve and me. More central than Milngavie. Jordanhill, maybe. Pity there are no big gardens around Byres Road.)

The pills carried Ailie off to the arms of Morpheus. A blackbird awoke her, and the sunshine got her out of bed.

(Broad daylight! Dear goodness, half-past eight! The bus! Mr Gray!)

Her adrenalin took her halfway across the room before she noticed that everything was different. Green Axminster, wall-to-wall. White marshmallow quilt. Full-length nightie in place of the baby-dolls. Different bed, different room, DIFFERENT HOUSE!

Ailie ran to the door with a scream at her throat and a bloated feeling around her tummy as if it were the setting of her moon (which it was not.)

"Jojo! She opened the door and shouted again, "Jojo! Jojo! Help me!"

Across the hall, another door opened and a stranger appeared. Bleary-eyed, scratching dishevelled hair with one hand and clutching at droopy pyjamas with the other.

"Whassa time?"

"Half-past eight. But . . . "

"Half-past eight! Aw Mum, how did you not waken me up? I'll get my books!"

He vanished back into the room. Ailie stood still for a minute or two, and then tapped and entered.

Dingy little room, with posters darkening the windows and clothes strewn over the floor. In the foreground, the fellow she had met was pulling up his underpants, so Ailie averted her eyes to the further away bed, where a sleepy-headed youngster was unbuttoning his pyjama jacket. The older youth pushed past her, shirt in hand.

"Get out of it, Mum! You're in the way!"

So she had heard it right.

"Where am I? What is this place? Who are you?"

The younger boy raised his head. "You're at home, Mum. What's wrong?"

"Mum? Mum? Why does everybody keep calling me, Mum?"

"Don't screech like that, Mum. What is it? Have you lost your memory?"

"I'm not anybody's Mum. I'm Ailie Lorimer and I'm only 18 years old!"

"It's Davie, Mum. Don't you know me anymore?" He ran past her out into the hall. "Hi, Crawfie! Something's up with Mum!"

"What is it?" came from downstairs as Crawfie banged out of one room and into the next.

"I don't know – she's lost the place again, or something. It's scarey!"

A toilet flushed. Davie ran downstairs and nearly collided with Crawfie rushing for the door.

"Look, I'm in a desperate hurry. I've had my last warning.

Tell me later!" The front door banged shut.

Davie trailed back upstairs and sidled past Ailie.

"Are you my son?"

"Course I am. Aw, Mum, don't go your funny way!"

"My . . . funny way? Listen, Davie, no, don't move away, please. What age are you?"

"Fifteen."

"And Crawfie?"

"Nineteen."

Ailie staggered back into the room she had woken up in. As she slumped into an armchair, a photograph caught her eye – herself a bride, Steve by her side.

"What year is it?"

"1989."

(Nineteen eighty-nine . . . nineteen eighty-nine . . . 20 lost years. A mirror!)

A wrinkled forehead, incipient pads of fat around the jowls. Short hair, salt and pepper over the fair. Two stone of extra flab around the midriff.

"Mum, don't cry!" Davie kept his distance. "Is it another funny turn?"

"Where's your father?" She grabbed him.

"Lemme go! Leave me alone!"

"Where's Steve?"

"I've got to go! If I dog it again I'll get sent to Guidance!"

(I can't even understand the language anymore!) "Look, I'll send a note to your school. Just tell me where I can find Steve!"

"I don't want you to start on about it again."

"About what?"

"Liz. That woman that works beside Dad."

"What about her?"

"The nights he doesn't come home . . . well . . . "

(I don't believe this! I can't believe this! I don't. I can't!)

"See? I just knew you'd start crying again."

"I want a doctor."

"Better not. You don't like doctors. You don't want to go back to the hospital, do you?"

"Back to the . . . " (It's a nightmare, that's what it is. You're a dream. I'm a dream. I must waken myself up.)

She saw a brooch on the dressing-table and plunged the pin into her hand.

"Stop it, Mum! I hate you when you do crazy things!"

(Real pain. Real blood. Of course, the very brooch is only a dream. How do I get back to reality, using unreal means?)

"Get me a doctor, right away!"

"You want me to phone the clinic?"

Ailie opened the wardrobe. Matronly crimplene dresses, and so long!

Outside, houses rose roofless to meet the sky. Beyond and around, bare space, and a mass of woven roads railed off and unreachable.

"That's the motorway. The M8. Cuts right through Glasgow. See my school? Cuts right through the middle of it."

('See my . . . ' I never thought a child of mine would be as broad as that!)

In the clinic, the psychiatrist listened to her story.

"Total amnesia over the last twenty years? Don't you even remember your children?"

"Not a thing since before my marriage."

"Your pregnancies, then? Childbirth?"

"I told you. Nothing."

"I see." The psychiatrist heaved a sigh. "Well, you've fairly done it this time, Mrs Carmichael. This latest episode. . . "

"What other episodes have there been?" Ailie followed his

gaze to a fat file on his desk. "Is that all about me?"

The psychiatrist leaned forward and spoke gently. "Do you yourself not remember having any problems at all?"

"I had meningitis as a child, and after that I used to take attacks of petit-mal. But I was all right as long as I took my tablets."

"And was that all?"

"More or less."

"More or less?"

"Well." (Why is he asking me? He must know all about it already.) "There were the Blanks."

"Tell me about them."

"Periods that I couldn't remember – that other people told me about."

"How long were these periods?"

"Sometimes short, occasionally long. There was one period of eighteen months . . . I'm sure it's all down there in the files."

"I want to know how much you can tell me."

"There you are, then. I do remember having the Blanks." Ailie tried to look young and appealing. This look had saved her from the tawse at school, and had delivered her unto kisses from Steve.

> *(You've got eyes of blue*
> *I never cared for eyes of blue*
> *but you've got eyes of blue*
> *that's my weakness now . . . )*

"What are you going to do with me?"

"Perhaps we should readmit you to hospital."

"Not a mental institution!"

"What kind of talk is that? You didn't mind your other stays."

(A loony bin! Me, living among weirdos, queeries, maybe . . . homocidal maniacs. Faces, like the ones that came in the night . . . ) "How long for?"

"Not too long, I hope. Just until we find out what's wrong and, hopefully, put it right." The psychiatrist scribbled on a pad. "Now, Mrs Carmichael, I want you to keep pestering that family of yours with questions, to read as much as possible about past events, anything to jog the old memory. Got that?"

Out in the waiting-room there were only four people and none was Davie. An old lady, a mother with a baby, a fellow with something familiar about him.

"Oh, I remember you!" (Coarse red face, stomach sagging over a tight belt, blurred jawline. Nights of gluttony and booze. Last time we were at the seaside together I thought he was a Greek god.) "But you looked completely different then."

"Davie phoned me at work and told me you were ill again."

"It was kind of you to come." (What bloodshot eyes! And he has hairs growing out of his nostrils.)

"How do you feel?"

"Fine, apart from the amnesia." (He can only be 46. Looks more like 60.)

"Come and I'll run you home." Steve led her out to a flashy white car. "You have to buckle yourself in, now." He showed her how. "It's the law."

For five minutes Ailie studied his fat-nosed profile, set in the driving position.

"You know, I really don't remember anything since the night we got engaged."

"I know. Davie told me."

"Is Crawfie working?"

"Clerk with a law firm. Next month he's moving into a place of his own, with a couple of pals."

"At his age?"

"You were even younger, surely, when you left home."
He shrugged. "God knows, there's little enough to keep him
with us. Mother in and out of psychiatric hospitals. . . "

"Is that my fault?"

"I know it's not your fault."

Anniesland Cross was a vast roundabout, still with the red
striped tower block in Crow Road. The Odeon Cinema,
where she and Steve had had their first necking session, was
closed down.

"Are you still a surveyor?"

"Na. When there's a slump on you steer clear of the
building trade."

"Is there a recession just now?"

"Over three million unemployed."

"What! It can't be three million."

"Near half a million in Scotland."

"But surely the folk would never stand for that?"

"In Scotland the people stand for anything. I'm telling
you. If the Government ordered them to slaughter their first-
born, you'd get some outraged letters in the *Herald*, then
they'd go and do it. NEMO ME IMPUNE LACESSIT –
what a hoot!"

"I suppose you have a job, though."

"I'm in business for myself. Selling videos."

Ailie waited, but he made no attempt to explain.
"Selling . . . what?"

The profile wrinkled in irritation. "Don't ask. It would
take too long."

"Do you sell a lot of them?" (Hope he doesn't. Hope he's
a failure.)

"I do all right." For a moment she thought he was going
to look at her, but the cool gaze went instead to the nearside
mirror. "Everybody has to have a video-recorder these days.
They're the in thing."

"Oh? That's nice for you, if everybody wants one." (Paisley Road West. Wish I'd noticed it more, in these jaunts down to Largs and Millport. I've no memory to compare it with.) "Do I have a job?"

"You!" He did glance at her this time. "How would you ever hold down a job? Ask me when you need money." He snorted. "Old sugar-daddy, that's me."

For the first time, Ailie noticed her house from the front. Red sandstone mid-terraced. Older than the house she'd grown up in. Big front room with bow window, high ceiling and carved cornicing. The home of her dreams. She sat down and Steve switched on the fire. It was gas, but burned with a naked flame, pretending to be a coal fire. There were individual 'coals' which could be shifted and played about with, using tongs.

"Where does Jojo live?"

"What makes you mention Jojo after all this time?" Steve looked at his watch and rose. "She went abroad."

"Abroad!"

"Yeah. She was talking about a kibbutz or some such enterprise."

"Do we have her address?"

"How would I know? I suppose you'd take it at the time, but she's probably somewhere else by now. She moved about a lot."

"What about Sandy? And my mother?"

"Look, Ailie, I left the girl in charge of the shop. I really must. . . "

"I can't have lost touch with everybody!" wailed Ailie.

"Their addresses'll be kicking about somewhere. You used to be quite close, didn't you? In a quarrelsome way." He rose and made for the door.

"Wait! Can't we talk about this?"

"What's there to say?" He turned the door handle.

Ailie strove unsuccessfully to bring her voice down to a dignified pitch. "You don't seem to care about my loss of memory. You haven't asked me. . . "

"I've had over twenty years of your aberrations, Ailie. There's no curiosity-value left in them."

Still Ailie sought to forestall him. "What about dinner? Do I have to. . . ?"

"In this house we all see to our own food. Look in the freezer – you'll see old sugar-daddy keeps it stocked." He left without a backward look.

After a moment's hesitation, Ailie went to the phone and dialled her mother's number. A strange male voice aswered, informed her that he and his family had owned the house since 1985, had bought it from a Pakistani family whose forwarding address they had lost long ago.

Ailie opened the book at Lorimer. She tried all the Lorimers. None were Sandy or even Jojo. She tried all the R MacLeods. None were her mother.

At the back of five the boys rushed in. Ailie kept out of their way. When they fried themselves hamburgers in the kitchen she perched on the edge of the couch in the living-room. When they moved themselves and their dinners into the living-room she escaped into the bedroom.

Her eyes lit upon a large handbag in the corner. (It can only be mine. Still feels funny, rifling through it. Packet of paper hankies. Comb and mirror. House keys. A sort of identity-card with a picture of me on it – TRANSCARD – whatever that means. A purse . . . my goodness! An absolute fortune! Twenty, thirty pounds – and all in tenners! No, this here's a twenty! Forty-one, two three four pounds! How did I ever get such an amount? And me with no job! Working, I only got £9.10s a week. This section's funny too – couple of florins and a whole lot of foreign-looking coins. Pretty wee square of plastic with 3D pictures on it. It's got my signature on it –

suppose I should ask one of the lads . . . No address-book.)

Ailie paced about a bit before venturing into the living-room. Bleep-bleep! Brrrrr! Bleep-bleep! Bleep-bleep-bleep! "Whow!"

"What are you doing, boys?"

Bleep! Brrrrr! Bleep-bleep! Brrrrr! "Hey!"

"What are you doing to the television set?"

David dashed his hand to his brow. "Mum, you ruined it! I was trying to beat Crawfie's score!"

"Ha ha! As if you had a snowball's hope in hell, wee man!"

"But I would've, if Mum hadn't interrupted. . . "

Ailie held out her purse to Crawford. "Do you know what these coins . . . ?"

". . . don't have any more time to play. Time for my football meeting."

"Get you down the road, Crawfie." Both boys rose and pushed past Ailie towards the door.

"But . . . when are you coming back?"

Crawfie favoured her with a three-second stare. "How do we know?"

The front door slammed. Ailie looked in the freezer and found it full of burgers, pies and pizzas. The idea of food made her stomach heave. She returned and pushed a few buttons on the television set. Nothing meaningful – just little coloured graphics floating about. She switched it off and went to brood in bed.

Byres Road was as she remembered it. She lamented the closure of the Grosvenor Cinema – but the Salon was still to the fore. Picture houses had been closing down wholesale even when she last walked that way. However, she followed a sign into a lane – and found Byres Road had developed a 'B' feature every bit as interesting as the 'A'! Two 'B' features, in fact. Everything was there to pass the time for a mad lady of leisure – classy cafes, arty restaurants, craft shops, galleries and two Grosvenor cinemas!

She visited the flat she had shared with Jojo, hoping to see again the stained glass landing windows – the Goose Girl, and Hansel and Gretel. The new intercom system at the closemouth barred her way.

She joined classes, when they started in August. SCE 'O' Grade Modern Studies, with a bit of paper at the end, and Scottish Literature for Pleasure, without.

Sometimes she told her menfolk where she had been, but usually she did not. Once or twice Davie asked, but hardly ever. Mobility was a smooth Transcard, freedom forty pounds a week from Steve and no interest taken.

(Wish I could be a tourist forever. Wish I didn't have to go into the madhouse. Wish I could find my first family. Wish I had a friend. Wish I was still 18. If Glasgow's miles better, and I am miles worse, Steve is the Wreck of Ages.)

In the pocket of an old broken handbag, she found a German address for Sandy. The paper was besmirched with blood. She wrote to him in hope.

The Aurora Hair Salon, renamed Ringlets Fair was under new ownership. It had developed sidelines – sunbeds, a coffee machine. No one there had heard of Dorothy.

On the morning she was to go to hospital Ailie came down to breakfast later than she should. Steve and Crawfie sat over bowls of fluffy cheesy scrambled eggs with no burnt brown bits.

"When will you know?" asked Steve.

"Know what?" ventured Ailie.

"A week on Friday," replied Crawfie.

The kettle whistled. Ailie poured it over a teabag, added milk.

"What about Carey?" asked Steve. "Couldn't he help you?"

"I asked him. Seems I'm not long enough in post."

"Where's Davie?" Ailie perched on the edge of a hard stool at the breakfast bar.

Steve noticed her. He held out a letter. "Here. This came for you."

A blue envelope, sickeningly familiar.

> *MR SANDY LORIMER*
> *MAYBACHUFER 11*
> *1000 BERLIN 44*
> *GERMANY.*
> *E M P F Ä N G E R*
> *U N B E K A N N T*

"When was it you started?"

"A year past in October. I'll be just three weeks short. That's why I think it's a ploy."

"And there's nothing you can do?"

"Not a damned thing."

Ailie cleared her throat and raised her voice. "Where's Davie?"

"Out."

"Out where?"

Crawford slammed down his cup. "How the hell do I know?" He turned his back to Ailie and his front to Steve. "So long, then, Dad. I'll see you." He thundered out of the house.

Steve glowered at his plate. Ailie looked at him, looked at her letter, looked back at him. "Wasn't . . . " she cleared her throat and began again. "Wasn't that amazing, these scenes on the telly when they started letting through the East Germans? After all this time." She smiled and shook her head. "It seems to have been an astonishing year."

Steve stared up at her blackly.

"The last year," she murmured softly, "of the second last decade of the millenium."

"Ailie," Steve hissed, "you are unbelievable. As a parent, you are unbelievable."

Nervously, Ailie glanced at the closed door. "What's upsetting Crawfie?"

"He thinks he's going to get the sack. They say it's for bad timekeeping."

"Oh dear." Ailie assumed an expression of concerned parenthood.

"He thought the union rep might be able to do something, but he can't."

"That's too bad. He'll just have to start looking for another job."

"With everywhere folding? Come on!"

"I'd forgotten unemployment was so high."

"You would."

"Steve, I am trying so very hard to catch up on current affairs. I've been getting books galore out of the library about twentieth century history. . . "

"You do that. Educate yourself." He rose. "I'm going out now. I'll be back in time to run you to the hospital."

"You don't have to."

"I know. But I will."

After he left Ailie looked in the pan, but there was no scrambled egg left. Fortunately it was a non-stick and therefore easy to clean.

# 2

AT THE HOSPITAL, Steve hovered about as she undressed for bed.

"You don't need to go to bed right now. Why don't you look around – get to know the place?"

"I'm very tired. I'd like a nap before tea. The nurse gave me a couple of pills." (Why am I justifying myself to him? This is my illness – it's up to me what I do with it.) She climbed into bed. "You needn't wait."

"All right – well – cheerio." He was gone.

(Tightly tucked-in bed. Must get my feet free. There – that's better. Much looser. Much . . . what . . . what . . . someone else in the bed!) Someone small, dumpy, asleep. A baby.

The child looked about a year old. Fair hair plastered with perspiration, tear-stained rosy cheeks, wet mouth sucking the thumb of a slightly sticky hand. As Ailie stared, a small boy came in.

"Mummy, wee Frankie's dropped milk all down the back of the couch."

Ailie sat up, shaking her head. Another boy rushed in from behind and shouted, "It wisnae me, Mrs Carmichael, it wis Andy."

From outside the room, she heard a key turn in the lock. She was no longer in hospital but back at home, in her dressing-gown, lying on top of the unmade bed.

"Daddy!" The first boy rushed towards the bedroom door just as the old, fresh-faced slim Steve came through it.

"What the hell's going on here? Do you know there are four strange kids rampaging through our living-room while you're snoring it off?"

He strode to the bed and dragged her onto the mat. The baby started to howl, and the room seemed to be full of wee boys ogling the scene.

"Steve, something's happened to me. . . "

"Too bloody right something's happened to you. Day after day I come home to find the place a pit and the dinner not bought never mind cooked. And look at yourself and the day nearly over." He shook her by the shoulder. "Your hair's right into your eyes. You're twenty-six and you're like the Hag of Barra."

"I don't understand this! What year is it?"

"If I could have seen you then, the way you are now, I'd have walked a thousand miles in the other direction from the Registry Office!"

"There's something terrible wrong with me, Steve. A short while ago. . . "

". . . you were in the Land of Nod and the kids were wrecking the place."

". . . a short while ago it was 1989 and I was nearly middle-aged. . . "

". . . you're middle-aged now without the birth certificate. . . "

". . . I'm telling you what happened. . . "

". . . I don't give a bugger for your dreams. If the dinner's not on the table for half-six, you'll not live to see 1989. . . "

". . . For God's sake listen! I'm going out of my mind!"

"You poor inadequate bitch."

"The children are total strangers!"

"What are you talking about?"

"Last time I saw them they were teenagers. That apart, I can't remember anything since 1969."

Steve regarded her for a long moment. He turned to the hushed audience.

"Home, kids. Show's over. Go on, scram."

When the last wee boy had gone scurrying down the street to tell the neighbours all about it, Steve resumed his gaze.

"My God. You've finally flipped." He sighed. "I suppose it's white coats and straitjackets this time."

"Don't joke, Steve. Not about that."

"Who's joking?"

Steve picked up the howling baby and caressed him until the howls died down. Crawford began playing with toy cars in a corner.

"I remember the night we got engaged. Then I woke up and suddenly it was 1989. I lived for a few weeks in 1989 and then I woke up into – what year is it, anyway?"

"1976."

"Now do you see?"

"I see that you're getting all worked up about some dream. . . "

"Oh, I'd give anything for it to have been a dream. But it was real, as real as now."

"It can't have been!"

"I know the difference between dreams and reality."

"Look, you said you'd forgotten the past. I can take that. It's just the kind of thing the likes of you *would* do. But this stuff about experiencing the future – that can't happen."

Ailie wiped her eyes. "I would have said so. Only it did happen to me."

"Have you been taking your tablets?"

"The pheno-barbs? I think it was maybe them that brought it on."

"The anti-depressants."

"I take pills for depression?"

"You've been taking them since we got married. Since that time you tried to do yourself in."

(SINCE THAT TIME . . . what time? . . . YOU TRIED . . . and failed? How? What damage did I sustain? . . . )

Steve shook his head. "Ailie, you're a mentally unstable person. Don't ask me what goes on in your woolly maze. All I know is that living into the future can't happen. What you had was a hallucination, not your first, undoubtedly not your last."

"But . . . "

"Drop it, Ailie. I don't want you to mention it again. Okay?"

"But . . . "

"Okay?"

"I want an appointment with the doctor," muttered Ailie.

This GP was of a different kidney to the last/next. Florid face, white hair, scientific scepticism boring out through thick glasses. So, Ailie imagined, must Pettenkoffer have looked in the moment he quaffed Koch's beaker of live cholera bacilli, and in the weeks afterwards when his survival proved to his satisfaction the non-existence of micro-organisms.

"What's the trouble this time, Mrs Carmichael?"

(Emphasis on 'this' to inform me of my status as a persistent offender.) Alie lowered her eyes and spoke softly. "I know you'll find this hard to believe, doctor, but I don't seem to be on . . . I seem to operate on a different time-scale to everybody else. . . "

"Eh? . . . What's that? What do you mean?"

"I mean, well . . . I seem to have lived into the future for a while, and then again. . . "

"Are the tablets not strong enough? Is that what you're saying?"

"It's nothing to do with the tablets. I feel so confused. My children are strangers to me. . . "

"Come, come. I'm sure it's not as bad as that."

"Oh, but it is! Last time I saw them they were teenagers. . . "

"Your children . . . how old are they, again?"

"Five and one."

A long, steady stare from the doctor. "Mrs Carmichael, what are you trying to tell me?"

(This time the emphasis on 'what' indicates his irritation. On the 'are' it would have indicated his disbelief, and on the 'trying' my inadequacy.)

"I'm trying to tell you. . . "(Away up in a scraich goes the voice. Bring it down, bring it down.) "I'm trying to tell you. . . " (down, voice, down!) ". . . to tell you about my problem with Time! I knew you wouldn't believe me." (Stop it! Back, tears, back! Don't dare show yourselves! Back in! Back in!)

"Is the depression worse?"

"Well, I can't help the situation getting me down. . . "

". . . I'll prescribe you a stronger brand of pills."

"But depression isn't the main problem! You're treating the symptom and not the cause!"

The doctor paused in his scribbling to look at her over the top of his spectacles. "Where did you do your medical training, Mrs Carmichael?"

(They wouldn't let me be a doctor or a nurse. Just a patient, the greatest expert of all.)

"I'm sorry. I don't want to sound as if I'm. . . "

"Just leave us doctors to sort out the causes and symptoms. Why buy a dog and bark yourself?" He handed her the prescription. "One three times a day, just as before."

"Thank you doctor." (Crawler.) "I was kind of hoping you might send me to a specialist."

"I'd like you to give the new medication a chance, Mrs Carmichael."

His forefinger moved towards the Next Please button, and Ailie moved towards the door.

She tried to phone her mother, several times. Once she took a taxi out and battered at the door while the taxi waited. The neighbour told her they were all away for an extended holiday, in Poland, she thought. Poland rang a bell with Ailie.

Her address book had no entry for Sandy. Steve told her she knew his phone number by heart and had never bothered to write it down after she had lost the old receipt where it was first noted. He was living in a flat with Pandora somewhere in the West End.

There were now eleven SNP Members of Parliament, and whenever one of them appeared on television in Scottish political programmes – they rarely appeared in network – she was reminded of Sandy and Pandora. Often she took the bus over and wandered up and down the main thoroughfares – Byres Road, University Avenue, Dumbarton Road, Great Western Road, Sauchiehall Street, walking fast through Kelvingrove Park and the Botanic Gardens, looking at the faces of the people and not the autumn foliage, pushing the buggy and with toddler in tow, trying to cover as much ground as possible.

The children were extensions of her body, it seemed. Where she went they went, regardless of her interest or lack of it. It never ceased to amaze her how they required an element of her attention every minute they were awake. It gave her new respect for the many people in the street. Each one must have taken up massive amounts of someone's time and attention. Each pathetic old down-and-out, each hardened young thug appearing before the courts, each downtrodden old pensioner, unloved in her flat, must at one time have been hand-fed, nappy-changed, nose-wiped, dressed, bedded, protected from falling, swallowing, wandering, running across roads, carted about everywhere, if not talked to, sung to, played with, loved and cuddled, hourly over years by some selfless soul, probably a woman. Those lacking such attention would die. It astounded her that so many survived.

On a night when Steve stayed in to look after both she trawled the popular howffs of the West, the Curlers, the Aragon, the Rubaiyat. She never stopped to hope. Finding Sandy became a mini-obsession with her.

The political scene itself was of only academic interest. After all, she knew how it would end up, this time around.

There was however, an address for Jojo.

> *Dear Jojo,*
> *Before I tell you about the strange things which*
> *have happened to me recently, I want you to*
> *promise that you will never under any*
> *circumstances stop writing to me, even if I at*
> *some point in the future stop writing to you.*
> *It's so weird setting all this down when I don't*
> *even know if this epistle will reach you. . .*

"Mummy!"

"What is it, dear?"

"Tell me a story."

"I'm writing just now."

"I've been asking for a story for a long time. I started asking before you started writing."

"Wa-a-a-a-a-ah!"

"There's Davie starting up now."

"Wa-a-a-a-a-ah!"

Upstairs, the door of Steve's study opened. She heard him coming down.

"WA-A-A-A-A-AH!"

The living-room door opened and Steve came in.

"Daddy!" Crawford ran and grabbed his father. "You tell me a story."

"Ailie. AILIE."

Ailie turned her head slowly.

"Do you not hear? The baby needs you."

"I'll see to him."

"Don't bother. I'll go, I suppose, though I had other things to do."

"It's all right. I can. . . "

"Look, you concentrate on that one. Tell him a story, for God's sake."

"But Daddy! I want *you* to tell me the story!"

Steve left and Crawfie came back to Ailie.

"A story. Now, let me see." (Wonder if I'll reach Jojo this time. Wonder what she'll make of the whole thing.)

"Mummy!"

"A story. Right you are. Once upon a time, there were three bears. . . "

"Not that one. A new story."

"A new story. Hmmm." (I really have to reach someone. Make some kind of continuity out of it all. . . )

"The story!"

"Once upon a time, there was a little girl."

"What was her name?"

"Her name was Ailie."

"Well? What happened to her?"

"She . . . she . . . No. We'll have another story. Once upon a time, there was a little boy called Sandy."

Steve came in again and Crawford ran to him. "Daddy! Please *you* tell me a story."

"Can't you even do that right?"

"It must be these new pills." (Back, tears, back!) "They make everything far away. It's as if there's a barrier between me and the rest of you."

"We should be so lucky. Look, tomorrow you take your sick head down to that bastard and get him to sort you out once and for all. Make him send you to a shrink."

"I'll try, but. . . "

"Stand up to him, for God's sake! Don't be such a doormat. You're no use about the place, the way you are. Come here, son. About that story. . . "

He sat in the armchair. Crawford clambered on his knee and snuggled up with his head against his father's chin.

"Once upon a time there was a boy called George, who wanted very much to have a dog of his own. . . "

Ailie slipped out of the room and out of the house. She walked round the block, into Bellahouston Park, past four shows of narcissi and into the Palace of Arts. She stared at over three dozen paintings by Glasgow schoolchildren. She walked out of the gallery, out of the park. In Paisley Road West the heavens opened. She stood in a close until it was over.

Afterwards, in the south above the hill of the park, a watery sun shone through. She crossed towards it, and looked back at the grimy maroon tenements. Within the decade they would blush rosy in a new dawn. For now the sky remained leaden to the north, bright to the south.

"Just the kind of firmament for a rainbow," she thought, and as she looked again one appeared. Deep, bright colours against the slate, overlooked by a paler shadow. Hope in the mist.

Dripping wet, she broke into a run. When she reached home, she had to ring the bell because she had forgotten her key. Steve opened the door with a grim face and no comment.

And still her head was not clear. Still, when she looked at Steve, she saw only Jojo. When she looked at Crawford, she saw only Sandy.

On a windy piece of land in Maryhill, where folk-remembered footpaths in the rank grass picked around rainbow puddles, stood a red sandstone block, dark with age, with crow-stepped gable boasting its classical Scots past, and the sparkling glass in the yard its humble present. Above the first storey nineteenth century hands had carved GLASGOW SCHOOL BOARD – GARSCUBE PUBLIC SCHOOL. Below this, immediately above the porch, hung a metal printed sign: GARSCUBE WORKSPACE.

Inside, on the first floor, a balcony with tiled walls surrounded the stairwell. Each classroom was now a mini-factory; a printshop, a small machines repair shop, a sewing room where twenty Asian women put together anoraks from daybreak to dusk. Behind the door of what had been the Primary Seven classroom, sat two men, separated from each other by crude hardboard dividers, each surrounded by accounts books. Each ran his left forefinger down a page while tapping intermittently with his right on a calculator.

Walter had drifted out of the business world when his firm, manufacturing asbestos, had closed down. At 52, in Central Scotland, the rising tide of competition for the dwindling number of openings had prevented his return. He sank, grabbing at various straws which broke his fall. The latest was this shaky new enterprise, in partnership with Sandy, whom he had met through the pages of a finance periodical. Walter had never put down roots, never escaped from the twilight land of temporary contracts and furnished bedsits. This old Quali exam room was his latest testing ground.

Sandy's degree was in French and German, although he wished it had been accountancy. What hope for a linguist who hated teaching? His hair and beard were fair, and for the past decade he had favoured gold rimmed John Lennon glasses. (Ah, '68, the year of fate – when all seemed fair, he was there! He was there! He only had to walk along by the left bank to be a student again – young, privileged and free; poor, Leftish and right.)

On offer was advice on stocks, shares, government bonds and unit trusts, both at home and abroad. Both advisers were untrained, but Sandy was already contributing occasional articles to finance journals. How hard for an all-rounder to select, to realise at 17 and completely in command of all school subjects, that an even greater bent lay in the world of pounds, dollars and marks!

To Sandy, the investment consultancy practice was still a part-time job. His security, and his misery, stemmed from the latter half of the week, when he attempted to teach in a comprehensive school with a roll of over a thousand and an ethos light years away from his own scholastic experience. The available escape routes lay South or West, but Sandy had long ago determined that if Scotland lacked quality jobs, he would forge his own. Until recently they had met in Sandy's flat, but pressure from Pandora's social life had prompted them to rent this room.

On his road home Sandy dropped in at the supermarket. He was eying up the frozen carrots when his glance was drawn to the mirror on the wall.

Something about her carriage, the shape of her face, the way she moved, the way she bent her head, the delicacy of her profile, of her hands. Often over the years he had glimpsed a girl who resembled her, her colouring, her hairstyle, the clothes she used to wear. Each caught his eye and his heart-strings, each revived the old memories, each burst his bubble, for none was she. This time it was, it was, it was, it was! It was the real thing. It was the old love.

She was even more beautiful than he remembered her,

and his heart began to thud. He whirled round, only to see her vanish round a rampart of tinned pet food. He nearly capsized an elderly gentleman in his haste to follow. She was at the cake mix counter. He walked right up behind her, stood trembling at her back, and gently touched her shoulder.

"Jasmine. It is you, isn't it?"

The thick hair swept her shoulder as she turned and raised her face. Her large eyes widened and glowed. Pink flooded her cheeks and he was bowled over by the smile he knew so well, wide, innocent, clean, soft.

"Sandy!" The very word was a declaration of joy.

"Jasmine. Jasmine! . . . Where have you been all these years?"

"I was in Aberdeen. I was married."

"I heard. A copy-writer, wasn't it?"

"But I'm not any more." Jasmine wasted no time. "We've been apart for nearly a year."

Sandy expressed the conventional, hypocritical regrets.

"We're getting a divorce." Jasmine's smile broadened, and her unsubtle glance sought his left hand. "You're not. . . "

"No," said Sandy hurriedly. A tiny voice bleated 'Pandora' and he quelled it. He pulled Jasmine out of the way of a rampaging, child-guided trolley. "Look. We can't stand here. We're blocking the passage. Are you based in Glasgow just now?"

"I've a flat in Broomhill."

"You give me your phone number. I'll ring you and we can arrange a date to talk over old times."

She gave it gladly, nor asked in return for his. After they parted he watched her bright figure all along Byres Road. She turned so often to wave that she blundered into people. Three times he blew her kisses. Amongst the rush-hour crowds, through the blurring rain, he could pick out Jasmine until she turned down Highborough Road.

Back home, he paused for a moment outside the living-room door.

"But there's no sense in getting involved in that sort of thing," Pandora was saying "just now when everything's going so well!"

"You reckon? When did Westminster ever give anyone anything without having its hand forced? You just wait and see what happens with this. . . "

Sandy walked in. The place littered with beer-cans and people. Three fellows he knew slightly, two strangers. The grey-faced character with yellow hair and fingertips cut off in mid-sentence, but Pandora took up the talk.

"I don't see any need for a separate Poetry Editor. A general Literary Editor would suffice, while we're small."

Sandy edged his way into the kitchen and put the kettle on to boil. He turned the gas up under the remains of yesterday's stew, added some curry powder, stirred, and reached for the instant mash. He hoped Pandora's magazine committee would leave well before bedtime.

He ate his dinner in the kitchen, where they had converted the old bed-recess into a diner. It was chilly and too dark to read, but more peaceful than it would be in the living-room amongst the strangers.

He washed the dishes and the pots and pans slowly, killing time. Then he had to re-enter the living-room, to get his work for the evening.

"I mean, if the place were to get like Northern Ireland," Pandora was saying, "do you honestly think. . . " She broke off as she spotted Sandy and cried, "Of course! He just got a new instant camera! Sandy, we want someone to take a picture of the whole new editorial committee!"

The six of them arranged themselves with much ribaldry on and around the couch. Three of the men sat on the couch, with Pandora stretched cheekily across their laps, while two peeped over the back with their elbows resting on a couple of shoulders. Sandy pressed the shutter, felt the exposure slide out.

"Now a second one, so we've got a choice." This time, after a bit of discussion, two of the men put their arms together to form a basket, which Pandora sat in daintily, an arm slung around each neck.

The yellow-haired fellow spoke. "How about one with the Literary Editor and the Political Editor together?" He wrapped his arm around Pandora and pressed her cheek to his. Through her freckles Pandora reddened and grinned, and Sandy, quietly outraged, took the snap.

A few more like poses were struck, and Sandy fleetingly wondered if Pandora were trying to stimulate him into a humiliating display of jealousy. More likely the drink was to blame. There followed the examination of the developed pictures, much giggling and exclamations of, "Oh look at me!" . . . "But what a sight I am here!" . . . during which Sandy slipped away and got stuck into preparing a lesson which could claim to have some connection with French while retaining attemptability by the non-certificate section of S4. . .

They left around three a.m. Sandy was still awake when Pandora, wearing a pair of his pyjamas, crawled in by his side.

"Is this some new project you're getting into?"

Pandora looked sharply at him. "What? Oh, you mean the literary magazine? Yes, I've been thinking of setting up in publishing for some time."

"You never told me that!" No reply. "Are you sure you've got time to start something totally new like that, when you've got your political involvement, the Rape Crisis Centre, the consciousness-raising workshops, your. . . "

"I'm looking for something that might be a staff and comfort in time," said Dora. "I can't spend my whole life writing little stories from the police courts. It's driving me into the funny farm."

"Well, Mrs Carmichael? Has there been an improvement?"

"It's hard to say, doctor." (Be brave, woman!) "I haven't had any more time lapses, yet."

"I told you the tablets would help."

"I don't know. They . . . perhaps . . . I don't like the effect they have on me. When I'm taking them I don't have a clear head."

"You don't get anything for nothing nowadays. As a housewife you should know that."

(As a housewife I know neither the price of bread nor of butter, but I do know which film star will become President, and how Indira Gandhi will die.)

"Tell me, which is worse, this sensation of distance, or the problem you complained of before?"

"But I don't know if they have cured the problem! I still go to bed every night wondering when I'll wake up."

"You ought to stop dramatising the situation like this. It doesn't help your case at all."

"Won't you please send me to a specialist?" (I'll burn him with my eyes, that's what I'll do. Send my will over to him. Make him do it. Burn.) "I'm no use to man nor beast like this – my husband says so."

"Mrs Carmichael, you seem to know so much about it. Exactly what kind of a specialist do you have in mind?"

A comfortable small room, with a pink plain carpet. Pot plants on the filing cabinets – a Busy Lizzie all in bloom, Wandering Sailor trailing down, Sweetheart Vine clambering up. Cheeseplant in the corner. Across the desk, a middle-aged woman with a face the shape and colour of a morning roll. A soft face, a sociable smile.

"I'm Dr Mathieson. Take a seat, Mrs Carmichael. The armchair is the more comfortable, I believe."

"Thank you."

Silence.

"What do you want me to tell you?"

"Whatever you want to tell me, my dear. Tell me all about yourself."

"Really, my life is pretty dull. Apart from my problem, that is. I suppose the likes of you would find that interesting."

"You have two sons, don't you?"

"If you say so."

"Do you like them?"

"No. They're a nuisance. I wish they would go away."

"Do you dislike them?"

"I've no strong feelings about them." (What have they got to do with it? They interfere enough with my exterior life without her dragging them into my insides, too.) "I don't feel guilty about them, if that's what you're driving at. Really, I don't think of them as my children at all."

"And your husband?"

Ailie stared at the desk. "I can't separate him from what he's going to become. The memory of him in the future puts me off him in the present."

The shrink was not one to let go. "And what is he going to become?"

Ailie raised her eyes. "Fat. Coarse. Adulterous. I can't bring myself to. . . " she faltered ". . . you know. I suppose it's easy for me, not knowing . . . well . . . what I'm missing." She giggled. "I'm a virgin with two children!"

"How does Steve feel about what he's missing?"

Ailie had puzzled over that herself. Once she had almost spoken of it, but had baulked at discussing sex with a strange man. "He never mentions it. Maybe we came to some arrangement in the past."

Ailie took the subway home. The nineteenth-century subway, dusty hardware fragrance and slatted floors. Mentally she superimposed the Clockwork Orange over the wooden Toytown cars and basked in superior perspective.

The visits to Dr Mathieson became her foundation. The other days were as chaff to Friday's wheat. "She finds me interesting!" she told Steve one evening when he caught her singing *Zippity Doo Dah* to the dirty dishes.

"You are a rare form of life . . . fortunately."

"Me, not just my illness. She listens to my moans and groans."

"That's her trade."

"And with all that education behind her!"

"Let's hope her education gets you sorted out."

Next morning Ailie dared to ask Dr Mathieson, "Do you believe me?"

Dr Mathieson's kindly eyes flickered to the Monstera Deliciosa. Then, well-trained in body language, she resumed her steadfast gaze.

"You see, it's not just whether . . . the real question is . . . where does subjective experience become objective?" She waited for Ailie's response. "Do you understand what I mean?"

"Yes. You don't believe me."

"That's not quite. . . "

"What gets me down," Ailie interrupted, "is the discontinuity. It's always different sets of people. I can't keep friends. It's always different doctors. I can't. . . "

"You've no points of reference."

"Right."

Dr Mathieson contemplated the Wandering Sailor for a minute or two. She rose and pulled a long strand out of the earth. She threw the withered bottom end in the wastepaper-basket and stuck the top end in a jar of water filled with Busy Lizzie cuttings.

"There used to be a theory, you know, about Time, which might go some way to explaining what you say happens to you."

"A theory?"

"A very far-fetched theory. I personally wouldn't give it much. . . "

"Tell me it!"

"Do you know anything about the Theory of Relativity?"

Ailie cast her mind back to her Maths 'O' grade course. "No. Not really. Just something about . . . if you're looking out of a train window. . . " She sneaked a glance at Dr Mathieson, who smiled and said, "Yes?"

"The cows in the field seem to be moving but you know that it's really you that's moving and they're standing still."

"And even when you can no longer see them, you know these cows still exist, just beyond the window frame."

"What's this to do with me?"

"The theory held that Time, like the cow, is stationary. What we perceive as past, present and future events actually happen simultaneously and constantly. We ourselves are the travellers and can only see the tiny part we're experiencing at the moment." She stopped. "Do you see?"

"I don't know," murmured Ailie. "I think I maybe. . . "

"According to this theory your consciousness is in a train which leaps from station to station at random, instead of in proper sequence."

"And the folk around me?"

"They experience their surroundings, including you, in normal sequence. As far as they're concerned, you're always there."

"No." Ailie shook her head. "I don't get it."

"It is a difficult idea to come to terms with."

"Oh, but I will. I will." Ailie leaned forward, resting her chin on her clasped hands. "Explain it all again."

"In the first place, all perception is subjective."

"I follow that bit," said Ailie cautiously, "but please remember, this person you're talking to is basically a wee girl not long out of school."

"I'm referring to the old conundrum about the invisible, unfeelable, inaudible tiger . . . you know that all empirical proof depends upon our senses. . . "

(School. Childhood. The Faces. The Blanks. The Blanks!) "Does this mean," Ailie broke into the Morning Roll's lecture, "that I'll experience my whole life sooner or later? Even if it's taken out of order?"

"Possibly, but. . . "

"That's it, then! We've cracked it!" (So I haven't missed anything, really. I'll get all my due – perhaps my threescore years and ten, or more, if I'm lucky . . . just like everybody else! There'll even be advantages. . . )

"I have to point out,"said the Morning Roll, "most schools of thought reject this theory of Time."

The summer of '76 dried up rivers throughout England and even much of Scotland basked in sunshine. The Glasgow City Fathers talked darkly about future water shortages, but everyone knew the faithful rain would not, could not, fail its protégé. The Carmichaels drove up the West coast and met with clouds aplenty there, mixed with patches of sparkling sun. Clouds, blue sky, sheets of rain, steaming sun, mist and even hail – all in one day. Louring mountains, dappled in shades of olive or gold. (Scotland is patchwork, like my life!)

The road was broken by tea-and-nappy stops at the main names: Crianlarich, far-heralded but tiny, Glencoe and the Great Glen, Fort William, Fort Augustus, Inverness, then across by single track roads past wide empty lochs to Ullapool. There they spent a week, largely separately, but in peace. Steve fished, while Ailie walked or took the children a boat trip to the Summer Isles, where the main thing was the Post Office and the surcharge stamps. Ailie sent a card to the Morning Roll and wished again that she knew where to reach her own family.

When she met up with Steve, at mealtimes, they exchanged careful pleasantries, talked about their respective days. Steve was still handsome, these days, with his thick, light brown hair grown fashionably down his forehead and past his collar, his features still sharp, his complexion clean. In the evenings he crawled about with Crawford on his back, or dandled the baby on his knee. Once or twice she thought she could remember a bit of what she had once felt, the old attraction. On the way home she was almost fond of Steve, in a negative way.

Back in Glasgow, the sun had continued to shine, but in August, about the time the shops put up their Back to School signs, the deluge returned. Ailie took her own education in hand and arranged for Steve to babysit twice weekly, while she took classes in Scottish Literature and in Modern Studies. Wednesdays – Glasgow University. Old-fashioned terraced house with a myriad of passages behind the oak-panelled door. Mondays – Langside College – dark grasslands in the drawing-in nights.

Towards Christmas she had another attempt at contacting her mother. This time to her shock, the receiver was lifted at the other end and a strange male voice, slightly foreign, answered.

"Could I speak to my . . . to Dorothy, please?"

"Hello?" Her mother's voice, at least, had not changed. "Ailie! What a nice surprise. We were just wondering, the other day, what had happened to you. Must be . . . what . . . six months, at least!"

"I tried to call you over the summer. . . "

"But I told you, dear, we were going away, to Poland, and

then again to Greece. And I expect you were away as well, weren't you?"

"Just for a week. Up north."

"Oh, that would be nice. Well, what about it, then? When are we next going to see your happy, smiling faces?"

"What about. . . "

"Listen, dear, we're booked to go round to Stan's daughter for Christmas dinner. But it would be nice if you could come over for New Year's Day."

"Well, I. . . "

"I'll be inviting Sandy and Pandora, too."

"Sandy and . . . All right. We'll be there."

At Christmas, Ailie got Crawfie to shout up the chimney to Santa, although what he asked for he would not get – a Time machine. She found decorations in the loft and enjoyed herself hanging them about the living-room, even if the novelty did not stay long with Crawford and Steve appeared not to notice. She found a bag full of tree ornaments, but no Christmas tree. Had she been in the habit of buying a real tree every year and throwing it out? She felt that such a waste.

Tentatively she broached the subject with Steve, at a moment when he looked as if he did not have too many important things on his mind. He took her to the back door and pointed up the back to a shoulder-high spruce in a pot. "You bring that into the house, and use it every year."

Filling the stockings was exciting, even if the reactions in the morning were not as she'd hoped. David was too young, and Crawford opened each toy faster than the last, without examining any of them, so that he was through them pronto, and bored and waiting for his breakfast. Ailie made a big effort for dinner, and with the aid of a cookery book stuffed and cooked a goose for them. The boys would not touch it and Steve proclaimed it the greasiest thing he had ever half-eaten. Afterwards she took the boys to Bellahouston Park, while Steve washed the dishes.

On the first day of 1977 the old family house looked just as it had back in the sixties. The regime had altered however, and it was a tall courtly man who ushered them in. Faded fair hair, foreign accent, well-kept forties or Peter Pan fifties, faintly familiar.

Sandy and Pandora were seated on the couch and acknowledged the entry of Ailie's clan with a nod. Clearly *they* had never sought *her* through park and precinct, shopping mall and museum, old address-book and telephone directory. They had never missed her at all. (So it is, of course, when you can keep track of yourself and others on the highways of Time and Space, when you are in love with your flatmate and can take your family for granted, at the other end of a phone call which you need never bother making.)

Steve slumped into an armchair and reached into his bag for yesterday's *Herald*. He turned to the sports pages.

Stan laid out the cutlery and uncorked the wine. Nigel was nowhere to be seen, but thunderous rock music pumped down from upstairs.

"He doesn't want to know any more about Burns' Night gigs!" lamented Dorothy.

"Since discovering his hormones," smiled Stan.

"Well, goodness knows, Burns' own hormones were perfectly in order! I told him if he wanted to sing about sex we could resurrect some of the bawdy ballads and do the working men's clubs!"

Sandy said, "The sex has to be in 20th century packaging, Mother. No teenager's interested in the urges of a 200 year-old corpse."

Pandora chanted softly, "*He's lost his falorum, di-diddle, di-dorum . . .* "

Ailie knew without looking that she would not find Roddy

in this house.

Dorothy was in the kitchen, putting the final touches to the roast lamb. A succulent roll of meat, basted in rich spicy gravy, with a completely ungreasy look to it. Dorothy greeted her daughter, pecked her on the cheek, and reached for the jacket potatoes.

"I take it you're living with Stan now, Mother?"

"What?" Dorothy rounded on her, outraged. "But we're married! Goodness, you were at the wedding in March! What's the matter, dear? Have you been having more of the blanks?"

"Just a wee one. What happened to Uncle Roddy?"

"Sounds like a big lapse to me. Are you still taking your tablets?"

"I've got three different bottles of pills at the moment, and I take them all regularly . . . Mother, I want to have a proper talk with you."

"Any more problems with the blackouts?"

"That's what I want to talk to you about."

"Don't tell me they're worse! Yet, the doctors seemed to think that once adolescence was over. . . "

"As far as I can see I've grown out of the petit-mal. Or at least it's totally under control. But. . . "

"Totally under control? No attacks at all, these days? Now, that's a great relief to me, Ailie. You've always been such a source of worry. All these different things wrong with your br . . . well, never mind, thank God if it seems to be better. That . . . those turns – they can be insidious."

"I know, Mother."

"In fact, they can totally damn a person's life. They can render it impossible to get a job. . . "

"I was refused entry into nursing, because of it. So I've been told."

"And your memory lapses! You say you still get them?"

Ailie pulled a 1976 calendar off the wall. SCOTLAND IN

COLOUR – all the old favourites – Eilean Donan Castle, Princes Street. Colin Baxter's artistic stuff had not yet come into its own. "What about Uncle Roddy?"

"It's very sad, dear. I really think he's on his last legs now."

"He's ill?"

"Self-inflicted, of course. The liver can only take so much."

"Is he in hospital?"

"What could a hospital do? Och, he's been in getting dried out . . . but then . . . well, the problem really lies in the character, doesn't it?"

"Where is he?"

"He's in a bedsit, somewhere off Queen Margaret Drive. Nigel'll show you, if you want to visit him sometime. But, for now, would you mind taking these dishes through? We can't let it get cold. Nigel! It's ready, dear!"

At the fourth calling, Nigel clattered down. Time had done little for his looks. His blonde baby curls had darkened and straightened and his complexion greyed. He wore dirty platform shoes and a sweaty T-shirt with BAY CITY ROLLERS emblazoned across it. He strode across to his meal, addressing himself only to the plate.

At the start of the meal Dorothy did most of the talking, about the holiday in Poland, about how they'd visited Stan's old home.

"His family were well-to-do, you know, before the war. They owned this huge mansion and 100 acres of forest. Stan never got any compensation for that, you know. The East German refugees, they got reimbursed by the Federal Republic, but not the Poles."

Stan shrugged. "The present Government of Poland would probably deem it a crime that one family had owned all that in the first place."

Pandora said, "Would you say they had a point?"

"Who were we exploiting? For goodness sake, we didn't keep serfs. The land was used for timber, and we gave employment to quite a few people."

"These few people doing the work, and your family raking in the profit."

Ailie looked from one to the other. (Should I say anything?)

"Either you have a system of private ownership," he said stonily, "or you have a system of State ownership. In those days, it was private ownership."

"In a few years' time," began Ailie timidly, "the communist system in Poland. . . "

"Which system do you think is more just?" demanded Pandora.

Dorothy cut in. "It was interesting to visit Stan's old home again. It's used for housing and offices for the forestry workers and their families. When we told them who we were, they let us look round the place."

Sandy said, "Must have been a bit galling."

"Do you find it galling?" Pandora asked him. "I mean you personally?"

Sandy flushed. "Why should I? It's nothing to me. I never saw the place, then or now."

"I mean, because. . . "

"How's your new operation going, Sandy?" Dorothy broke in. "Getting plenty of clients?"

"Not a lot, just now. I'd been hoping I might cut back on teaching, maybe go half-time. But I reckon, with this new mortgage we've taken on. . . "

"What a pity. And with all your high qualifications. . . "

"Mother, I've told you before. High qualifications count for nothing in this game. What matters is making contacts. Getting your name known in the right places."

"I still think, if you were to take that conversion course and become a proper chartered accountant. . . "

"I told you, Mother, it's out of the question. I wouldn't get a grant."

"What about that Carnegie Trust business. . . "

"I explained all that," said Sandy wearily. "It only pays the fees. How would I live?"

"Pandora's working, isn't she?" began Dorothy.

Stan cut in. "What about you, Steve?" He shared out the last of the wine. "How's your job going?"

"Okay." Steve picked up the *Record* and turned to the sports page.

"Ailie said last spring that you were thinking of giving up the surveying, going on to a new line?"

"Aye, I was." Steve raised his eyes briefly. "Bad time just now to start a business." He dropped his eyes again.

Nigel rose. "Gotta go an see a pal," he muttered.

"But Nigel, there's still the Xmas pudding and brandy sauce!"

"Don't want any."

"Nigel!" growled Stan. "This is a family occasion. You'll spend today with your family. You may phone your pal and tell him you'll see him tomorrow."

"Oh aye? Well, you're not my family, so that's good. I don't have to spend it wi' you." Nigel moved with a graceful slither towards the door. Dorothy and Stan exchanged glances.

"Nigel, come back here!" Stan bellowed, while Dorothy sat cold on her dignity. Too late. They heard the front door slam.

"That boy needs . . . something." Stan shook his head and helped himself to more stuffing.

"Did he take it badly," asked Sandy, "when . . . well, all the changes there've been?"

"He's adapting." Dorothy rose and began to gather in plates. "I suppose it'll take a bit of getting used to, that's all."

Ailie longed to ask questions, but waited until Dot and Stan were both in the kitchen.

"Look, Sandy. I think I told you about my Time lapses."

"Yes, have they been. . . "

"Just fill me in on the story to date. When and how did Roddy leave the scene?"

"For a long time he didn't want to go," said Pandora. "Then they paid him off."

"Now, Dora, it wasn't quite like that. He was given a sum of money to compensate for his half of the house. . . "

"Water under bridges. Whisky down your belly. Money down the drain."

"Once he was on his own, it was up to him what he did."

"Everybody could predict what he would do. Particularly with all that bread in his hand. We didn't need your wee spey-wife here to tell us that."

"Roddy is an adult. You can't nurse him forever. If a person's determined to pickle himself to death, nobody can prevent it. You can only get out and save yourself from being dragged down with him."

"Particularly once an option hoves in sight in the shape of someone else's husband."

"Mother," said Sandy icily, "had him first. You don't believe in marriage anyway, so what's all this moralising?"

"But when did all this happen?" bleated Ailie. "And what about Stan's wife?"

"She took it badly," frowned Sandy, while Pandora encircled her throat with her right hand, stuck out her tongue and mimed pulling a rope with her left.

"You mean she. . . "

"Course not."

"Nearly. . . "

The door opened and Stan entered with the Xmas pudding, singing heartily in a good tenor voice.

> *O bring us some figgy pudding,*
> *O bring us some figgy pudding,*
> *O bring us some figgy pudding,*
> *and bring it right here!*

"Dot says to warn you, youngsters, it's full of shillings!"

The night before school was due to return after the holidays, Sandy beavered away at his desk, sunk in gloom.

"If I could even make enough out of the consultancy business to cut back on the teaching, without giving it up altogether. . . "

"I told you," said Pandora, "success in business is five percent talent, thirty percent hard work, and sixty-five percent getting yourself known to the right people." She scribbled on a bit of paper for a while and then laid it on Sandy's desk. "That top one would be your best bet. He's a good pal of mine from Uni days. He started up a firm dealing in linseed oil and it's totally taken off. That other approached the paper when he had a problem and I sorted it for him. He's something big in Novco, the American car fleet company. With both of these guys you'd have to mention my name first though, or they won't even read your letter."

"You know I can't stand sucking up to folk whom. . . "

". . . you consider your inferiors."

". . . whom I don't like, just to get something out of them."

"Well, that's the system we live under. If you're too haughty to take advantage of it, hell mend you."

"Pandora, it's not that I don't appreciate. . . "

"Sit," said Pandora, "and wait for the world to beat a path to your door, and you'll be teaching till you're an OAP. . . "

The bell rang.

Sandy grinned ironically. "You were saying?"

"You don't imagine it's for you?" Pandora slipped out and Sandy heard her admitting two of her cronies. From the kitchen Sandy heard their voices undulating, heard the fridge door opening, heard glasses clink. Pandora rarely took work home, and was not carrying on an extra career on the side. After a while he heard the front door slam and then there was silence. This time they had forgotten the token offer for him to accompany them to the pub.

He looked down at Dora's piece of paper for a long moment and then folded it and placed it in his wallet. He rose, crossed to the phone and dialled.

Over the miles he could hear Jasmine's breathless excitement. "I thought you'd lost my number!"

"I wouldn't ever lose your number, Jasmine." He paused for effect. "Look, I want to talk to somebody. Fancy coming over to the Shish Mahal?"

"Oh, Sandy, I've just eaten!"

"What about tomorrow, then?"

"Actually," she paused, then went on shyly, "I'm a vegetarian, now."

"Oh!" Sandy's voice showed its disappointment as the vision of a cosy curry with Jasmine, of many future cosy curries with Jasmine, faded. "How long has this gone on?"

Jasmine thought his tone implied that it was a juvenile phase on her part. "Four years. Why don't you come over to my place tomorrow, and I'll cook you something? Something really good, I promise. You'll never miss the meat at all!"

A once-grand terraced house, bluish-grey paint peeling off the sandstone. Ailie found MACLEOD amongst the myriad of paperscraps while Nigel rang five times. After a while he rang five times again. A girl in faded denims opened the door.

"Is it old Roddy you're wanting? Go right on down."

In the day of the rich big families the hall of a grand mansion, it was now half-way reverted to common close. The floor was mosaic, the sweeping stairway wooden with wrought iron balustrade. The ornate dining-room now housed Chilean refugees, the drawing-room on the first floor a Polish music-teacher. The bedrooms of the Master and Mistress and of the Junior Misses were home to three students and a couple of nurses from the Western Infirmary. Roddy's dwelling-place was humbler, down an unadorned spiral staircase to the dark quarters of the lower orders. Next door to the common kitchen, handy for mealtimes, but inconvenient for the light of day.

Roddy opened the door to them, looking about a hundred. However, when he saw that Ailie was with Nigel, in her honour he slipped in his teeth, shedding a couple of decades.

"How's it going, Dad?"

"Got a bit of a cough." Roddy wheezed as he led the way to his hearth and a one-bar electric fire. He sagged into the armchair. Under his old dressing-gown his pyjama trousers rode up, exposing mottled shins. Granny's Tartan, Dorothy used to call it. Seldom seen, since the demise of the coal-fire.

"I brought you a wee tin of spam, and some tomatoes," said Ailie. She looked about for where to lay them. The table was littered with the debris of at least three previous meals, plates and cutlery, unwashed milk bottles, whisky bottles, Tennents lager cans.

"Thanks. That'll do tomorrow's tea."

"What about cigarettes?" Nigel placed a once-fawn cushion at his father's back. "Are you okay for smokes?"

Roddy's dull eye showed a spark of light. "Got any with you?"

"I can get you some. Tomorrow. I'm meeting a pal, but when he goes to do his evening paper run I'll come round with the fags."

"Which pal's that?"

"Gary."

Roddy's face grew ruddier. "Steer clear of that one!"

Nigel grinned lop-sidedly at Ailie. "For some reason Dad doesn't like Gary. Don't know what it is. I mean, Mum doesn't like him either, but that's cos she's a snob. Dad's never met him."

"You know why I'm warning Nigel off him." Roddy took Ailie's hand beseechingly. "You tell him."

"I don't know what you're talking about."

"But it was yourself told me!" Roddy screwed up his face, brought his hand down in a clumsy sweep. "Ach, years ago." He turned again to Nigel and waved a warning finger. "The day you ride off with him will see us both into the sunset!"

"Blethers, Dad, blethers!" Nigel smirked in embarrassment. "Hey, Ailie, let's try and tidy the place up a bit for Dad."

"All right." As they rose and started shifting bottles, Ailie murmured in a low voice, "I don't know exactly what Uncle Roddy means, but if he tells you to avoid that boy, avoid him!"

"What!"

"If he says I said that boy spells danger, then I did. And he most assuredly does!"

"You too?" Nigel's lip curled in disgust. "Adults! You're all alike. Well, Gary's my best mate, and he's never let me down, unlike everybody else, and I'll not let him down either!"

Jasmine opened the door to him, her face wreathed in smiles. Sandy took pride in never commenting on clothes and such trifles, but he noticed the trouble she had taken to charm him. She wore a loose white lacy blouse against which her sunny skin glowed, and her face was made-up, light blusher and red lipstick. Pandora never wore make-up, and Sandy too, maintained disapproval. Yet, the idea of Jasmine's gilding the lily just for him – after all, they weren't going out – was flattering.

Could she cook! Her mushroom pakora was crisp and light, her vegetable masala melted in the mouth, and her rice pudding, with all grains separated out, luxuriated in a sweet cream. Since wine does not accompany curry, she had provided beer, and at the end a couple of Drambuies which went straight to his head.

They discussed his work, and hers. She was a dental hygienist at the local Child Welfare Clinic. . . They discussed her marriage.

"It wasn't anybody's fault. I guess we were just too young. We developed different ways."

"How?"

"Well, Iain got more and more tied up in his job. Particularly when he joined this new advertising company. When he had a deadline to make he wouldn't come home until ten or eleven at night."

"Knowing he had you waiting at home for him? Incredible."

"It was expected of him. They all did it. Occasionally they just stayed the night in the office – didn't come home at all."

"All I can say is," Sandy's eyes washed over her face, "it takes all kinds."

"I could understand, he had to build up his career. He was in a competitive field."

"So who wants competition?" Sandy reached out and brushed her cheek with his hand. "Give me collaboration, any day!"

"But even when he did come home," Jasmine frowned slightly, "he seemed to have nothing to say. He just pored over his work all the time, or watched the telly. He never wanted to talk, or . . . anything."

"Manifestly a screwball of the first order," pronounced

Sandy, "and a man of no taste, forbye."

An electric organ stood in the corner. Jasmine admitted she could not play a note. "It belonged to Iain. When he went, he left it behind. He meant to come back for it, but I suppose he forgot. Can you play?"

"I've never tried. Still, a keyboard is a keyboard." Sandy sat himself down. "These buttons must be various sound effects. And these others will be the accompanying rhythms?"

He footered around for a bit, trying out various beats. He found out that by pressing a magic chord button he could attain the effect of a backing band to support his melody.

"This is fun! Like being in charge of an orchestra!" He glanced round, and caught a bored look on Jasmine's face. So he switched off the backing, set the tone to violins, and played and sang *Black Eyes* to her, but changing it so that he sang,

> *Where the Kelvin flows,*
> *a sweet Scottish Rose,*
> *set my heart aflame,*
> *Jasmine was her name.*
> *Her dark Indian eyes,*
> *seemed to hypnotise.*
> *My heart skipped a beat,*
> *when we two would meet.*

She rose and came to him, laying her hand on his shoulder.

> *Eyes of ecstacy,*
> *always haunting me,*
> *always taunting me,*
> *with your mystery;*
> *Tell me tenderly,*
> *you belong to me,*

> *for eternity,*
> *black eyes talk to me!*

"That was beautiful!"

So was she. As he looked up at her, close and radiant, Sandy was seized by a passion so strong that he trembled. His breath quickened, and when he rose he felt faint. To steady himself he reached for her, and she came into his arms as if she had been made for them. Her lips were soft and full, and there was a fragrance about her hair which made him pull out the band and run his fingers through the waves.

Jasmine kissed him again and again and clung to him as if they would never part. Then she took his hand and pulled him gently out of the room. In a red haze Sandy allowed himself to be led to the bedroom, and watched Jasmine unbutton her blouse and slip out of her skirt. He caught only a glimpse of her golden body before she was under the sheets.

A small voice muttered 'Pandora' but he had overcome it before he was out of his trousers. The sheets were cool, Jasmine warm, and to his shame he climaxed before he even entered her.

"I'm sorry," he murmured. "I don't . . . " He stopped himself before telling her of the wonderful control he and Pandora had achieved together. However, Jasmine smiled gently, kissed his hand and placed it on her breast so that he became ready again, and this time all went perfectly, with a text-book finish in tandem.

After a last cup of coffee, drunk against a background of John Denver's *Annie's Song*, Sandy took his farewell of Jasmine, promising to come again, but still not giving her his own phone number or address. Out along Crow Road the very stars seemed to yell out – You've done it! And he felt as if he had newly lost his virginity. All jumped out in stark reality, as if he were intoxicated, the ragwort under the hedge, the pale moon above the tenements, the scent of the year to come.

As he was waiting for the bus home, a hoarse fellow hove in sight selling morning papers. Sandy bought a *Daily Record*, and read it en route. On the front page was a story about four members of the so-called Scottish Provisional Army helping the police with their enquiries into a plot to blow up imperialistic symbols and rob banks.

Sandy put his key in the lock in trepidation, preparing his story. He had had to meet a client over a drink, to discuss a very complicated portfolio, and they had ended up having dinner together. However, he had no need of worry, for Pandora was very far from concerned about Sandy and his whereabouts. He found her sitting over a flaming waste-paper bin, dropping in letters and pamphlets and photographs. He asked no questions, and neither did she.

On his fourth visit to Jasmine, while they were lying in bed, post-coitally, with her hair spread out on his shoulder and his hand below her breast, he broke it to her.

"You recall Pandora MacAlpine? Well, I've been living with her for the past eight years."

Beneath his palm Jasmine's heart began to thud. She answered, serenely enough,

"You don't want to marry her?"

Jasmine would assume that it was the male who baulked at marriage.

"No," he lied, in knowledge of the three proposals of marriage Dora had received from him to date.

"Do you still. . . "

"Make love? Only occasionally." (Whenever we happen to be in bed and awake at the same time . . . about once in three weeks.)

"Do you not . . . " (find her so attractive any more?) . . . "

How does she . . . " (compare with me as a lover?) "If . . . "
(only we could be on equal terms, instead of you with another
woman and me with only you!)

"When I make love with Pandora, I always get the feeling
her mind's elsewhere."

"You mean, she's frigid? Does she not reach orgasm?"

"She reaches orgasm every time. But somehow, it doesn't
seem important to her. It's as if she's planning her next
project, even as her body's responding to . . . " He stopped.
How could he betray Dora like this?

"So orgasm is just a mechanical thing to her?"

"Let's not talk about it."

"Just like scratching an itch?"

"I said, I didn't want to talk about it!" (How could he
sully Dora and her intellectual approach to sex, to love, to
life, discussing it in terms worthy of a women's magazine!)

"I'm sorry!" (But, surely, he should be the one to apologise,
two-timer that he was?)

"Jasmine, if you feel you'd rather not see me again. . . "

"No!" Her arms tightened around him. "I don't want to
lose you!" (Could it be true? Would she accept this, to be
concubine to Dora's spouse? A beautiful creature like Jasmine,
taking second-best? Could he support this role, deceiving
Pandora indefinitely – for Dora would never take this, if she
knew!)

As, indeed, she did. She greeted him on the stair landing.
"How goes it with the fleshpots?"

"What do you mean?"

"Jasmine Patel. Fresh from the sheets of whom you are."

"I. . . "

"Don't waste your breath denying it. Remember, I have
my spies everywhere."

He tried attack. "And you called me megalomaniac!"

"Don't try to twist things. I'm the wronged one here."

"I thought you weren't the jealous type. What happened to free love and independence?"

"For a person like me it's impossible to have respect for anyone who is attracted to a bovine little clinger like Jasmine."

"Hah! A woman scorned always descends to personal abuse. Don't tell me what Jasmine's like. You've never met her."

"Was I wrong?"

"Jasmine's . . . indescribable."

"Like Pakora."

"She's lovely, and above all *good* in a way you couldn't understand. . . "

"She's good in the sack," asserted Pandora.

"Well, yes. That too." Sandy glared at her. "That is important."

"Okeydoke. Make your choice. Me or the Perfumed Garden."

"Well . . . I . . . "

"Right now. Forever more."

Sandy sighed. He looked at Pandora for a bit, stretched out and touched her hair, all wild and fly-away as usual. She jerked away.

"No sloppiness, please. Choose."

"I can't . . . we can't just discard all we've built up over the years."

"That's settled, then." She bustled in. Sandy followed and timidly closed the door. She rounded on him. "Only understand this . . . if you ever step out of line again, with Old Creeping Vegetation or anybody else, that's it. Curtains."


"Considering you haven't touched a note in five years, you're not too bad." From Steve, a compliment!

Ailie shut the piano lid. "Last time I heard the opening sequence of the Warsaw Concerto, Sandy was playing it in the school hall for prayers." She crossed the room and began pulling pieces of plasticine out of the carpet pile. "Dr Mathieson's going to hypnotise me tomorrow."

"What good's that supposed to do?"

"She says it'll help us to find the real me. If only it works! I want to be a proper member of the family."

"I know you do." Steve gave her a kind smile.

"I'd be happy enough to stay at this age and carry on from here. I'd only have missed out on a few years. There'd be loads of time left to get to know my boys." She laid her hand on Steve's arm. "All of them."

"Don't talk that way. Gives me the creeps," said Steve.

# 3

DR MATHIESON'S FACE waxed and blurred into a floury bab. Her watch dangled in the foreground.

"Tick tock! Tick tock! Tick tock!"

"I'm a wee bit scared of losing consciousness," murmured Ailie.

"You won't be really out," soothed the Morning Roll. "Aim for a nice relaxed state. Don't try to talk yet."

"Tick tock! Tick tock! Schizoid! schizoid! schizoid!"

Ailie opened her eyes. A pair of button eyes looked back at her. Mary Ann, her old rag doll. Across the room, Jojo's bed was empty.

From the east the sky grew grey and the last of the stars disappeared. The sun rose big and red through the fog, melting the frost on the bungalow roofs and greening the front lawns. The avenues where the owners of all the parked cars lived were deserted, and only the winter birds noticed the figure emerging from No 46, running down the drive, weaving among the parked cars towards the river.

As the morning drew on, smoke rose out of the chimneys of the church-attending residents. The mist dispelled, the bells pealed, and ladies in tall hats, men in sheepskin jackets trotted out of their porches and into their cars.

Inside No 46 Dorothy rose, washed and dressed, and put the kettle on. While it was heating she strode into the living-room, gathered up the bottles, and aroused Roddy with a wet dish-cloth.

"Wha-a-a-ss-a time?

"It's eleven o'clock, but don't worry. It's Sunday."

"Did I not go to bed last night?"

"You did not. Nor the night before. The kettle's on." She yelled up the stair "Time to get up!"

While Roddy and his sore head competed with the kids for the bathroom, Dorothy poured herself a cup of tea and drank it over the *Sunday Post*. Sandy reported, "Jojo's gone again, Mum. Her bed's rumply, and she's away."

"If she's not here she'll get no breakfast, that's all." Dorothy washed out her cup, opened the fridge door and started cracking eggs into the pan.

Roddy and Ailie came in together and sat down at the table. Dorothy gave Ailie her cornflakes.

"Did you have a good night, dearie? . . . Ailie? I'm talking to you!"

"Yes, Mummy."

"None of the nasty dreams, or faces, or anything?"

"No, Mummy." (Best keep it simple!)

"Could I have a pint mug of water, please, Dot?"

"Turn the tap and you'll get as much water as you want. Toast, kids?"

"Yes, please, Mum."

"No thanks, Mummy."

"Did you remember your tablet, Ailie?"

"Yes, Mummy."

"When do we have to be at the old folk's home?"

"Two o'clock."

Ailie frowned, and ate a couple of spoonfuls of cornflakes. Presently she asked, "What are we supposed to be doing this time, again?"

"Ailie! Even you can't have forgotten. That stuff we've been rehearsing all week!"

"Ailie goes round in a dwam, doesn't she, Mum?"

"Do we have to go?"

"We have to. You don't want to disappoint all the nice old ladies and gentlemen, do you?"

"O-o-o-h Dot, pet, could you pull the curtain a bit more? The sun's streaming right in on me." Roddy cupped his hand around his left temple.

"Take another Alka-Seltzer if your head's bad. There are more potato scones if you want them, Sandy."

"You know, Mum," Sandy remarked, "you're fairly putting on the weight. I think you're fatter now than Mrs Patel."

Dorothy closed her eyes.

Out by the Allander, Jojo sat on a stone looking for fish in the running brown. Beside her, the grass sparkled like emeralds. She was a sapphire in a sea of emeralds. She drew her anorak around her against the moist West wind. (Cold it is, and sharp and wet the ground, but rather here than back there. If I ran and ran straight as an arrow, across the river, over the brown, grey and green fields, jumping over the rocks and the wire fences, how long would it take to reach these hills? What if I could fly?)

"Catchin fish, hen?" An old man in a long coat. (Nuisance of an old man, disturbing my solitude with his white bristly chin, his watery blue eyes, his brown scarf and bonnet. Poor old man, probably with no home of his own.)

"No. Just looking."

"Lookin, eh?" The old pest sat on the rock beside her, mud-caked boots at the water's edge. Jojo slid off her stone onto the ground. The grass soaked cold into her ski-pants. (Chill in the kidneys. Piles.)

"Ah hud a wee lassie like you, hen." His breath stank like Uncle Roddy's. "Lovely black hair." He reached out and stroked her hair. Jojo drew away sharply and stood up.

"Aw, sugar, ah'm no gonnae touch ye." He felt inside his coat and pulled out a half empty bottle. He took a swig and wiped his mouth. "Hoo dae they ca ye?"

(I must not tell him my name! I shouldn't!) "Josephine."

"And wherr dae ye stey, Josephine?"

"Over there." She waved vaguely towards the bungalows back in the civilised world. "I'll have to be getting back, now." She stepped away. (He's spoilt it all, the lovely primeval scene, the grasslands and the brown hills where the Picts must have trod the self-same ground and gazed upon the self-same scene!)

"Will ye no stey for a wee blether?" He held out the bottle. "Want a sup?"

"No thanks. I really must be going."

"Whit age ur ye, Josephine? Sixteen?"

"Fourteen." She started running up the hill. Better even back there than here, now.

"Ye wee fuckin snoab! Awa hame tae yer swell hoose an yer Daddy wi his big caur!"

Back home. "Clear out!" ordered Sandy. "We're having a private discussion!"

"So, discuss! It's supposed to be a free country." Jojo poured Cocopops into a bowl and got the milk out of the fridge.

"Mummy told us. . . "

"Shut up. This doesn't concern Jojo."

"Tell me or don't tell me. See if I care." Jojo settled down with the *Sunday Post*, turned to the HON Man page and began to munch.

"Mummy says she's going to have a. . . "

"Ailie! Do you have to tell every Tom, Dick and Harry?"

"What a pair of sweetie-wives!" Jojo's heart sang. (That'll put their noses out of joint. I'll get the baby over to my side. Then the odds'll be evened. Funny. I somehow can't picture Auntie Dot letting Uncle Roddy . . . Suppose she did it to boost Glasgow's population or something. Or maybe just to show that she still can.)

"So, madam! You're back!"

Jojo swivelled in her chair and rested her eyes on Auntie Dot's tummy.

"I'm waiting for your explanation, Jojo."

"I was out."

"Obviously, you were out. I want to know where."

"Just out."

Dorothy stepped closer and peered. "What have you done to your ears?" She paused for a reply and none came. "You've had them pierced! At your age! You silly, silly girl!"

"What made you do a daft thing like that?" asked Sandy.

"They'll all take you for a rag tag and bobtail, now," scolded Dorothy.

"When did you get it done?" asked Sandy, the troublemaker.

"Up the town. Robin Hood Gift shop."

"I said when. What time of day?"

"Friday afternoon."

"Are you telling me you weren't at school? Jojo, what am I to do with you?"

Jojo offered no suggestions.

"I haven't the time for all this nonsense. Well, don't look to me to write you a note. You can get yourself out of this mess."

"The thought never crossed my mind."

When Jojo finally laid the *Post* to rest and wandered into the living-room, Dorothy was splendid in a long tartan skirt, Sandy and Ailie in kilts and red velvet jackets.

"Auntie Dot. Auntie Dot. I want to ask you something."

"Not now. We're far too busy. Jojo, while we're gone you must look after Uncle Roddy. He's not very well today."

Jojo cast a glance at Uncle Roddy, white-faced, tousle-haired, clutching a cup of tea and staring red-eyed at nothing.

"All right, Auntie Dot."


"Fine lass you have there, Mrs Macleod. She looks so wee to be up on the stage."

"Ailie's small for her age. She's eleven."

"Eilidh! Now that's an uncommon name down here. Have you Highland connections, yourself?"

"I don't, although my husb . . . well, actually, we don't spell it the Gaelic way. It's A-I-L-I-E."

"I see. Is that not a bit of a halfway house? Was it a compromise you wanted?"

"It's short for Alison." (And what has it to do with the minister's wife, anyway? Cheeky besom. Her man puts on a dog-collar, and she thinks she's the Queen of Sheba.)

"And you, young man, will be Sandy Macleod."

"Sandy Lorimer. The name's Lorimer."

Dorothy broke in quickly. "First, Sandy and Ailie will sing a well known favourite, *Annie Laurie*. If anyone feels like joining in, please do." She seated herself at the piano and struck the first chords.

Ailie found to her relief that the words flooded into her mouth almost without passing through her memory. Even when Dorothy changed key for *Jessie the Floo'r o' Dunblane*, the lyrics seemed welded to the melody at a level below consciousness.

"Now, Sandy will play and Ailie will perform for you one of the dances favoured by the Highland aristocracy of olden times, the Highland Fling."

Sandy's fingers flew over the keyboard.

"What a pianist!" enthused the minister.

"The instrument isn't really suited to the dance," fretted Dorothy. "Maybe I should start sending him for accordian lessons!"

"He certainly has the hands for a keyboard! And the girl has a good pair of legs. I mean, she's a dainty enough dancer."

By concentrating hard, Ailie camouflaged the rusty parts. The audience noticed nothing amiss. Although it was some years since her last performance, she did have a decade and a half of experience tucked up in her juvenile frame.

Halfway through the tea-break Dorothy finished her crumpet and made her way to the Ladies where she checked her hairdo and renewed her lipstick. Back out, she gave the nod to the minister, who clapped his hands for silence and a return to the seats. This time Dorothy took the centre stage herself. Her children stood respectfully by.

"In case you think I let my children do all the work. . . " (Pause for polite laughter) "Mr Nicholson has kindly offered to play for me while I sing *Flowers of the Forest*."

Hushed silence as the minister sat at the piano. The first key he offered was too high, but the second was just right. Her timing, her enunciation of the Doric, her pitch – all was perfect. No one would guess her condition. (And yes! there are two old ladies with tears glistening in the crevices. Applause is the breath of life!)

"That was truly moving, Mrs MacLeod," declared the minister. "A fitting climax to the afternoon's entertainment."

"Ah, but it's not the end," smiled Dorothy. "We don't want to finish on a sad note, do we? The children will now give us *Bonny Dundee* and again, they would appreciate any help with the chorus."

She gave the starting chord.

*To the Lords of Convention. . .*

What was this? Only Sandy's voice ringing out, singly, in the hall. The audience appeared worried . . . Dorothy stopped playing and stood up. There stood Ailie, in the centre of the stage, body rigid, eyes white and dead.

"It's all right, Mr Nicholson. No thank you, there's nothing you can do. She'll be all right in a minute."

"Would a cup of tea help?"

"No, really, it's not necessary. She's just over-tired. She was ill when she was small, you understand, and she's suffered from these fainting turns ever since. I'll just take the children home." (Yes, better away from all the pitying looks. How could Ailie give me such a showing-up!)

Back in the car, Dorothy glared at Ailie. "I thought you said you took your tablet!"

"I thought I did." (How hard to be blamed now for the tiny neglect of ten, twenty, thirty years ago!)

"She didn't, Mum. I saw her. She opened the bottle and looked inside and then shut it again."

"Why, Ailie? You knew we had a performance today."

(Yes, why indeed?) "It's a long time since I had any blackouts, Mummy."

"That's because you were taking the pills, you silly girl! . . . Well, well, no good blubbering now. Tears never solved anything yet."

The atmosphere hung about them as a dark cloud all evening. Dorothy recounted the tale to Roddy as she made the meal and Ailie got another lecture, this time in the sorrowful how-could-you-do-this-to-your-mother mould, from a Roddy full of Alka-Seltzers, eager for the good books and ready for his tea.

Only Jojo was openly delighted.

Jojo waited all evening for the right moment. Along with Roddy she washed the dishes while the other two played Monopoly. She started to her homework without a telling and finished it all before coming down to watch TV. At half-past nine Dorothy said, "Up to bed!"

"Auntie Dot, the thing I wanted to ask you. . . "

"Will it take long? I'm very tired, dear."

(Dear! A good sign!)

"It's just . . . " (How I hate asking favours!) "You know I'll be going into Third Year after summer?"

"Hmmmm?"

"Well, I was wondering . . . I'd like to . . . could I go to St Kentigern's instead, please?"

"What! You want to go to a Catholic school?"

"Yes, please. If I could. It would save you money, Auntie Dot. It's free."

"And, of course, you are always so concerned about saving me money. Come off it, Jojo. Cut the hypocrisy."

"It isn't just the fees. . . "

"What is it, then? Are you turning Catholic?"

". . . it's the price of the books. And the uniform too, if you like. I could wear anything to school."

"That would look great, wouldn't it? I send my own two to a good school and my stepdaughter has to make do with Middenhead Academy!"

"St Kentigern's isn't like that, Auntie. I know two of the kids who go there and they seem very nice."

"Since when have you been interested in religion of any kind?"

"It isn't the religion, Mum," Sandy revealed. "It's the Italian."

"Oh, the Italian business. Are you still on about that?"

"Look. . . "

"No, you look. You're no more Italian than I am. Your precious mother walked out through the front door and she never looked back. She left your father with two babies and do you know what she said?"

(Could I fail to know? I know this script better than the five times table!)

"She said, I'll take this one. He can walk! That was your wonderful Italian Mama for you. I'll take this one. He can walk." Dorothy glanced at Roddy who duly nodded. "It's been good Scots folk who've had the upbringing of you, my dear, so don't give me this Italian stuff!"

"I just want to learn Italian. I must learn it. Could I go to classes?"

"You think your marks are so high that you can take on extra subjects outside school?"

"She only got 9 out of 20 in her maths test last week," said Sandy, the cub reporter.

"Sandy and Ailie have their music and dancing classes!"

"So would you, if you showed the slightest inclination in that direction. Believe me, Jojo, it's been a sorrow to your Uncle and me that you've let all your chances go. Remember? When we tried you with piano lessons you wouldn't practise. Your only spare time interest is running wild."

"You should be an example to the others," put in Roddy. "You're the eldest."

"And a worse model they couldn't find."

Jojo looked from one to the other. She screamed, swept Roddy's glass from the table, pushed Ailie against the wall and pulled her hair, rushed upstairs.

"How dare you exhibit such temper! Come down here and apologise to your sister!"

"Uch, Mummy, just leave her. It doesn't matter."

"Why is Jojo always so bad, Mum?"


Thoughts of the night.

(Back to the old days – lying, waiting, wondering if there will be faces tonight. If they're nice ones, I won't mind at all. I feel nostalgic for the nice old Faces. Daddy's, maybe. He

always seemed kindly. If only . . . There, there it is. O-o-o-h
– a really bad one. Dark, hollow eyes, fixed desperate grin.
It's coming for me. There's nothing I can do. Struggle is
useless. If I could only move . . . call out . . . it's coming
closer . . . with the pillow . . . the pillow . . . ooooph. . . )

As Ailie flailed against the suffocation Jojo watched her.
After a few moments she heaved a sigh and went for Dorothy.
Ailie wrestled with the monster, grappled with the pillow,
threw it to the floor. She stared at the creature of darkness
and saw it was her mother!

(Dot when I first met her. Beautiful, strong, vivacious.
Married with three children, but clearly the one for me. I
cannot resent her contempt. If I were Dot I would despise
Roddy. As Roddy, I despise Roddy. Roddy as a teacher,
Roddy as a husband, Roddy as a stepfather, Roddy as a
father-to be. Coward slaves, every one. Fridays and Saturdays,
anaesthesia and vomit. Saturdays and Sundays, sore heads,
cold shoulders. The brass neck to check Jojo for her bad
example – and I didn't even win Dot's approval by it. Why?
Did the rot start with my parents, speaking Gaelic to each
other but English to me?)

(I hope the new baby is a boy. I have more success with boys
than with girls – or men. What's wrong with me, that I land
up with weak men? Two useless drouths in a row. At least
Joe left me the capital and the nice house. What'll Roddy
leave behind, once his liver screams to a stop? If he keeps his
job we'll be lucky. Yet, when I remember how he sang like
an angel, how his eyes were once blue as the sea, blue as
innocence. . . )

(Silly weak Ailie, with her fits and nightmares. How could
someone like me get a sister like her? School tomorrow. Can't
wait for the judging of the End of the Tramcars poetry

competition. Hope they make a big thing of it – announce the names of the winners at Prayers.)

(I am Italian! I am, I am, I am! Hate Auntie Dot, hate Uncle Roddy, hate Sandy, hate Ailie. Hate the house. Hate my school. Hate Sunday night. Hate Monday morning.)

At school, the following month, Sandy won first prize in the poetry competition and chose a history book. Nobody mentioned his triumph at Prayers, and so he typed out a piece about it himself and stuck it on the notice board. Ailie paused to read it and got fifty lines for coming into her own class late. Her teacher, scraichy of voice and fly-away of eyebrow, had the habit of ending mental arithmetic lessons with the catchphrase, "For the last five minutes before the interval I want you all to sit with your hands on your heads."

(Morning: the Lord's Prayer and Good-Morning-Miss-Dalziel – said with a curtsey or a salute. Schonell's Spelling List and Mental Arithmetic. After the interval Formal Arithmetic and Problem Arithmetic. Pounds, shillings pence, halfpence, farthings (it's an old book). Hectares and acres. Miles and furlongs. Runaway trains and unplugged baths. After dinner particular analysis, Old Subject, Tom Predicate and all. Last come the 'fun' subjects: history, geography, occasionally singing or drawing. Beyond the afternoon interval sewing traycloths and knitting dishcloths for the sex whose expected future lies in close contact with such skills and such objects. Handwork for the future breadwinners. Regularity, discipline, competition, the belt. How would Crawford and Davie find this classroom?

Ah . . . *the bell, the bell, the b-e-l. Tell the teacher ah'm no well.* A rhyme I learnt on holiday in Cullen, where there are bairns. Not here where there are children.

Down the stair in a crush. There are some girls from my

class playing at ropes. I ought to join them, if I want to live my childhood to the full.)

"Getting a good look?"

"What?"

"It's that creepy Ailie Lorimer. Spying on us."

"Can I play too?"

"Will we let her?"

"Mebbe. I suppose it's a shame for her. She doesn't have any friends of her own."

"HIGH, LOW, SLOW, MEDIUM, DOLLY ROCKY HOPPY PEPPER. HIGH, LOW. . . "

"Caw higher, Ailie!"

(I'll never manage when it's my turn. Not after all this time. There's a game of Stroke the Bunny over there. That would be more my line – plenty of running about, but no skill. It wouldn't even bother me to be het – I could get all that into perspective now.)

"Gimme the rope, Ailie."

(Now for it. Hope I don't make too big a fool of myself.)

"HIGH, LOW . . . Ooops!"

"That was tails. Tails don't count."

"It was counted with me."

"We didn't count it with Helen."

"But it was counted with me. It was, it was!"

"Look, Ailie, do you mind being out again so quickly?"

"That's all right." (Blessed are the meek, for they shall inherit the rough end of the rope.)

"Thanks, Ailie. You're a sport."

(Fee-paying school charm, borrowed from *School Friend* and the *Girl's Crystal*).

Ailie tried to take bets on the sex of Dorothy's baby. Unfortunately the others all seemed to concur that it would be a boy and she got no takers. Nigel arrived with the first frosts. Ailie warned Roddy not to take his car when he went to visit the new sprog, but he heeded not her advice and so lost his headlight and his no-claims bonus.

On the day of the Parade of the Last Tram Ailie took a sheet of sugar paper and painted on it in black poster paint,

> FIRST PERSON ON THE MOON
> NEIL ARMSTRONG
> JULY 20th 1969

She had used up both sheets she had taken from the school Art Department before she learned to judge the size of the printing, so that in the end it looked like an optician's testing board.

Dorothy had planned to take all the children into the city centre to view the Transport Pageant, but the dull blustery weather, and snuffles from Nigel, put her off. Sandy went, with two pennies and a ha'penny to bend under the wheels, and Ailie also sneaked out, with her poster rolled under her arm and Roddy's Brownie camera over her shoulder. She did not like to stop an adult in case she sounded cheeky, and she feared to stop a boy in case he mocked her, and so in the end she got a girl to take her, holding the poster towards the camera, with the Transport Parade to her back.

Roddy used the rest of the film up on his only begotten son. However, when it was developed, what with the rain dinging, the girl chittering and the cheap camera, the photo was more porridge than proof of second sight.

On her 40th birthday Dorothy looked in the glass and the image therein was pleasing to her. Flawless makeup, camouflaged flaws, and sculptured auburn coiffure – a credit to the trade. Slimming biscuits had seen her figure back to its pre-pregnancy state.

As she turned down Crow Road she was irritated at having to go to work on such a rare day. On the nearside, railway cottages glowed rosy in the morning sunlight, while across the road trees bent fresh foliage over the fence of the High School's playing fields. (If only I could get advance warning of a day like this! Ah, June, June!)

Under Jordanhill Bridge and into Broomhill. On the stroke of 8.30 she parked the car, grabbed her bag and swept in.

"Good morning, Barbara."

"Good morning, Mrs MacLeod. The kettle's just boiled."

Dorothy perched on the reception desk and sipped the unsweetened coffee.

"Today's my birthday, Barbara."

"Many happy returns!" (35? No. She'd be better preserved than that. 40?)

"Yes, I'm Gemini."

Barbara opened her magazine and flicked to the appropriate page. "Stick closely to your usual routine. Today is not a day for taking chances."

"Hmmmm?" Dorothy sipped. "You know, Barbara, I was a seven-months baby."

"Really?" (Self-centred bitch. Thinks everyone should be interested in her life story.)

"Yes. I've always felt I should have been Leo. Leo is more suited to my personality." (And Roddy's Cancer. Fire and water never did mix.) "What has Leo to say?"

"A day for enjoying life to the full. Promising new relationships may develop."

"Ah." Dorothy grew tawnier by the minute. The door opened. Sadie, the junior, entered. "Well, well, miss!" Dorothy glared at the clock. "And what's the story this time?"

"Slept in!" Sadie flounced through to the back shop. Dorothy raised plucked eyebrows, gulped the rest of her coffee and followed after.

"Now, Sadie, do you really want to be a hairdresser? Tell me honestly, now."

Silence.

"You know your mother was keen for you to make a go of it here."

Silence.

"When I took you on it was as a favour to your mother. She's helped me so much with Nigel. Do you want the job?"

Silence.

"Answer me if you've got a tongue in your head at all!"

"Aye, well, the pey's no that great, is it? Twenty-five boab. Mingy!"

"Pardon?"

"Ah sayed it wisnae very much."

"That's because you're learning a trade. You're a lucky girl, getting the chance of an apprenticeship. You know I would send you to college in August if you wanted."

"An ah like ma Setturdays tae masel."

"We discussed that at the interview. You know hairdressers always work on Saturdays."

Silence.

"For your mother's sake, I'm going to give you one last chance. Try to smarten yourself up. Comb your hair and don't use so much lacquer. Wash your overall more often. Remember you're representing Aurora Hair Salon to the clients. I'll be speaking to your mother about this little talk."

As Sadie slouched out, Barbara brought in the mail. "Mrs Douglas phoned. She cancelled her appointment with you for this afternoon."

"You have remembered to keep my diary free for tomorrow afternoon?"

"That's right. Sandy's prizegiving, isn't it?"

"Yes."

Barbara smiled. "I take it Sandy's walked off with the best

prize as usual?" (Stuck-up wee swot. His mother over again.)

"Second, this time. I'm glad to say he seems to be coping as well with the secondary curriculum as he did with the primary one."

"Second in the class, eh? Must be marvellous to have brains like that." (Only second? He would get a bawling-out that day!)

Dorothy slit the first letter with a red-tipped nail. "Ah! Here's the note from the company repairing the hairdrier. It's ready."

"Was that in Ayrshire?"

"Largs."

Barbara left. Dorothy crossed to the window and drew aside the net curtain. Across the street, at the foot of the tenements, were gardens. In one of the gardens was an ornamental cherry, lately in bloom. No bird was to be seen, but wafting across from that tree, across the noise of traffic, was as sweet a song as blackbird ever sang.

June warbled, beckoned, summoned Dorothy. She looked at the sky, the sun, the streets, the tenements, the cars. She walked into the main salon. Already two of the girls were hard at work.

"Barbara, I've decided it would be quicker for me to drive down to Largs myself and pick up the drier. After all, we don't know how long delivery might take."

"The firm was reliable enough last time. And we don't urgently need it."

"No. It would be best if I picked it up."

"Whatever you think." (Wish I was the boss!)

Dorothy almost danced out of the Aurora Hair Salon and into her car. She turned her face on the new Clyde Tunnel, the south, the west, the sun, the country roads, the hills, the sea, and her back on the shop, the clients, the husband, the kids, the high buildings and dusty narrow streets.

A tree-lined drive swarming with blue-garbed figures. Four doors for four family members: primary girls' door for Ailie, secondary boys' door for Sandy, secondary girls' door for Jojo, main door – Doric pillars – for Roddy. Past the gold scroll of pupils who Gave Their Lives, past the decorated plaque of dux medallists to which Sandy would one day aspire, past the framed photographs of prefects from the black stockinged largely short trousered 1900s to the box-pleated grey flannelled 1960s. All these things Roddy passed without seeing, for it was five to nine, he had a headache and he had passed them all a thousand times before.

Men's staffroom – black coffee and a musty gown. The bell rang before he had finished drinking and he had to pour it out and hurry down for Prayers.

*God be in my head and in my understanding. . .* (Oooh! my head!) Under the observation of the other teachers Roddy closed his eyes and moved his lips.

Mrs Nichol at the keyboard and seven hundred piping voices. *Stride manfully onward, dark passions subdue. . .*

(Dark passions? In these fledgelings from well-feathered nests? Myself, now. . . )

The Lord's Prayer came to an end and the Rector read out the announcements, from what the first fifteen had achieved at the weekend to what extra preparation time was being given to the Bursary Group. Then Mrs Nichol struck up her Sousa march and the crowd left in single file, like blue knitting unravelling. All except six, caught talking, who waited behind to be told which Psalm they must copy out, thrice.

Roddy unlocked the cupboard in his classroom. First Year, *Midsummer Night's Dream.* Second Year, *As You Like It* and *Merchant of Venice.* Third Year, *Henry V* and *Julius Caesar.* Fourth Year, *Macbeth,* Fifth, *Hamlet,* Sixth, *King Lear* and *Othello.* So it was, had been, and evermore would be.

This period he had a Third Year class, but as the Academy

believed in forward planning, they were already well into
*Macbeth.*

"George, Macbeth, Sheila, Lady Macbeth. On you go."

> . . . *That which hath made them drunk hath*
> *made me bold.*
> *What hath quenched them hath given me*
> *fire. . .*

Roddy's attention wandered through the window, out to the
playing fields where thirty skinny youths were sprawling about
after an egg-shaped ball, interrupted by shouts and whistles
from their dwarfish teacher. Period Two would bring Fifth
Year inside and the tennis-players outside. Roddy liked
watching tennis. His teaching experience was lengthy and
uniform enough for him to follow a match while picking out
routine points of difficulty.

"Stop there, Philip! What is meant by Hyperion to a satyr?"
(Game to the pretty blonde girl in the extremely short tennis
skirt.) "That's right. On you go again, Philip." (Good they're
changing sides, so Blondie is at this end now. Wonder whose
English section she's in? Nice tanned thighs – must have
been abroad at Easter.) Yes, Roddy preferred tennis to rugby.

> *Had he not resembled*
> *My father as he slept, I had done't . . .*

Sheila intoned. The old memory returned and Roddy
wallowed in it. In a macabre way he enjoyed thinking the
thought right there in front of all these gently-reared innocents.
Even after all these years, parts of Macbeth still awakened the
guilt. Midsummer Might's Dream was so much safer.

The noise level in the classroom reached its usual mid-
period peak. Roddy mostly ignored the racket unless he

thought it would attract investigation from elsewhere. Stuck at the end of that corridor, it was unlikely. Grumbles from the success-oriented pupils about not being able to hear were to him as water off a duck's back.

Ice-cream at Nardini's! Dorothy sat back in a wickerwork chair and looked through the door to a pyramid of foil-wrapped chocolate and sugar. To her right was the wild western sea. White wings bobbed where once there had been longships.

"Dottie MacCallum!"

A stranger, so blond he could be a Viking. Yet, what stranger would call her by her earliest name?

"Stan!"

He sat down beside her. "Dear Dottie! How long has it been – fourteen years?"

"What brings you to Scotland?"

"I never left." He ordered a knickerbocker glory for himself.

"Never . . . Why didn't you write to me? Why didn't you tell me?"

"But I did. I wrote to your lodgings and the letter was returned."

"You were so sure you were gone forever. If I had thought for one minute . . . "

"In London I met some of my fellow-countrymen. They told me . . . well. I could never go back. Not after what they told me. Not for good."

"I left the bed-sitting-room a couple of months after you went away." (Curse! curse! curse! It could all have been so different!)

"I have been back a few times recently."

"Mmmm?" (My whole life! Bloody, bloody hell!)

"I stayed with my brother and his family each time."

"Waldek, wasn't it? How's he keeping?" (I still can hardly believe it!)

"Fine. He has four children. My own parents died a few years back, you know."

"I'm sorry to hear that." (One tiny misunderstanding!)

"Now we stay in Gourock."

"We?"

"Carol and I. We have two children."

(Of course. Carol and two children. Curse, curse, curse!)

"What about you? Did you marry?"

"Twice. My first husband died."

"Children?"

"Three of my own and one step. Are you on holiday here?"

"I am not as lucky. I had to attend a business conference this morning. Now I should go back."

"When I knew you, you were hoping to study engineering back home."

"Instead of which I went to the Royal Tech. Now I'm a design consultant."

"That sounds very grand." Dorothy smiled. "And I run my own hairdressing salon."

"So we are both successes in life." He patted her hand. "From the beginning it was predictable."

They paid the bill and left. Before them sprawled Cumbrae, and to the left, the Arran peaks, sharp and clear. Behind them, children played on the mechanical amusements, rockets, satellites, horses.

"Let's go to the miniature zoo." Dorothy pointed along the promenade. "Have you seen Bimbo, the woolly monkey?"

"I have a better plan than that." Stan pointed to the Millport ferry, just approaching. "Let's play truant together. We can hire bikes and cycle round the island."

"Sounds wonderful!"

"We will visit the Marine station. We will have a picnic tea at Lion Rock."

"Lion Rock. I remember taking the children there, once, long ago. Jojo found a slow-worm." (Only, it wasn't Jojo. It was. . . )

"I always think you Scots are so impervious to the charms of your own land." Stan smiled like an angel. "Have you heard about the Millport minister who prayed for the islands of Great and Little Cumbrae and for the adjacent islands of Great Britain and Ireland?"

"Everybody has heard about him." (And there are charms which leave me anything but impervious, oh yes there are!) "I still can't get over it, that you stayed here, after all. After our big farewell scene, and everything." (And not only that, not only that!)

They boarded the ferry and stayed up on deck. For Dorothy, water rolled back under bridges and the sands of time poured up. His brown arm close to hers, his breath like caller air (without a trace of whisky on it), her heart thumping in anticipation. (Like last time, only better, because I no longer sweep up the trimmings in someone else's shop, and his statelessness is but a romantic bit of his past.) As they rounded the headland Stan almost put his arm around her shoulder and she almost rested her head on his breast. And, almost, she told him about it, what there was to know.

"There's the Crocodile Rock!"

But not quite.


Four o' clock at last. Sandy generally walked to the bus-stop alone, through the back lanes.

Around the corner, two serge-garbed lurkers. Michael Kenny and William Robson.

"What do you know! If it isn't Swotty Lorimer, Brain of Britain!"

"Hurry on back, son. You're missing homework time!"

"Skedaddle, troglodytes!"

"What did he call us?"

"I don't know, but it wisnae very nice!"

"Is your case heavy?"

"Probably full of encyclopaedias and dictionaries. (Snigger) He needs them for talking!"

"Let go of my schoolbag!" Sandy pulled, the others also pulled. William grabbed Sandy's cap and threw it over a hedge into a garden. "Oops, sorry, my hand slipped!"

Sandy sized up the stranger's garden. Missing, that cap would cost a hundred lines or a Psalm copied out thrice. "My hand's going to slip all over your face in a minute."

"What's this, wee man? Threats of violence?"

"Here's what I think of his threats." Michael wrenched the schoolbag away, opened it and turned it upside-down over the hedge. Books, jotters, pencils, even his precious flask disappeared with a flutter and a crash. "Now wipe your hands all over my face if you dare. Come on, now! Do what you just said!" Michael advanced, pulling Sandy's tie awry, twanging his belt, pulling his hanky from his pocket, butting him in the face. "Aw, the shame! And his mummy keeps him lovely!"

"He husnae the guts!" William reached down towards the hem of Sandy's kilt. "Let's see if he's a true Scot!"

"Leave him alone!" Hands grabbed William's shoulders and shoved him into the hawthorn hedge, face first.

"Who the fuck's she? Is she his girlfriend?"

William struggled upright. "Naw, too old! Wee Swotty wouldnae know what to do with a big developed girl like that!"

Michael pointed and whispered to William. Both boys sniggered.

"Hey, you lassie. Beady here wants to ask you something!"

"Naw, I don't!" (Snigger).

"Go'n. Ask her."

Jojo followed Sandy into the garden and helped him gather up his belongings. Neither spoke. They hurried out before the owner of the garden should see them.

"Here, does your bum bleed every month?" Both boys collapsed into laughter.

"You horrible wee rats!" Jojo flung herself on them. "If you ever, ever, ever," she banged William on the ears, "bother my brother again. . . "

"It's his sister!"

"Cowardy, cowardy custard, hides behind his sister!"

"Two against one says you're the cowards, not Sandy!" Jojo pulled Michael's hair and thumped him on the nose. The boys took to their heels, casting back, "She's not a girl, she's a steamroller!"

"She's too much woman for me!"

"Pansy Potter, strongman's daughter!"

"Thanks for nothing!" muttered Sandy, when Jojo caught up with him.

"Oh, is that your attitude? Sorry I interfered, and you coping so magnificently! Them losing all your books, that was all part of your great plan, was it?"

By the time they caught a bus it was half empty. They sat in separate seats all the way home.

Nigel could already toddle to the coffee table. He lifted a biscuit, sucked a corner of it, thrust it at Jojo. "No want!"

Jojo took and ate the thing, while Nigel made the return trip for another. He avoided Sandy, who scorned him, and Ailie, who prodded his soft neck like the harbinger of doom.

In the bedroom, Dorothy fussed over Sandy's black eye. "Today, of all days, Sandy! You never get into fights!"

"I told you, Mum, it wasn't my fault. Two of them jumped me."

Jojo lifted Nigel and wandered through. "I was the one who stopped them from beating him up."

Dorothy carried on putting make-up over Sandy's eye.

"If I hadn't come along it would have been much worse."

"What was it, Jojo? Are you the only one with the right to bully the children?" Dorothy did not raise her eyes for even an instant.

"The clock tower, do you see it anywhere?"

"Mummy, how are we ever going to find our way out in the dark?"

"The Southern General isn't as bad as Stobhill Hospital was! That's out in the sticks and no mistake! Anyway, it won't be dark when we come out. These days the sun doesn't set till after eleven."

"Mummy, that's not the first time we've gone round that circle!"

"Stop talking, both of you, and look for somebody to ask."

"Mummy, why do I always have to dress so stupidly?" (Like a strawberry creamola foam, frothy in pink lace with a big satin bow in my hair.) "If we have to be Americans, why can't we be modern Americans? Sonny and Cher, for instance."

On the platform, Dorothy pounded out honky-tonk, while Sandy, hand on heart and panama hat in air, strained, *Oh, I want a pretty baby and it might as well be you, Pretty Baby . . .* Ailie sidled in, tap-dancing furiously, *Pretty Baby, Pretty Baby. . .*

After the *Cakewalk*, while the children changed into their costumes for the Old West spot, Dorothy's trained voice delivered *America the Beautiful*. (Soon, Sandy's voice will be breaking, and he will have to concentrate on the piano for a while, letting Ailie and me carry the vocals. How will we manage? Ailie's such a greeting-faced creature. Just never looks capable of enjoying herself. Such a face doesn't go down well, no matter how skilful the performance. What has she to be so miserable about? Nice home, caring family. Her illness doesn't affect her life, yet.)

(Hope these troglodytes don't spread it round that it was a girl that chased . . . that helped me get shot of them. What total, total troglodytes, the pair of them!)

(If they only knew! I could tell Sandy something of great interest to himself, but I won't. I'll leave it up to someone with vengeance to seek and no love to lose. I could tell Mummy something appertaining to Nigel, but I won't. I don't want her to hate me. Or should I? Maybe she could forestall it. I just know she wouldn't believe me, that's all. Nobody believed me even when I was an adult – and who takes the word of a child? Oh, what a weight I have to bear until the First of July – and what will happen then? Where will I go when this big Blank is filled in?)

Performance over, tea and cakes over, home sweet home.

"Why do I never get any support from you? I've to run the house, my business, the performances. Why can't you see to a simple thing like repairing the toilet cistern?"

"You're better at that sort of thing, dear," said Roddy, mildly.

"And what is it that you're better at? You're a non-fare-paying passenger in this family, Roddy, a bit of baggage. That's right, reach for another drink. Solves everything."

To hear them fight made Jojo feel warm and excited. She lingered until Dorothy chased her upstairs. She entered the bedroom silently.

"What are you saying?"

"Nothing." Ailie turned her face to the wall. Jojo bounded to the bed and pulled her round.

"You were saying something! What was it? Were you talking to yourself?"

"No."

"You were so!"

"I wasn't. I was talking to people."

"What people?" Jojo looked around. "You're nuts!"

Ailie tried to pull the covers over her head. Jojo hauled them back.

"Tell me, Ailie! What people were you talking to?"

"You wouldn't believe me."

"Try me." Jojo lowered her her voice and assumed a kindly smile.

Ailie stared at the ceiling. "I often talk to people."

"What kind of people?"

"Folk. Like Daddy, for instance."

Jojo started back. "Were you praying?"

"No! I talk to Daddy, that's all. And he answers."

"Aw, come on! You must think my head buttons up the back!"

"I've always talked to Daddy, and sometimes he answers. I talk to other people too, but I don't always know them."

"Do you see them, too?"

"Sometimes. Sometimes they look bad."

Jojo stared at Ailie for a minute. "You're crazy." She undressed, climbed into bed and switched off the light. The shadows drew across and reached her. Whenever a car passed they looked alive, like teeth on the ceiling. Jojo hated the night indoors. Lengthy and unloving.

"Ailie."

"Yes?"

"Could you get Rosita?"

"Rosita. I don't know. I wouldn't know her if she came."

"Promise not to tell, and I'll show you something." Jojo climbed on to Ailie's bed and shook her. "Promise!"

"I promise."

Jojo switched on Ailie's bedside light and bounded to a

drawer. Vests, pants and liberty bodices tumbled to the floor. From the back Jojo retrieved a carton of paper hankies. She stuffed the undies back into the drawer and brought the carton to Ailie's bed. From under the hankies she edged out a small framed photograph. Identical twin girls.

"That's us when we were four years old. Can you do it?"

"I'll try."

Jojo stared at her for two minutes, then, "Are you getting anything?"

"Not yet."

Another breathless wait.

"What about now?"

"No. It's no good."

"You wee cheat!" Jojo hit Ailie on the side of the head and pulled her hair hard. "I knew you were having me on, you stupid liar!" She shook Ailie by the shoulders until her sister's eyes turned up dead to the world. Jojo hissed, "You crazy epileptic!" and pushed her out of bed. The photo fell to the floor and the glass broke. Jojo sneaked downstairs, taking care to miss the fourth and sixth step. She disposed of the frame deep down in the kitchen bucket and returned to her room. She was about to find a new hiding place for the photo when she noticed an address scribbled on the back.

MARIA – XXX SUNNYBANK STREET. The number was impossible to decipher.

Somewhere in Scotland's industrial capital Jojo had a real mother and a brother. A full-blooded brother, none of these halfs and steps. A big brother who would take her part.

November. The dreichest month of all the year. Towards the end the sun grows weary of life, rising later and retiring earlier below hills, tenements or sea, so that workers on regular shifts get themselves up, away, into shops, factories and offices and out again without ever cheering their souls on the white light of nature. Vision is all-electric – the round bulb of home, the blue square of television, the flicker strip of work, the yellow sulphur of the black streets.

In such a black street one shiny wet night stood a group of boys. Three sported the Brylcreemed quoifs and drainpipe trousers which were already passé in more fashionable circles, the smallest still agonised under the straight fringe of childhood.

"Heh, did ony o' yese see the pictur that wis oan at the fleapit last week?" asked Drew. "*The Seven Samurai* – fantastic."

"Ach thae films is fur weans. Ah go mair fur Brigitte Bardot." Woody sniggered. "Whit a boady."

"Ah go fur sex in films an aw," announced wee Willy.

"Whit wid you know aboot it, son?" snorted Woody.

"Me an Anne-Marie Devlin. . . "

"Uch away back tae school!"

"Don't go tae school the morra!" jeered Willy. "It's St Andrew's Day!"

Tony dropped the stub of his Woodbine and tramped on it like a man. "Fancy a bevvy?"

Woody and Drew cast nervous glances down the road to where the Rob Roy spilled yellow light through frosted windows.

"Whit like ur they aboot servin ye?"

"Uch, come an we'll jist go tae the caff," proposed Willy.

"Haw – jist cause he's nae chanst o' gettin served!"

"Who's nae chance?" However, he made himself scarce when the others pushed open the door.

The pub was not crowded, but seats were few and most of the customers stood around the bar. Shrunken wee bauchles in dark grey jackets and checked bonnets, burlier National Dried Milk generation in tight trousers, slicked hair and sideburns, thin bomber jackets arrogantly open to the winter chill. At the far end games of darts and dominoes were in progress.

The boys, right sex but wrong age, slunk into a pew near the Gents, where they might remain hidden from the bar staff.

"Gonnae you take the orders, Tony? You're the biggest."

"Whit yese a fur, then?"

"Pin' a heavy."

"A hauf n' a hauf."

"Aw, Woody, ye're at it! Pey day isnae till the morra."

"Okay, make mines a pin' a heavy an aw."

At the bar, Tony stood on the brass rail, raised his chin, lowered his voice and the barmaid never gave him a second glance.

"Were ye at the club game on Saturday?"

"Aye, magic, eh? D'ye see the second goal wee Malky pit in?" Woody punched the air. "Ya beauty!"

"He's goat glory in his feet, that yin."

"He telt me he wis tae get a trial fae Celtic."

"Izzat a fact? Here, did the same thing no happen wi his brither? Naw, naw, ah tell a lie. He wis tae get a trial, but he never took it up because he goat the chanst o' a motor mechanic apprenticeship wi Saunders."

"Haw, trust big Eddie tae make a fuckin hash o' things!" crowed Woody.

"Noo, insteid o' a fitba player he's an apprentice mechanic, a second year apprentice mechanic, and," he paused for dramatic effect, "a redundant second year apprentice mechanic!"

"Whit!"

"Aye, did ye no hear? Saunders closed doon a week past therr."

"Heh, ma uncle works therr!" squawked Drew.

"Well, he disnae work therr ony merr."

"Heh, did youse two hear aboot the two players, wan Catholic, wan Proddy, baith equally good?"

"Aye," grunted Tony.

"Naw. Gie's it."

"Which wan does Celtic take?"

"The Catholic?"

"Naw. The Proddy. That wey, Rangers cannae huv either o' them! Heh-heh, good, eh?"

"Auld as the hills," remarked Tony.

At ten to ten the switching on and off of the light and the opening of the doors to the night frosts signified the legal end of Scottish hospitality.

Tony scuttled to the bar for last orders and carried back six full pints. No time now for conversation. The boys opened their mouths and poured to finish as much as they could before shoving-out time.

The zig-zag way to the fish and chip shop was punctuated by detours round the backs of closes. Lost in an anaesthetising haze, the boys munched out of fragrant newspapers, until Drew's stomach poured its carry-out, still fighting, over the pavement.

"Haw haw! Wee Drew cannae haud it!"

"It wis the haggis supper! Rank rotten, so it wis!"

"Maybe aye an maybe hooch-aye!"

"Maybe the sun's shinin the night!"

His manhood at stake, Drew looked around for a distraction. "Hi – therr wee Maggie Morrison! Woody used tae go wi hur!"

Two girls, wobbling home, peerie heels and straight skirts. The lads closed in and a cloud of scent assailed their nostrils.

"Hello, lassies, wherr youse wans gaun the night?"

"Naewherr wi youse, that's fur shair!"

"Uch, c'moan, be nice an we'll gie yese a chip!"

"Keep yer stinkie chips – we're no needin nae chips, ur we, Senga?"

"Senga?" Woody squeezed in between the girls. "Ah wanst knew a lassie wis yer mirror image, so she wis! Wull ah tell ye hur name?"

"That's the line they aw try on me. Gonnae gie it a rest?" Senga let out a squeal. "An keep yer manky paws tae yersel!"

"If ye've nae objection," Woody informed Maggie, "Ah'll take this wan fur masel. Ah fancy yer pal mair'n ah fancy you."

"Ah fancy the haill world mair'n ah fancy you," Maggie told him.

Woody burst into song:

> *If you were the only girl in the world,*
> *and I were the only boy. . .*

"Must be full moon," remarked Tony.

"Fur Chrissakes," Drew leaned against a closemouth, holding his midriff. "Pit a sock in it, gonnae?"

The girls allowed themselves to be drawn through to the back of the close. Woody and Maggie, leaning against the wall, took up their relationship where they had left it in June, abandoning Senga to close encounter with Drew.

"C'moan, hen, don be ro'en. Jist a wee kiss. C'moan."

"Uch, gie's peace!" Senga turned her head to the right, out of the way of the thick wet lips. Further along the passageway that led to the back court, Woody seemed to be trying to push Maggie through the wall. One hand was flat against the grey stone and the other was lost inside Maggie's angora jumper. His eyes were closed, his face red, his mouth clamped like a lamprey on Maggie's. No help there. Senga looked to the left. Tony stood at the closemouth, in profile against the light, a red spark of a cigarette in his hand, his own thoughts in his head. He was the very spit of James Dean, only a wee bit darker.

"Whit's yer pal's name?"

"Tony. Ye're . . . an awfu nice-lookin burd. Ye've a lovely boady. C'moan, gie's a brek."

Drew's breath was overpowering, his saliva sour and hot. His tongue was in her mouth and his sweaty palms were everywhere. Senga pushed him away.

"That's enough."

"How's it enough? Uch, Senga, hen, ye don't know whit ye're daein tae me. Ah'm crazy aboot ye, so ah um." He pulled her back to him and once again she was enveloped by his body and his stinking breath. When he backed off for oxygen Senga again sought support.

"Maggie. . . "

She stopped. Under her coat Maggie's skirt was right up over her hips and her pants hung loosely around one ankle. Woody's jeans were baggy at the seat and open at the front where his body was thrusting against Maggie's. Senga belted Drew over the ear with her fist. As he reeled, she lunged for the closemouth, nearly falling as she bent to snatch her handbag. She ran up the street, coat flapping, nylons splashing until her heel snapped. One skinned knee, two laddered nylons, one coat muddied, one white skirt split up the front.

Tony behind her, his hand on her arm. "Moan, hen. Ah'll walk ye hame."

"Beat it!" She shook free and scrambled to her feet. "Ah'm no as green as ah'm cabbage-lukkin."

"Ah know ye urnae."

"An ah'm no a lassie like Maggie, neither."

"Ah never thought ye were."

"Ah don't dae that soarta thing. Ah believe in keepin masel pure, n' that."

"That's aw right wi me." He waved his hands in the air.

"Ah'll no lay a finger on ye, ah promise. Ah'm jist takin ye hame tae yer maw."

(Maw. What had she said? "All men are wolves, and a gentleman is just a patient wolf.")

# 4

ON THE FIRST OF JULY Ailie went with six schoolmates
to the shows at Glasgow Green. It was the first time her
mother had allowed her so far from home on her own. She
went on the Waltzer four times in a row. On the fourth cycle,
she felt the world receding, along with the shouts, the laughter,
the Everly Brothers.

(What now, what now? On the first of July long ago, I
woke up in hospital where they had taken me. They tried to
make me remember the past eighteen months, and then they
sent me home to my mother. This is a hospital, if I'm
not wrong. White bed. White room. White people. No, not
totally white. Just very pale, very old and in washed-out
clothes.)

Ailie moved to rise out of bed. How stiff she felt. She
pulled the blankets off her legs. Legs! Broomsticks wrapped
in creased hospital issue. At the second attempt the
broomsticks obeyed the commands of her brain and she rose
unsteadily to her feet. Her surroundings swam. In the right
hand corner crouched an aged crone with wispy white hair.
Her vacant eyes were fixed on her left hand as it tenderly
caressed her right hand, patting the back, tickling the palm,
stroking each finger carefully into position and smoothing the

nails. Against the wall opposite stood an equally wild-looking dame with long grey straggles past her shoulders, that put folk in mind of the auld Witch of Endor. This one's face was twisted in anguish and her hands were the feet of a hen. What a selection. After a moment's hesitation Ailie started to make for old Greylocks, who looked in partial touch with the world of here and now.

"Get you back to your fuckin bed!"

Ailie turned in alarm, to see a large woman with piled-up hennaed hair bearing down on her. The woman grasped Ailie by the wrist. "Ah'm no gonnae tell you again! Get yer face doon on that fuckin pillow. Ye've been warned!"

The valkyrie tried to pull Ailie back to bed by force. Ailie glanced back to see if Greylocks would assist her, and to her dismay found herself looking into a large mirror!

"Now, now, Marie. Leave poor Ailie alone!"

Two nurses, chosen as much for their brawn as their tender loving care, sprang up from nowhere. The male one escorted Marie back to her place.

"Please," Ailie asked the female "What year is it?"

"Never you mind the year. You're supposed to be in bed. It's nap-time."

"I'm not tired!" How thin her voice! "Tired is the last thing I am!"

"Never mind. You're still to be in bed."

Ailie dug her heels in.

"Hey, Eric! Gonnae help me with this one?"

Eric deposited Marie in her bed, pulled bars into place around the sides, and strode back down the room. His face assumed an expression of coy charm.

"Now, Ailie, I want you to behave yourself again like you did yesterday. Will you do that for me?"

"Was she good yesterday? She's never good for me."

"Och, but she likes me. Don't you, old girl?" He tweaked

her playfully on the waist. Ailie glared at him. He went on. "She ate all her lunch yesterday and slept like a baby. Didn't you?" He chucked her under the chin.

(Please, Please, may I escape soon from this stage?)

"Well," said the female nurse, "I don't know how you do it. I find this one one of the worst. She's a crafty old get, mind you. . . "

"Oh, she's crafty, all right. She tries to get round us in her own way, don't you, Ailie?"

They had reached the bed. Eric prodded her to get her on to it.

"Please," she clung on to him as he shoved her down. "When was I seen by the doctor? How long have I been here?"

"You've been here a good while." Eric began prising her fingers off his sleeve. He got her forefinger off.

"How long?" He got her middle finger and ring finger away.

"I don't know. Since before I came here." He pulled away her pinkie and her forefinger and thumb clamped on again.

"And how long have you been here?" Ailie's skin broke out in gooseflesh.

"Let me go, you daft old rabbit!" He wrenched his arm away.

"Are we talking about weeks? Months?" Sweat trickled down her brow. "Years?"

"I've been here two and a half years. Satisfied?"

"No! No! No! No!" Ailie lashed out and caught the female nurse on the nose. The nurse jumped back with a yelp. Eric forced Ailie down and deftly pulled the bars into place around the bed.

"Are you okay, Linda?"

"Think so," snuffled the nurse. "It's no bleeding."

Ailie rose to a kneeling position. Eric forced her back.

"That was very, very bad, what you did just now to poor Nurse Watters. Lie down!"

"No! Let me out!"

"LIE DOWN!"

Ailie sat down. "Please, I want. . . "

"LIE DOWN! RIGHT DOWN!"

Ailie lay down.

"There you are, Linda! Don't take any nonsense from her. It's as simple as that."

Ailie began banging with all four limbs on the bars. Linda the nurse disappeared. . .

"Now, Ailie, what's all this banging in aid of? It doesn't do any good, you know."

(I want out, I want out, I want out, I want out.)

"Is there something you want?"

. . . and reappeared with a syringe.

"No! no! Please let me . . . expl . . . Aaaaagh!"

"There, there. All better now."

"I . . . want . . . to see . . . a . . . doctor. . . "

"There's no doctor here just now, dear."

"What . . . year . . . is . . . it?" Her voice was not only slow, now, but deep . . . like . . . the . . . Great . . . Bell . . . of . . . Bow.

"Sure she asks the year like other folk ask the time?" remarked Linda to Eric.

And . . . here . . . comes . . . a . . . chopper. . .

Eric's head detached itself gracefully from his shoulders and floated around the frame of her vision, bantering grin and all. The whole ward dwindled to a mound of white. White pillow. Sunlit pillow. Her pillow. Her bed. Her room. Half-past seven on her alarm clock.

(I'm back! I'm back! It was all a dream! It never happened! I'm normal, normal, normal, normal, normal!) She kissed the pillow, kissed the counterpane, the clock, every dear familiar object. (It's worth having a nightmare, to feel this good afterwards!)

"Jojo!" She burst through to the kitchen where Jojo was drinking tea. "Oh, Jojo, I've had such a terrible dream!"

"What was that, Ailie?"

"I dreamt I lived into the future! No, it wasn't that simple. I dreamt that my consciousness wasn't fixed properly in Time."

"How do you mean?"

"I was experiencing my whole life, but not in the same order as everybody else."

Jojo drained her cup. "I still don't get you."

"It is very hard to explain. . . "

"Then don't try." Jojo carried her dishes over to the sink and turned on the taps. "It's over now."

"Over now! Jojo, you don't know how happy that makes me! Everything was so unpredictable. I ended up in this horrific sort of hospital for crazy old folk."

"A geriatric ward."

"I guess so. If we could all see what lay ahead. . . "

"Cut it out! You've got a lot to look forward to. There's your wedding coming up. . . "

"Oh yes, Steve!" Ailie laughed. "When I see him I must tell him about his part in my dream!"

"What was that – Bluebeard?"

"Sort of."

"Maybe it wasn't a dream after all."

"Don't say that, Jojo. Not even in jest."

Jojo went out and returned with her coat on. "Hate to shatter your lovesick thoughts, but are you not bothering with clothes today?"

"That's right," beamed Ailie. "I've got to go to work!"

"Must be nice to feel that way about your work."

"I've still to tell them all at the office!"

"About your dream?"

"No, silly, about Steve's proposal last night! About my engagement." Ailie chuckled. "Can't wait to see Shirley's face."

"Ailie. . . "

"You remember me telling you about Shirley? She was the one used to . . . Jojo, what's wrong?"

Jojo gazed at Ailie, then closed her eyes and turned towards the door.

"Come back! What is it?"

"Nothing."

"It can't be nothing."

"It is nothing. Only, you might think it was something."

"Tell me Jojo. Damn it, tell me!"

"Steve didn't propose to you last night. It was eight months ago. Your wedding is next Tuesday. Look on your finger, there."

A sapphire and diamond ring. The very kind she had wanted.

"Look, Ailie, it doesn't mean anything."

Ailie continued to stare at the ring. (How could I have missed it?)

"It's just another Blank."

"Is it?"

"You've had them before, and longer than this. Look at that time when. . . "

"When I was eleven. I know. I know."

Jojo hovered for a minute before the door. "Are you all right?"

"Yes. I'm all right."

"Are you sure?"

"Yes, yes. Of course. You go on. Don't be late on my account."

"Maybe you should take today off after all. Phone in and

say you've caught a tummy-bug."

"Rubbish. It was only a dream."

"I don't like to leave you like this."

"Just go. I have to think things out."

"Look, Ailie, we'll talk about it fully when we're home again this evening."

"That's what we'll do."

"Or you might want to phone. . . your mother about it."

"Honestly, Jojo, it's not that important."

"All right, then. I'll bring in fish for the tea tonight. Okay?"

"Okay."

The front door shut.

(I wonder if I can do anything to stop it? Probably not. It seems to be planned in advance.)

Ailie rose and shut the windows, curtains and door. As she opened the oven door and took out the pans and shelves, she considered her confused life. (This time, I'll be in comprehensive company. Everybody dies sooner or later.) As she knelt down, turned on the gas and laid her head inside the oven her last sensation was of discomfort.

(Hard floor. Crick in the neck. Sickening smell. Makes me gag. Fancy so many choosing to go in this position. Would I have been better to have taken tablets? But then I might have found myself . . . in a go-chair! Yes! Wheels whirling, pavement flying past. Other children skipping along-side . . . Jojo, Sandy . . . Rosita!)

As she had fixed as a gloomy child on Nigel the infant, so the infant Ailie fixed gloomily on Rosita the child.

Two yellow dresses, two pink parasols, Sandy's big blue ball. Into the postcard shop on Seafield Street, past the houses painted pink, blue, green and black against the salt winds, under the viaduct along which trains would still thunder for the next nine years, and onto . . . the beach! Cullen Sands. Yards of sands, pails and spades. Sandy built a complicated castle with windows and a hole for the door, but the twins' castle had a moat and even a flag! Jojo found a baby crab and let it walk from her hand onto Rosita's and back again.

After the picnic, Dorothy and Ailie paddled in the water, while the three older children played Piggy-in-the-middle with Sandy's ball. Taller and stronger than Sandy, the twins kept it permanently beyond his reach. Sandy made a great Piggy until he went in the huff.

"Here it is, sulky Sandy!" Rosita ran into the sea clutching the ball, with Sandy after her. "To you, Jojo!"

"Here, Sandy!" Jojo held out the ball invitingly, and threw it to Rosita as Sandy approached. A great game. Sandy began to cry.

"There's your stupid ball!" Rosita hurled the ball as far as she could out to sea.

"I'm telling!" Sandy waded back towards his mother.

"Rosita! Come here!"

The twins trailed up the sand to Dorothy.

"You two think it's great fun teasing your smaller brother, don't you? Well?"

Rosita fixed her eyes on the sand.

"Rosita! Look me in the face when I speak to you! Why did you throw Sandy's ball out to sea?"

"For fun," whispered Rosita.

"We were just playing," whispered Jojo.

"Let's see how Miss Funny here likes playing the same game with someone bigger." Dorothy pulled Rosita's parasol out of the bag, marched over the sand to where the waves lapped, and flung the parasol out to sea. It caught the wind, all pink fragile paper and thin matchwood sticks, fluttered like a dying butterfly, plunged into the waves. It floated for a while, a pink patch on the green briny.

Rosita roared with rage. She started to wade out after the parasol, but Dorothy held her back. "Don't be silly, girl. It's far too deep out there. Maybe you know now what it feels like."

Rosita pulled away from Dorothy and ran up the beach, crying.

"You can have my parasol," called Jojo. "Come back, Rosita, here's my parasol."

"Pay no attention to her," ordered Dorothy. "Help me gather everything up. It's time we made tracks."

By the time everything was piled into carrier bags, Rosita was up at the far end of the beach from the steps which led down from the street.

"That's us away, Rosita!"

"Are we going to leave her behind?"

"She knows the way back as well as we do. It's just across the street and up the brae."

(Should I say something? What should I say? What did happen to Rosita, and when? Wish they'd talked about her a bit more in the days when. . . )

"Please come up, Rosita," called Jojo from the pavement.

"Don't leave her," said Ailie. "Something might happen."

A baby Cassandra. (Again, perhaps it wasn't today. Or even this year.) Dorothy called back once more, "If you don't buck up you'll get no tea."

Back at the caravan Daddy, who was not well, lay in bed while Dorothy prepared the tea. She set Sandy to laying the table while she and Jojo hurried back to the shore.

They looked where she had last been seen, scuffing her toe in the sand. Only seagulls wheeled and screamed. They asked a fisherman in a navy jumper and peaked cap. They asked a woman in a Paisley headsquare hanging up clothes in the yard between her gable and the sea.

The tea was cold and the shadows long when men trawled her out of the harbour, seaweed and white legs. Ailie and Jojo howled all night and into the morning.

"I killed her!" shrieked Ailie. "I killed her!"

Dorothy gave her two junior aspirins and when no one was looking Daddy, crying into his cups, gave her a slug of his whisky. After that she went out like a light.

Empty whisky bottles. Empty beer cans. And a sore head.

"Ooooh!" groaned Ailie. "I feel hellish!"

"So do I, Mum."

The kitchen table, the early morning light and David.

"What's been happening? What year is it?" She looked on the wall where the clock used to hang. "What time is it?"

"It's seven o'clock in the morning and it's 1994." Davie stretched. "Guess we had quite a night of it."

"It never ends!" Ailie laughed hysterically. "Just never ends!" She washed out a pint mug and filled it with soft clean Loch Katrine water. She drank it and filled it up again.

"Where are Steve and Crawford?"

"Crawfie's married and away, living in England. Got a girl pregnant last summer."

"A baby!"

"Deborah, they called it. Born a couple of months ago."

Crawfie came in, waving his hands in front of his face. "You two still up? Phew, what a stink of booze. Open a window, for God's sake." He crossed the room and threw up the sash.

Ailie and Davie shouted in unison:

"What you doing here?" – Davie.

"I thought you said Crawfie had. . . " – Ailie.

"What's this?" said Crawford. "You ganging up on me? Trying to put me out the house?"

"But where are Jill and Deborah?"

"Who?"

"Crawford, you. . . " David stopped. "Oh no. Jesus wept. Not again." He closed his eyes. "Mum, I take it all back."

"What the hell are you on about?" Crawford shook his head and made for the door. "You should put in along with Mum for a brain transplant."

"Maybe I should."

"David," (Surely not. And yet. . . ) "did you . . . did you mistake the year just now?"

"I guess so." David covered his face with his hands.

"You didn't seem too surprised."

"No."

For a long moment nothing broke the silence but the thudding of Ailie's heart. "Has it happened before?"

"Yes." David poured himself a pint mug of water and drank it. "What about cereal? Cereal is a nice clean thing to eat after a dirty night. Let's see," he opened a cupboard. "Och, we've let it run down. We used to have a much better choice than that. You can have Weetabix, Bran Flakes, or Coco Pops."

"Coco Pops."

He poured Coco Pops for Ailie and a mixture of all three for himself. "On my sixteenth birthday," he said between mouthfuls "I got pie-eyed for the first time in my life. On Drambuie."

"Well?"

"I woke up on an oil-rig, with no idea what I was doing there."

"What age were you?"

"25. As far as I was concerned, I hadn't evenfinished school and there I was supposed to be a roustabout. So I left."

"Where did you go?"

"Crawfie was married and Dad had set up with his fancy bit. You were on the funny farm. So I just knocked about hostels, drawing Income Support for a year or thereabouts. Till the next switch came."

"And then?"

"Then I was 19. I thought I still was, till Crawfie put me right just now. Suppose I must have slipped a year." He finished his cereal and pushed the plate back. "You know, I haven't sat my school leaving exams yet, but people tell me I flunked in all subjects. Wonder why I bothered to sit them."

"Our condition stops us from carrying out long-term projects, like studying for exams. I was in the bottom stream for most subjects at school. It was," she put in hurriedly "a selective school, you understand."

"What do you think causes it, Mum?"

"I suppose it's hereditary." For the first time in her consciousness she kissed her son on the hand. "Davie, I'm so glad I'm no longer alone!"

"Oh, but you are." Davie pulled his hand away. "We're both travelling through Time on yo-yos, but they're different yo-yos."

"Simply to be believed!"

"I've believed you since 2001. Much good it's done us."

"Is there no way we could use this ability of ours?"

"You mean disability."

"Don't you see, it's a blessing as well as a curse?" (What were all those arguments put forward long ago, or long ahead, by the Morning Roll in the pot-plant consulting-room?) "Most folk would give anything for the chance to avert future mistakes."

"No one will believe us."

"Surely there are others like us, somewhere."

"I've never heard of them."

"I could try again to trace my relatives. I'm sure Sandy doesn't have it. He's never had to come to terms with anything in his life. In the sixties, when rebellion was in fashion, he had to go out seeking problems to get hung-up over. I wonder about Jojo, though."

"There's nobody else."

"She didn't seem over-astounded, the time I started to try to explain it all to her."

"It's no use. We're quite unique."

"On the other hand, she's never shown any signs. My mother, she's far too successful to have had any of these troubles. Then there's Jojo's brother . . . "

"I want to kill myself."

"Listen. I know I'm going to end my days in hospital. So what? Most people end up there. They just don't know in advance."

"Yes, but. . . "

"And at least I know that I will still be there, and whole in body at ninety – or whatever! Think of that! Until I'm ninety I don't need to have any fear of death, or mutilation. Think of the risks I can take now, with impunity!"

"That's all very well. . . "

"Tomorrow, you could wake up suddenly at eighty, ninety, or a hundred. It's not so bad. You know one day you'll be eighteen again."

"But the worry of not knowing how long you're going to stay at ninety, or a hundred. . . "

"Other folk who are a hundred know it's forever. Folk like us – we can enjoy our hopes and our memories at the same time!"

"I suppose, when you look at it that way. . . "

"It's the only way to look at it."

David snorted.

"Meanwhile," decided Ailie, "we must publicise what we have to offer."

"Seeing the life you've had," said David, "I'm more inclined to keep it quiet."

"Palaver!" New strength surged through Ailie. "Prophets always suffer a little persecution. And they go right on prophesying."

"What do you suggest?"

They racked their brains.

"For a start," decreed Ailie, "a wee phone-call to the *Record*."

"You mean . . . the *Daily Record*?"

"And the *Express*. And, – why not? – the *Herald* and the *Scotsman*. Tabloids and qualities, all."

"What about the *Evening Times*?"

"And the Sunday papers, too. We want the best offer on an exclusive."

"Are you saying," David chuckled, "we should make money on it?"

"And why not?"

David rose and paced about a bit and sat down again. "When I was 25, it didn't seem to me that I was that rich."

Ailie shrugged. "Maybe it was all lying in some bank account."

"And didn't you end up old and forgotten?"

"For all I know it was an expensive nursing-home."

"Maybe I shouldn't kill myself yet."

"David, I've been where you are. Take it from me, this way's more fun."

David got excited. "Do we need to hire an agent?"

"We'll get one with the first profits."

"Let's drink to that." David opened a can of Tennent's.

"Nothing for me."

"*Slainte!*" He took a gulp. "Another way to make money – we could tell famous people when and where they're going to die, so they know not to go there."

"But we don't want to use the gift only to make money."

"We don't?"

"We also want to be of service to the world."

"We do?" David considered. As an optional extra, okay. "How?"

Ailie thought carefully. "There's the scientific knowledge to be gleaned from the future. Inventions, cures for diseases. . . "

"We wouldn't understand all that, though. Not well enough to remember and repeat it."

"All right then, what about politics? We could tell Cabinet Ministers how future generations will view their present actions."

"And forecast the results of elections. In fact, with us around, they wouldn't even need to bother holding the elections."

"Maybe we can stop another war from happening."

"Or at least," said David, "get our own show on TV. . . "

Ailie spread her hands impressively. "Focus on the Future, with Carmichael and Son."

"Carmichael and Mother."

Crawford wandered in again, with an envelope in his hand. "You two still yakking? Do you know your voices carry right up the stair?"

"Poor Crawfie," crooned David. "He so badly needs his beauty sleep."

"Beats me what you find to say to each other." Crawford ripped open the letter and scanned it. "Aw, shite!"

"Bad news?"

"Aye," sniffed Crawford. "Bloody travel agent's messed up my holiday in Benidorm. They're fucking over-booked!"

"What a shame," David commiserated. "Never mind. If you go to Majorca instead, beware of brunettes whose names start with the letter J."

"Who says I'm going to Majorca instead? I booked for Benidorm and it's there I'm going. I'm going down town this afternoon and I'll sort them out."

"And if you can't be good," put in Ailie, "be careful."

# 5

THE KNOWLEDGE THAT SHE was not destined to be killed or permanently injured removed Ailie's fear of motorways, and she took up driving lessons. Unfortunately the charm did not extend to her driving instructor's car or other vehicles or, for that matter, to the driving instructor and other road users. Lesson followed lesson, driving instructor followed driving instructor, test followed test and twenty-pound note followed twenty-pound note. With each backward-rolling hill-start, each reverse on to the middle of the pavement, each three-point-turn that lost its way, her confidence sickened, and with a bashed nose across a GIVE WAY it died. On the eve of her fifth test Ailie was so burdened with the weight of responsibility for the lives and property of all these anonynous vulnerable fellow road-users that she risked a refreshment or three.

She awoke to the winter of the year, the spring of her life and the life in her ankles, for her private dancing lessons had been supplemented by school jigs, reels and schottisches in preparation for the Christmas Party. She must have been having a mid-afternoon nap, for she was fully dressed, and on the pillow beside her lay the newly-read copy of Paul de Kruif's *The Microbe-Hunters*, the book which had inspired her to fill out all these doomed applications for nurse training, once she had realised that she would not pass the Highers necessary to be a doctor or a scientist.

Across the corridor, Dorothy put the finishing touches to her make-up, checked the hang of her skirt and left without her boots. Down the MacLeod path, or drive as it was called in the neighbourhood, past the neat lawn with its bare sticks and sleeping roses, up the Patel driveway with the rockery hard as iron.

Mrs Patel was small and plump, with a fresh, young-looking face and hair piled-up behind an Alice band. She wore a safe, straight shift dress in an inoffensive puce shade, little black pumps on her feet.

"Mrs MacLeod! So pleased you could come. The others are already here."

A sparsely furnished, well-carpeted lounge. Three ladies perched on a three-piece suite, sipping coffee. An ornamental glass clock with four gold balls inside on the fawn tiled mantlepiece. A good print hanging over the hearth – no other pictures in the room. Nothing exotic or even foreign to be seen – a strictly occidental room. Not even the Indian husband was in evidence.

"Do we all know each other? Mrs MacLeod, Mrs Meiklejohn, Mrs Ross, Mrs Thomson. Mrs Ross was just telling us about their redecoration."

"Yes, well, the big problem was what to do about the kitchen curtains. I really loved the pink pair, but now that the colour scheme is orange and white. . . "

"Dorothy. You don't mind my calling you Dorothy, do you? We're all first names today."

"Not at all. Go ahead."

"How do you take your coffee, Dorothy?"

"Black. No sugar."

"Ah, so you're like me. Watching the weight!"

"Well, not r. . . "

"Aren't we all!"

"Thet little shop at the corner sells rether nice cirtain material."

"Oh?"

"Yes, I heppened to notice yesterday."

"I came across a good diet in the *People's Friend* the other day. Based on eggs and salad."

"Sounds more painless than most diets."

"Yes, I'm not really all that concerned about. . . "

"But would silk brocade not be rather lavish for a kitchen?"

"Of course. I was relly looking for bedroom cirtains at the time."

"I put on a whole four pounds last festive season, and I've never lost them."

"Thank you for telling me, anyway. I'll pop in next time I pass."

"Would you like to try the cream meringue?"

"I think I'll stick with the crumpets."

"The only sneg is thet the shop won't make them up for you. You hev to do thet yourself."

"That's all right. I enjoy dressmaking. I make all my own clothes."

"Relly? Thet dress you're wearing – I was thinking what a pretty blue it was. Did you. . . "

"It's dreadful that we girls find it so much easier to put on weight than to take it off!"

A tear trickled down his cheek and landed plop! changing the golden loch into a salty sea. (The single positive act of my life was a negative one. If I could turn the clock back . . . ah . . . I would do it all over again. Wildness and weakness. Cursed combination. Suburban living sapped the one – the other remains.)

"My hubby, now, he takes these fits when he gets out the old tracksuit, the woolly hat, stuffs the ancient bags. . . "

". . . Inside his socks!"

"You've seen him!"

"I should think the whole street has seen him."

"Men! They're so funny!"

"Jasmine, pass round the Dundee cake."

"Jasmine's fairly stretching. You'll be into your teens now, Jasmine, eh?"

"They're all teenagers nowadays , aren't they? In my young day there were no such things. It was the awkward age, plain and simple."

"Mmmm, delicious. Your own baking?"

"I'd like to take the credit, but I have to confess, Jennifer brought it over."

"Clever Mrs Meiklejohn! Now, if only I could bake like that . . . "

"It always makes me feel so inadequate when I taste really good home baking and think of my own efforts . . . "

"What about you, Dorothy? Do you bake?"

"No." (And never feel so inadequate either.)

"And what does your husband do, Dorothy?"

"Teaches English at Scotus Academy."

"He must know my sister-in-law! She teaches French and German there!"

The door opened and he met the cold gaze of stepson Sandy. He turned quickly away, brushed his cheek with his hand, sniffed.

"Can I borrow your copy of Burns? Thought I'd start practising *Tam o' Shanter* now so's to have plenty of time."

Roddy did not trust his voice to answer with dignity. He waved his hand in the direction of the bookcase and, as the door closed again, he finished the dregs, poured himself another and downed it in one. He stood shakily, with the warm courage in his veins, the clouds in his head and the knocking at his heart.

"We are lucky in the Avenue to have as a neighbour Dorothy MacLeod, who owns the Aurora Hair Salon in Broomhill. Dorothy has very kindly agreed this afternoon to give us a demonstration of modern hairdressing. Who would like to volunteer to be the first model?"

> *My Mary's asleep by thy murmuring stream,*
> *Flow gently, sweet Afton, disturb not her*
> *dream.*

(Thank goodness I'm doing songs instead of spoken verse at this year's Burns Supper. You want to give as much help as possible to the memory when you know the shutters might come down at any minute.)

The fuzzy world beyond the condensation turned a deeper blue and the street lights came on, pink at first and then yellow, except for one – there always is a maverick – which remained pink and flickery. Not long now.

Reflected in the pane she thought she saw a Face, a sympathetic Face sharing in her thrill, but nobody was behind her.

(I will give it five minutes more. Then I will shut the book and go down and save him, with Sandy as witness to my timely intuition.) A prickle of excitement, of pleasureable anticipation, the complement to the let-down of hearing, years ago, the second-hand account of her glory.

"I never did approve of French combing, even when it first came in. Soon the public will find out what the professionals know – that French combing only serves to break the hair."

"It's the only way I know of getting the required height to the style . . . "

"But I don't think we should overdo the height. Not with prominent cheekbones and a heart-shaped face like yours."

"Jasmine, put the kettle on. We'll have tea for the next round. Mrs Thomson, the last meringue? It won't keep, you know."

"Ai'll leave the hendsome husband for little Jesmine."

A microscope on the table and Left Bank posters on the walls. Under the table, a heavy tape-recorder. Shelves illustrating the development of an all-round Renaissance puberty, from the red binders of *Look and Learn* to the constitution of an Opposing Op-art Society which Sandy had tried to found at school.

"Where's Uncle Roddy?"

"Away and don't interrupt me. Get your own practising done."

"I can't find him."

"Why do you want to?"

"I think I know where he is."

"Good for you. So you go seek, if you're that keen."

"I want you to come with me. I want to show you."

"Show me what?"

"Sandy. We have to get a move on. He's in danger."

"Eh? How do you know?"

"Please come, Sandy."

"Oh, cease your wailing, woman."

"So, as you see, bringing the hair back here and letting it fall forward there can create an illusion of fullness across the lower part of the face."

"What about lacquer?"

"With proper setting there should be little need for heavy

lacquering in this style. It should hold itself naturally. Nowadays the emphasis is on the natural look. Even in make-up, you'll notice, although heavy eye-make-up is modish, the fashion is for pale lipstick, as a reaction to the unnaturally red vampish lipstick of the past." She teased forward Jennifer Meiklejohn's left kiss-curl. "In the same way as the Flappers over-reacted to the Edwardian wasp-waist by unnaturally flattening their own figures."

The door bell went. "Jasmine, get that, dear."

"Could I ask Mrs MacLeod her opinion of the new fed amongst young gels for ironing their heah?"

Coatless, with his breath condensing before him, he was kept warm by his mission. When the door opened the warmth spread to his cheeks, for the girl before him had long shiny hair, flawless tanned skin and lustrous eyes. He recognised her as Ailie's playmate of lang syne, before Ailie's perjinketies and Jasmine's sojourn in India had separated them. Sandy despised boys who lusted after girls, as he despised everyone who differed from himself. He cleared his throat and mentally reorganised. "Is my mother in?"

Ladies in crimplene two-pieces or dark day dresses, ladies with arched eyebrows and narrowed vowels, nails and lips of burgundy, moulded tinted hair. Sandy approached the one who was his mother.

"Could you come back over, right away?"

"Why, what's happened?"

"It's Uncle Roddy."

Dorothy felt the eyes and her tone dropped. "What's wrong? Is he . . . ill?"

"He's in the garage. You'd better come. We can't move him."

"Is there anything we can do to help, Dorothy?"

"No thanks. It'll be . . . all right." (As if it is an everyday occurance for my husband to be lying in the garage.)

"What is it? Hes Mr MacLeod taken ill in the gerage?"

"Look Dorothy, are you sure you don't want our help?"

Roddy's first sensations were of a whirling ceiling and a raging dervish far, far away.

"You blinking idiot! What in Christ's name were you trying to do? You drunken sod, you could have killed someone."

"Mum, I don't know that he was trying to drive off. . . "

"You keep out of this, Smarty-pants! Of course he was trying to drive off! He switched on the engine and then he fell asleep before he opened the garage door!"

"Why did he shut the garage door in the first place?"

"Because he's an inebriated wreck who doesn't know if he's coming or going."

"Dot. . . "

"I'll dot you! Do you know you owe your life to Sandy?"

"He doesn't owe it to Sandy – he owes it to me."

"If he hadn't found you and opened the garage door and switched off the engine you'd be dead by now."

"I was the one made Sandy look."

"Anybody in the street who didn't know about your drink problem won't be left in the dark after this!"

"Want me to tell you how I knew he was there?"

The doorbell rang. "Ailie, get that."

"But. . . "

"Don't let anybody in, for God's sake!"

Ailie opened the door to Jojo and Nigel.

"Auntie Dot! I've taught Nigel a new song! He'll be up on the stage with you soon. Come on, Nigel – let it rip!"

> *My Aunt Jane, she took me in,*
> *She gave me tea, in her wee tin.*
> *Bread and butter with sugar on top,*
> *And three black balls out of her wee shop!*

*My Aunt Jane has a grand wee shop,*
*Lucky bags and lime juice rock. . .*

"Not now, Jojo, can't you see your uncle's ill?"

"But I thought you'd be pleased. We practised so long. . . "

"Away and practise somewhere else."

Jojo glared at the prostate Roddy (What's all the fuss? Tanked-up again – hardly a unique occasion!)

The doorbell again.

"Hello, dear. I just thought I'd pop over on mai way home to see if your mother needed any help."

Dorothy flew to the door. "Oh, hello, Mrs Thomson. Very nice of you to call, but it's all right now."

"End Mr MacLeod? How is he?"

"Much better, thank you. It was just a dizzy spell. He's fine now, really. He's resting."

From the front room came the sound of Roddy retching. Sandy rushed into the hall, into the kitchen, and re-emerged with a basin.

"I'm so gled. You hed us all worried beck there!"

Back in the front lounge "Christ, the carpet!" said Dorothy, and she sent Sandy back to the kitchen for cloths and soapy water.

"What's on his breath?" asked Jojo. "It's not just drink and vomit. . . "

"Carbon monoxide," said Ailie.

"He'd fallen asleep with the engine running," snorted Dorothy. "He was damned lucky we found him."

"I knew where to go to find him," said Ailie.

"How come?" asked Jojo.

"Because I'm able to. . . "

"It had to happen when I was nextdoor with half the neighbourhood. My God, he picks his moments!"

Jojo smiled. She slipped her hand into Roddy's and

whispered, "Don't worry. You're not the only one."

Roddy's eyes were half-closed. This could have been due to the toxins, but Jojo thought they might screen the resentment which surely smouldered there. Tenderly she stroked his forehead and kissed him for the first and last time in her life. "You shut your wee eyes, Uncle Roddy, and I'll make you a cup of tea."

Sandy had not known Jasmine, but she had known him. In his garden, in his den (through the wall from the room she shared with her sister), she saw him and felt him. At Assembly she heard him sing with gusto or watched him play them in or out, noticed his eyes rebelliously open during prayers. On Sports Days, while her classmates were sighing over some rugby hunk, Jasmine's eyes were on Sandy, keeping himself fastidiously clean at the expense of the match, courting unpopularity with disdain, deliberately, superciliously weedy. At debates she observed the ease with which he addressed the audience, the way he tossed his fair head and laughed. At Prizegivings she watched him sweep the board. What comprehensive talent. Music, languages, even maths and science. What complex ideas in such a head, probably all at the same time! How flattering to have such a mind seek out her company! What challenge to keep a brain like that interested in what she had to say! She recognised, of course, the way in which he had responded to her at the door. She knew that look well, had received it from lots of boys and not a few grown men. Coming from the boys, the gaze produced in her a frisson of vanity, coming from the men a shift of unease. Only when the message emanated from Sandy did she experience this thrill of something more than flattery. How delightful that this refined, clean, good-looking, clever, quick, confident, selective, Renaissance Prince should feel his body reply to hers in the age-old urge to pass on his inheritance! To mix his line with hers. What superior children they would be, too, assuming his abilities, his versatility. His powerful genes would assuredly dominate in such fields over her own ordinary ones!

Henceforth, Jasmine had a primary aim over and above her past one of pleasing her parents. She would nourish Sandy's spark of fancy, she would fan it to a flame, she would widen it to include his mind as well as his body, she would marry him and have her children by him.

Thus began her campaign. Whereas before, she had washed her hair and left it to its lustre, now she styled it, ironed out the kinks, converted it into romantic curtains such as framed the face of Sandie Shaw. As an intellectual, Sandy would favour natural-looking hippy styles, however laboriously produced, over lacquered bouffant. Whereas before, she had left her complexion to its golden nature, now she spent ages peering for imaginary flaws and covering them in *Light and Lovely* foundation, in applying lipstick of the palest peach (white or shell-pink, more fashionable, did not suit her at all), enlarging her weekend eyes in sooty mascara and eyeliner, and panicking with Dettol and creams at the infrequent plook. She shortened her skirts, including the school uniform ones, to six inches above her knees, and took to wearing *American Tan* nylons. Under penalty of a hundred lines, she had to wear her school hat at all times when outdoors in uniform, but she bent the brim and put the school badge at a rakish angle until, on her, it was an accessory instead of a toadstool. To keep his attention, once won, she borrowed books from the library on subjects dear to his heart, such as politics and music, and made assiduous notes. Sandy would not accept a dunderhead as a wife. It was too late in her school career to transfer to the Latin section, but by dint of extra study she made it to the top of the domestic science section. She badgered her father into talking more Punjabi at her. If she could not equal Sandy in school subjects she would at least retain some corner of knowledge he could not share. In this she would be a mystery.

Whenever she saw him, going in or out of the school gate, coming up or down his garden path, fear of the importance of the thing made her hunch her shoulders and poke her head forward before she scurried to say Hello and flash her best smile. More was not her place. The first three times she was rewarded by a flush of colour, the fourth by an invitation to come in and play Scrabble.

# 6

JASMINE WAS NOT THE ONLY ONE, that summer, to discover *plaisir d'amour*.

"They left under cover of darkness . . . " As they always did, paragraph after paragraph. Jojo's mind was centuries from Livy's *Hannibalian Wars*. She had already counted heads and sentences and wrestled her way via the back of the book to the meaning of the one which would fall to her lot. Now she was free to think her own thoughts as the passage crawled its way around the room.

"Barry Wilkie fancies you." Three weeks ago, a statement by a girl Jojo did not like, about a boy she had never looked twice at, opened up a whole new side to life.

She now looked forward excitedly to lunchtime, for Barry also attended dinner-school. From her lonesome position amongst the other Fourth Year girls she kept her eyes on her grey mince and scooped potato and hoped that his were on her. Now and then she would laugh uproariously at some half-heard unfunny comment at her table and she would strain her ears for his voice. The changeover of periods found her running to make it round detours which took in the classrooms where he might be found, then striding by with head high and sulky, licked Lollobrigida lips. Four o'clock was a time for scanning the horizon for a flying figure on a red bike. She washed her hair without persuasion. Lacking Jasmine's skill with the needle, she rolled the waistband of her school skirt over four times and stretched a waspie around the bumfle. The material was navy serge, the style box-pleated Jean Shrimpton. Detectable make-up was out of the question, but she turned Aunt Dorothy's *Evening in Paris* upside-down over her wrists every morning and had her hair cropped in the Mary Quant geometric style. Just in case she should develop a weekend social life, she bought herself a jockey cap and white *Evette* lipstick.

Baldy Bain, desperate for a smoke, heard the last pupil stutter out one of Livy's immortal lines, and glanced at his watch.

"Right, class, finish the rest of the passage in your jotters." He hovered for a minute, then left.

The period limped by in mutterings and scribblings. Jojo gazed out of the French window beside her desk. The classroom had been built as a hut on the roof at the time the post-war baby boom hit Scotus Academy. Along the roof to the right was a skylight looking down onto the classroom where Class 4D was masticating algebra.

Jojo let her hand slide to the latch and the French window swung open.

"Hey! Jojo's opened the window!"

"What did you do that for?"

"Just wanted a bit of air. It's like an oven in here." Jojo took off her school jumper. It was December and the temperature in the classroom was 55°F.

"Maybe she wants to go out there," sniggered Judith Campbell. "I know what it is – she wants to go over and look down on lover boy."

"Who's lover boy?"

"Barry Wilkie. She's fancied him for ages."

"I haven't the faintest what you're on about," sniffed Jojo.

"Oh, sure!"

"Aye, aye! Up the Clyde in a banana boat!"

"If I wanted to go out there I would. Old Baldy wouldn't stop me – if I wanted to."

"Pull the other – it's got knobs on!"

"All right then." Jojo climbed onto her desk.

"She means it! She's going!"

"She's crazy. Serves her right, if Baldy catches her."

Jojo swung through onto the slates. They were covered in ice and in some places insecurely fastened. As she edged towards her goal, the frosty wind whipped her hair, froze her arms through her blouse, bit her knees until they were rosy.

Skirt and blouse billowing, she knelt by the skylight and scrutinised the heads until she lit on Barry's. Short back and sides as in the regulations, heavy fringe shooting out at the front where the natural wave came.

A few people saw her. They pointed, muttered. giggled. Then Crabbit Carruthers, the Gorgon of the Maths Department, glanced up.

Jojo slithered back into her own classroom and shut the French window behind her.

"What happened? Did somebody see you?"

"Serves you right. What a caper! It could only be Jojo!"

"Did you see Barry?"

"After this he'll think you're just a silly wee girl – and he'll be right."

"You should leave the boy to do the chasing."

"He's too young for her, anyway."

"Jojo likes them immature – like herself."

Just as Jojo covered herself completely in Hannibal's elephants, the classroom door opened and Baldy and Crabbit billowed in in dreadful tandem.

"Josephine Lorimer! Step out here!"

Trembling, Jojo obeyed.

"Are you a monkey? Eh?"

Silence.

"We don't have monkeys at this school, do we, Mr Bain?"

"Nor do we want them, Mrs Carruthers."

"What will we do with her, Mr Bain?"

Baldy slid to the desk, opened it and took out the tawse. Jojo's face froze in disbelief.

"You've a choice, girl. You'll take the strap, or you'll come with me to see the Rector."

You could have heard a pin drop in that classroom. Jojo's mind raced. She'd had the belt often enough in her younger day – Miss Reid had had a policy of belting all those with more than two spelling errors of a morning – but at nearly sixteen! On the other hand, what could an interview with the Rector lead to? The 'O' grades were imminent – "I'll take the strap."

Thwack! Thwack! Thwack! Jojo's hands were no redder than her face, but she avoided the final humiliation of tears, and thanked God that Barry was not in her class.

"And, I must say, it's a dreadful thing for a girl of your age to be strapped – I can't recall it ever happening before. Can you, Mr Bain?"

"Never before at our school," responded Baldy, reddening himself as he slipped the tawse back in his desk.

Jojo avoided her schoolmates for the rest of the day. At lunchtime she hung about the cloakroom or the toilets with no appetite for the lunch she was skipping. At four, skulking to the bus stop by the back lanes, she heard a bike being wheeled behind her. Barry, and another boy whom Jojo scarcely noticed.

"Hello," Barry mouthed.

"Hello," she mouthed back, heart thudding.

Barry advanced as his second lagged tactfully behind. "I

was wondering if you were doing anything on Friday."

There was only one answer.

"Well, would you like to come and see the film *From Russia With Love?*

Jojo took pride in despising James Bond, and only the other week had publicly announced that no bribe on earth would ever entice her to a cinema to watch such rubbish.

"All right."

Friday the 13th was Ailie's school dance. Half-past four found Ailie surveying her reflection. Her besocked legs and bare arms stuck out like twigs from the froth that was her party dress. Her hair was flat against her skull, and despite her mother's efforts, frizzed out where the pigtails had been.

At least half the girls in her class had started their periods, but her own were four years away. The skin of her chest still stretched tight over her ribs. Ailie went to the box of paper hankies and stuffed a handful inside her liberty bodice.

Dad was standing at the corner of the room as she turned to leave. She told him, "I'm going to a school dance tonight. I don't remember what this one was like, but I think I had a good time at some of the later ones."

Dad smiled his support and sadly faded away.

Across in the room that was Dot's and Roddy's, Jojo was due to leave in twenty minutes and yet had not decided what to wear. Her own leisure wear consisted entirely of ski-pants and woolly jumpers, out of line for The First Date.

Shakily, she opened Dot's wardrobe – and saw the very thing. A red crepe dress with a straight skirt which clung all the way to her knees and a scoop neck which exposed her straps until she pinned them out of the way. Unfortunately Dot took a different size in shoes, but Jojo's own black school shoes served the purpose. Terrified of interruption, Jojo applied the shell-pink lipstick and blue eye-shadow which had accounted for half her week's pocket-money and finished the job with a heavy application of Dot's *Chanel No 5* to wrists, hair, ears and bosom. Checking the coast was clear, Jojo nipped downstairs, grabbed her duffle coat, and sneaked out below the evening star.

The room was a-trot with tulips. Girls fluttered in bright dresses, marched to the music on dainty gold sandals. The boys padded alongside, flat-footed in sandshoes, formal in school uniform or kilts. Over all, the record-player wailed out *The Thistle o' Scotland.*

Ailie was a wallflower, as usual. She loved Scottish Country Dancing, especially the fast polkas. Sadly she watched – forward pad pad pad; backward pad pad pad; forward pad pad pad; backward pad pad pad; twirl twirl twirl twirl twirl twirl grip; polkapolkapolkapolkapolkapolkapolka. Actually there were more boys than girls in the class, but the minority of boys in the class who spurned dancing outweighed the surplus. Ailie's skills went on show only in the rare Ladies' Choices.

Next dance was the Dashing White Sergeant, which employed circles rather than couples and so offered a reed of hope. Unfortunately most of the incomplete circles required an extra couple rather than an individual.

"A preparation for adult life," thought Ailie as she attempted to foist herself on a foursome. Horrible William Robson was unkind. "Aw, no, not creepy wee Ailie! What you after, you wee spook?"

Ailie slipped back to the benches along the wall and watched the dance begin without her. Had she been a real child she would have gone somewhere quiet to cry. Her fingers twiddled with the Shetland stole which her mother had draped around her shoulders. Was it her personality? (I don't laugh enough.) Was it her clothes? (Mummy always dresses me like a toddler. Pink nylon dress, sticking out paper nylon petticoat, ribbons in my hair. She never dresses Jojo that way. She thinks I'm stuck at three years old.)

The path to the Golden Sedans was long and involved. They groped their way to the seats, sat down facing the screen. After a minute Barry's arm, as expected, crept around her shoulders and Jojo's heart began to thump. Her grown-up life was beginning!

Strip the Willow. Another favourite. If it could only be the way it was in the practice sessions, when the teacher actually placed boys and girls together! From her elevated perspective, the groans of the partners would wash over her unnoticed, and she would get her dance! Staring into the eyes of each advancing boy, she caught the eye of Stephen Paterson and rushed to stand opposite him in the row. The record-player began.

"Hey! Stevie's got two partners!"

"Did you think I was picking you, Ailie? I was picking Lesley, here."

Ailie fled. Usually the girls' cloakroom smelt of old gymshoes and dust. Tonight there was an overlay of scent and talc. From below, the strains of *The Barren Rocks of Aden* made music to her moans.

Dragged awkwardly across the Golden Sedans, Jojo closed her eyes and presented her lips for her first kiss. With a bit of luck she might not have to look at any of the film at all. Barry's breath smelt hot and slightly sour. She prepared her soul for orbit.

His mouth came down heavily, with a clink of colliding teeth. How rough his skin was! Lots of shaved stubble, even though he was only fifteen-and-a-half. The kiss lasted a long time, during which Jojo opened her eyes twice and closed them again.

Why don't you tell me about it?" Mr MacKinnon, one of the teachers from the English Department. Young, soft Highland voice. Ailie slipped into the thirteen-year-old niche.

"Nobody will . . . sob . . . sob . . . dance with me! The night's nearly over and I've not even had w-w-one dance! And I'm good at dancing! The boys in my class are horrible!"

"Come on downstairs and I'll dance with you," soothed Mr MacKinnon. "What's your name?"

"Ailie Lorimer. Why do the boys always get given the right to choose?"

"It's an unfair world. The next dance is the Eightsome Reel. You like that one?"

"Yes," murmured Ailie, "but that's not the point."

"You're losing your hankies." One bunch was popping out of her puffed sleeve, the other had reached her navel. Her chest was quite flat again. Angrily she pulled out the six at her sleeve and blew her nose in the lot of them.

They stepped off the bus and walked up the road with stinging lips. The frost was down and the sky was clear. Jojo fixed her eyes on Orion the Hunter. "See that red star? It's a burnt-out giant called Betelgeuse." (How do you converse with a lumber anyway, when the kissing's over?)

Inside the garden he pulled her round the back and pushed her against the cold sharp harling of the wall. Nyeuch! His mouth was open this time and his tongue poked right into her mouth. His saliva tasted warm, bitter and germ-laden. She tholed it as long as she could, and then pushed him away.

"What's up? Did I do something wrong?"

"No. . . " This was the famous French Kissing which fed

the gossip in the common-room. Why did she wish it was over? Why was she always the maverick?

His hands were inside her duffle-coat, pressing, rubbing, probing her be-creped breast. This was less unpleasant – she could put up with any amount of it. She stood placidly, running over the levels of involvement as graded in the common-room: Stage One – kissing. Stage Two – above the waist, over the clothes. Stage Three – below the waist, over the clothes. Stage Four – above the waist, under the clothes. Stage Five – below the waist, under the clothes. Stage Six. . .

"Please, Barry, don't!" A finger on her nipple – Barry had discovered the armholes – jolted her back to the here and now.

"Don't do what? Did that hurt?"

"Keep your voice down!" Too late. The back door opened sending yellow light streaming down the path to the rockery.

"Who's there?" Familiar wail. "Is that you, Jojo?"

"See you!" Barry gave her a quick peck and disappeared round the side of the house.

"What are you doing skulking about the garden at this hour?"

In the kitchen Dorothy scrutinised Jojo with a suspicious eye, while the rest of the family gathered to see the fun.

"You're painted like a clown – lipstick over half your face. And what a reek . . . You had somebody out there with you, didn't you?"

By the time Dot had strutted to the side of the house and barked, "Anybody there? Show yourself!" Barry was halfway to the bus-stop.

"Let me go!" screamed Jojo, straining to go upstairs.

"Not so fast, m'lady. Let's have a look at you. You're half undressed. Did he do that to you?"

Ailie played the young innocent. "Has Jojo been out with a boy?"

"Och, Ailie, you're quick!"

Jojo rounded on Sandy. "Enjoying the show, Sanctity Personified? And where have you been all the day, Sandy boy, Sandy boy – playing Monopoly with Jasmine?"

"Scrabble, actually."

"Sure! Next thing Jasmine'll be having a Virgin Birth!"

"You foul-mouthed slut!" hissed Dorothy. "You're not fit to speak to Sandy – you're not fit to breathe the same air. . . Oh!" A final tug removed the duffle coat. "My good dress!"

Crushed, baggy, choc ice on the lap and sweaty fingermarks on the bodice. Dot threw herself at Jojo, boxing her ears, slapping her cheeks. "How dare you wear my clothes to go necking!"

"Now, Dottie, there's no real harm done. . . "

"Jojo bad!" Nigel had got out of bed to be with the action.

"She'll take it off! She'll take it off here and now!" Dorothy hauled the dress over Jojo's head. It came away with a slight ripping sound and Jojo shivered in her underclothes. "Not even an underskirt! And she's torn it!"

"So I'm a bad girl?" Jojo was crying now. "I'd rather be a bad girl than a murderess!"

Dead silence. Roddy looked at Dorothy, who popped her eyes at Jojo so that the whites showed all round. "What . . . did you say?"

No answer. Dorothy yanked her head back by the hair. "I asked what the hell you're talking about?"

"You killed Rosita!" screeched Jojo. "The only friend I ever had in this house. . . "

"I see! You've been nursing this imaginary grudge all these years, have you? Of all the self-pitying, self-centred, sick. . . "

"I'm sick? In this house you should know sick people when you see them. There's old Drouthy-Features looking for his next support – and what about that wraith in the corner? Look at her, shaking because the attention's on her! Going to take one of your bad turns, dear? We're all watching!"

"Get her out of my sight!"

"I'm going now. I'm going for good. I'll never set foot in this cursed house again." Jojo fled upstairs and struggled into her jumper and ski-pants as Auntie Dot yelled Good riddance! from down below.

As Jojo left the house behind the drama of her situation gave way to the cold tedious misery of the night. She had £2.10/4d in her shoulder-bag and the clothes she stood up in.

"I'll get a job." She thought with a pang of regret of the 'O' Grades in April. She would never even get to know her prelim results. "A job in a shop . . . or a factory." All quite wild – she had no idea how to go about finding work.

The stop was deserted but she managed to catch the last bus into town. All the way she stared out into the blackness in case the two other passengers would notice her frightened tears. The thought crossed her mind that if she stayed out a couple of nights the folks back home would get worried and maybe . . . but no! She would never return! Never, ever, ever!

By Anniesland Cross a forlorn idea had entered her head, and at George Square she looked up Sunnybank Street in the big map there.

"Aw by yersel, hen?" An arm swept round her shoulder as she peered in the dark. Whisky breath filled her face. "Wherr ye lookin fur, eh? Lemme show ye – wherr is it, eh?"

"It's all right. . . "

"Naw, tell me, hen. . . "

Rough-skinned old drunk. Harmless enough, but she unwrapped his arm and escaped into the shadows of Queen Street Station and hung about until he was surely gone. Back at the map, she found at last what she sought – and made off through the darkness of Ingram Street to Argyle Street, shuttered and empty.

The pubs had been shut for nearly two hours, but still a couple of stragglers lurched along the Gallowgate. In London Road two sang mournful dirges to each other and the stars – *The Bonny Wells of Wearie* and *Dae Ye Mind o' Lang lang Syne* – things the family entertained the pensioners with on other occasions – only delivered at half the pace. Crotchets in place of Quavers, Breves or Tied Breves in place of Minims. By an umbrella-shaped shelter an old man clutched a stack of Saturday morning *Daily Records*. Bare fingers and woolly mittens.

The heavens opened, and the streets, the sky, the driving rain – all was at one with the blackness within her. And the bowl of night emptied itself over her head, soaking through her anorak to her very soul.

The seventh close in Sunnybank Street yielded a Lorimer, two up on the right. No doorbell. Jojo knocked. No reply. She knocked again, and rattled the box. A shout from ben the house and an answering grunt. A door opening and feet padding towards the front door. A male voice. "Who's therr? Whit dae ye want?"

"I want. . . " What did she want? ". . . to talk to Mrs Lorimer."

A disgruntled grunt. "Ach . . . " The door opened on a youth in crumpled pyjamas. "She's in her bed."

Jojo stared for a long minute. "Are you Tony Lorimer?"

"Aye. Who wants tae know?"

"I'm Jojo!"

"Jojo who?"

"Josephine Lorimer. Your sister."

Tony looked her up and down. Then, without asking her in, he yelled "Ma!" and hurried back into the lobby. After some time he returned. "Ye've tae come in!"

He showed her into a room containing a black vinyl three-piece suite, a formica coffee table, a television set and a two-bar electric fire, which he switched on. Jojo perched on the edge of the couch and the two of them gazed at each other anew. Same colouring, same features except that Tony had the male version – slightly coarser.

"Whit age are ye?"

"Fifteen. I'll be sixteen in February."

"I'm seventeen."

"I know."

Another silence.

"How did ye find out wur address?"

Jojo explained about the photograph. Tony ran out of talk again until, in embarrassment, he moved to the door and once more shouted, "Ma!"

"Here I'm coming!" A squat little woman bustled in, spread her arms and cried, "Josie! My wee Josie!"

Jojo gasped for breath against the ample bosom, and released, sank back on the couch.

Maria wore a floral quilted dressing-gown and her perm was black streaked with grey. Unless she normally wore perfume and make-up in bed, she had put them on especially for Jojo. Her eyes glittered like black jewels.

"Away you, Tony, and put on some tea." Maria sat beside her daughter and scrutinised her. "So you're wee Josephine."

"I'm usually called Jojo." Jojo looked away from her mother's eyes, round the room. Fawn tiled fire surround, big print of a Spanish dancer with mantilla and fan, three china ducks in flight to the left.

"Take your jacket off. You're soaked to the bone. What made you come out on a night like this?"

"Just . . . I wondered what you were like."

"Are you still with Dottie MacCallum? Do they know where you are the night?"

"Of course they do."

"Hmmmm." Maria hung Jojo's anorak on the back of the door. "Well, well, wee Joseph . . . wee Jojo. We often wondered how you'd turned out. Are you still at school?"

"Fourth Year. I sit my 'O' grades this April." (If I'm still about.)

"My! You're clever, eh? And well-spoken, too."

Jojo was disappointed in her mother's voice. She'd expected a foreign accent.

"Aye, Tony coulda went in for 'O' levels and a' that and all. Passed his Quali wi flying colours and got to the senior secondary. But he got the chance of a good trade and he took it. He's serving his time as a turner down at Fairfields."

"Do you like it?" asked Jojo.

"'S okay." Tony shrugged.

"Come on, son, what kind of attitude is that? It's a good job. You're always secure if you've got a trade." Maria poured out the tea. "And how's everybody at home?"

"Fine."

"Dottie's got two weans of her own now, has she not?"

"Three."

"Three! Och, aye, I mind now. She married again, right after . . . How do you get on wi them all?"

Jojo shrugged. "One's a prig and the other's a banshee. The last one's too infantile to count." (And if I never see any of them again it'll be too soon!)

"What's that?" Maria laughed. "A prig and a banshee? Ah, you've got a fine turn of phrase! What about Dottie hersel? How do you get on with her?"

Tony was sprawled in the armchair in the arrogant space-taking posture beloved by teenage boys – legs stretched and straddled. Maria sat beside Jojo on the couch, saucer in her left hand, cup in her right, hospitable dimple in her cheek.

"Why did you walk out on us? Why did you leave us behind?"

Maria's eyes shifted to her cup and her lips lost their smile. "Your Dad and me – we weren't suited. We just didnae get on, dear. I was used to a big family, parties, noise an all that. He was older than me. He wanted a quiet life."

"He did like drinking."

"Och aye, he drank, all right. That was another thing. I don't mind drink in its place. In a pub, or at a party. Your Dad just wanted to drink quietly every night on his own. No singin, no pals in, just sinkin the tumblersful o' whisky."

"Funny," mused Jojo, "Uncle Roddy's just the same."

"Aye, well, thon must be the kinda bloke she goes for."

"I don't think she goes all that much for him. Not nowadays, anyway."

"She musta liked him at the start. She married him quick enough after. . . "

"'Spose she did." (Coming home day after day, finding them practising duets at the piano, sometimes even sharing the stool. The pair of them seated on the couch in front of the telly, long after the twilight's last gleaming. Were they really holding hands? Was Roddy's arm around her shoulders or only along the sofa-back? Was Daddy even dead yet?) "What made you go for Dad in the first place?"

"Beg your pardon?"

"From what I remember of him, you seem different types altogether. What made you get married to each other?"

"What made us . . . aye, that's a good question." Maria settled back in her chair and gazed gloomily into the fire. "See, I was very young at the time. He was a friend o' the family. He'd helped my Daddy out a lot when his chip shop ran into trouble during the war. There was a lotta hooliganism in those days, you know, a bit of anti-Tally feeling. . . "

"How did he know you?"

"His mother was part-Italian. . . "

"I never knew that!" (So I'm more Italian than Scottish.

More warm than chilly. More arty than prim. More brilliant than grey. Of course!)

". . . and he was involved with the Italian club where he met my Daddy. Well. He liked a drink, my Daddy liked a drink, my Daddy told him his problems and Joe helped him out!"

"How?"

Maria rubbed the tips of her fingers together. "Joe was well enough off then. He'd taken over his own faither's factory, makin gas fitments, mantles and the like, and he'd married a widow with a bit put by."

"He was married!"

"Haud on, haud on. His wife died about 1943 or thereabouts. TB, ye know. They hudnae any weans, and I suppose he was looking for somebody to inherit his fortune."

"Fortune! What fortune?"

"I guess there's no much o' that left now. But at that time, he was like a millionaire to us ones, that was crammed nine to a dozen in a wee tenement flat, all living off the one chippie."

"So you married him for his money."

"Look, when the war ended I was eighteen and I'd a been in Scotland about twelve years. I didnae know whatta hell I wanted, to tell ye the truth. But Joe took a fancy to me, particularly one night after he heard me singin *Santa Lucia* at the Italian Club New Year do. I was good-lookin in those days. It was the shoulder-length perm that was in fashion then, but I still had my hair in a great big long plait down my back. My Mama and Dad wouldnae let me wear lipstick or powder like the other lassies did, but then I didnae need it because my skin was that fine. So Joe took his notion. And my Mama and Dad thought it wid be a good idea to go along wi it all."

"A sort of arranged match." Jojo sensed a hint of aristocratic glamour about Maria's plainness.

"No exactly either. I cannae really blame anybody but myself. Anyway, it's all water under bridges now, poor old Joe."

"What happened to him?" Tony came out of his shell. "We heard he died, but naebody tellt us whit of."

"It was his heart." Jojo recalled the snoring heap in the bedclothes, the sitting shadow staring. "He had angina, and I suppose the drink didn't help. Look, M. . . " (What to call her? Mum? Too familiar. Mother? Too soppy. Maria? Too democratic. The woman is old enough to be my. . . ) "I understand why you split up with Dad. That's okay, no problem. But. . . "

She stopped. Maria shifted in her seat, as if she knew what would come. The moment grew until Maria was obliged to break it.

"But what?"

Jojo leaned forward earnestly. "But why did you leave Rosita and me behind and take Tony?"

A long, long silence. Maria covered her face with her hands. Then she took her hands away and assumed a frank expression. "Put yourself in my position. The only place I could go was my brother Luigi's, and he had a houseful. Two weans and a third on the way, and the lotta us in a two room and kitchen. Tony and mysel, we had to sleep in the kitchen bed-recess. I had to work in Luigi's cafe." Maria's eyes filled with tears. "It was a hard life, thon. You cannae understand, you've always had it easy. Believe you me, you were better off where you were."

"Money isn't everything."

"So you say," sniffed Maria, "you folks that's never wanted for nothing. I say it's better to be miserable with money than without."

"But you didn't even visit us! You could've written. You could've let us know where you were! You abandoned us. . . "

(. . . in the camp of the enemy!)

"I thought it was for the best," soothed Maria. "Why drag it all out? Best a clean break and let you settle down. Anyway, Joe knew where I was. Dottie used to let me know when anything important happened." For a moment Maria remembered – two wild wet faces, two screaming mouths red in the night, two constantly sodden nappies, the tot girning for attention and the melancholic critic in the winged armchair. "But I'm delighted to see my big daughter again, and her turned out so clever and good-looking."

"One thing's sure, you'll never see Rosita again."

"I'm sorry I never made it to the funeral. I was that upset, I was right no well when I heard, wasn't I, Tony?"

"She was greetin." Tony helped out.

"The tears were pourin down my face . . . I couldnae sleep for thinkin about it, my poor wee baby. . . "

"I wasn't at the funeral either," said Jojo coldly. "Auntie Dot thought that children shouldn't go."

Tony went to his bed. Maria gathered up the cups and made yawning and stretching movements, but Jojo showed no inclination to rise.

"You said you couldn't look after two babies. How was Dad meant to?"

"Ah, but he had money. He could advertise for living-in help."

(He got an answer no bother, worse luck!) "Wonder what possessed Auntie Dot to answer that advert. Child-minding isn't her scene!"

"I suppose she was desperate for a place to stay and a job."

Jojo tried to picture Dorothy desperate for something. "But she must have been working as a hairdresser."

"Well, she couldnae do that with a wean to look after."

"But she didn't have us to look after until. . . "

"Not you. The baby she brought with her."

"She brought a baby with her?"

"Aye. A wee boy, just new-born."

". . . Sandy? But I thought his father was my father." (His blood my blood. His brains my brains.)

"Is that what they told you?" Maria laughed "Naw, naw. There's no way auld Joe coulda been yon baby's Dad. Thought your own sense woulda told you that. There must be no much more than a year between you and the boy."

"Fifteen months. But I thought we were just a few weeks old when you left us."

"Jesus wept. Whatta web they've spun you. You were a year past." (The worst age: able and unable to walk, needing a helping hand, four helping hands, four watchful eyes, into a mess, into danger, into everything, wetting, crying, demanding, all in stereo.) "Goodness knows what other lies they've told you. You were about four when your Dad married Dottie. Divorces don't happen overnight."

"So she got a name for her baby and money to start her business. And he got a nurse for his hangovers."

Maria stood up. "Look, it's awful late, and I'm working the morra afternoon. You can sleep here in the front room wi me, Jojo. But we should let your folks know where you are. Are you on the phone?"

"No."

"Surely you've got a phone, living out in Milngavie?"

"No phone."

"But your folks'll be worried!"

"Nobody's going to worry about me. Anyway, I'm with my folks!"

Maria sighed. "Okay, well. Come and I'll find a nightie for you."

With her folks or not, it was strange and slightly distasteful for Jojo to put on someone else's nightdress and climb into an already slept-in bed which she would share. She turned her face to the wall. She had neither washed nor brushed her teeth and hair.

Just before she retired Maria searched Jojo's handbag until she found, in a school diary, the information she needed.

Long before the winter sun rose over Glasgow to glint weakly at the bungalow panes, the family in No 46 was up.

"Are you sure you have no idea who that boy last night might have been?" asked Roddy.

"She isn't in my year! How can I keep track of the folk she knocks about with?"

"Why should Sandy know if you don't?" Dorothy leapt to the defence. "You teach in that school, after all . . . if you call it teaching."

"It's nothing to do with that boy," said Ailie. "She's with her mother."

"Rubbish! She doesn't know where her mother lives."

"Yes, she does."

"Suppose, Miss Know-all, you tell us where Jojo's mother stays."

"I don't know. But Jojo does, and she's there now."

"You leave this to the grown-ups, Ailie."

"Should we try to contact Maria?" wondered Roddy, "just in case?"

"What! You're as bad as she is. Fine fool I'd look, after all these years . . . anyway, how would I find her? There never was a phone number, and if I had her address I'm sure I lost it long ago."

"Well, then we should call the police."

"By we you mean me, I suppose." Dorothy tightened her mouth and strode towards the phone. Sandy thrilled in anticipation of the almighty row when Jojo would finally appear.

The telephone rang before Dorothy reached it.

"Is that Dorothy MacCallum?"

Only one person called Dorothy by her maiden name. But this was a woman's voice. "It's Maria Lorimer here."

Dorothy's heart gave a thump. She closed her eyes and controlled it. "Yes?"

Sandy was jostling her, pushing his face in front of hers, trying to listen. "Is it her? Is it Jojo?"

"I thought I'd better let you know Jojo's a'right. She's here wi us."

"Oh, I see. Well, we're all very relieved to know she's safe. Would you want us to . . . or would you prefer . . . " Dorothy paused, delicately, hopefully.

"You can come for her whenever it suits you this morning."

Dorothy's heart sank.

"Mum, is that the police?"

Jojo awoke and stretched. She was alone in the bed. For a few minutes she regarded the high carved ceiling. Dusty white plaster cornicing and a central rosette, faded red, gold and green. Such ceilings were rare in the homes of her acquaintances, and becoming rarer as people lowered ceilings to keep in heat, covered up door panelling to keep down dust, went for the clean plain modern line. Light streamed through a bow window – you wouldn't see that either on these new high flats.

Then again, a new flat would have a bathroom. Jojo wondered how her mother and Tony managed, at that kitchen sink with the single brass tap. Did they snib the kitchen door, take off everything and lather themselves as they stood before a basin? Did they have a zinc bath stashed away somewhere out of sight? Or (horrors) did they do without? She hoped they did not do without. Not her mother, not her only brother.

At the last school dance the Master-in-Charge had called out during the elimination dance, "Sit down all who had a bath last night in front of the kitchen fire!" Everybody had laughed, no one had sat down. Everyone in her class had a proper bathroom. Or, at any rate, no one would admit to being without.

Voices, out in the lobby. Auntie Dot's voice. Jojo was out of bed in seconds. The door opened before she could hide.

"Get dressed, Jojo. I've come to take you home."

"No!" Jojo shook her head vehemently. "No, no, no!"

"Don't make a scene now, dear. We can discuss things in the car outside."

"I won't! I don't want to! I will not!"

"Maybe, if she's that upset . . . we could let her stay here a couple of days?"

"That wouldn't be suitable," declared Dorothy. "No, she leaves now, with me, or she stays for good."

"It's no bother to me to. . . "

"No, no. She makes up her mind now and for good. We can't be doing with shilly-shallying. We must know where we stand."

Jojo's hope flared. "Could I. . . "

"Look, pet, it's not that I don't want you." (And died.) "But there's your schooling to consider. No point changing schools in the middle o' your exams. And to be honest wi ye, there's no much room here. If I had a bigger hoose . . . Or, tell ye what – maybe once you've left the school. . . "

Jojo stopped listening and padded over the cold cracked lino to the chair where she had left her clothes. On her way out she gave only a fleeting glance to Tony. Maria's voice floated out after her into the car, "You'll have to come and see us often! Mind an no lose touch, now!"

Dorothy switched on the ignition and Jojo put her mother away for good. Back home, she opened the envelope she found on her bed. A Christmas card of the big padded kind, from Barry.

"I love you!" she whispered, although really she did not like him much at all.

# 7

A FEW DAYS AFTER JOJO'S ESCAPADE Ailie decided she was tired of being thirteen. She had not enjoyed the year first time around, being much closer to the old term 'the awkward age' (which Mummy favoured) than to the teen scene. If she could have made full use of her powers things would have been more interesting, but in her gymslip or in her puffed sleeve frocks no one took her seriously. One evening, then, she overdosed on phenobarbs in hope of finding David.

She awoke on the back seat of a car. A stranger was driving and no one was in the front passenger seat. There was something different about the car . . . about the driver. He was sitting on the wrong side! That was it! She was in a foreign country.

Where, then? She looked for clues outside, to the broad clean pavement whizzing by, to the shop names and the street signs. BÄCKEREI flashed past and BLUMEN. Germany . . . or Austria or Switzerland. She concentrated on the driver. Who could he be? What was her relationship with him? Why wasn't she on the front seat?

An internal sensation drew her attention to her abdomen. It swelled out in a globe and, as she peered, a ripple broke out on the surface of the globe, which immediately returned to its smooth shape. She touched her stomach, expecting it to be soft and blubbery. It was hard and firm like a balloon.

Someone was in there!

Which one? What age was she? What year. . .

The car pulled up at a tenement and the driver turned to her. "*Maybachufer. Welche Nummer?*"

"I'm sorry," said Ailie. "I don't speak your language."

After a moment the driver said in English, "Which number, please? In Maybachufer?"

"Number? Oh, I don't know. . . "

"You don't know? This is Maybachufer. Which number, please?"

"I can't remember." (What a fool he must take me for. He thinks . . . he knows I'm crazy.)

In exasperation the driver held out his hand. "Twenty-five marks, please." (So it's a taxi. All is explained. I need fumble for a relationship with this fellow no more. Now, do I have any money?) She felt in her pockets, in the handbag on her lap. A purse yielded some banknotes, blue, green, brown. She read the denominations and gave him three blues, tens. Then she was out on the pavement, pregnant, alone, with the taxi roaring away down the street. On one side a half-broken tenement loomed above her, while across the road ran a gloomy canal.

But wait! As well as the money, her hand clutched a scrap of paper. A scrap with a familiar look to it. Only clean, this time.

> *SANDY LORIMER,*
> *MAYBACHUFER 11,*
> *1000 BERLIN 44.*

Dreamily, she found the right entrance, and opened the street door. The close inside was unlike those in Glasgow – more like the inside hall of a grand mansion fallen on hard times. Wooden stairs and panelled house doors with carved handles. Little light filtered through the stairhead windows and she had to peer at every nameplate until she reached the top without finding any Lorimer.

Now what?

She could not stay there forever, and began the descent. As she rounded a corner, she collided with a young woman. With her new clumsiness, she lost her balance and tumbled to the next bend in the stairs.

"*Entschuldigung!*"

"Sorry!" (If this were a movie, I would now go into labour, if there was time. Or lose the baby, if there weren't.) And then (But this is no movie. This baby gets to be born, and gets to live. This I know.)

"*Alles OK?*" The young woman helped her to her feet. She saw that her knee was bleeding, and felt in vain for a handkerchief. The only thing she could find was the scrap of paper with Sandy's address on it, and so she used that.

"Do you speak English?"

"I am a student of English."

"Oh good. Could you help me?" Ailie showed her the piece of paper, now in its familiar, smeared state. "I can't find the name on any of the doors."

"I suggest you try the *Hinterhaus*." The girl pointed through a window, and Ailie saw why so little light managed through the glass. Within the backcourt was another tenement building, just as high as the building which looked on to the street. The door stood ajar.

The close in the *Hinterhaus* was darker and more decrepit than the front close. With difficulty Ailie made out LORIMER amongst three chits of paper pinned to a door on the second floor and tirled the key which worked the bell. A young man answered and showed Ailie into a hall. Large hall, with a suitcase in the corner and what looked like a payphone on the wall. Facing her were high, panelled, double doors inset with frosted glass. They flew open in answer to her knock.

"Ailie!" Sandy embraced her and drew her in. "You made it. I've just been to collect your luggage – it beat you to it – see?" He indicated the case.

"Sandy! I found my way to you!"

Sandy led the way into a spacious room with high carved ceilings. In size and embellishment the room could have been up a Victorian close in Glasgow, but French windows opened onto a wrought iron balcony. (Balconies had only arrived in Glasgow with new housing schemes, once Mediterranean travel had broadened the minds of the city architects.) A mattress lay on the floor, and a table with two chairs stood near the window. A television stood on the floor in one corner, beside a set of bookshelves. There was an old overstuffed armchair and a green velvet chaise longue. She plumped down on the armchair.

"What are you doing here . . . wherever we are?"

"Ailie, you're the most . . . Jojo would say you were 'spaced out' . . . " Sandy narrowed his eyes at her. "Sometimes I honestly wonder. . . "

". . . if I'm the full ticket." Ailie cast about again. "Where are we?"

"Berlin, of course."

"Berlin!" Ailie hurried to the window. No sign of a Wall or, for that matter, even a street. Back court on all sides. "East or West?"

"Och, Ailie, think, now! They'd hardly send me for my year abroad to the DDR!"

Ailie turned again to the window. How could she start explaining things to Sandy? Yet she must, if she was to expect him to explain things to her.

"If you're looking for Jojo," Sandy remarked, "she went

out last-minute shopping. I'm expecting her back any minute."

"Is Jojo here?"

"Well, of course she is!" Sandy looked at her askance. "Remember! That was why you had to postpone your visit till now – because she dropped in last week, and there wasn't room for you."

"Dropped in? To Berlin?"

"You know Jojo. To her and her rucksack a continent's a garden and an ocean's a pond."

"So if she's here, why's there room for me?"

"It'll be a tight squeeze. But she didn't want to miss you. So you two can sleep in my bed tonight and tomorrow night. I'll have a shake-down on the floor. On Friday Jojo catches the night train to Munich. Uch, but Ailie, I told you all that. It's awfully annoying when you can't retain anything in your noddle!"

Ailie thought it was awfully annoying when he patronised her from a position of ignorance, but she kept tactful silence. Sandy disappeared and returned with a steaming pot.

"German coffee. Much stronger than our stuff. I've grown into an addict to German coffee, schwarzbrot, and leberwurst."

"So you like living here?"

"Well, it's different. I like working in the school. The kids are much more mature than the Scottish variety. Of course, I miss Dora, and all of you."

"You must have made friends here."

"Oh, yes, of course. There are a lot of folk I'll be keeping up with after I go home. Especially since I hope to come back regularly on holidays."

"You like the folks here, then?"

"The differences are greater than I expected. On the one hand they're more enlightened in most matters. You see children running about naked in the gardens – no one thinks anything of it. In Scotland it wouldn't just be the weather that would militate against it! On the other hand there's a certain smugness that's hard to define – a sense that their way is the best and only definitive way – a way of looking at other people objectively, to snigger at the heresies . . . it's difficult to put my finger on it." He smiled. "The English have the same attitude."

"What about the place itself?"

"I miss curries, and free museums – here they cost a bomb. And the Scottish accent. Here they're all taught to talk English in a parody of R P which I find intensely irritating, particularly when I have to reinforce it. They're drilled to distort the pure German vowels so that they end up overcompensating with the-fet-cet-set-on-the-met."

Ailie giggled. "So you try to put the case for the Doric over to them?"

"Of course not. Not to the kids. I've brought it in once or twice, but naturally they're not interested. The few that'll ever visit Britain will get no further than the London area. I do try to put it to them that Scotland shouldn't be included in the term England, but I doubt if they believe me, in the face of all the evidence."

"Some folk would say what's in a name?"

"That's what Jojo says. Och, she does see that it isn't a question of semantics. The disappearing name is the symbol for the disappearing culture. But Jojo says her origins aren't part of her essence – she doesn't identify personally with slights or compliments to them. She introduces herself as Scottish rather than British. If they then proceed to make the usual mistake she lets it go."

"To most people, it must seem a mountain out of a molehill."

"Well, it is, if they don't share our national hang-ups. I find it particularly hard when meeting adults, socially. They ask me where I come from, and I tell them. Later, they're bound to refer to me as English. How often do I correct them? And do I leave it at that? Do I take the chance each time to make the political, as well as the semantic points? Dora thinks I should, that's it's my duty as a Scot abroad, to correct world opinion wherever I can. But it's so wearing to go to parties knowing that at every turn you'll have to make a political issue out of your very identity."

"I'm sure you cope." Ailie sipped her coffee. "I see you're still into making speeches, anyway."

The doorbell rang and Sandy crossed to the window and looked down. "It's Jojo." He went out through the double doors into the hall, pressed a buzzer, and returned. "That'll be her coming up now. The button in the hall opens the front door. It's a security measure."

"I know," said Ailie. "In a few years' time the tenements in Glasgow . . . " she stopped. (When I tell him, I'll be best to start at the beginning.)

A creak outside and the doors flew open. Jojo, bronzed and Latin-looking. Jojo, loaded with carrier bags in a way that only Jojo could carry them, as if they were bouncing feathers. Jojo, shining eyes and a wide grin. She tossed her burdens onto the chaise longue and herself on Ailie. "Ailie! How long has it been?"

"I haven't the faintest!" murmured Ailie. She returned Jojo's hug. "You're grown-up! I've always preferred you grown-up."

"Of course I'm grown-up! And so are you." Jojo patted Ailie's stomach. "Grown up and out. Are you hoping for a boy or a girl?"

"It's a boy."

"You reckon?" Jojo shook her head. "Guess a boy would please that rampant misogynist you're wedded onto, but I'd find a girl more company, myself. Have you thought of any names?"

"What year is it?"

"What . . . ? 1970, of course."

"Then I'll call him Crawford."

"Crawford? That's funny for a first name. Is it after anybody?"

"Couldn't tell you. Maybe somebody on Steve's side." Ailie shrugged. "Anyway, that's his name."

Sandy and Jojo exchanged a look. "I've always found Ailie a bit bizarre," said Sandy.

"I like bizarre people," said Jojo. "They're more interesting than the usual nose-to-the-grindstone tramliners."

"You're wasting your breath," said Sandy. "I long ago grew immune to your insults."

"Sandy! Did you inspirationally see yourself? And here I wasn't meaning you at all!" Jojo grinned.

"Talking of tramlines," said Sandy "I'll have to be taking the *Strassenbahn* along to the university library. Some of us bores have grindstones to get our noses to."

"Well, you do that, Sandy," said Jojo. "And while you're sharpening the old proboscis I'll take our baby sister around the fleshpots of Berlin."

As they wandered out into the street Sandy gave them the run-down on local history. "That canal across the road. The *Landwehrkanal*. That's where Rosa Luxemburg and Karl Liebknecht met their ends. Murdered and thrown in."

"Who were they?"

"Oh dear, Ailie. I'm going to have to take your education in hand."

"Wish somebody would. I feel I've missed out."

"Never mind what he says," Jojo squeezed her arm. "You can read, write, sing, dance. And you never wanted to be Dean of the Faculty, anyway."

"There are some halfway stages," pointed out Sandy, "betwixt the good Dean and Mother Hubbard's dog."

"What a pompous wee sibling we've got! His mother over again," she tweaked his cheek, "only softer."

Sandy walked up to a tenement block on the same side of the street. "This has its points of interest too. Are you looking?"

"We're all fascinated admiration. Or is it admiring fascination?"

"This doorway here – it's only a frontage – see?" They walked through the doorway and were immediately in the back-court. "Bombed during the war and left as a memorial. There's a church in the city centre kept ruinous for the same reason." He laughed. "If this were in Glasow, it'd long since be demolished as a danger to the public. Our architectural heritage be damned."

"I hear Glasgow looks a lot like this back-court just now, too," remarked Jojo.

"Does it? Why should it?"

"Planning blight. They're building a Ring Road. I'd have imagined you knew, Ailie, just coming from there. Charing Cross is a giant dusty pit, Buchanan Street is a permanent building site, and St George's Cross a desert with the subway station sticking up like a beacon."

"Is that what Tony said in that letter?" asked Sandy.

"Your brother! Are you in regular touch?"

"Only when I have a fixed abode. He wrote to me care of Sandy last week, you see."

"What's he doing?"

"When last seen he was working on the Upper Clyde. Or Govan Shipbuilders, it's called now. He seems to be getting interested in radical politics. He's joined a crowd called the . . . now, what was it again? . . . The Revolutionary . . . no . . . . . . The People's Party of Scotland. He draws up pamphlets for them. . . "

"The People's Party of Scotland?" cried Ailie. "Tell him to get out, fast."

"What? Well, now, I don't believe he'll take orders from me as to his political allegiances. . . "

"Come here!" commanded Sandy. They hurried up, Ailie puffing, Jojo lolloping. "Here, you get an underground train which actually runs through the first floor of a tenement building."

"Are all constructions in Berlin as crazy as this?" asked Jojo. "I mean, this is just a normal residential street, isn't it? Not thrown up for the tourists, like Disneyland, or anything."

"Rather, thrown down by the Allies," smiled Sandy. He came to a stop. "This is where we part."

"Right." Jojo took Ailie's arm again. "Don't wait up for us. I know you need all the sleep you can get, to look beautiful for Pandora next month."

When he had disappeared, Ailie said, "He seems to have become more nationalistic than before. Is that the effect of living abroad?"

Jojo shook her head and put her finger to her lips. "*Cherchez la femme*, m'dear. *Cherchez la femme*."

"Pandora MacAlpine? Has he totally broken up with Jasmine, then?"

"Why, where have you been all this time?"

Ailie smiled. "Whizzing through Time and Space."

"Sounds fun. Somehow, when you say incredible things, I almost believe them."

Jojo led her to an underground station. "I don't have the hang of the buses and trams here. But I do know we can take a *U-bahn* to the *Ku-damm*! We'll maybe see the inside of that flat yet! Wonder what the rental is? Germans are hypersensitive to noise – I could probably get them to pay me to let it give me a good home, if I should want to settle down here!"

From a machine Jojo bought a five journey ticket. "Now we have two-and-a half trips each. Do you have any German money?"

"Don't know." Ailie looked in her handbag. "Yes, a few notes. And . . . what looks like travellers' cheques."

The platform was built to the scale of the pavements outside. Plenty of benches. Jojo studied the map for a bit, and then indicated the side they should wait.

"You should see the Metro stations in Moscow."

The train roared in and they took their places. It was the rush hour, but a seat was soon found for Ailie. She was pleasantly surprised – she had forgotten she was pregnant. Across from her sat a little white-blonde boy in lederhosen.

The *Kurfürstendamm*. A wide pavement, wide enough to accommodate all sorts of goings-on alongside the fast, aggressive causeway. Glass display units ten metres out from the shops which owned them. Pavement artists galore. Everywhere the lederhosen boys, the dirndl girls.

"It's as if folk in Scotland really did wear kilts!" whispered Ailie. "I mean, people apart from English tourists."

"You should see it in Munich. The babies in prams there are bedirndled!"

They found a bank and Ailie cashed a cheque. "What about you," Ailie asked. "Are you really without a base?"

"Just now," said Jojo "I'm doing Germany. I was three months in Munich, then Berlin for a couple of weeks. Before Germany I did Amsterdam. After Berlin it's back to Munich, and then I'll spend the winter in Italy, where it's warm. It's how I like to run my life."

"But do you not find it lonely?"

"Not as lonely as living in the one place was. After you left I'd nothing to hold me in Glasgow. I knew a school pal of mine had got a job in Amsterdam. So I took off there. She introduced me to a whole new network. In Amsterdam, I was never short of a friend's pad to crash on."

"Why did you leave?"

"Got to be a bad scene. The hippy bit was swinging, and

the flower-power bit was fantasmagorical, but it got a bit too druggy. So I split. Some of the crowd knew of this guy in Munich, looking for go-go dancers for his new disco." She stretched. "And so it goes on."

"Must be exciting."

Jojo laughed. "Think so?"

"I mean it. All that variety. . . "

"Look, Ailie, you don't have to pretend. I know it wouldn't be your scene. See, I'm not like you, with close family ties. Who knows," she grinned "Maybe I'll find some family ties in Italy!"

"I'm not that good at keeping up family ties myself," murmured Ailie. "I travel a bit too."

"Sure! You made it here! Package holiday from Cook's."

"What do you live on?"

"Och, black economy jobs are easy come by. And well paid! Back home I was only getting £20 a week, and I had to pay tax off that. Here, when I'm working, I can make double. I even made enough for a long weekend in Moscow, last winter!"

"Goodness! Troikas in the snow?"

"Oh, yes – they lay all that on for the tourists. Otherwise it was pretty different from how it was in *Dr Zhivago* – which was what gave me the notion in the first place." She grinned. "Still, you see what the German economic miracle has brought me – and plenty other hippies! Though it would be easier if we were in the Common Market!"

"But what do you actually do?" They passed a young woman standing in a white skinny-rib jumper, a black leather mini and a bored expression. Ailie looked into her listless eyes, and wondered. . .

"Mainly, I work in bars. Sometimes I'm an art school model."

"You mean, without. . . "

"In the buff? But of course. Every bump under surveillance."

"But are you not shy? All these men!"

"Och, they don't look at us that way. Least, if they do, they're not allowed to show it, so it comes to the same thing."

"Would you not want to do something better? You've got Highers."

"I've got Higher English and Art at band 'C', and I got German and History at the second attempt. Not a great basis for the academic life. Anyyway, I'm not into the work ethic."

"How do you mean?"

"Look, all over the developed world a new order is supposed to be forming. Suddenly lounge lizards are out and horny-handed sons of the toil are trendy. Lucre is filthy and the Fuzz are Pigs. Down with authority! Power to the People! When you get unemployment you get Right to Work marches and they all chant, Heath Out . . . as if a change of personnel would alter anything. But what about a real change in things? What about the right the ruling classes have always kept for themselves? Why does nobody ever want the Right to Leisure?"

"The unemployed have plenty of leisure. . . "

"They get other problems. Hassled over assault courses to get their basic needs. . . "

"I never knew you were so political!"

"I'm not. All I want is to use the only life I'll get in a free way, with enough time to travel, to read, to get culture. Leisure time isn't valued by Trade Unions or bosses – only money is – and since the only way they can dream up more money is through work, everybody wants more boring, mind-shrinking, bloody awful work!"

"You could always change jobs now and then."

"And lose all pension rights? You get rewarded for servicing the same rut for forty years! Christ! what a shitty deal!"

Two people of doubtful gender were leaning against the

wall – one long-haired, one cut into the skull, both in traipsy sleeveless shirts, tiny minis, heavy make-up and five o'clock shadows. One puckered up his or her lips at them as they passed. Ailie blushed and Jojo stuck out her tongue.

"Have you ever. . . " Ailie began, but lost her nerve and finished, "modelled for people other than the Art school?"

"My body," said Jojo "is my possession. Right?"

"Of course, but. . . "

"Any way I use what's mine to earn money is honest. Right?"

"I'm not criticising. I just thought you might think that . . . well, that encouraging folk to think of you as a sex object was against feminism."

"Against what?"

"Against Women's Lib."

"Well, of course it's against Women's Lib! Here – let's eat in Café Kranzler, since it's an occasion."

Mirrored splendour, interwar for the main part. Reminiscent in some ways of The Glasgow Style, of Mackintosh even, although not a ladderback chair was in sight and the looking-glasses, which were everywhere, were devoid of roses. In a daze Ailie accompanied Jojo into the glass lift and floated to the balcony. There they sat and shared a *Wienerschnitzel*, while marvelling at the warring night traffic, the cars on two wheels round the roundabout, the bikers on one wheel leaving the lights, the screaming drivers, the whooping gangs, the buskers, and the pavement fire-eaters.

"I hope this isn't veal," said Ailie. "I know how veal is got."

"Do you approve of how chicken is got?" asked Jojo. "Actually, in my experience, they're much more conscious of that sort of thing in other European countries than in Britain. That's why I like them."

"What sort of things?"

"Ecology."

"Eek . . . what?"

"Our responsibility to the planet, and its life-forms and all that. Sandy could tell you more about it than I could."

"So you manage to talk to Sandy?" Ailie smiled.

"Oh, yes. He and I had a big discussion about it last night. He's not such a stuffpot as he used to be. Old Germany's broadened his mind."

"He thinks you don't stick up enough for Scotland."

"Uch, it's not that I'm ashamed of it. I mean, I've come across folk in my travels . . . there was one girl from Dumfries who always introduced herself as English. Saved hassle, she said. Saved explanations."

Ailie smiled. "I know you're going to tell me her real reason."

"Really, she did it because, if the Scots have an image at all, it's a negative one. Backward bumpkins. Poor mindless hooligans. Certainly not middle-class, which is what she wanted to be recognised as."

"But you think the other Europeans are ahead of us in their thinking."

"So they are. The Northern Europeans, anyway."

"Then the Scottish inferiority complex is justified."

"Not at all. The Scottish complex is entirely with reference to the English – after all, we've been cut off from the rest of the world for 200 years. To me, the rest of the Brits are as backward as the Scots. Except maybe in London, which is full of foreigners anyway. Honestly, you wouldn't believe how liberal they were in Amsterdam – and Germany's the same."

"Is it not maybe that the Northern Europeans don't have the basic worries – like jobs and housing – so they've space for long-term issues?"

"But the Scottish professional classes don't have these worries either. Catch them organising demos!"

"We do get demonstrations against the atom bomb. . . "

"Any I've been on have been organised and dominated by English people. No, the remaining Scottish bourgeoisie just lie low. Gutless, they are. Rather be acceptable than free. And that's why Sandy and Dora'll get nowhere with them."

Ailie paid the bill and they wandered out. Despite the lateness of the hour the streets were thronged with drifters. Hippies had set up jewellery stalls on the broad pavements. Everyone wore summer clothes, no one carried a cardigan just in case.

"See what a way of life we could have in Scotland if we could depend on the weather from one minute to the next?" sighed Jojo. "And if we didn't have to hide all the drink behind frosted glass. Come and I'll show you a side of Berlin Sandy won't – if he even knows about it."

They dived down some side streets and found themselves in a world of strip-joints and official brothels, where women in camisoles smiled from shop windows, beckoning to the American sailors who sauntered past. There were micro-skirted prostitutes of both sexes, and flashing neon-signs advertising PEEPSHOWS, SEX-SHOWS, LESBIANS and GIRLS, GIRLS, GIRLS for the benefit of the monoglot tourist. Ailie kept her eyes down for much of the time, and shuffled after Jojo.

"The have the same red-light area in Amsterdam," said Jojo. "What price Blythswood Square now?"

"How do you know about these places?" asked Ailie. "Is it safe for a woman alone to walk down such streets?"

"You're not too happy here, are you?" smiled Jojo. "I'll tell you what – on the way home there's a nice pub that even Sandy approves of – in fact, he introduced me to it."

She led the way down dark leafy avenues, well away from the neon buzz. From time to time she stopped under a street light and scanned the city atlas she carried in her trouser pocket, but mostly she strode confidently ahead, earrings and hips swinging, ignoring overtures from kerb-crawlers and pack-hunters.

"The trick," she murmured to Ailie, "is to look like you know where you're bound. If you don't, they take you for a natural victim. Even if you're pregnant."

"That's all very well," puffed Ailie, "but I can hardly keep up with you."

"Sorry." Jojo slowed down. She pointed to a banner stretched across a building – BERLIN WAR NOCH NIE SO JUNG WIE HEUTE. "See that?" She translated it for Ailie's benefit. "That's a campaign they've got going just now. Sandy told me all about it. Actually, it shows just the opposite. Only a city scared of its aging population invents a slogan like that."

"They all look young enough from what I can see."

"That's at night. Respectable German pensioners retire at nine sharp, even in the middle of a telly programme."

"Why should there be so many old people?"

"Who wants a three hour trip to the hinterland? In Berlin you get tax concessions for having babies, you're exempt from military call-up. But still, to me the typical Berliner is an old lady with a trilby and grim expression. Prussian mothers, I call them."

"In time to come," said Ailie dreamily, "the Wall will tumble down."

"Sure. The Russians'll turn Tory. And the Pope'll join the Wee Frees."

"Close. And Glasgow'll also adopt a slogan – Glasgow's Miles Better."

"Better than what?"

"Don't know. Better than other towns, better than it used to be . . . but the puns! Glasgow's Smile's Bitter. Glasgow's Males Batter."

"How do you know this?"

"I told you," Ailie smiled. "I'm a traveller in Time."

"No, really."

"Stickers amongst my sons' stuff. You know what teenagers are like."

Jojo grasped her shoulders. "What are you saying?"

"Remember, years ago, when I was . . . when I tried to kill myself."

"The neighbour got to you."

"I told you around then about my problem with Time."

"That was sorted out. It was a dream or something. You apologised in hospital for the bother you'd caused."

"Don't know about that. Haven't lived that bit, yet."

Jojo screwed up her face "Here. Into this wee pub and let's have it again."

The wee pub was actually a pillared mansion, opening at the back to a walled apple orchard where festive people lounged round tables under the canopy of the night. Women in tuxedo suits, men in make-up.

"The name's pretentious enough," remarked Ailie, feeling a yokel in her pastel print dress.

"Café Einstein? It was a private house till recently. I like it because it's always full of would-be writers. You see them sucking their pens, staring at the sky, scribbling something, then staring at the sky again."

"Really?" Ailie looked around again. No one seemed to be in a group of less than four.

"Now you must try a *Berliner Weiß*. Don't worry, they're hardly alcoholic at all. They come in green or red. Don't know why they describe them as white unless it's to describe the head."

"When do the pubs shut here?" It was already half-past midnight.

Jojo shrugged. "Don't know if they do. I've never hung about long enough to find out."

After the waitress had taken the order Jojo leaned

conspiratorially across the table. "Right. Come on with it. Your tale."

With the luxury of a listener again, Ailie was unsure where to start. "It's like I told you. I'm living my life in patches, but the patches are out of chronological order."

"How do you mean?"

"I mean I don't know anything of what went immediately before I woke up in the taxi this afternoon. I haven't lived that bit yet. As far as I'm concerned, just before I was in that taxi I was only thirteen."

"And do the separate bits never join up?"

"They haven't till now."

The waitress brought the drinks. Fluffy-headed globes, green for Ailie, red for Jojo.

"But you still expect to experience all the parts of your life eventually?"

"All I have to go on is the Morning Roll's theory."

"The Morning Roll?" Jojo laughed.

"My psychotherapist. If I ever live over a part twice, I'll know she was wrong."

"Still I can hardly credit it, Ailie. I found it hard to take when you first told me, and I don't completely accept it yet. Why has no one else had this thing?"

"This ability, you mean. Maybe they weren't believed." Ailie patted her tummy. "Not this baby but the next will inherit the tendency. We have a standing arrangement to keep in touch once he's grown up."

"It's a thing of the genes, then?"

"An inherited faculty, yes. I wondered at one point if you maybe had a wee bit of it in you."

"Definitely not." Jojo shook her head. "I have some funny traits, but nothing as way-out as that. But then, you always were the banshee."

"The banshee!"

"Are you still in touch with the dead?"

"Not since this ability appeared. I wonder if the others, the Faces and so on, were only the precursors to this."

"They could only be the precursors if they preceded the others. Which came first?"

"First and last are without meaning in my condition."

On the way back Jojo asked "And will Glasgow be Miles Better?"

"Och, I think so. Believe it or not, Glasgow will be designated Culture Capital of Europe in 1990."

"Fantabulous! A lot must be due to happen."

"New theatres, new museums. . . "

"Still free? The museums, I mean."

"Still free. New market halls, annual cultural festivals, rehabilitation of the Victorian architecture. The concrete and glass stuff they're throwing up now will be condemned as ugly and inadequate. . . "

"What about the deprivation? The unemployment?"

"That will get much, much worse before it gets better. People will accept 16%, 17%, 18% unemployment."

"But what about the Trade Unions?"

"Totally powerless."

"So Heath will beat them after all?"

"No, they'll beat him. It's another Tory Government that'll destroy the unions. And to a large extent the Welfare State."

"Another Tory Government?"

"Led by a woman."

"What!" Jojo snorted. "That isn't quite how I pictured the first woman Prime Minister. I thought by definition she'd have to be a left-winger."

"No, no. Her great god will be money."

"But money-worship is a male attribute. Look at all these men, going hell-for-leather for promotion, after overtime, even never seeing their families. . . "

"Well, you know what they say about converts being the most fanatical of all."

When they tiptoed through the door they nearly fell over Sandy, dreaming sweetly in his sleeping bag behind the door.

"Good," said Jojo, "when the cat's aslip the mice can trip." She fumbled in her rucksack and pulled out the gear. Deftly she rolled up a joint and offered it to Ailie, before putting it in her own mouth and feeling for matches. "You're probably right. Wouldn't do the wee bugger's health much good. But then, why shouldn't the unborn have a bit of unhealthy fun too?"

She sat with her back against the wall, closed her eyes and took a long draw. Against the moonlight streaming in through the balcony door, her profile was aquiline, the picture of tired nobility. Her real experiences had only started when Ailie moved out to get married, but already, to Ailie, she looked like a citizen of the world. She had lost all her Scottish gaucheness – her cotton khaki ranger trousers and her desert boots had a look of battered quality, as if Naomi Mitchison had worn them to cross the Kalahari.

"Is it fair to smoke that stuff here?" asked Ailie. Yokel for asking, but abusive of Sandy's hospitality if she did not. "Couldn't Sandy get into trouble?"

Jojo sniggered. "Mamby-Sandy caught sleeping it off in a roomful of wacky baccy! What a turn-up for Mummy that would be."

(Might have known it was hopeless appealing to Jojo's sense of legality. She doesn't care if she gets into trouble with the law, so why should she care if anyone else does? Strange to think of her having been a twin – she's so independent now – so very single. On the other hand maybe it's because she's got to be it for herself and Rosita now. Maybe she sees herself as the continuation of both of them, so she's not so alone in her mind. Phew! that smell is strong! Just a minute . . . what was it I wanting to say to her before? I wanted to warn her. When was it? Was it before or after the Café Einstein? Before or after the Café Kranzler? Was it herself I wanted to warn her about, or was it . . . Not Nigel. I've warned him already, many times, directly, though whether he believed me . . . Might be better to tell him nearer the time, when he's more receptive . . . Teenage boys! They're the pits. Anyway, is there any point to it? Can I forestall something which I know has already happened? Is it worth forestalling something which, as far as I know, didn't happen, although it might have? . . . It was Tony!)

"Talking of trouble," said Ailie "I meant it about Tony and the Scottish People's Party. He should get out."

"I rea-ll-y don't seeee . . . that it's oooouuer business."

"I'm serious! Sometime next year . . . I don't know when as I haven't lived through it yet, but sometime in 1972. . . "

"Can't we discuss it in the morning?" Jojo had lost her noble look. Her eyes were still shut and a smile played on her lips. She looked foolish.

"Sometime in 1972 the leaders of the PPS will be put in jail."

Jojo lost her smile. She frowned, and still with her eyes shut said, "What for?"

"Robbing banks."

Jojo smiled again. "Tony's a bi-i-i-ig boy now. I think we should credit him with a le-e-e-etle sense. Un poco, un poco sense." She crooked her forefinger and thumb together in an Italian affectation which annoyed Ailie.

"Listen, this is big stuff. The main protagonists will get the longest sentences ever passed in Scotland. About 25 years each."

Jojo opened her eyes. "Do they kill people?"

"No, although a shotgun gets fired, I believe. One of them

makes a long political speech in court, and that goes against him. The Judge says he's an enemy of the State."

"Enemy of the State!" Jojo shook her head. "People's Party of Scotland! Both sides always deal in such clichés!"

"Enemy of the State," repeated Ailie, "or words to that effect."

Jojo said, "I really don't reckon that Tony would be daft enough. . . "

"I believe the PPS men pled not guilty. Anyway, whether they were guilty or not, the sentences were for the fact they were politically motivated. Ordinary bank robbers don't get sentences like that. Nor do murderers, for that matter. So anyone in that party could be tarred with the same brush."

"How do you know this, if you haven't lived through the period yet?"

Ailie took a deep breath. "During my trips to the future I try to pick up information that might be handy for other periods. I spend an hour or two a week browsing through old newspapers on microfilm. This story caught my eye because of one of the headlines – WORKERS OF THE WORLD UNITE – IN JAIL!"

Jojo whistled. "And in this paper, did you see any mention of Tony?"

"No, although of course I wasn't looking out for him."

Jojo sat with her head resting on her knees for a while, until Ailie thought she had fallen asleep. Timidly she attempted to rouse her. "Wish I could recall the exact date."

Jojo grunted, "the date?"

"When it all happened. The trial of. . . "

Jojo flung her head back again so that it hit the wall. "If you feel he should be warned, go and warn him yourself. You'll be in Glasgow before I will."

"He'll never believe me. He'll think I'm a Government agent."

"I'll write him a letter, to back up your case."

"Okay then, if you give me his address." Ailie was without enthusiasm – but, after all, she wanted to make use of her gift. (Trouble is – will my oratory match up to my clairvoyance? Can I sell an idea to a stranger?)

"In fact," went on Jojo dreamily, "you should go and warn the ones that did get the jail sentences. So they'll not rob the banks in the first place. Or disband their party. Or whatever they were put in jail for – not do it. Or undo it, if it's done already." She drew on the root and blew the smoke lazily out of her nostrils. "If you can find them."

Ailie drifted off to sleep. The noise of church bells awoke her. She went to the bathroom and found the door snibbed. Twenty desperate minutes later it was still locked, despite all her pleading. She roused Sandy.

"I think Jojo's flaked in the bathroom." She desisted from revealing the cause.

"There's still an old *Klo* on the stair landing. Key in kitchen cutlery drawer."

Sandy rolled over, Ailie went, and soon she too was asleep again.

When she next opened her eyes, it was to Sandy's angry voice.

"Jojo! Are you responsible for what's in the bathroom?"

Jojo, curled up in the bed beside Ailie, grunted and pulled the covers over her head. Ailie followed Sandy through.

"It's beautiful!"

"Maybe so," said Sandy grimly, "but she forgets I share this flat with six others. And painting and decorating are not allowed."

The bathroom was an interior room, about two and a half metres square, papered in white Anaglypta. On one wall, using coloured chalks, Jojo had drawn a vision in Van Gogh colours, corn yellow and cobalt. Flames burst out of the head of a handsome, arrogant-looking youth and from the head of a lion beside him. From the scalp of an identical youth poured water and crabs, which he caught in a jug. The whole was framed by a thorny briar.

On the wall opposite was a whitescape of icy caverns and Matterhorns, overlooked by a woman with a face like a prune, carrying a bow in one hand and a jug in the other.

The third wall was mainly green, with a giant willow sweeping through the whole, into the waters of a burn jumping with fish. On a green bank grazed a sheep and further along, a bull, oddly mounted by a baby human.

The last wall featured rust and orange, and a rosy, fat-cheeked woman weighing bowls of fruit in a pair of scales.

"It's the seasons," wondered Sandy. "Where did she get the materials?"

"She bought them in an art shop while we were out. But where did she get the time?" asked Ailie. "At most she must have had only seven hours."

"Where did she get the talent?" Sandy felt a pang of jealousy, and nobly pushed it aside. Of course it was right that Jojo should surpass him at something. "Why did she never show this skill at school?"

That night Sandy and Ailie saw Jojo off at the *Bahnhof Zoo*. While Sandy was away getting *Die Zeit* the girls said their last goodbyes.

"Why do we get on so well whenever you're grown-up?"

"Couldn't we also say whenever *you're* grown-up?"

"But I'm always grown-up. Or never."

"Then we must ask why we didn't get on as kids."

"You were so hard, such a troublemaker. . . "

"You were such a drip."

For the rest of the fortnight Ailie spent the mornings in bed, rising in time to get coffee and *Brötchen* ready for Sandy's return from the *Gymnasium* where he worked. Sometimes they went for lunch to a café in the student quarter, or in the city centre. In the afternoons, Sandy took her round the official sights – the Reichstag, the unapproachable Brandenburg Gate with the Soviet soldier, in isolation, guarding his metre of West, the Siegesäule, the Wall. She shopped in Karl-Marx Strasse, for baby dungarees in colours brighter, trendier than anything in Scotland, and a pair of boy's lederhosen.

On the Thursday evening they dined in a small Greek restaurant in Bleibtreustrasse.

"Romantic name, isn't it? Remain True. James Joyce mentions this street in *Ulysses*." Sandy studied the menu. "What are you for?"

"I've never tried Greek food. What's *souvlaki*?"

"*Schaschlik*. I mean, kebabs. Bits of meat on skewers. Out here Greek restaurants take the place of the Glasgow curry-houses. Except there are fewer of them."

They ordered and Ailie wondered if she should start telling Sandy about her oddity. He was regarding the tablecloth, through John Lennon spectacles, with nothing to say to her and no cares on the matter.

Ailie leaned across the table. "Sandy," she leaned closer (Why's the damned table so wide? Never mind, if I speak quickly and with especially Scottish intonation, maybe they won't understand.) Sandy had raised his eyes to meet hers, with no noticeable change of expression and was waiting for her pearl of wisdom. Ailie flustered and blustered, and what came out was, "John Lennon will be shot dead in 1980."

Sandy's eyes widened. "Is that supposed to be a joke?"

"No. It's true. I. . . "

The gypsy violinist who had been playing softly at the next table had reached theirs. "*Engländer*?"

"*Schotte*."

The fiddler beamed, lifted his bow and gave a passable rendering of *Loch Lomond*, then *Greensleeves*. Ailie said no more.

On the Friday evening Sandy took her to a party held by the senior teacher who was his supervisor in the school. The party was held out in the garden, with little lamps hanging from the plum and apricot trees, and the cooking done out at a fake wishing-well, which really was a barbecue. No one sang, but a megaphone belted out American pop-music for the guests to dance to. The children of the guests, bright blonde and splashily dressed, scrambled on the climbing equipment on the middle of the lawn, all apart from one of them, a *Berliner Pflanze* as Sandy called her, with an upturned chin, who followed them about asking repeatedly, *"Und deine Schwester, kann sie gar kein Deutsch sprechen? Überhaupt kein Deutsch? Wieso?"*

Ailie, uneasy at her lack of conversation, kept with Sandy. Although there were teachers of English at the party, most of them wanted to relax in German, and abandoned Ailie after a few polite sentences. At last she came out of the toilet to find Sandy in conversation with another Scot. A tall, dark-haired fellow, pale like herself, with strange grey eyes.

"Ailie, I think you two know each other?"

Ailie looked blankly at the other. His beard, as black as his hair, circumvented his chin, leaving his upper lip bare. It gave him an open, honest look somehow, like an archaic Dutch farmer, a pioneering Quaker. An Amish, that was what he looked like. However his eyes, they were not Amish. Anything but. Large, with glass-grey irises outlined in black. They reached from his aura to hers. She found it hard to tear her own eyes away.

"I see you don't recall the occasion, although I do." His voice spoke of the twilight of Gaeldom. "Do you not remember? Pandora's party last March? I was with Willie."

"Willie?"

"Now, you surely remember Willie."

"I'll put her out her agony," said Sandy. "It's Don John!"

"Don John Bain," added the other. "Where I come from there are a lot of Don Johns. And you're Ailie, who put us all right about Time."

"I did?" muttered Ailie nervously. His hair looked so thick and shiny – she wanted to run her fingers through it. But she was married and pregnant – and it would not do.

"Eilidh, now, that's a. . . "

"I would like to say it was," cut in Ailie, feeling guilty for some reason "But I spell it the Anglicised way. A-I-L-I-E."

"Our mother has internalised our colonisation," smiled Sandy. "She thought English words were more comprehensible, therefore to be preferred." He went on, "Don John is doing his year abroad in Hamburg. He's here for a few days to see Berlin, swopping accommodation with another student who wants to see Hamburg. Well," he heaved an obvious sigh of relief, "since you've been introduced, I'll leave you to catch up on things."

"Let's sit down here," Don John indicated a sofa under a cherry tree beside a bird bath floating with little perfumed candles, "to do our catching. Now, where were we with Time?"

"I haven't the faintest," sighed Ailie. "I haven't lived through that bit yet."

"You haven't lived through. . . "

Ailie found herself explaining to this perfect stranger all about her situation.

When she had finished, he took a long sip of his beer. "Right from the start, I knew there was something strange about you."

"You mean, you believe me?"

"And why should I not?" He leaned forward and transfixed

her with his wondrous eyes. "There are more things in Heaven and Earth than are dreamt of in . . . Sandy's philosophy."

It should have been corny, but two elements saved it. His expression made him look an acknowledged expert in the field, and Ailie, struggling as usual to enter into the mood of the times, recalled that the sixties had been a more psychic-friendly era than most. What were these ideas? Ouija boards? Transcendental meditation? Dragon lines? Lucy in the Sky with Diamonds. . .

"My baby," she patted her stomach, "will be a boy called Crawford. I know him well. . . "

"Of course you do."

". . . and he won't be all that congenial. But my next son – on him I pin all my hopes."

"Seeing you know just what you're doing, I'm sure they will bear fruit."

(What is this? Is he only spinning me a line? Surely he wouldn't try to chat up a woman six months gone?)

"It's not that I'm trying to chat you up," he said. "My old dear claims to have the second sight. Do you know what that is?"

"I think so." She squinted up at him. "Have you a bit of it yourself?"

"Maybe." He smiled gently and half-entranced, she did something she would never normally have done to a strange male at a party. She did it because she felt safe. He seemed so other-worldly that it was inconceivable that he would interpret the gesture in a sexual way. After all, there was no sex in the matter, was there? No sensuality, pure sensuousness. She reached up and ran her fingers through his hair.

Thick and slightly oily – sebaceous gland-oily, no Brylcreem involved, smooth and strong and soft and tangle-free, like willows, like seaweed.

"So this is what you're up to!" Sandy's voice broke in. "I can't leave you alone for a minute, can I? Don John, she's a married woman, as you can well see."

Don John kept his eyes on Ailie. "Don't mind him. He's not of our world." He turned then to Sandy, "I'll away and see what this grill business is all about."

Ailie did not leave Sandy's side for the rest of the evening. When darkness fell, the children were each given a paper lantern, with a candle, and they paraded out along the street, soft colours shining under the moon, high voices singing, "I*ch gehe mit meiner Laterne, und meine Laterne mit mir!. . .* "

"Very pretty!" exclaimed Ailie. "But that boy, there, is he not holding it at the wrong. . . "

The lantern in question caught fire. The boy dropped it, and adults quickly stamped it out on the pavement. The little parade meandered back, now only six glowing globules in the blackness of the neo-rustic night. Then the adults whisked the children off home, or into bed. Ailie sought Don John, but he had left.

"Sandy," said Ailie when they got home, "I want to talk to you about something."

Sandy yawned and stretched. "Will it take long?"

"Yes. It's very complicated."

"Will it keep till tomorrow?"

"I suppose so."

Next day, by the time Ailie arose, two of Sandy's colleagues were there, ready for the trip of the day. Ailie felt off-colour, but out of politeness she stuffed down the breakfast Sandy had prepared.

They took the U-bahn east through the sector boundary, non-stop past windy, gloomy socialist stations abandoned to the border guards, to Friedrichstrasse. They cleared the rites of passage – three separate routes for the West Berliner, the West German, and the foreigners – and stepped out to meet in a dank main-line station with a smell like a public lavatory.

Out of the station again, into a clean, bright, impossibly broad, almost empty main road bordered on both sides by concrete megaliths. Of the few people in the street, about half were in military uniform. This gave Ailie a strange, knotted feeling in her stomach.

(I hope I don't disgrace Sandy in front of his friends. If only I can keep the coffee and the *Spiegelei* down . . . Aahhhh! The coffee! Do-o-on't think about the coffee! Black, coffee, thick, bitter . . . Don't think about . . . think about . . . the *Spiegelei*! Fried egg, dripping in grease . . . No! I won't! Think about the buildings. Think about . . . the television tower! Big silver ball – reminds me a bit of a chocolate Christmas decorat . . . no, I mustn't think of food! I've seen it all over the West sector – now I'll maybe get to go up it! Is it true what Sandy said – that the Eastern Tower was built after the Western one – and that's why it's slightly higher? Will I be able to see Sandy's flat from up there? This must be the shopping sector. Hmmmm . . . mainly bookshops, or strange galleries. Looks a bit like a Glasgow housing scheme. But they do have the odd street café – there's one over there serving big glasses of pink ice cream. Nothing but big glasses of . . . No, I will stop thinking about food. Who's this coming?)

One out of uniform approached them and tagged onto Reinhold, muttering, pleading, looking about him. Reinhold hesitated, glanced at the others. Sandy frowned, Ulrich shrugged. Reinhold followed the other into a shop doorway for a moment, to reappear moments later, tucking something into his inside pocket.

"What were they doing?" whispered Ailie.

"Ssshh. Changing money, of course."

"But we already changed money, at the border. Remember, you said they were so hung-up about getting foreign currency. . . "

"Keep your voice down! You want to go on television and tell them about it?"

"I'm surprised they allow just any old body on the street to change money if they're trying to keep control of it all."

"Och Ailie!" Sandy smiled weakly and ruffled her hair. "Why did you cut off your pigtails? They suited you."

"I don't remember doing it." Ailie felt a bit huffed. "When I find out I'll let you know."

"Anyway," said Sandy "now we've got plenty of Eastern money to spend on this side of the Wall."

Unfortunately, Saturday was the early closing day. All big shops were shut, and the streets grew more deserted until, it seemed, only militiamen were about. They made for the tower, but it was closed too, either because of Saturday or because it was new.

"*Laß uns nach Hause gehen.*" Sandy felt that every passing uniform could see inside Reinhold's wallet.

Reinhold and Ulrich put up a protest.

"What's the problem?" asked Ailie.

"We're not allowed to take the money back," explained Sandy. "Sometimes they check purses. If we can't find something to spend it on we'll have to eat it!"

They entered a café, where they found to their consternation that communist fare, though plain and of little choice, was incredibly cheap. Eating her way through forty marks worth of horse-meat sausages, world-weary *Brötchen* and pink ice-cream, Ailie grew sicker and sicker. Afterwards, in a daze, she followed the others as they wended their way back to Friedrichstrasse, where the reek caught her like a punch in the throat. They pushed their way through a crush of embracing relations exchanging cabbages and fresh flowers.

"Look," whispered Sandy in her ear, "they have a box where you can donate spare Ostgeld to the Vietnam war victims! We didn't need to stuff down all that horse-meat and ice cream. . . "

Ailie never knew how she made it on time to the litter basket. Only a little landed on the ground, and although a uniform made a slight move towards her, he backed off again when Sandy came to her assistance.

"You gave me a fright, there," he whispered once they were through the border. "I thought your kid would be an East German!"

Next morning she flew home. She had not told Sandy about her gift. However, Pandora was to have a week's holiday in Berlin and then Sandy and she would return to Scotland. Ailie promised to visit them there.

"I look forward to meeting *meinen ersten Neffe oder Nichte!*" beamed Sandy, at the airport.

"And I look forward to telling you all about . . . it."

"Not all!" pleaded Sandy. "You don't want me passing out on you!"

# 8

THERE WAS, OF COURSE, no direct flight to Scotland. By the time the London train rolled into Central Station she was relieved to see Steve waiting for her. As she clambered into the car she hardly noticed the rain.

"Did you have a nice time?"

"Yes. Jojo was there as well as Sandy."

Silence.

"We went to East Berlin for the day."

"What was that like?"

"I was sick all the time." She giggled nervously. "Wasn't the fault of the city. If it hadn't been the half-day it might have been interesting."

"Good weather, was it?"

"Oh, yes."

Silence.

"Look, would you mind if I just let you off in town? I've got to go to this important meeting."

"On a Sunday?"

"It's the only day that suited everybody. Would you mind?"

"Suppose not."

"You can get a bus at this stop." He drew up. "Have you got money?"

"I think so."

"Here, take this fiver."

"It's all right. I've got money."

"Don't worry about your stuff. I'll keep it in the boot until I get home. Nothing you need?"

"No."

"Sure?"

"I'm sure."

"Got your keys?"

"Yes."

More silence, lasting until they left the city streets. It was only as she watched Steve drive into the middle distance that she realised she did not know whether she was yet staying at the address in Bellahouston.

She was.

Apart from the absence of toys, the house looked much as it would in 1977. When Steve came home at ten p.m. and, indeed, all the other nights when he came home at ten or later, Ailie would search – in a dreamy, academic way – through his pockets, his briefcase, the drawers of his desk. There were never any signs of activity other than work. In a way she was disappointed. A fight over another woman would have given some point of contact, would have provided an excuse to spend more than five minutes together in the same room, would have offered some excitement. No rose-scented letters amongst the bills of quantity, no lipstick on the estimates.

On St Andrew's Day, when Steve was not at home, she went into labour. She left a note for Steve. Fourteen hours later he arrived at the maternity hospital, to be followed twelve hours after that by his first-born son. By the time the forceps hauled Crawford unwillingly into the world Steve was back at his desk. The labour had taken more time than he had anticipated.

Ailie, her body a saggy stretch-marked battlefield, regarded her fruit and tried to think of him as worth the effort. He was red and wrinkled, with slits for eyes and a fuzz of mousey hair. Had it been David she would have been fonder, but she kept seeing Crawfie the adult, Crawfie the bore. Dutifully she pushed his mouth to her breast. The baby fought and yelled. Ailie tried for a week to suckle him – each day he grew more antagonistic to the idea and at the same time hungrier and lighter. The paediatrician said he looked starved. The African Sister spoke severely to Ailie, telling her that Western women did not know how to nurse babies, tweaking her nipples until she shivered. And still Crawfie was devoid of the rooting reflex. Eventually, after seven days and nights spent mainly behind curtains, Ailie brought in the bottles and Crawfie put on the weight.

"So you disliked me from the word GO," she murmured to him on the first night home. "And if we'd been in the wilds – what then? Would you have stayed proud unto death, or would you have taken my offerings?"

In a cupboard she found a few baby clothes. She dressed him up and took him to see her mother. Dorothy was preoccupied – Nigel was in trouble again. He had been caught amongst a group of children, some of whom were shoplifting. He might have to go before the new Children's Panel. Dorothy glanced at her first grandchild and made some light-hearted comment about, "He can only improve!"

"Wouldn't be too sure," muttered Ailie darkly.

Roddy was in his cups and grunted inaudibly. Neither showed any willing to touch the new bud on the family tree.

One evening, when Crawford was a couple of months old, Steve came home earlier than usual, at eight o' clock. Ailie put the baby to bed and a cup of tea in front of Steve, behind the *Evening Times*. Without looking up from the paper Steve said, "What about it then? Will we start it up again, then?"

"Start what up again?"

"You know." To her amazement he glanced up from the article he was at, gave a lop-sided grin, and caressed her hand.

"Sex!" she thought excitedly. "At last I'm going to know what it's all about!"

Before going to bed she had a bath, covered herself in talc, put perfume behind her ears and at her cleavage. She put on a clean nightie and fresh sheets on the bed before sliding luxuriantly between them.

At eleven o' clock her lover ascended the staircase. Without glancing at Ailie – she had spread her hair over the pillow like a net – he undressed to his pants, went to the drawer and took out a short length of rope.

Ailie's heart began to thud. She propped herself on one elbow and stared at the cord, and at Steve. Without a word he hauled back the quilt, pulled off her pink brushed nylon nightie with the dainty embroidered yoke and tied her wrists to the headboard.

"What. . . what are you doing?"

Steve looked surprised. "Tying you up!"

"Why?"

Steve frowned. "But we always do it this way!"

"We do?"

"What's wrong? It's not hurting you, is it?" He checked her bonds. "Did I tie it too tight?"

"No, it doesn't hurt. . . "

"That's all right then." He put off the lamp, removed the rest of his clothes and clambered on top of her.

With his bulk pushing and grunting at her, and her own restricted movement, the whole business was more uncomfortable than painful. Fortunately it was soon over. Steve squeaked his last, clambered off, untied Ailie's wrists and put on his own pyjamas. In a few minutes he was in the Land of Nod.

Ailie stayed awake the whole night. (Is this normal? Is this *permissiveness*? Wish I'd lived through the past two years. Am I prudish? Am I frigid? Do other couples do this? Why does Steve want to tie my hands?) She thought of several possible sensations he could be getting out of binding her hands – each darker than the one before. She was only starting to drift off the subject and into the world of dreams when Crawford let her know it was time to stoke the engines of the new day.

Ailie took Crawford to visit Sandy and Pandora. She telephoned first to let him know she was on her way and he met her at the door. In the living-room a red-haired girl was sitting over some papers. She smiled in recognition. "Hello, Ailie. Sandy, away and see to the coffee." She waved at the papers. "I'm just going over some old canvass returns."

"Oh? That's . . . nice."

Dora looked as if she expected more interest.

"Are they . . . promising?"

"You'll be happy to know the returns are particularly high for the two streets you leafleted last summer."

(I was delivering political leaflets? As far as I know I've never even voted!)

"So this is your wee boy!" The girl held out her arms and Ailie placed Crawford in them. The baby grinned toothlessly.

"So you were right. Last time I saw you you were sure it would be a boy."

"I would be."

Dora bounced Crawford on her knee. "I saw Willie last week. He was asking for you."

"Was he?" (Willie?)

"You seemed to hit it off quite well, didn't you? Not that I closely followed your conversation – all this philosophical stuff about Time. . . "

"Were we discussing Time?"

"Time," remarked Sandy, coming in with a tray of coffee,

"is Ailie's favourite subject. It's like you and Scottish politics."

"For an expert in Time," said Dora, "you'd seem to have a short memory. I thought Willie made quite an impression on you."

Sandy tutted. "She's a married lady."

"What's that to do with it? Don't be such a prude."

"I'm sorry I don't remember Willie. You can tell him it's nothing to do with his . . . memorability. I just haven't lived through that part yet."

"There she goes again!" Sandy turned up his eyes helplessly.

"You can tell him I look forward to experiencing our discussion."

"Do you understand your sister when she talks like this?"

"No. When we were wee I thought she was just dopey."

"Nothing new there. You thought everybody was dopey when you were a kid."

"But I thought Ailie was particularly dopey. Now I see she's really enigmatic."

"Let that be a lesson to you." To Ailie she added, "Since I've had him I've jagged his bubble in a dozen places. You wouldn't know your Sandy at all!"

The baby smiled, opened his mouth and posseted all over Dora's shoulder. Ailie apologised and scrabbled for a tissue.

"That's all right. He just wants to remind us he's there. Don't you?" Dora kissed his head. "He's a lovely boy. You must be very proud."

"I'm working on it." (Should I tell all?) "I know how he's going to turn out, that's the trouble."

"And how's that?"

"A non-communicative, selfish, cold bore."

"A West of Scotland male, in other words!"

"I've got higher hopes of the next."

"Better make sure it's a girl!"

"I can't. I mean, it won't be. That's pre-ordained. But it will take after me in essential features."

Dora threw a chuckle at Sandy. "Your sister kills me!" And to Ailie, "Are you saying you can see into the future?"

"I'm saying I can live into the future."

"But not into the past. Otherwise how could you forget poor Willie?"

"Into selected parts of the future and the past."

Sandy and Dora looked glazed. Sandy said, "You're serious."

Dora said, "Explain."

Ailie did. After she had explained once, she explained it all again. Then, because they were still unclear on some points, she explained a third time.

Sandy said, "That's the strangest story I ever heard. I can't believe it."

Ailie said, "Now you see why I don't know Willie."

"You must give us some proof," commanded Sandy. "Tell us something that's going to happen, and we'll see if it does."

Ailie considered. "It's difficult. If I only knew which period I was going to land in next, I could look up the newspapers for the month and give everybody news items for their immediate future."

"Surely there must be some big story about to break."

"No doubt, no doubt. But to *remember* . . . If I asked *you* what was the main news story for, say, April 1966. . . ?"

"Well," Sandy drained his cup, "you'll have to offer something more if you're to convince me."

"Let me see. I did memorise all the biggest stories over about twenty years, just in case . . . Ah, yes. The next Olympics are to be held in Munich."

"We know that already."

"Yes, well, something dreadful will happen to members of the Israeli team."

There was an uncomfortable silence.

"What kind of thing?" asked Sandy.

"Shouldn't you warn them instead of us?" said Dora.

"It doesn't seem in very good taste, somehow, just to prove a point. . . "

"A sort of party trick. . . "

"What do you want?" pleaded Ailie. "You asked for a sign. Can I help it if things like terrorist outrages are what stand out in the news?"

"You should warn the victims. That way you'd make practical use of your gift."

"You reckon they'd believe me? A total stranger . . . I don't even know their names. . . "

"You could try."

"It's the old story," said Sandy, starting to gather in the cups. "Ailie's always been the meek, passive type. Line of least resistance."

Ailie felt a pang of guilt. This was what she and David had planned – to do good by the world, to use the gift. But to do it alone without David? She grew angry at herself, and then at Sandy.

"You haven't changed either. You're a . . . a . . . smug old grandpa. Always quick with the advice. What do you know about any of this?"

Dora applauded. "You were saying, Sandy? Passive wee thing, was it?"

"I was wrong. She has changed."

"Experience increases your confidence," said Ailie. She picked up the baby. "You'll know what I mean when you're forty. Must go." She was out of the house almost before the others could get out of their chairs.

Sandy said, "I still don't believe it."

"You don't want to believe it. You don't want your simple

wee sister to have a speciality denied you."

"No, it's just such a preposterous. . . "

"I don't know. I want to discuss all this further with Ailie. But let's get on with what we'd planned to do."

"The campaign."

Three o'clock found Sandy and Dora in an unfamiliar part of town.

"Which do you want? Tenements or four-in-a-blocks?"

The tenements looked crumbly. The closes smelt decayed.

"Four-in-a-blocks," said Sandy.

"Good. I don't like four-in-a-blocks. Too many dogs with territorial instincts. Wonder how their owners ever get mail. I'll do this street, and you do Achnasheen Street round the corner. It's only a dozen or so houses. I'll meet you at the far end."

As Sandy crossed into Achnasheen Street the heavens opened and he began to realise that there were advantages to tenements. He had neither brolly nor hood, his election literature was in a battered cardboard folder which rapidly grew soggy. The piece of the electoral roll on his clipboard was marked out in blue felt-tipped pen which ran in streaks down the page and, when he tried to protect it, down his coat.

At the first gate there was no dog to be seen in the garden, and he strode up the path boldly enough. However his knock at the side door produced a furious snarling and growling from behind.

"Hope they hold it back," he thought. He preferred arguing with hostile get-tough Labourites or hostile up-on-irrelevant-statistics Tories to debating with anyone in the presence of canine hostility. Canvassing was the worst – with leafleting you merely pushed open the letter-box with one hand, shoved the pamphlet right through with the other and never, but never put a finger near the space.

The door opened a crack and the hugest, blackest Canadian bear – no, it was an Alsatian – sprang out and launched himself at Sandy's jugular. He was prevented from attaining this objective by a little silver-haired old lady who had him on a choke lead and hauled him back with her full six or seven stone.

"Goo-good evening. I'm here on behalf of your Scottish National Party candidate, Jim McElroy. I wondered if we could count on your support in the local elections, next week?"

The creature sat on his haunches, licking his lips and staring at Sandy's bobbing Adam's apple. Neither the choke lead nor the old lady looked strong enough to hold him back should his interest become more than theoretical.

"The SNP?" Without warning the old lady flung the door open wide. Sandy, eyes on the dog, stepped back smartly – and then he noticed what he was meant to see. A huge saltire was stretched across the back wall of the hall, and a banner beneath proclaimed FREEDOM!

"I see you're one . . . one of us!"

"That's me! Staunch Nationalist. It's no jist thae young wans that's sick o' the wey London dictates tae us!"

"That's . . . most . . . yes, very encouraging, Mrs . . . Gillespie. Are you a member of the Party?"

"Naw, naw. Me wi ma bad back, like, arthritis, ye know – ah couldnae dae much fur yese. But if ye gie me a poster ah'll stick it in the windae."

The clouds burst anew. It was like a pall over his head.

"It's an awfy day fur yese tae be oot. Here c'moan in till it settles doon a bit. Ah'll pit the kettle oan."

Sandy looked at the dog.

"Och, don't bother yersel aboot Jezebel. She'll no touch ye. Long as ye don't make ony sudden movements, like."

"If you don't mind I'll pass your offer by this time. I've only just started this street, and I've a lot to get through."

When Dora reached her last close she went, as always, to the top landing to work her way down. This way, if anything untoward happened, she would not have to pass the same door twice. Such funny-looking doors some people in these old tenements had! This door had no name-plate, but a piece of coat or something was wedged between it and the door-cheek. Dora knocked tentatively, and passed on. She should have gone to the bathroom before starting out. That last can of export had done for her. She would ask the next female FOR voter for the use of her toilet.

Unfortunately of the three people who answered the door none was FOR. One, however, engaged her in five minutes' heavy discussion from which she only with difficulty escaped when he revealed himself as a Labour activist.

"Blast. Why can I never resist an argument?" Rapidly growing desperate, Dora crossed the road to rejoin Sandy.

On her left was a dark block of tenements more ramshackle than the last. A reek of tom-cats assailed her nostrils as she passed each close. On impulse she entered one – perhaps she could go round the backcourt, or something? Dreadful if she were spotted, though, a real vote-loser.

Up the first flight of cracked, uneven stairs, on the half-landing, a door gaped ajar. Pandora pounded up, hurried in, pulled the door to until it clicked. Only then did she see why this stairhead lavatory was open.

There was no door-handle.

Dora quelled the welling panic. She tried shouting, but either the door was as sound-proof as it was escape-proof, or else no one was in one up.

Anyway, rescue from such a situation was unbecoming. Bad for the image. If anyone answered, she would quickly remove her badges. Then, what would be her excuse for sneaking into other folks' closes, other folks' toilets?

Could she wait for Sandy to miss her and come looking?

Hardly. This close was not on the list. By the time they did a thorough enough search the police would be in on it, maybe even her friends in the press. What a laugh that would give them all.

As a last resort she scrabbled through her handbag. Oh joy! A pair of scissors! It took her five minutes to force back the rusty old sneck.

Over the next few weeks Ailie put in a bit of effort to love Crawford. She referred to him exclusively (and tried to think of him only) as Wee Crawfie. Technically he was wee, but his face had sharp, adult features which defied the usual diminutives – podge, wee dumpling and all. He was the first thin-cheeked baby she had seen.

On the rare occasion his eyes met hers they were furtive, darting. Usually, once he could focus, he pitched at a point beyond Ailie, searching for Steve who adored him.

(Which came first? Did he turn out nasty because I could remember how he had turned out nasty and therefore rejected him from the start so that he in turn rejected me? Chicken or egg?)

1971 brought decimalisation in the spring, and with it Ailie's 21st birthday – a family party at the old homestead, with Roddy morose, Dorothy cutting, Nigel obnoxious, Steve taciturn, Jojo absent, and Sandy and Pandora absorbed in each other.

The municipal election came and went. The SNP lost most of the gains they'd made in 1968, and Pandora went on a bender which lasted two nights and a day. On the Thursday morning at eight a.m. she rang the bell of the flat and Sandy, in his pyjamas, let her in. Her face was wreathed in smiles. His wasn't.

"Sorry to get you up. I think I lost the key to the storm doors somewhere along the way."

"Where the hell have you been? I've spent a fortune ringing

all your cronies. I even rang your parents, so your mother's up the pole with worry. I spent yesterday looking for you through all the pubs in the West End. . . "

"I thought the big dream was over, but it isn't." She flung herself into an armchair and her arms into the air. "I've been talking to Ailie. She says we do really brilliantly in the mid-seventies, when there's a Labour Government and people are hopeful again. I believe her."

"Hmmm, yes. I must say, my pleasure in it is a bit marred by my having to . . . "

"Aw, for God's sake, stop wittering on. Did I ever offer you a job as my minder?"

"This is a city, Dora. A lot of funny folk are loose in a . . . "

"It's my city, and I love it. Dirt, rubble, guts hanging out and all. Any angst you had over my going walkabout in Glasgow is not to be allowed to sully this moment . . . we'll be into Parliament in strength!" Again she made her victory salute.

"Thought we mainly wanted out of Parliament."

"You stoop to conquer. Playing on words instead of feeling. Gold star from the Lit and Deb. Is this the Sandy I once l-l-l-l . . . iked?"

"I'll get you a black coffee. Guess you could do with one."

He strode to the kitchen, filled the percolator with water, reached for the coffee jar. It was empty. Of course – all these lonely hours wondering if Pandora was at the bottom of the Kelvin, raped up a dark alley . . . or celebrating the SNP's future with her mate Tam. He shut the jar, switched off the percolator and reached for the Nescafe.

On a winter's morning before the year was out Ailie took the subway to Kinning Park and painfully carted Crawfie and buggy separately to the top of the stairs. Keeping baby and buggy together was forbidden, but no one came to help her as she folded them up the officially approved way, with child on one arm and bags and pram on the other. On Paisley Road West she realised she had come out on the wrong stop – Shields Road or even West Street would have been closer. Nothing for it. She cut through to Govan Road and started along the way. After the pale, smooth pavements of Germany she was always conscious of the state of them in the poorer parts of Glasgow. Broken, cracked, patched in a range of greys, covered in rubble, dogs' dirt, rotting garbage . . . The rubbish of 1971 was rather more bio-degradable than that of a decade or two later. More old cabbage, more ash, more whelks, less cellophane, polythene and polystyrene. More pungent, less lasting. The rubbish seemed to be more low-lying, too. Most gathered in the gutter where the rain quietly rotted it until it reached a texture to swirl down the stanks. The few trees lacked their favoured 1990 adornments of unravelled cassette tapes and grey polythene shreds.

She wondered why the pavements in poor areas were invariably messier than the pavements in the likes of Milngavie. More wear? (Fewer cars). More dogs? (More crime). Less civic responsibility? (More cynicism). Lower standards? (Lower expectations). The waste ground, too was just that, covered in generations past of ruined buildings, broken glass, sickly balding grass and puddles even when the weather was dry. No one could ever describe such as a meadow, or even a field. Were the Germans – and most other European peoples – naturally tidier than the Scots, or just naturally more bourgeois?

Before she had completed her train of thought she found herself at the shop. For a while she peered in the window and the door, and then she plucked up her courage to enter. It was poky and dusty, and the person behind the counter was long-haired, young-looking, and unfamiliar.

For a while she browsed amongst the books and

pamphlets – works of Lenin imported from the USSR, the Thoughts of Mao imported from China, a pamphlet produced by the John Maclean Society – *Ireland's Tragedy; Scotland's Disgrace.*

"Is there anything ye want to buy?" asked the young fellow at last.

"Oh!" Ailie nearly jumped out of her skin. "No. That is, well, it's not that I want to buy anything just now. . . "

"I'm sorry. It's not that I'm chasing you out. It's just that we're about to close."

"Right! well, em . . . " She picked up a leaflet which started off SCOTSWOMEN UNITE! YOU HAVE NOTHING TO LOSE BUT YOUR BRAINS!

"That's seven and a half new pence."

As she fumbled for her purse and looked away from him, she plucked up courage. "Could I have a word with the person in charge?"

"You're looking at him."

Ailie took a deep breath. "I know you'll think me a crank, but I'm not. I'm here to warn you."

The man behind the counter regarded her stonily.

"I know this sounds bizarre, and I don't expect you to believe me, but the fact is, I have lived into the future . . . "

Still the stony gaze.

". . . and I'm here to warn you that some of your number will be going to jail for a long long time."

No response.

"In fact, for the longest sentences ever given in a Scottish court. For 24, 25, 26 years." She cleared her throat. "Soon."

The young man narrowed his eyes. "Who sent you?"

"Nobody. I came myself, to warn you."

"What is it you want?"

"Nothing. I'm just warning you."

"I see. Well, now I'm warnin you." He came round the

back of the counter and Ailie backed away towards the door. "If you don't get your bum oot my shop pronto ye'll be pickin yer teeth oot the back o' it."

Out on the pavement, Ailie realised she was still clutching the pamphlet (which, after all, did not say Brains, but rather Drains). Should she go back in and pay for it, or at least return it? She gently pushed open the door. From the back shop the man's voice drifted through, "Bloody agents. They're usin young lassies wi weans, noo."

Ailie replaced the pamphlet on the counter and softly made her exit. As she scurried down towards Shields Road subway, an old man loomed out from a doorway, blocking her way. Thick white fuzz on his chin, shining stream from nose to mouth. A bottle bulged from his jacket pocket and his clothes stank of sweat and urine. His wet eyes lit on Ailie, and then on Crawfie.

"Eeeehhhh . . . !" A broken fingernail reached out to chuck Crawfie under the chin. Ailie wondered frantically if she had a coin to give him. What did people give beggars nowadays? Was ten pence too much?

"Ehhh ye wee champion!" slurred the old fellow, a playful little leer about his features. "Ach you don't need that dummy. Ach, you're too big fur that dummy. Ach gie me that dummy!"

To Ailie's horror, before she could stop him, he pulled the dummy out of Crawfie's mouth, shoved it in his own, gave the teat an exaggerated sook, and returned it to Crawfie's mouth. Crawfie sucked on, regardless.

Ailie tried to hurry on, but the old man grabbed her. "Haud oan, haud oan . . . " He felt in his pocket and brought forth a shilling, which he pressed into Crawfie's hand.

"Fur luck, fur the wee man."

Ailie thanked him and went on her way. At the subway station she threw the dummy in the litter bin and Crawfie screamed for it all the way home.

She sent a warning letter to Golda Meir in Tel Aviv, and to the Olympic organisers in Munich. At the last minute a fear prevailed of how life might go on for a person of interest to the Israeli Secret Service, and she sent them unsigned, and so of course there was no reply.

Ten foot by six and no windows. A table, a chair and a typewriter.

### WHEN THE CONNING HAS TO STOP.

*This Government has carried out a REAL CONTRICK on the working classes of this country.*

Tony reached for the correction paper. From the living-room voices passed through the cupboard door as if through nothing.

"She did not!" Was that Senga's voice, or her mother's?

"Withoot a word o' a lie!" Must have been Senga's, because *that* was her mother's.

"Piece n' Yodel!" – Donna.

"Aye. Help yersel. Whit did you say?" – Senga.

"Ah telt hur straight, so ah did. Ah sayd, don't you talk tae me aboot doctors, hen. Ah sayd, ah've hud ma gall-bladder done, the hysterectomy, the lot. When they opened me up, they sayd they'd never seen a uterus like it. The head surgeon came up tae me hissel, when it wis by, a nice-lookin man, an he sayd, Mrs Halket, says he, I don't know how you suffered in silence so long, says he. So just don't you come it tae me aboot doctors."

Too bad he hadn't noticed in time. Maybe if he went over the T, R, and I and then shifted the page slightly he could get a hyphen in and still squeeze in all the letters?

"Yodel aw done!"

"Gie's the new jaur, ah'll open it til ye . . . So whit did she say?"

"Cannae reach it. Too high."

"She sterted tellin me aboot aw the pills she wis oan fur hur nerves.Wid ye credit it? Tellin me!"

He held the correction paper in place with his left and started to type with his right forefinger.

"Gonnae you get me it, Ma?"

"You'll get whit fur, if ye don't gie me a break!"

"But ah waant i' the noo!"

"Shut yer geggie!" cut in Mrs Halket. "Ah'm talkin! Wherr wis ah?"

"Ye were sayin aboot Mrs Watterson comin it aboot hur nerves."

"Aye. Well, ah says tae hur, says I, don't come it, says I . . . "

Another whine. Donna again. "Tiny Tears's went n' broke. Gonnae you soart ur?"

"Ah'll soart you if ye don't pit a sock in it!" That was Senga's voice. At least, he thought it was. Latterly it was more and more difficult to distinguish it from her mother's.

"Away an get yer Da tae fix it. He's daein nuthin useful!" – Agnes.

"As usual!" – Senga.

The inside door handle began to lower. Tony took the correction paper away. The white I was way out of line.

Saved, by a ring at the door.

"Fur cryin out loud. Who might that be?"

"Wan o' Tony's sisters sayd she'd be roon."

"Zat the toffy-nosed wan?"

"They're aw toffs. But it's no Jojo. It's . . . whit dae they cry hur. . . ?"

"Ah've no met hur. Whit's she waantin?"

"Sayd she'd a message fur Tony."

"A message? An she couldnae say it over the phone?"

"She sayd it wis personal."

The doorbell rang again.

"God, it must be the revolution startin at last! Hi, Double-O-Seven! Yer emissary's here!"

Ailie perched on the edge of the settee and smiled her greeting to those present. Senga bent over the new nephew. "Aw, the wee man! He's gorgeous, so he is!" Her features had become heavy, like those of her mother. Strong jaw, close-set gimlet eyes. Same tight frizzy perm. Once she lost her teeth she would be her mother over again.

"Well? How ye daein?" asked the old woman, briskly.

"I'm fine. How are yourselves?"

The old woman started up, "That's a question ye shouldnae ask me, hen. Ah've nae respite wi this stomach o' mine, an as fur the waaterworks! Well, ah jist don't know where tae stert. . . "

"We're okay," cut in Tony.

"Ehhh! I beg your pardon!" The old woman's eyes opened wide. Granite marbles were her irises, beneath eyebrows of steel wool. Rolled-up sleeves with forearms like a wrestler's. Granny's tartan on her shins showing through the sheer Pop-sox.

"Don't you break in when ma mammy's speakin!" chided Senga. "Ye got nae manners?"

"Disnae know the meanin o' the word!" snorted the old woman. "Ma Senga's like me. Let aw the bonnets go by waitin fur a hat. An luk whit she ended up wi!"

"Couldnae huv been that many bonnets," observed Tony. "She wis only nineteen."

"Thur wur plenty bonnets!" retorted Mrs Halket. "Ma Senga wis the maist popular lassie in the street."

"Mammy, piece n' Yodel!"

"Aye, aye. Ah'm gonnae pit the kettle oan. C'moan ben."

Senga shuffled through to the kitchen, with Donna in tow.

"Ye said ye had something to tell me?" said Tony quietly.

Ailie appraised Tony. She knew him scarcely better than the others. She had been told she had accompanied Jojo to his wedding, and later to the christening of his daughter, and in time to come he would turn up to surprise them all at Roddy's funeral. She shifted her gaze to the mother-in-law who fielded it in a parody of all the mother-in-law jokes of which she and Jojo had disapproved together. (Why were there no stepmother jokes, Jojo had complained. Quite apart from fathers-in-law and stepfathers. Wasn't it nearly always a stepfather to blame when a baby, on five 'at risk' lists and dripping with social workers, was found battered to death?) At any rate, the old woman, lowering expectantly, was not one to take a hint. Ailie returned her stare to Tony, widening her eyes, trying to send the message. He glanced from her to his mother-in-law, sucked in his cheeks slightly, and looked back at Ailie. He saw the hint but was afraid to take it. Over to Ailie.

"Could we . . . would it be possible to speak to you alone?"

"Eh-eh-eh-just-a-wee-minute-noo! Let's get wan or two things straight, here!" Agnes leaned forward, jaw jutting, finger to the fore. "This is ma hoose, ah'll have ye know. Onythin ye huv tae say tae Tony kin be sayd tae ma face jist the same as behind ma back." Her eyes narrowed. "Whit wey wid you huv secrets wi Tony onyhow? Thought yese'd never met, hardly!"

"That's right," said Tony, glumly.

"Yet yese're apposed tae be brother an sister? Wee bit funny that, eh?"

"Half-brother and sister," corrected Ailie.

"We wurnae brought up thegither," mumbled Tony.

"Zat a fact? An so Senga an me, that widnae know this dame if she came up an landed us wan in the gub, is supposed tae take yer words fur it that she's yer long-lost relative?"

"Aye, that's right!" An aggrieved note entered Tony's voice.

The matron leaned even further towards Ailie. "Kin ah talk plain?"

"Please do." Ailie drew back.

"Ah know nothin aboot you or whit ye choose tae dae, an ah care less. Whit ah dae bother aboot is ma wee lassie. That's hur man therr. Ah waant ye tae remember that."

Ailie wondered if the woman was drunk. She waited for Tony to laugh. She nearly laughed herself. Then embarrassment won. Tony she thought the most incredible of all. How could the brother of Jojo land up subject to such attitudes? Jojo, strong as an ox and free as a bird . . . but they were still looking at her. Did they, did Tony expect her to grace this with a response?

"What I have to say to Tony is something to do with politics."

"Ah knew it! Ah jist . . . whit wis ah efter sayin . . . Senga! C'mere, hen !" The mother's face glowed with triumph. She all but flung her fists in the air for joy.

Senga scuttled through, teapot in hand.

"Sure ah sayd jist today that aw thon extremist politics wis gonnae get Tony intae trouble?"

"Aye, ye did."

"Aye. Well noo this dame that makes oot she's his long-lost sister says she's got a secret message aboot politics fur him! She says she disnae waant us wans tae hear! Whit dae ye make o' that, eh?"

"Ah'm no intae aw thon party political stuff masel. Ah've been tae the Liberal Club. That's jist a good laugh. . . "

"'At's no the point, but!"

". . . Ah think aw thae politicians ur the same. Chancers, wan an aw. . . "

"'At's no the point, neither!" Senga's mother shook her

head in exasperation at her daughter's obtuseness. "Look here, Mrs Lorimer – or whatever ye cry yersel – Tony here's a faimily man noo. He's got responsibilities. Whitever loada shite – 'scuse ma French – he gets hissel intae – it'll be his wife and wean'll suffer fur it."

(Should I just leave? Even if he's so scared of them, surely he could get in touch with me later. Surely he would have the sense to follow this through. Anyway, I could no more picture Tony robbing a bank than . . . On the other, hand, perhaps he's one of their ideas men. Maybe he gets involved in this desperate business to compensate for his treatment at home. Maybe. . . )

Tony cut into her thoughts. "I think, if it's to do with politics, we should talk about it ben the bedroom." He rose, and led the way. Ailie followed, gathering up Crawfie on her way. In the bedroom, he placed a finger against his lips and a chair against the door. He crossed to the far end of the room and sat on the bed, indicating that Ailie should join him.

"Just say what it's about," his eyes were on the door, "and then we can go back."

"I don't want to know any of your business," began Ailie "and I especially don't want to know if you're involved in anything illegal."

Tony turned to face her as she passed on the warning. At the end of it he said, "I jist write pamphlets for them, that's all."

"I said I didn't want any details from you."

"Still, I've been noticin recently – well, ah think ma phone's been tapped. . . " He laughed. "Whit um ah sayin? Everybody gets their phones tapped. The CP, the CND, the SNP. . . Christ, even the Labour Party mob gets thur phones tapped!"

"I heard a funny story about that," said Ailie. "My brother Sandy knows this old Swiss German who's lived in Glasgow for ages. He told Sandy that one time, during the War, he was phoning his sister, when a voice cut in. It said, Please could you restrict yourself to High German on the telephone. Our tapper can't understand Swiss German."

"Whit's High German?"

"It's the kind of dialect that's official in Germany. A bit like Standard English here. Or even RP."

"Oh aye?"

Ailie rose. "Well, I've warned you, anyway."

"Here, wait a minute!" Tony hauled her down again, eyes narrowed. "Where did ye get aw this fae? You got inside information?"

"That's right."

"Naw, but they'll waant tae know. Whit can ah tell them? You got a lumber in Special Branch, or whit?"

"No." Ailie looked down at Crawfie, who squinted up with furtive little eyes. Almost as if he were taking notes. The Wee Watcher, Steve called him, affectionately.

"Well, then, how dae ye know?"

"If I told you you wouldn't believe me," said Ailie heavily. "I tried to warn them at the shop, but I think I blew it."

"Try me."

So Ailie did. At the end he said, "Ye're right. I don't believe ye."

"I knew you wouldn't."

The rap of authority came to the door. "Heh, whit's gaun oan in therr?"

"Aye, aye, we're jist comin." To Ailie he whispered, "I'll pass the word on, but ah don't suppose they'll believe ye ony mair 'n ah dae masel."

"It's the truth. I know of no other way to put it."

Back amongst the teacups and Yodel pieces Senga pounced on Crawfie and gave him the bottle Ailie had brought. He gurgled with glee and wound her wiry thatch around his fist.

He seemed to take to everyone more readily than to Ailie.

"How do you like living in Greenock?" asked Ailie politely.

"Uch, it's okay," mumbled Tony.

"Ah miss the big city," sighed Senga. "Aw the cinemas n' at. It's jist no the same."

Tony sniggered. "Whit she means is the pubs."

"You watch yer gob, Mr Rude, Crude and Unattractive! If ma Senga says picture-hooses she means picture-hooses. Sure you've no been near a pub since the wean wis born?"

"Chance'd be a fine thing!" snorted Senga.

"Bein in Greenock's no stopped Mr Red Oan the Bed fae launchin the Revolution fae a fresh boozer every Friday!"

"You'll get a bit of sea air here, though?" Ailie ventured. "Better for the wee one."

Senga and her mother both burst out laughing. "Sea air?" yelped the mother. "Och aye! The sweetest of pongs is the pong of the Clyde!"

"It will get cleaner in time," Ailie reassured them. "Once the heavy industry's gone, the salmon'll return, and . . . "

She stopped when she saw them all staring at her.

"Whit ye mean, wance the heavy industry's gone?" demanded the mother.

"Heavy industry's why we're here at aw," said Senga. "Ye kin keep yer sea air an salmon."

"Ah came here tae work for Scott-Lithgow efter the UCS debacle," Tony told her. "Seemed mair secure, like, fur the faimily."

Ailie shook her head. "You might have been better to stay where you were," she said sadly.

"How'd ye mean?"

Three pairs of eyes on her. Two pairs granite hard, one pair soft brown.

"Scott-Lithgow will fold in the 1980s. Govan Shipbuilders will survive, although in a truncated form."

Mother and daughter exchanged looks. "And whit makes ye think that?"

Tony spoke. "She says she's lived into the future."

There was a moment's silence, and then Mrs Halket burst into a guffaw. "She's whit? Ma Goad, we could dae wi her doon at the dugs!"

Senga chided, "C'moan. We're no as green as we're cabbage-looking. Whit'd she really say?"

"It's the God's honest truth," said Tony. "That's whit she telt me."

His mother-in-law stopped laughing. "This you tryin tae take the mickey, hen?"

"It's true," said Ailie, "but I knew you wouldn't believe me." She began to gather her possessions together.

"Heh, ye cannae jist leave us wi that!"

"There's no point in going on about it. It would take too long to explain and you wouldn't believe me anyway. I've done what I came to do."

Mrs Halket's eyes narrowed. "So, whit wis the big story?"

"Ah telt you. It wis aboot politics."

"Politics." Mrs Halket shook her head. "Aw the politics ye need is in Rabbie Burns." She fixed her expression on Ailie and beat time with her forefinger while chanting tunelessly,

> For aw that, an aw that,
> It's comin yet for aw that,
> That man tae man the world ower
> Shall brithers be for aw that.

"Aye, never a truer word."

"Aye," grunted Tony "But it's no gonnae happen withoot a bit o' help fae us revolutionaries."

"Wad ye listen tae Trotsky Lorimer here! Sure if they wait

fur help fae you they'll wait till it snaws in the Kingdom o' Hell!"

Tony gave her and Crawfie a lift down to the station. At the barrier he started to say goodbye to her. Suddenly a known face hove in sight. Tall, fair, classical rather than middle-aged, with an un-Scottish poise – Stanislaus Karpinski! Behind him, undoubtedly Scottish from her short legs and squat body up to her homely, honest face, trailed his wife, Carol.

Ailie calculated. Stan did not yet know her, although he already in all senses regularly, heavily and clandestinely knew Dot.

"Well," said Tony, "I suppose we'll see you again sometime."

"Eh . . . 'spect so," murmured Ailie, eyes on Stan.

"Be sure and look us up if you're in the neighbourhood."

"I will." If she approached Stan now, how could she introduce herself? And what could she say to his wife?

"Zat somebody you know?"

"Eh? No, not . . . yet." She would have liked to have taken this chance to meet Stan at an early stage, away from Dorothy. . .

"Mind and tell Jojo I'm asking for her if you see her again."

"Uhuh. . . " But to do what? Appeal to his fine side? The thing was nothing to do with her. Stan and Dotty were well matched. Poor Roddy. Poor Carol.

". . . And your husband too, of course. Well, I'll away, then."

"Cheerio." Ailie turned her attention to Tony. He was already gone. She whirled back. Stan and Carol were also gone. She sought them in the first two carriages of the Glasgow train, but eventually had to sit down as the places were filling up and Crawford was weighing a ton.

Before the train left Greenock Central Crawfie glugged down both the bottles of milk Ailie had prepared for the journey home. As the train was pulling out he soaked through all his nappies, right into her lap. He then screamed with hunger all the way back to Central Station.

Ailie risked leaving her bags and buggy long enough to walk him up and down the corridor. To no avail. She resisted the temptation of the moment to open the train window and toss him quietly out, in case she got sent to Carstairs. Instead she returned to her seat and laid Crawfie beside her on one leaf of her newspaper, picked up the rest of it, and tried to concentrate on Angus Og, hoping people would not think they were travelling together.

Had it only been David she would not have minded at all.

1972 came and went. The political extremists were jailed (Tony having left the movement in good time), the Israeli team were massacred, and Ailie appeared to have had little effect on events.

In 1973 Ailie called a halt to the bondage. "I really don't enjoy it this way."

"But you never enjoy it anyway!" Steve shot her what she used to see as his angry young man face, in the days when she imagined his head full of deep thoughts. "That's your problem. At least let me enjoy it the way I like it. You don't *hate* it, do you?"

"Not exactly hate. As long as it's over quick I suppose it doesn't bother me too much. . . "

"Well, if we do it the way I like then I get excited fast and so it is over fast. Savee?"

"But I expected more from . . . surely at the beginning we didn't do it this way?"

Steve went red. "Is that your memory away again – you don't even remember . . . ?"

"But what do you get out of tying me up? I mean . . . it means I can't really respond to. . . "

"We went through all that too!" His voice softened. "I told you my fantasies once before. I don't want . . . you can't expect me to go through it all over again!"

Ailie rose and put her arms around him. She nuzzled his cheek and spoke as gently as she could. "You don't need to be scared of me. You know I'm not prudish. I'm . . . I hope I'm broad-minded enough to accept anything you want to tell me."

"I'm . . . you know I hate talking about this sort of thing."

"Go on . . . darling." His body felt nice and solid and she found herself hoping that they could make love the normal way in a minute. If they could only reach understanding. . . "Tell me all about it. Don't be shy." She sat on his lap and gave him an encouraging peck on the lips.

"Well, all right then." He turned his face away. "I told you before . . . with you I only make it these days if . . . if I fantasise. . . "

"Yes?"

". . . I'm the owner of a plantation and you're my favourite negress." He spoke in a rush. "You don't really want to do it with me, but you must, because you belong to me. So anything I do or say you have to go along with, even though you don't like it. For my part, I do my best to be gentle and not hurt you unnecessarily, just so long as you give me as much pleasure as I need, every time I command it."

Ailie perched on his knee, rigid.

"Another fantasy is that I'm a Roman senator and you're a new slave I've just bought in the market. I've got to try you out, break you in. . . "

Ailie jumped off his knee. "But that's . . . " She stopped, as she caught sight of his face, open for the first time since her return from Germany.

"You were going to say, horrible, weren't you?"

"No, no, not at all. . . "

His lip curled. "And you were broadminded. You were not prudish."

"It's not exactly prudishness . . . you can't do it in the normal way? Couldn't you ever?"

"Och, yer bum!" He snorted. "You were the one that changed."

"So at the very start it was okay?" She cast her mind back. "You certainly seemed . . . normal when we were . . . " (Sandy, keeping the language alive, would have said, winching.) ". . . courting."

"Ah, were you not different then, though? None o' this crazy . . . this. . . "

"This what?"

"Och, what's the use. I've explained myself. Take it or leave it."

"Could you not just keep the fantasies to yourself and do without the props? That way I could have my fantasies, too."

"But that's what would stop it working! Knowing you were having your independent fantasies . . . I need the rope to make my dreams come true. Don't know what you're complaining about. You don't like it any way I do it. You didn't much like it the old way either. You told me so."

"Well, I don't want you to tie me up, ever again."

"That it, then?"

"That's it. Unless you can do without the rope, you'll have to do without all of it." She folded her arms.

"We'll see about that. You know there are plenty women out there who'll be happy to do it with me any way I want?"

Ailie's heart began to thud. In the corner she thought she glimpsed the shade of Old Joe shaking his head, in disapproval or in sorrow, but she kept her eyes on Steve and her voice as low as she could manage.

"If you're going to bring home a dose of something nasty, you can forget the whole thing with me for all times!"

"I wasn't talking about paid women. I'm not a bad-looking bloke. There's plenty'd jump at me. And with somebody a bit more exciting I won't need the rope." He kicked off his slippers and went for shoes and Ailie wondered if he had someone in mind right then. "So we know where we stand, anyway. That's our conjugal relations over and done with, for all time. Least, I'll get it again, though I don't expect you will."

(Oh, I'll get it again, before now, if not after!) Still, she was depressed as he stormed out of the house, and even more so as she realised her mistake. Here, she had killed off her sex life, and David was not yet conceived.

Was Steve even now scouring the pubs? Kerb-crawling round Blythswood Square? She cared little, but enough to drown her sorrows in enough whisky to carry her away from all this.

# 9

"OOOOOAAAAAHHH . . . " She shifted her arm and her head struck a rock. Ailie sat up. She was on top of a cliff, lying on high billowing heather like a horsehair mattress without the covering. Below gleamed shell-white sand and a turquoise sea. There were people about, dropped on spots on the heather just as she was. They were gazing about, clambering rocks, eating sandwiches, taking still and moving pictures of the sheep, the seagulls and each other. They wore strong, good-quality clothes in natural fibres, and they did not seem to belong there.

She rose and approached a young man nearby. "This sounds silly, but I suffer from amnesia. Would you please tell me the year and where I am?"

"Amnesia? That's rough. It's 2008, and you're on Mingulay."

"Mingu. . . ?"

"Mingulay. You know. *Heel ya ho, boys.*"

"Ah, Mingulay! The island." She smiled politely and looked around. "Is there a village, or something?"

He indicated a roofless stone shell. "The original village is mainly in that condition. The population evacuated itself to Vatersay during World War One."

"Evacuated? Like St Kilda?"

"And others, I daresay. St Kilda gets all the publicity."

"I didn't know about Mingulay. I thought the wives were still waiting on the bank. . . "

"In a sense, they are again. There's a new settlement round the back of the island. That's where the rest of the party went."

"What do they live on?"

"There's a pottery and a craft shop. They sell hand-spun woollens. . . I think a few of them have private incomes." He pointed to a machine on the brow of the hill. "That's the village helicopter. Airlifts the kids to their schools every day."

"That's a big improvement on the old way of sending the children into digs at eleven or twelve years of age!"

"The Mingulayans are lucky. One of their number is a retired RAF pilot. They clubbed together to buy the chopper."

Ailie wandered up over the hill. At the foot, yellow flag irises indicated bog, but as she climbed higher, the turf was springy below her feet. From the crest of the brae she looked down on a scattering of new looking houses, all odd architectural shapes, triangular, rhomboid, triple-peaked. She hurried down on turf which sprang and bounced beneath her feet.

The first building she came to was the Post Office. She wandered in and began looking at postcards. The woman behind the counter was gossiping with one of the locals.

"And sow Mrs Cunningham wown't be inviting the Weatherbys to her next function, I take it?"

"I should jolly well think not! Little Melanie was telling me her mother plans to be having a cheese-and-wine in the gahden at the weekend of the summah soastice."

"That sounds like fun. Depends sow much on the weatha, of cawss."

"Of cawss. Anyway, everyone is invited as usual, except. . . "

"What about the Pilkingtons?"

"She's gowing to invite them, for foahms sake. But I shouldn't think they'll show theah faces, would you?"

The two women giggled conspiratorially. Ailie gave up hoping to find out what the Weatherbys and their accomplices the Pilkingtons had committed, and drifted outside. In the main street four small girls were playing hopscotch, as she had once played peever (and no doubt would one day again.) Ailie watched them for a while, feeling glad that the old customs of playing in the streets seemed to be undergoing a revival.

"Emma! Wheah'd'you put the choke?"

"It's oh used up!"

"Ow now! Box numbah six is sow woashed up, you can't hardly read it anymoah!"

"I got moh at howm."

"Ow, do be a spawt and fetch some out."

How did games like beds and skipping compete with television? Ailie glances up at the roofs. No aerials were to be seen. Of course, that proved nothing. Perhaps technology had overcome the need for outside aerials, even in this far-flung spot. Indeed, one house sported a large saucer.

She meandered back over the hill. The young man she had addressed was cupping his hands and calling out to the tourists around him, "I think we'll begin making our way back to the boat, now."

"Excuse me, Mr. . . . "

"Jeremy." The young man turned and grinned. "Just call me Jeremy."

"How long have you stayed here, Jeremy?"

"On Barra? Three yeahs. I was bohan on Skye."

"You were?"

The tourists were making their way slowly down the side of the cliff, over the rocks and on to the tiny primitive jetty, where another young man assisted them aboard the boat bobbing in the swell. Ailie followed them down. She looked around vaguely. "Excuse me again, Mr . . . Jeremy. Did you notice . . . was I with anybody here?"

"You do suffer from amnesia, don't you?" He pointed to an elderly woman seated in the prow of the boat. "As far as I could see you were with that lady over there."

Ailie quickly ran over in her mind some of the women and girls she'd known in any lasting way. None of those who would be in their seventies or eighties in 2008 looked anything like that one. Yet there was a ring of familiarity about the crinkled face, the high cheekbones, the long jaw. Ailie tried several times to catch the eye of the older woman. The crossing was longer than she had expected. By the time they reached Castlebay she had remembered where she had seen the woman before. Long ago, it was, at the foot of her bed.

"Excuse me, we are together, are we not?"

"Well, of course we are!" There still existed one person, at least, with a Highland accent. "What were you doing, running off and leaving me?"

"Running away? I was with the party all the time!"

"You were supposed to be with no party. You were supposed to be with me!"

"But. . . "

"I help my goodness. I never saw anything like it. You raced up yon hill like a blooming sherpa and left me peching like I don't know what. . . "

"I'm sorry. . . "

"Then when I make it to the top . . . what do I see? You've fallen asleep on the job!"

"Job? What job?"

"What job? Gracious, to hear yourself you'd think you were on holiday!"

"Am I not?"

"So it's that you're on holiday now! Would you just listen to yourself!"

Ailie laid her hand on the other woman's shoulder. "I'd rather listen to you if you'd explain the situation to me. I know you find it strange that I should require any explanation, but . . . well . . . I've got this sort of memory problem. . . "

"It's myself that's due the explanation, and it's myself that'll be getting one, just as soon as I get through to thon Scottish Enterprise and see what they're playing at."

The woman vanished into a hotel in the shore street. Ailie wandered along to the village school, and looked over the railing at a couple of sheep grazing contentedly in the playground. She strolled back to the square.

More sheep in the car park. And Scottish Enterprise? What did she associate with that?

In the middle of the bay, Kisimuil's Castle was a lump of grey against a sky now white with clouds. It began to spit with rain.

"Scottish Enterprise!" Ailie hurried into the hotel. The old woman was in the lounge, sipping tea. Ailie plumped down beside her.

"Who are you?" she asked breathlessly. "What's our relationship?"

The woman turned to stare. "Who am I? It's who are you, is more to the point. I'm Catriona Mackinnon, as you're well aware. . . "

"I'm sorry for asking this, but I suffer from a kind of amnesia. . . "

"Indeed! And the SE in their wisdom sent you out to look after me! Talk about the blind leading the blooming blind!"

"Am I on a scheme for the unemployed?"

Catriona looked out of a pursed-up face at her. "I suppose you are, although it's a long time since I heard them called that. The usual name is Community Duty."

"So what's my job? How long is it supposed to last?"

"Are you sure you know your name, m'dear?"

Catriona bought some postcards in the mini-market. Ailie found herself listening for accents everywhere. (I'm getting as bad as Sandy!) The girl at the checkout spoke in English, but in Highland tones.

"So there are some Gaels left!"

"Shift of population," sniffed Catriona. "The Highlanders can't wait to get to London, and the Londoners all pour up here. The grass on the other side."

"Only, next generation the London Highlanders will all be Cockneys, but so still will the Highland Londoners."

"Aye, too true. It's the way of the world. Some lots last and others don't. Look at the Picts, and . . . what were they called . . . the Incas."

"I knew around the North-East, where the oil was, it was all English accents you heard in craft shops and hotels and schools," said Ailie. "But I thought the Gaelic was still strong here. What's the effect on the bi-lingual education policy if there are so few native speakers here?"

"There are still some," said Catriona. "But it's true, the English have been moving west for generations. It's not a bad thing, I'm thinking, except maybe culturally."

"How do you mean?"

"Well, the incomers are great ones for the committees and all that. They don't let the Government away with anything. You just have to say Nuclear Dump or Army Testing Range or School Closure and right away there's committees formed against it. Very successful they are. Whereas the old people would have been thinking about it in terms of the jobs they might be given out of it, or at best would be running around looking for somebody to tell them what to do."

"But what about the Gaelic language?"

"Och. They still teach it in schools," Catriona reassured

her. "A few of the newcomers wanted their children to have a bit of the Gaelic, for interest's sake. So they teach it the same way they teach French. Right enough, I don't suppose they pick up much. If their parents think they're learning something then that's what matters."

Back in her hotel room Ailie failed to find a handbag, or even any money.

"You had a wee bag when you got off the boat at Mingulay," said Catriona.

"Will I be able to get it back?"

"I should hope so! Do you expect me to support you during the last two days, or what?"

"Well. . . "

"You could phone Mingulay. Or just ask the folk going on tomorrow's day trip to pick it up for you. Must be somewhere on yon first wee brae."

"Did I not go anywhere else?"

"Not you! Sure, you exhausted yourself that much, galloping up to the top like a sheep after clover."

Ailie got her bag back the night before they left. Purse with loose change, credit, chequebook and hole-in-the-wall cards. Bunch of house keys. Diary with an address for herself in it, and with the bank PIN

Boy's

cunningly disguised as Phone. Seashells. Sweets. Broken comb.

In

Naples

Address book with addresses familiar and unfamiliar. Book of Gaelic phrases. Five-year diary with a few significant dates recalled from the future already filled in.

Glasgow airport looked bigger than she remembered.

"And so it has to be," said Catriona, "with flights from all over the world coming in and out. Not far off the size of Manchester Airport, now."

"So people don't have to pay an extra hundred or two to get to London before they go abroad!"

"A hundred! That wouldn't take you anywhere near London nowadays, unless you went by bus or Shanks' pony!"

"Still, more direct flights! That must be a great help to the tourist trade."

"Well, it's an absolute necessity to anything calling itself a holiday destination. And tourism is Scotland's number one industry these days."

"What about Prestwick airport?"

"That went years ago. Too off the beaten track." Catriona stared at her. "I get the feeling I'm blethering to Rip Van Winkle, here!"

"That about sums it up. If I thought you'd believe me I'd tell you my story, but it would only serve to confirm in your mind I've a screw loose."

"Well, since I'm absolutely convinced of your loose screw at the moment you've nothing to lose by it. It's a long time since I heard anything really out of the ordinary. And, you never know, I might believe you. By the way, that's mine there," Catriona pointed. "The green leather case. Do you think you could grab it off the belt and put it on the trolley for me, with my bad heart and everything?"

On the taxi out to Catriona's home in Dennistoun, Ailie related the saga.

Catriona gave her verdict at the end. "I would say there's a thirty percent chance you're telling me the truth," she declared. "There's a sixty percent chance you're away with the fairies, and a ten percent chance you're taking a loan of me deliberately, though what you would get out of that I can't begin to imagine. Now, would you prefer tea or coffee?"

Catriona being the only soul Ailie could be sure of knowing in this strange new world, she made a date before leaving to visit again in a few weeks' time. She made for the nearest

Bank of Scotland branch, put her card in the slot and learned the worth of her current account. ECU387. It meant nothing until she could ascertain the value of the currency. She drew some out and took a taxi to the address in her book, a flat in the West End. The flat was unfamiliar, but she knew the furniture, and wandered about for a while caressing and even kissing bed, table, piano and armchairs. "If Catriona could see me now," she chuckled to herself, "she'd drop the credibility rating to twenty!"

She searched the flat in vain for a rent book or a trace of mortgage payments. The phone was dead, either broken or disconnected. In the pantry she found long-life milk, tea, coffee and biscuits. She switched on the television and saw a reporter standing in a pretty tree-lined street with pavement cafés to either side. He was talking about something called Youth Service. It was only when the camera widened its angle that Ailie realised, by the old underground station at the foot, that he was standing in Buchanan Street.

Next day Ailie walked into town down Great Western Road, along St George's Road, much improved with small bright shops facing onto the motorway, and up Sauchiehall Street. The pedestrianised part of Sauchiehall Street had glass canopies up both sides, supported by concrete and some-times wrought iron pillars around which twined flowering plants.

Under the canopies pubs, cafés and restaurants (there seemed little difference) spilled their tables and chairs onto the street. Apparently there was some kind of festival on, for Ailie counted two sets of street theatre, one white-faced robotic dancer, two jugglers, one fire-eater and four individual buskers.

In the centre of George Square a piper and a couple of fiddlers accompanied two sets of professional dancers performing an Eightsome Reel.

Ailie sipped a beer shandy in a hotel on the north side of

the square before phoning Sandy. To her amazement he was still at the address in her diary. She knew his voice at once, carefully educated but deliberately Scottish, pure vowels, all Rs carefully enunciated, but Ts as well.

"Where are you? Ah, you mean 1820 Square! I take it your . . . heid's been away and come back?" (Sandy often sounded as if he had quotation marks around his Scotticisms.) So he knew, then.

Ailie wandered out again, to wait for Sandy to pick her up. Watching the piper, she felt the old familiar life twitch in her ankles. (And why not? I, with no control over my reputation; what care I for passers-by? But what about my health – am I in the habit of regular exercise? Will it be too risky? What age am I?) She took off her spectacles and slipped her mind into the frame so familiar in her recent theatrical childhood, fudging the sea of faces, pretending she was practising alone before the triple wardrobe mirrors in Dot's boudoir. And she sprang into her own wild reel, a combination of pas-de-basque, jig and schottische. Within minutes (though she saw them not) she had her own audience, all clapping the lady with the flying straggles, the birling skirt and the high-kicking woolly legs.

Soh-te-doh! Soh-te-doh! Soh-te-doh! Te la soh – fa/la/fa/la/fa/la/fa/la ray/doh/te/soh/la/te/doh! Soh-te-doh! Soh-te-doh! te la soh – fa soh la fa me – ray soh te doh! screamed the fiddles and . . . "Hooch!" scraiched Ailie to the mists around her. She forgot the age she was supposed to be until a fit of palpitation and a loss of breath reminded her and she sat down plump in the middle of her acclamation. The sky and the faces swam above her. Her face was suddenly wet. (Sweat? Tears? No, the beautiful sun is gone and rain is spitting down from on high.) A gentleman took her elbow and asked her if she were all right. A familiar person, longish grey hair, goatee beard, thoughtful eyes, haggard cheeks.

Ailie clutched Sandy's green corduroy sleeve and helped herself up.

She drank him in at arms' length and gave an extra little skip of excitement. "It's really you! It is, it is! At long last!"

"Let's get out of here," muttered Sandy. "They're all staring at us."

"What do I care! Let them gawp!" (A Scotticism of her own would please him.) She embraced him until he pushed her away. "Oh, Sandy, I've been so lonely!"

"Well," Sandy gave an embarrassed chuckle. "That depends on your point of view. After all, you came to dinner only last week!"

They had to take the subway to Sandy's car. He explained that cars were no longer permitted within a square mile of 1820 Square. They disembarked at Cowcaddens and made their way to an underground carpark.

Great Western Road looked much the same as ever, although Anniesland Cross was now a roundabout.

"Why are you driving so slowly?"

"There's a speed limit of 30kph within the city limits, and 60kph overall," Sandy told her. "And they really mean it! If you're caught you lose your licence. Caught twice, you have to resit the test. Three times, you lose it for good. It's as unusual now to break the speed limit as it is to go through at red."

"Sounds like the anti-car people are in power at last," commented Ailie.

"If you're asking whether the Greens have inherited the Earth, well, in a sense they have. They're in power in Sweden and in Norway, and are a powerful lobby in Germany. In more backward states like Britain the Green Party is still struggling against the system, but Labour and the Democrats have adopted a lot of their policies. The SNP always did share most of their policies, of course, anyway."

"So that's the story of Europe, then."

"When did you say you were last with us?"

Ailie thought. "Mid-1989, I think."

Sandy whistled. "Then you missed some of the changes. Europe's much tighter now. There's no East or West. We're one fat happy family."

"I remember Poland and Hungary weren't as communist any more, but. . . "

"Towards the end of the century they got a sort of liberal in charge of the Soviet Union. He let them all go."

Ailie thought back. "Gobblechop – or something? With a mark on his head?"

"That's the one. Anyway, he loosened the reins slightly – and you should have seen the satellites spinning away. More than a generation of education into the communist way of life – and the Soviet brand of communism – and yet after all it turned out they were only being kept in by sheer force. When the force went so did they – within months!"

"I recall they were starting to let Easterners through the Berlin Wall."

"It got chopped down and sold as souvenirs."

"You must give me notes of the exact dates all this happened," said Ailie, "and I'll make a point of being there."

"Just avoid Romania," advised Sandy. "Only there was blood shed."

"You mean they all went? Bulgaria, Czechoslo-vakia . . . what about Russia?"

"We're all the one Europe, now. We've got common passports, common money, free trade, and they're at last back to teaching languages properly in schools. I find it much healthier, being one in a combination of many, rather than an appendage of a giant. . . "

"I know, I know. And better for the teaching profession too, eh?"

"I'm out of teaching. For sixteen years I've been a full-time financial consultant."

"But you never trained in that field!"

Sandy smiled. "Twenty years ago they changed the rules – opened up chartered accountancy to all graduates, regardless of discipline."

"But. . . "

"Naturally, graduates from the field of accountancy tended to get preference over others in the jobs stake. I was lucky. I fell in with an old pal from university days, somebody who used to speak against me in debates, would you believe!"

"Not a Tory!"

"How did you guess? Anyway, I never mix business and politics. He gave me an apprenticeship, and I took the professional exams through correspondence courses. So here I am!"

"And is it . . . better than teaching?"

"It's certainly more lucrative. I've a lot of big firms on my books. Many still ask for me although I've been semi-retired for a year now!"

"That wasn't what I asked."

"I was always interested in money," said Sandy. "What I should have done – I should have used my languages to study economics in Germany – and maybe banking in Switzerland! It wasn't possible in my time. It is now."

A chill came between Ailie and Sandy. An unexplained chill, an undesired chill. Ailie sought to dispel it.

"Shame that the communist experiment had to end so absolutely. Don't you think so? It was founded on principles of unselfishness."

"Impracticable principles. People are born selfish, and won't behave otherwise unless they're coerced."

Ailie sighed. The chill had deepened. She settled herself back in the soft seat. "What about the world at large? Give me a rundown for future reference. I'm always hoping to use my knowledge to good purpose in another time. Somehow, so far, Fate has thwarted me."

"Well, the USSR is no more. It split into its constituent parts. Russia's getting richer, now that they're getting help from the USA and don't have to make as many bombs. The two Empires got together to send an unmanned spacecraft to Jupiter."

"You mean they've revived the space race? Maybe we'll get a chance yet to see the world from out there?"

"No, this was a one-off. They called it MIRPEACE and it was supposed to symbolise the new attitudes. Nothing more. I think the superpowers have lost enthusiasm for Space now that they lack the incentive to extend the boundaries of war. Space was always primarily a military interest."

"So America prevailed in the end. Consumerism, Christianity. . . "

"Some other countries got to be important too, and that blurred the old rivalries. China is coming to the fore. Germany's firmly set into a strong united Europe. Strong economically, that is – like Japan."

"Not, I trust, militarily." Ailie smiled to herself at her own turn of phrase. She seemed to be developing an elder stateswoman jargon to go with her grey locks. Maturity, it was not as bad as it was cracked up to be.

"I always feel," Sandy was saying, "that Europe is too civilised to waste all its treasures on machines of destruction. And Japan was of course forced by history into taking the same enlightened attitudes."

"But how do all the commercial interests feel about there being no excuse to make bombs?"

Sandy grimaced. "Well, if they want another bogeyman they're going to have to build up on China."

"What about you and Pandora? Still involved in the SNP?"

Sandy glanced at her and turned back to the road. "Goodness, you've been out of things a long time."

"Is Scotland independent, then?"

"Not . . . in the old sense . . . We've got a reasonably strong Parliament of our own, to deal with home affairs. . . "

"Devolution."

"We-e-ell. The Tories are trying all the time to tighten links with Westminster and loosen those with Europe, while the other three main parties try the opposite."

"Nuclear bombs being still a London option?"

"More and more a Brussells option." Sandy smiled. "Nuclear bombs don't seem as relevant anymore now peace is in vogue."

"Surely they'll always be relevant to us as long as we're hosting bases."

"We're working on that," said Sandy, "through the European courts. Actually the Edinburgh Parliament's semi-permanently fighting Westminster in the Euro-courts over some issue or other. Oil revenues, for instance . . ."

"But what about the real issues? Is Scotland the better country for having its own Parliament?"

"I think so," said Sandy cautiously.

"Well, you'd be biased, of course."

"I know, I know. But I think our philosophy is a bit more moral for having ditched the old imperialist notions that were still holding down Britain."

"What way?" Ailie beamed on her brother. There was good in him yet. He did not immediately equate Better Country with Richer Country. Pandora surely wielded influence here.

"We may be a poorer country than . . . some, but we're a better country to be poor in. A big proportion of tax is spent on welfare, on education, the National Health Service. In England they've hardly got a Health Service any more – it's gone like America, with insurance companies making more medical decisions than doctors. And their schools vary dramatically, with lots of excellent schools for those who can pay for them, and Middenhead Secondary for the large minority who can't. We're less obsessed with breast-beating than England still is, even these days of big power cooperation. We're always trying to cut down on our defence contribution, and we contribute a much bigger percentage of our budget to overseas aid than England does."

"They haven't slowed down the colonisation of the Highlands," said Ailie. "The Gaels have kept a toehold in the Western Isles, but in most places it seems you never see a Scot at all."

"Och, that's gone on for generations," said Sandy. "What can we do? You have to let people live where they want. But there are limits on the amount of land that can be owned, and the uses it can be put to. And we don't allow absentee landlords. Only persons domiciled in Scotland can own it."

"An old Highland lady I talked to thought it was a good thing, that the English had taken over."

"The Gaeltachd always was full of Uncle Toms."

"But should we not be flattered that they want to come and live here? They must see some superiority here, after all."

"I don't think we should be flattered that they find our topography superior, if they find our ways so inferior that they ignore them and impose on us their own."

"What if our ways are inferior?" murmured Ailie. "Anyway, I can see that you and Dora are just as committed . . . " she paused at her own choice of words ". . . as ever you were."

Sandy pulled into the side of the road, braked, and switched off the ignition. They were on an empty road, with nothing but hills to the horizon. "Is this where you stay? Where's the house?"

"I stay in Fintry. We'll see it, quite suddenly, round the

next corner. But first, there's something you must know. Pandora and I split up long years ago."

"What! But you seemed so . . . I just thought. . . "

"You remember Jasmine?"

"Wee Jasmine Patel! You used to play Monopoly. . . "

"Scrabble. Wee or big, I've been married to her many a year now. We have two grown-up daughters."

"Grown-up nieces! "What are they called?"

"Kirsty and Sorcha."

"Not much of the Punjab about that. Am I right in thinking that you chose the names?"

"It wasn't like that. Jasmine was quite happy with those names. She's totally Scottish herself."

"Doesn't she speak any Indian?"

"Och, her Dad taught her a few words of Punjabi at one point, but I'm sure she forgot it all long ago. Her parents have been dead a good many years."

"Did she never teach the girls any Punjabi?"

"I sent them to a Gaelic school, and we reckoned two languages were enough," said Sandy.

"You don't speak Gaelic yourself!"

"Just a bit I picked up at night school. Not enough to back up what they did at school. Sorcha never made much of it, but Kirsty got the Higher."

"Don't you ever visit India?"

"I've been a couple of times. Jasmine still goes occasionally, and when the girls were wee she sometimes took them. But it costs a lot, you know. And it's a depressing place. So much poverty. The girls prefer going with their pals to the Med or the Adriatic. Or sometimes the States."

"Have they found no solution to Third World poverty even yet?"

"The solution is as clear as it always has been – for the governments of rich countries to devote time and resources to it. There's more hope now than before, since the two main powers have stopped concentrating on war effort and are looking for another cause to fill the gap."

"But surely it's more likely that what will fill the gap will be something attractive to the big companies, something with a profit in it?"

Sandy shrugged his shoulders. "We must wait and see."

"And the poor of the world wait and die?"

"That's the way it is."

"So the Indian part of your daughters' heritage. . . "

"I told you that side doesn't mean anything to Jasmine," said Sandy. "If she doesn't care about it, why should the girls?"

"I see."

Sandy started up the car again. They drove into a sleepy village, where flowers, wild and cultivated, still encroached on the main street. Sandy pulled up outside a grey detached house. Rabbits bounced and nibbled in a wire run on the lawn, and in a corner up the side, white fantails perched on a doocote wound round with honeysuckle. Six sunflowers with faces like dinner-plates stood guard along the wall of the house.

"What a lovely garden!" exclaimed Ailie. "I remember Mummy never had any success with sunflowers. If she could see these now. . . !"

"We don't get the cold winters we used to," said Sandy. "Spring and autumn are warmer too, although the summer's still nothing to write home about."

Jasmine came to meet them. As a young girl her looks had been perfect – clear complexion even at fourteen, large eloquent eyes, glossy black hair. Now that the blackness had softened and the corners of her countenance were overwritten with her character, the effect was a more indirect charm. She carried herself in a shuffle, shoulders hunched, head poked forward.

"Come in, come in. I've made coffee." She leaned forward to kiss Ailie just as Ailie did likewise, and their cheeks bumped.

They sat down in an expensively furnished room, green velvet upholstery, onyx coffee table. Above the marble fireplace hung a Pre-Raphaelite-looking painting, red green and gold, while against the back wall, bathed in a fluorescent glow, old-fashioned people hovered on horseback on a vibrant shore. As Ailie moved across, she could swear that the old hunched rider in the foreground shook his head in sorrow.

"What's that?"

"It's *The Last of the Clan*, by Thomas Faed," Sandy told her. "The Art Galleries bought it by public subscription many years ago."

"But, I mean, *what* is it? It's not a picture. . . "

"It's a hologram, of course," said Jasmine.

"Now, Jasmine, remember what I said. Although we saw Ailie just a fortnight ago, she doesn't recall that. Or anything since . . . when was it?"

"It's . . . a bit more complex than that," said Ailie. "Let's just say I don't remember ever having been here."

"Goodness. That amnesia's a terrible thing. We've been in this house . . . what is it . . . surely fifteen years now."

"Seventeen, actually," said Sandy. "Anyway, I thought you'd said you'd made coffee?"

"Right. I'll go and get it now." Jasmine disappeared.

"Are . . . sorry, I've forgotten their names . . . your daughters. . . "

". . . Kirsty and Sorcha."

"Are they out at the moment?"

"Och, they're both away, now. Kirsty's lecturing in the Computing Department at Heriot-Watt, so she only comes home occasionally at weekends or during the university vacations. Sorcha's a physiotherapist, working out in Saudi Arabia at the moment."

"So your daughters are successes, then. That's nice for you, to know they're settled in proper careers."

Jasmine came in just then and smiled. "Yes, Kirsty especially seems to have it all. She gets her brains from her father and her looks from me."

"Och, come on, Jasmine. I'm sure you've plenty brains of your own."

"Of course she has!" declared Sandy. "She was even doing a course at the Open University a year or two back."

"Oh, how did you get on? I would have fancied doing something like that if only . . . things had been different."

"I didn't . . . "

"She didn't stick it," interrupted Sandy.

Jasmine coloured. "It was at the time Sorcha was going through a bad patch.She broke up with her fiancé just at the time of her final exams."

"Still no reason for you to abandon your own studies," grumbled Sandy. "That's Jasmine all over. Vicarious living."

"I just found I didn't have enough time. . . "

"Spends too much of it watching soaps."

Jasmine threw an apologetic grin at Ailie. "I know they're all rubbish, and the plots don't hold water at all, but somehow they get a grip of you. . . "

"And then the day's gone and you haven't anything to show for it. We know. Anyway," Sandy rose, "what did you come in to tell us? Is the coffee ready?"

"Oh . . . yes. If . . . if you'd like to all come this way. . . " She led them through a wood-panelled hall to a round room with a mahogany table set in the bow window. On the table was a steaming pot of coffee, scones, crumpets, apple tart, whipped cream, butter and raspberry jam.

"You didn't need to go to all this trouble!" gasped Ailie.

"Jasmine," smiled Sandy, "is a mistress of the housewifely arts."

Ailie's eye was caught by a bright little scene on the sideboard.

"Can I look at this?" She crossed the room. "What a dainty wee . . . object!"

Set out like a miniature tableau in three dimensions, brightly illuminated, was a classical Bacchalian scene, rosy-garlanded beaming figures draped on couches around a table groaning with roasts, fruits, wine, artistically moulded loaves. Tiny hands grasped golden goblets, filaments of fabric floated on an unfelt breeze.

"Jasmine likes all that sort of kitsch," Sandy remarked between mouthfuls. "She'd have bought a hologram of *The Last Supper* for this dining-room, if I'd let her!"

"But that was different," protested Jasmine. "It wasn't like that one, posed by actors. It was taken from the original work of da Vinci. . . "

"Yes, yes. Very tasteful."

Unnoticed, Ailie returned to her seat. Jasmine said, "I still think taste is a subjective thing. Surely one man's meat is another's. . . "

"There are certain accepted standards, Jasmine."

"Accepted by whom?"

Ailie said, "Are you in touch with Jojo these days?"

Sandy hesitated, then laughed. "Jojo. Now, there's a name to conjure with. Where will we begin, Jasmine?"

"Well, where did Ailie leave her?"

"I don't know," murmured Ailie. "I think it was Germany. . . "

"Ah. So then you missed the Art School experience. . . "

"Did Jojo go to. . . "

"Not to mention the Tinker. Sorry, Traveller. Mustn't use disparaging descriptions."

"And the baby," beamed Jasmine.

"Did Jojo have a baby to a. . . "

"And the kibbutz. Which is where we left them."

"Do you have the address of the kibbutz?"

"Keeping up with Jojo's vaccillations," Sandy shook his head, "would have required a private eye on a retainer basis."

"You don't tell me you let her walk out of your lives?"

"Look. There are two sides to it. We were happy to keep up with Jojo's movements, increasingly. . . "

"But. . . "

". . . increasingly bizarre though they were." Sandy raised his voice to override Ailie's. "But if she doesn't answer our letters, if she makes no effort at all, if she makes it clear she has no interest, why should we chase after her?"

Ailie's eyes filled with tears. She got her mind off Jojo – she would see her again one day. "Nigel?"

"He emigrated to Canada and married out there. But I've just heard that they plan to come back. So you can meet them soon."

"What about you? Are you still working?"

"I plan to slow down gradually," said Sandy. "As for pension, I'm in a private scheme. There's no employer's contribution of course, so expectations won't be as high as if I'd been an employee."

"Still, I daresay you've a bit put by."

"Och, yes," Sandy smiled. "We won't starve."

"What about you?" Ailie turned to Jasmine.

Sandy cut in. "Jasmine never wanted a job."

"No, it's not that I don't want a job. . . "

"She feels she's got it cushy enough as it is. The house, the garden, the pets, letters from the girls, coffee with the neighbours. . . "

"Now, I don't have all that much to do with the neighbours. . . "

"Sleeping in the morning, shopping in the afternoon, theatre or telly in the evening, sleeping at night."

"Come on, it's not all like that!" Jasmine laughed shakily.
"Holidays abroad, holidays in the Highlands. . . "

"You make me sound like a . . . "

"Lounge lizard?"

"I do work about the house."

"You do? Then what am I paying Mrs Buchanan for?"

Ailie said, "Jasmine, you don't have to defend yourself to
me. I'm not into the work ethic either."

"But I did want to work!" Jasmine protested. "It's just
that it's difficult to get back into paid employment when
you've been away."

"That's what that course in the papers was for, helping
women back into a job," grouched Sandy. "You should have
applied when you saw it advertised."

Jasmine regarded him with hurt eyes. He stared back
imperviously. To Ailie it seemed as though their faces naturally
settled into these long-accustomed expressions.

Jasmine turned at last to Ailie. "How are Crawford and
David getting on?"

"I was hoping you could tell me that. I've a standing
arrangement to meet David at Glasgow Green on the first of
the month, which I'm hoping he'll keep. I haven't seen or
heard of the adult Crawford in many a long. . . " she paused
for thought, "during my last few visitations, anyway."

"Visitations. I like it," chortled Sandy. He poured himself
another coffee. "Crawford took over his old man's firm."

"Steve's business. Videos, wasn't it?"

"More computers, I think, latterly. Anyway, he sold out."

"So is Steve retired, then?"

"He's dead. I thought you knew."

"I didn't. When did it happen?"

"Quite suddenly, last year. His heart. You know he was
grossly overweight. And he smoked forty a day till the end."

"What about his new wife? They had family, didn't they?"

"One daughter. Actually Liz wasn't his wife. You still are. You never got round to divorcing him."

Jasmine leaned across the table. "By law, you'd probably be entitled to a bit of his estate."

Ailie shook her head. "I wouldn't want anything of Steve's."

"Why not? If it's yours by law. Goodness knows, you could do with it."

Jasmine said, "You lived with him many a year, even though he didn't make you happy. This could be your pay-off."

"I don't need paid off. Steve wasn't happy either. In fact, it was my condition that made us both unhappy. So if it was anyone's fault it was mine."

Jasmine said, "But he made no attempt to understand your illness. He did nothing at all for you. And he was a womaniser. . . "

Sandy cut in. "Drop it, Jasmine. It's up to Ailie. If she doesn't want to take her share, that's her decision."

Jasmine gathered up the plates and took them through to the kitchen, refusing Ailie's offer of help.

"Why do you put her down?" asked Ailie.

"You always accuse me of that. I don't put her down. On the contrary, I'm trying to get her to make the most of herself."

"Why not just take her as she is? You've destroyed her confidence."

"What? For years I've been actively encouraging her to go for Higher Education, trying to persuade her to get out of the house and take a job. . . "

"Don't be so critical. Isn't she a good wife to you?"

"For me, a good wife isn't enough. I want a soulmate. I've tried to interest her in politics. . . "

"Does she have the same attitude as you there?"

"Well, she votes the same way, but she's not really interested in active involv . . . "

"How do you know?"

"How do I know what?"

"That she votes the same way."

"Of course I know. She. . . "

"Is it not still a secret ballot?"

"Why should she make out she votes the same way if she doesn't?"

"Just a thought."

"I don't like the way you're casting me as some kind of bully. Jasmine's a free person. I'd be disappointed if she didn't support my political views, at least passively, but of course I accept her right not to do so."

Jasmine re-entered. "If Ailie doesn't remember the last few years she won't know about David!"

"Just a minute," put in Sandy. "Jasmine, what did you vote last election?"

Jasmine's eyes widened. "Why are you asking me that?"

"Because I don't think I asked you before."

"Last election," Jasmine shifted her stare to Ailie, "there happened to be a Global candidate standing, and I voted for her."

"What's Global?"

"A minor party that purports to concern itself with world issues," Sandy frowned. "You know, the redistribution of wealth from the rich half to the poor. Originally it's a Scandinavian idea, but they put up a sprinkling of candidates in elections all over the world. Of course, this means that even if they occasionally got in (which they don't) their base would be too thin for them to accomplish anything."

"At least they have ideals," Jasmine pleaded. "At least they try."

Sandy said, "Just because your old man was Indian doesn't mean you have to prove it all the time."

"I'm proud of my Asian background," said Jasmine, quietly.

"What Asian background? English was spoken in your home. Your mother and sibs were totally Scottish . . . so was your Dad, more or less."

"That didn't save Paul from being beaten up."

"What?"

"My brother Paul." Jasmine cast a sidelong glance at Ailie. "Paul got beaten up once coming out of a disco by a group calling him a Paki bastard."

"How could they tell? He's hardly darker than you."

"That," hissed Jasmine, "is not the point."

"It was outrageous that he should be set upon. Did he tell the police?"

"He was only fifteen at the time."

"Well, of course, teenage boys are always picking on any excuse to beat each other up. Any little difference will do. . . "

"What is it, Sandy?" asked Jasmine. "Are you playing the old song, pretending there's no racism in Scotland?"

"There are thugs everywhere," said Sandy, "Scotland included. But surely there's more to Indian culture than getting called names?"

"I never said that was . . . I mean . . . Och, Sandy, you twist everything. . . "

The silence was heavy until Ailie cleared her throat. "You said David was up to something?"

Jasmine smiled weakly. "He's founded some kind of sect!"

"In actual fact, he doesn't refer to it as a religion. He calls it a philosophy."

"They're living in some horrible place . . . is it a squat, Sandy?"

"Don't exaggerate, Jasmine. It's . . . one of these change of tenure places." He turned to Ailie. "Used to be a council house until the Tories resurrected the private landlord system."

"Anyway, it's pretty much of a slum."

"Now, now," Sandy remonstrated. "Don't give Ailie the wrong idea."

"But Sandy, you mind that time we went, it was awful-looking."

"I've seen worse. In rural India, for instance. There, it would class as a palace, with its bathroom and electricity."

Jasmine flinched at this fresh, unprovoked attack.

"Sandy, you've surely changed!" interjected Ailie. " You were never so . . . How can you be a Scottish Nationalist and a cultural imperialist at the same time?"

Jasmine rushed out, slamming the door.

"I'm sorry. I don't know what gets into me." Sandy rubbed his beard. "Jasmine seems to bring out the worst in me."

"Don't blame it on Jasmine."

"She's so timid and unsure . . . it annoys me more than if she were into stand-up fights."

"There's a bit of the wife-batterer in you, Sandy, I do believe."

"Oh, never say that! I don't want you to think that of me."

"I was speaking figuratively, of course."

"Of course! So was I!"

"And apologise to her. Not to me."

"I will." Sandy grinned uneasily, and rested his hand on Ailie's shoulder. "Anyway, what about you, Ailie? How are you coping, really?"

"Just . . . finding my feet."

"Must be very confusing for you. How are you doing. . . " he slapped his pocket in an embarrassed fashion ". . . with the old finances?"

Ailie was doubtful. "Well, I'm not flush, of course. I got some pay for this temporary job I had, escorting an old lady on holiday. The blind leading the blind, she called it!"

Sandy laughed gently. "And what about when that pay

comes to an end?"

"I found a bank book, and there's two lots of money going into the account every month. So I suppose I get some kind of a pension."

"If you don't mind my asking, how much might that be?"

Ailie told him. He whistled. "Good God, that wouldn't last us a weekend, never mind. . . "

"Och, but I manage," Ailie told him. "I don't need much. And I might still be on the books of this agency that got me the last job."

Sandy looked thoughtfully at the floor. "Looks like you're due a rise."

Ailie laughed. "I should be so lucky!"

Sandy regarded her gently. "You must have forgotten where the second payment comes from. The one that isn't the State pension."

"Where does it. . . " Ailie caught his eye. "Oh no! You can't mean . . . "

"It's not like that, Ailie. . . "

"I don't want money from you, Sandy. These payments must stop."

"But, Ailie, don't you remember. . . "

"No, I don't, nor can I imagine what I was thinking of, to accept. . . "

"But we had an agreement. . . "

"Then we agree to disagree again. How can I have any kind of equal relationship with you if I'm a parasite on your back?"

"That's exactly what we have. An equal relationship. A partnership."

Sandy eased himself into an armchair. "Sit down and I'll explain."

Ailie resisted. "I won't be on the take from you. I was born your sister, and. . . "

Sandy waved his arm about. "And if it's all due to you?"

"What is?"

Sandy smiled. "17th October 1987. Black Monday, the financial institutions called it."

"I know. I read about it, somewhere. While I was trying to catch up on old newspapers, probably."

"The biggest money market crash since 1929."

"Didn't you get people flinging themselves off skyscrapers? Or was that the time before?"

"Mostly the time before. Anyway, you warned me."

"What!"

"I was dabbling in shares and unit trusts, just as a hobby, while trying to set up my accountancy firm. When you told me what was in the offing, I spent the Thursday plunging everything I had into cheap put options. The following Wednesday I sold them all at massive profits."

"But at whose expense?" (Will I have lost my conscience when that time comes round? Can Sandy see anything wrong in it at all?) "Did any of them jump off skyscrapers?"

"Nobody suffered. Not unless they'd written put options they couldn't cover." (No, he sees nothing wrong. I'm just over-sensitive.)

"Anyway, I made . . . a good bit . . . that way, and our agreement was that I would give you a regular share. So, anything you want, old girl," he slapped her shoulder again, "just squeak out."

# 10

THE ADDRESS WAS UP a close somewhere between Garscube Road and Springburn.

The door in the front of the close had at one time boasted a controlled entry system, but now what caught the eye was a slogan above the door – NAE DOPE, NAE BOOZE; NAE BREAD, NAE BROOS. The stairs were stained and uneven, and smelt of urine. Grafitti writhed around the walls.

A teenage girl answered Ailie's knock with a generous smile and showed her into a front room covered with photographs, sepia, black and white and coloured.

David sprawled beside the gas fire. On the arm of his chair perched a red-haired, pregnant youngster. Another waif, with a pinched face and thin, nippy clothes knelt at his feet.

"Mother! Come in! Come in!" David rose and to her astonishment hugged her like a bear. "Mother's mind has just returned from another plane," he announced, "and so she won't recognise any of you lot."

The girls stared blankly with the indifference of youth to age, as though having your mind visit another plane were an everyday habit.

"Mother, this is Jackie, a good friend from down the road."

The girl at his feet murmured surlily, "pleased to meet you," and dropped her gaze.

"And this," he threw an arm around the girl on his right, "is my wife, Karen."

Karen took Ailie's hand in both of hers and rose so that their noses were inches apart. Her own eyes were pale blue, and her complexion had never been south of Rutherglen. "I knew you before, Mrs Carmichael, but I'm honoured to meet you again."

Ailie smiled. (How strange that even now girls like Karen struggle to eradicate their Glasgow accents while the outside world adopts ethnicity as the badge of fashion. Scots never could see themselves as anything but out of date.)

"Please come over here." Karen waved her hand across the emptiness of the room. "There are two people I would like you to meet."

A snapshot from a Brownie, another age. A woman in a check shawl, traipsy dress and bunned hair. A man in working clothes.

"Mrs Carmichael, I'd like you to meet Patrick Rafferty and Agnes Ross. My great-grandparents on my mother's side."

Ailie glanced from the picture to Karen and back again. "Very . . . nice."

Karen patted her stomach gravely. "The genes of Patrick and Agnes are mixed with yours for all eternity, Mrs Carmichael."

Nearby, Ailie recognised a couple of snaps of herself, and the wedding picture of Dorothy and Joe. There was another wedding picture beside it, a coloured one of David and Karen with herself and another middle-aged couple in the background, Karen already distinctively swollen.

"When did you get married?"

"Three weeks ago. We called the banns as soon as we knew the foetus was healthy."

"Our philosophy doesn't allow us to marry until we have tested our reproductive systems."

"Surely that's hard on infertile people?"

"What's wrong with living together? David and I did it for eight months, before we started to want a family."

"In practice," said David, "I don't think infertile folk would be too attracted to our beliefs. They don't offer much for them."

"This religion you've set up. . . "

"It's not a religion," said David. "We don't need superstition. We base it all on reason."

The girl who had opened the door to Ailie came in carrying a plastic tray of tea and biscuits.

"You know Sorrel, of course, don't you? No? Sorrel's a relation of ours."

"How's that?"

"Remember Jojo's brother Tony?"

"Don't tell me! She's his daughter!"

"Granddaughter."

Sorrel smiled widely. "You're a legend in our family, Mrs Carmichael."

"My. How time flies."

"Especially for us." David raised his cup of tea. "Your very good health, Mother, and Junior's too." He patted Karen's stomach. "To the meeting of the generations."

Ailie went to the bathroom. Above the washhand basin was a hand-drawn text, framed, illustrated with skulls, gravestones and silhouetted yew trees.

*SIX STEPS TO OBLIVION.*

*1) You die.*

*2) The last person who knew you dies.*

*3) The last person to share your timespace dies.*

*4) The last person who ever heard of you dies.*
*5) The last person to carry any of your genes dies.*
*6) The last person to owe existence to you dies.*

*EVEN AFTER SIX DEATHS,*
*YOUR ATOMS LIVE ON!*

She returned to the living-room. "These ideas you've got going. . . "

"Our philosophy, Mrs Carmichael."

"Our *modus vivendi*, Mother."

"More concerned with dying than with living, surely? That drawing in the bathroom. . . "

"It's good, isn't it? I got Karen onto doing that. She's very artistic."

Karen slipped her hand into David's. "He told me what-all to do for it and I just done it . . . did it."

"I thought of getting her to include the last step of all. You know. The absolute end of the matter that went to form us. Wherever these atoms might be at the time, in our galaxy or far, far away."

Ailie frowned into her cold teacup.

"But I decided against it. After all, we'd be entering the realms of speculation."

"That's right." Karen grinned comfortably. "Nobody knows if matter had a beginning, or if it's going to have an end. Do we?" She directed her happy beam at David. He let go her hand, rose, and stood with his back to the fireplace, swaying slightly.

"That's why we take the gene as being the only immortal part of us."

"To those before, we owe. . . " (Here Karen paused, and Sorrel and Jackie chimed in with flat voices and downcast eyes), "Research, Remembrance, and Participation. To those after, Nourishment, Teaching, and TLC."

"It sounds a bit Chinese to me."

"It owes nothing to Chinese ancestor worship," David assured her. "Although I did study a bit of Buddhism before. . . "

"I mean the presentation more than the content. The way you. . . "

"It's our obligation to find out about our ancestors," said Karen earnestly, looking at David rather than at that ancestor of his whom she hoped to convince.

"Their names," put in Jackie.

"Aye, who they were, what they did, what lives they led."

"Photies."

"That's right," agreed Sorrel." Relics. Things they made or loved."

Jackie warmed to her subject. "We've got tae display them and pass them onto wur ain wee ones, so that all thae old folk can go on taking part in daily life. Sure that's the idea, Davie?"

"Just think, Mother. At every single point along the last 200-odd million year continuum, we each have direct ancestors living who have not yet reproduced, but who will."

"Well, of course. Every line has ends."

"Also, no matter what high ratio of infant mortality pertained, we each come from an unbroken line of survivors into adulthood. Think of the odds!"

"Aye, n' the cats an aw," put in Jackie.

"Cats?"

"That was a little discourse we had the other day," Sorrel came in on it, crossed blue jeans on the rug. "A huge proportion of cats get the operation. But all the moggies around today are from an unbroken line that didn't. So each time they get it, it's a first for their line." She waved her hands languidly. "Comprendi?"

"I think so."

"It's not important, anyway. What matters is that our descendants will have the same obligations to us."

"What about the folk without any descendants?"

"Everybody should try to get descendants," said David firmly. "We do keep an eye on the childless tangents, aunts, uncles, but priority goes to the direct line. It's only fair. It's a thank you for our very existence."

"What if your descendants don't want to know about their obligations?"

Karen looked shocked. "Mrs Carmichael. I plan on bringing up my children so they know their duties well."

Sorrel stretched her lanky limbs and remarked, "If the parent and the kid have a positive meaningful relationship then the rest follows – it stands to reason."

"To make it easier for them," enthused David, "we leave as many relics of ourselves as possible. We all keep written diaries in the computer, and we've made videotaped messages." He crossed to the television, selected a tape and switched on. Ailie appeared on the screen.

"Hello. I was born in 1950 as Ailie Lorimer, although my married name is Carmichael. I am now fifty-two years old. Let me show you a bit of the world that surrounds me today." There followed a few frames of her flat, of the streets outside. Ailie watched, fascinated. She had never seen herself on television before.

"Is it not very time-consuming? All this keeping of records . . . Does it not keep you from enjoying life now?"

"Are you joking? You've seen how many hours people in the past wasted in praying to an imaginary God."

"You're sure God's imaginary."

"Mother, I'm surprised to hear you say that."

"Well, how can you be absolutely 100% positive? That would make you as blinkered as the religious dogmatists."

David spoke slowly, as if delivering a lecture to a class of simpletons.

"In the old days, they thought the Earth was the centre of the Universe. Naturally enough. Now we know it's an insignificant member of a minor system on the edge of an ordinary galaxy. Most if not all the other planets and stars are dead cinders or poisonous iceballs. Why would a Creator have wasted his energy making all this set-up if he only wanted to suit us?"

"There could be a Creator without Life being the most important thing to Him . . . or rather It," reasoned Ailie. "Maybe we're just one of many different phenomena found throughout the Universe. After all, you and I, above all, know that there are more things in Heaven and Earth than are found in the orthodox philosophies. You know the apparitions I used to see. And did I ever tell you what happened to Nigel?"

"I know all about that. Was that supposed to prove the existence of an immortal soul?"

"It did give me pause."

"It shouldn't. Look, before conception our atoms are scattered to the four corners of the globe and our consciousness doesn't exist. After death again our atoms slowly scatter. Why should our consciousness continue? Except to satisfy some wishful thinkers who can't let go."

Jackie put in, "If ye went on bein conscious, like, after ye were deid, ye know, then you an David could experience bits of it, know whit ah mean, an come back an tell us."

"Face it, Mrs Carmichael," Karen slid an arm around her waist in a way that made Ailie's blood freeze, "we're all ye've got in the way of immortality."

Ailie pulled away.

"It must get unwieldy, though. I mean, as you go further back there are more and more ancestors."

"You're forgetting natural wastage. Illegitimacy, adoption,

wars, bombings . . . look at Sandy. He knows very little about his father's family. And I haven't so far got much on my own father's side, although I still hope to track him down."

"For your own sake, just hope your descendants don't live through interesting times!" chuckled Karen.

When the girls retreated to wash the dishes David lolled back in the chair with his legs spread over as wide an area as possible.

"You've the life of a pasha here," declared Ailie. "Is it only wee girls that follow your lead?"

David scowled. "We do get a few older folk . . . and some males . . . coming to our meetings. I suppose it's the family thing that appeals to females."

"That Karen could almost be your daughter."

"She's mature for her years, Mother. She's a quick learner. I'm teaching her everything I know."

"Very nice. What happened to all our plans for a career in show-biz?"

"We tried them out. It didn't work. Och, after a lot of waylaying of BBC personnel we managed to get an interview on *Reporting Scotland*. But they were very patronising. They made it clear we were only in for curiosity value. The whole time. . . "

"Stop it!" Ailie put her hands over her ears. "I haven't had that bit yet. Let me travel hopefully, at least."

"Sorry. Let me tell you about the baby. Or would that spoil the surprise?"

"Is it good?"

"Oh yes. She's a girl. I saw her when she was between eight and ten years old. She looked a lot like you."

"So you've been to lots of different times since I last remember you?"

"I've actually been at this stage for four years now. It's quite useful – I managed to build up the Genecists. I even fitted in a long trip to the USA last summer. You know how the Yanks are always open-minded about new philosophies."

"Did you make many converts?"

"I convinced a few people, I think. At least, we have a few Americans now on our mailing list. Sorrel came back with us. She hails from the Bible Belt. You know Tony's daughter Donna married a sailor from the Holy Loch."

"Were you at any other periods?"

"The last one was quite far in the future." He looked directly at Ailie. "I saw you out."

Ailie had to sit down. Her skin crawled and her heart pounded. David was still looking at her and she knew she had to be careful what she asked.

"I don't want to know when. Please don't tell me *when*. Just let me know . . . was I in an institution of some kind?"

"You were in my home. Not here – a better place. There was no pain, it was quite a good death. There was a high turnout at the funeral. . . "

"That's enough," snapped Ailie. "Don't tell me any more."

Dunbar the Makar, in the days of death the house guest, had written:

> *Sen he has all my brether tane*
> *He will naught lat me live alane;*
> *On force I man his next prey be. . .*

Once, these lines had followed her out of her Scottish literature class and into the next day, she wondering, in the lack of any evidence, if her condition might allow her an escape clause, if the Reaper might miss her stalk.

Fog closed over her head. She shut her eyes, leaned back and surrendered to the whirl of it. Before it was over she opened her eyes and her father was standing there with wasted smile. She rolled her eyes back again. When she next came to, Old Joe had transformed into David, bending over her, patting her cheeks.

"Are you all right, Mum?" He gazed at her searchingly. "You haven't done the old shift, or anything?"

"I'm fine." She sank back in the chair. "At least I know my time won't be up for a while!"

"I've never seen you take one of these turns before! I thought you'd grown out of them."

"So did I."

"I was just saying, there, I've learned to control the Time travel thing a bit. If I totally lay off the booze and the tablets, I remain stable. Then, if I want to get out, I drink myself legless and concentrate, as I slide into oblivion, on the period I want to see."

"I take tranquillisers when I want to go," said Ailie. "Must try aiming for a particular bit. Sounds hopeful."

"Aye, well, as I say, it's worked twice for me."

"Do you ever run into Crawford these days?" (Sometimes I forget I have another son.)

"Crawford," announced David, "is a poison-puker."

"A what?"

"A poison-puker. It's a polite word for a sonofabitch, a piss-artist, a mother . . . oh, never mind."

"You don't get along, then?"

"We have nothing to say to or about each other. End of story."

"I'm surprised to hear you talk like this," remarked Ailie, "after all your serenades about family ties."

David snorted. "Don't expect any RRP from that quarter! Uch, his daughter Debbie's quite nice. She expressed interest in our movement, in fact, and for her sake I made one or two videos of folk from her end. But since she emigrated I've had no occasion to contact the old sibling – no occasion at all."

"I'd like his address, all the same."

"He's in the phone book. Lives in Edinburgh. Take my advice and steer clear of him. You'll only shatter any tender memories you retain."

"I don't think I have much in the way of any kind of memories of Crawford," mused Ailie. "What's he done, anyway? Is he a mass-murderer? A war criminal?"

"Just a poison-puker, plain and simple. They don't come more toxic than Crawfie-boy."

David phoned for a taxi to take her home. People who didn't have cars usually travelled by taxi now, he told her, unless they were within reach of a subway. "But this administration is trying to improve the bus service, for the first time in decades. The service to this area may be only one an hour, but at least you can trust it to always turn up."

While she was waiting for the taxi Ailie put on another tape.

"Hello. I'm Stephen Carmichael." She switched it off hurriedly. "David!" she shouted "I thought you said you didn't ... " Her voice tailed away and she switched it on again.". . . with my wife Lizzie and daughter Ann. Lizzie and I used to run a high-tech shop, but we've been retired for some time."

He was balder and fatter than ever, and enunciated the text syllable by syllable, like someone who had newly learned to read.

"Ann studies Business Economics at Paisley University. Here is our house in Bellahouston. Let me take you inside. Our living room is large, typical of Victorian architecture." Ailie watched in fascination as she was shown around her old home. She supposed that was Lizzie, lambswool dress and sculpted grey coiffure, sitting on the couch and not knowing what to do with her hands. She recognised the drinks cabinet at the side, but the rest of the furniture was new to her. It was as if she, Ailie, had never lived there at all.

She switched off and ventured out to the rusted balcony. To her left loomed the Red Road student bedsits, monuments to a lost century. Their silhouettes blocked the marbled skies which rolled around the ribbon of the M8 to meet the amber mass of Glasgow.

A few landmarks she still recognised – Ruchill Park Tower; the Cathedral, floodlit and fairy-like above the ground. A superannuated crane marked for tourists the banks of the river that had made a Glasgow of another time. She raised her eyes to the westerly heavens. The other world beyond the stratosphere, the lochs of cloudland, grey fiords, white ridges, red seas, layer on layer.

David came behind her and stood in silence, resting his hand on her shoulder.

"I know why the ancients put paradise in heaven," she mused. "If there is life after death, it should be up there." (Fluttering forever where the sun shone golden, down again through the flossy drifts, back under the soft mists and drizzle, up again sharply, leaving Earth behind, soaring unscathed and immortal through the body of the Sun and out beyond to Sirius, to Vega, to Quasars, to witness the strangeness of yellow skies, purple landscapes, twin stars, white dwarves, red giants, black holes, back again to bathe in the blue atmosphere of Earth, to talk with other ghosts, seek out ancestors, await descendants. The freedom of the dimensions, at a will, up, down, left, right, past, present, future.)

"If there is life after death," said David, "why should it be heavenly? Life before isn't. Only because nothing is known of it, its possibilities are intact, and imagination can give free rein to hope."

"Wishful thinking," declared Ailie firmly, "is creative and enjoyable, and causes harm to nobody."

"Well, goodnight, you eternal dreamer," David helped her into the taxi. "And beware of the Crawfie-puker. I really mean it. That one would sell his mother to buy trimming for his jacket."

"Then who would sew the braid on for him?" smiled Ailie. "Goodnight, David. I'll be in touch."

Back home, the flat was bleak and chilly. Ailie glowed with satisfaction at the thought that, unlike most older people, she would experience the comfort of living in company one day again. For now, she was lonely, and tucked up in bed, she strove in her mind to see again the Faces which had frightened her long ago. It would have to be a friendly Face, Daddy's perhaps, or even the kind young lady with slanty eyes. She opened and shut her own eyes several times, she meditated with them closed, and then with them open. The Faces had abandoned her.

Next week, while rummaging through a drawer, she found a payment book for local income tax. She was two months in arrears. There was no indication as to where she had to go to pay it. Feeling foolish, she knocked on her neighbour's door armed with the tale of amnesia. A young man answered and gave her the address she required.

"Can I do anything to help, Mrs . . . ? Goodness, I'm your neighbour and I don't know your name!" He held out his hand. "I'm Fergus Mackay."

"Ailie Lorimer." She had said it without thinking. "That is . . . well, yes. Ailie Lorimer." (Why should I carry his name through all the more important parts of my life?)

"Lorimer?" mused Fergus. "I know someone called Lorimer. My brother's girlfriend. Roxy Lorimer."

"Don't know anyone of that name." She smiled. "I'm sure the phone book must be full of Lorimers."

She took her shopping bag down to Charing Cross. Sauchiehall Street was looking good, with trees down both sides, pavement cafés spilling out from the huge brick centre under a canopy of glass, stalls and buskers galore. If the department stores of yore were gone, at least some of the big chains remained, Littlewoods, C&A, M&S, BHS. Apart from that, nearly every doorway let into a warren of shopping arcades.

Ailie drew money out of a machine, paid her tax, bought herself a new dress of the kind favoured by young girls, thin voile with a short flouncy skirt and a tight bodice. She then called round to see Catriona Mackinnon.

Catriona stayed up a tiled close with a stained glass window on the stair landing – a classical-looking maiden kneeling under a willow by the banks of a stream. It always reminded Ailie of the song *Flow Gently Sweet Afton*. One of Dorothy's favourites for Burns Nights. Catriona's own door was polished panelling, with a brass bell-pull (probably one of the last in Glasgow), brass handle and a flylight of Hansel and Gretel. Inside, she had a large fern in a brass pot on a table set in the oriel window, and a traditional high tea laid out for Ailie on the table. White linen tablecloth, haddock and jacket potatoes, silver cake-rack with home-baked scones. Somehow Catriona had succeeding in marrying *nouveau siecle* materialism – she had a dishwasher, a freezer, an instant cooker, a video recorder, an ansaphone and even a computer – with the style of her youth.

Ailie found this period of her life to her liking. Her income was small, but her needs were few. She owned her flat outright – a settlement by Steve in lieu of the three years' maintenance he was required to provide.

Sandy paid for wallpaper and David's girls among them decorated her flat – dues paid by acolytes to the ancestor of the founder of their sect. She visited all the parks of Glasgow – there were more than ever, and it surely beat not only Europe but the world by now – and pinched cuttings, which she planted in margarine pots and cossetted. She visited David every Tuesday and Sandy every Sunday. Saturdays she visited museums – Glasgow had thirty-three by now and she would soon have been round them all. Thursdays she visited Catriona MacKinnon and sometimes went a bus trip with her. Mondays and Wednesdays she shopped for food or walked round parks or changed her books in the library, and Fridays she sometimes went to the pictures or the theatre. Sandy and Jasmine promised that she would accompany them on their next Mediterranean holiday. Had she to be a gooseberry she would have refused, but as things stood, her company would provide them with relief from each other's.

One evening in December, she came stamping in out of air so sharp it cut the throat. She unwrapped her muffler, took off her coat and emptied her Indian carry-out onto a plate. Half for today and the rest for tomorrow.

The spices of the Orient filled her room with warmth as she put her feet up on the pouffe, lifted her tray, and felt for the TV remote control. The main general news now came from Scotland, with happenings in Scotland following immediately after world events.

The first item related to an overhaul in the school exam system, replacing Standard Grades with something more suited to a wide range of abilities.

Nothing ever changed. The next item, however, caught her attention.

"Ms Pandora MacAlpine, Minister for Tourism, this morning strongly denied allegations made by an English newspaper of former links with a terrorist group."

With a name like . . . Sure enough! The red hair was faded to a sandy buff, the freckles, if anything, more numerous. Ailie spent the first minutes marvelling that Pandora should be a Ruler, a TV personality, a Member of the Establishment, so that only latterly did she take in what was under discussion.

". . . Of course there is no basis of fact!" exclaimed Pandora. "Anyone who has ever known me will vouch for it that I have always abhorred violence above all, have always sought out the legal means to any end!"

"The person who makes these claims. . . "

"Lacks the smeddum even to identify himself. All public figures attract the attention of cranks."

"You don't deny it is you in the picture?"

"It's me, all right. Taken when I was very young. . . "

"The development date on the back is 1976, when you were already over . . . "

"That's when that print was made. I don't recall when the exposure was taken. Anyway, these men were mere acquaintances, friends of friends met at a party . . . you know how it is when you're young."

"If you'll forgive my saying so, Pandora, you give the impression of being much closer than that to these men."

Ailie peered at the blurred snap shown on the screen. Where had she seen that before? Had Sandy not given it to her, in the days when she had collected snapshots as part of her obsession with Time?

"We were young and impulsive," Pandora went on. "Gestures then were freely given . . . "

"And the letter?"

"A complete forgery. I have never seen that before in my life."

"So you were unaware that. . . "

"I have never had truck with terrorism," said Pandora firmly, "nor with any terrorists. I've said it before and I say it again. I never have and never will."

"Pandora MacAlpine, thank you."

Ailie lifted her giant album out from the foot of the wardrobe and flicked through the pages. She found no trace of what she sought, but the snapshots she did find set her into transports of nostalgia (over what she had had) and curiosity (over what was yet to be). Pictures of herself and

Jojo – with a baby in a buggy – seated beside a life-sized model of an old sailor outside a white cottage; of Jojo and the baby placed about the background of a peculiar fake oil painting; of herself with the baby in an open-topped tram. All very surreal. She did not close the book until four o'clock in the morning. As she wrestled to wedge it back in place, she felt a few smaller books underneath, blocking the way, and she pulled them out.

They were five year diaries of previous decades. As she opened the first one, a piece of paper fell out. A poem.

### *TO AILIE, ENIGMA*
### *MARKS OF CAIN*

*SSSS! Who comes?*
*I am a fault in the air*
*a crack in the atmosphere*
*a space in the present*
*where the past shows through.*
*I am a time lurk*
*I am what happened*
*where sudden violence*
*instant death*
*unexpected terror*
*carved its scar*
*down black shafts of minings*
*up wind torn clifftops*
*forgotten battlefields*
*dungeons, castles, houses of murder*
*you find me. Who goes?*
*I am the sound of the sorrow*
*drudging through history.*
*The strength of my constancy*
*gives immortality*

> *in packed slums*
> *Satanic mills*
> *frozen fields*
> *and generations of the starved*
> *I make my moan.*

*DJB*

Ailie read the poem twice, shivered, pulled her chair round so that her back was more fully to the wall. She recalled the feel of hair pulled between her fingers, thick, black, supple, the steady gaze of clear grey eyes. Perhaps she would one day know true love, or at least a whirl of it.

Such a verse! Such a lover!

After she switched off the lamp, she thought she glimpsed for a moment a Face – a little dark-haired girl, smiling and friendly. Jojo as a child, perhaps, or even Rosita? Anyway, there was no threat there, and the Face had faded as she realised its presence. Full of well-being she sprawled across the electric blanket.

Sandy and Jasmine had also been tuned into *The View from the Capital*, played in three dimensions on a broad screen usually concealed behind tasteful mahogany doors. The air was thick with the emotions which word of Pandora always engendered: insecurity, inadequacy and nausea, frustration, envy, nostalgia. Always unspoken. At the end of the interview Sandy continued staring at the screen even after Jasmine switched off, whether out of genuine concern or merely to annoy her, to drag out the unpleasant moment, she neither knew nor cared.

"I'm away to bed," she announced, and went. She was still awake when Sandy climbed in, half an hour later, still awake when the doorbell rang at two a.m. Sandy, grumbling, put on his dressing-gown and went. Moments later, all thoughts of sleep left her as a hated voice sounded in the hall.

"It's been so long!" breathed Sandy. "You've hardly changed at all."

Pandora came straight to the point. "This is not a social call. Did you see me on the hot seat this evening?"

"Yes. I thought you . . . "

"Were you responsible for sending in those stupid photos?"

"What? You're crazy. How could you imagine that I would . . . "

"It's not your style, I know. But you're the one with the opportunity. And I know you hate me."

"Why should I . . . "

"For turning out successful only after leaving you. For getting more applause than you."

"Your later attempts at relationships were even less successful."

"So you follow up my love life. Now I know you're obsessed with me."

"And I know you've turned megalomaniac." Sandy smiled faintly. "Not dictator of the world, not even Prime Minister of Scotland. Minister for Tourism. That's all it took."

"The dirty tricks brigade are out to get us. Not just me. You'll have seen about Drew Maxwell?"

Sandy nodded.

"They've got goods on Gerry McGlone an' all. It'll be all over the English tabloids before the week's out. Destabilisation is the name of the game." She slumped into an armchair. "I've thought and thought about those pix ever since they surfaced. I know they were taken in the flat we shared. I never saw them since we split. Therefore you must have retained them. Ergo. . . "

"Wait . . . wait . . . I don't think I've seen them since either. How do you know one of these characters didn't take them?

Are you still in touch . . . "

"You're jesting! The day they got wheeled off to the Bar-L I burnt all correspondence from them, even all these badly-printed, wild pamphlets they used to ply me with. . . "

"In those days you were proud to overlook the spelling, even the logic of a leaflet, if its heart was in the right place." Sandy shook his head. "You've become a politician, all right. You're stuffier now than ever I was."

"There was a box full of photos. Most had been taken with your camera, and I'm sure when I threw out yourself and your stuff, that went too."

"Do you want some coffee?" Sandy made for the kitchen. "Or something stronger?"

Some of the fight seemed to go out of Pandora with the sigh she heaved.

"A wee dram would be fine, though I'm trying to cut down . . . Look, I'm sorry for coming round at this dreadful hour. I took a taxi right from the studio. That interview upset me quite a bit. This could be my Parliamentary career on the line. You know what the Party's like about respectability these days."

Sandy poured out two generous whiskies. They clinked glasses and Pandora chanted, "*Slainte mhath agus Alba gu brath!*" She screwed up her face at Sandy. "So emotionalism still embarrasses you? You should go to Russia. There they make about forty different toasts in an evening, each one soppier than the last."

"I've been to Russia," said Sandy stiffly. "I think we can excuse them their bit of sentiment."

"But not the Scots. Sandy, Sandy," she stroked his cheek and he pulled back. "I never thought *you'd* fall prey to this thing of supporting every country's grievance save your own."

The door opened and Jasmine shuffled in, pink nightie, fluffy slippers.

"Och, it's the fair Ophelia!" cried Dora. "Get thee to a nunnery!"

"That whisky isn't your first tonight!"

Dora ignored him. "What about you, Pansy, or Dahlia, or whatever you're called. Can't be very nice being married for years to a torch-bearer! Especially when the deity regularly invades your own hearth!"

"Never mind her," said Sandy. "She's a drunken megalomaniac."

"Now, wouldn't *you* be tempted to put a wee spoke in my wheels? Don't be ashamed to admit it. I'd rather admire you for it. It would prove that you're not only milk and water, despite appearances."

"I came in," mumbled Jasmine, "to say that I know what happened to these photos. I gave them to Ailie, long ago."

# 11

AILIE AWOKE to the realisation that it was already past noon. She had really enjoyed this sleep, positively wallowed in a dream Paradise unexplored since leaving childhood for the first time. She rolled over under the quilt, stretched, luxuriated, felt the hard cover of one of the diaries beneath her cheek. She pulled it out and browsed through it for some time, knowing that she would have to get up and get her breakfast, but that there was no hurry.

She sat up quickly as she read the entry for Wednesday, 17th August, 1988:

> *Went to the Garden Festival with Jojo and*
> *baby Roxy. Rode on old Paisley tramcar,*
> *sailed on Festival Belle, went through Magic*
> *Forest, and up the Tower. Stewards very*
> *helpful – looked after buggy for Jojo every*
> *time. Tea in the Stakis Showbar – very*
> *Mississippi – coffee served by a black waiter*
> *in a Panama hat! Heard the Phoenix Choir*
> *in the Rendezvous Point. Avoided Roller*
> *Coaster in case it sent me on my way again.*
> *Had to wait to cross back over bridge as*

> *Waverley was passing through – took half an*
> *hour. Last time for Jojo as she's off to kibbutz*
> *on Friday.*

Ailie took a long look at this, jumped up, and pulled on her clothes before crossing the landing and knocking on Fergus Mackay's door.

After hearing Jojo's voice on the phone, if even only for a few moments, and arranging a meeting at Sandy's house for Boxing Day, Ailie was so filled with well-being she had to arrange to meet someone else. Nigel was probably still in Canada, Dorothy and Roddy were dead. She went into town and browsed through the Edinburgh phone book. A bit of courage and she had fixed up a visit to Crawford's home for next Saturday.

Crawford lived in a 1980s Leech estate. The trees had matured, dwarfing the timber-frame English-style houses but creating an overall look of respectability.

Crawford's wife Jill was pleasant enough, as she showed Ailie into the open-plan sitting area. Crawford was in the best armchair, reading the *Evening Times*. When Ailie entered, he glanced up but did not smile.

The very picture of the 1976 Steve.

"Hello, Crawford. I don't know when I last saw you. For me it was when you were still a bachelor . . . "

"Goodness!" trilled Jill. "That's a long way back. Surely you remember when he was doing his sales rep, and later in the Met Police, and then . . . "

"Shut it, Jill," snapped Crawford. "Of course she's seen me since then. She just doesn't remember. As per usual."

"Was that the London Police? Did you want a change from Scotland?"

"It's easier to get into the Metropolitan," explained Jill.

"They're always desperate, and they don't ask for the same in the way of. . . "

"I said, shut it, woman. You're a bloody parrot, wittering away, there!" Crawford rose, swayed, and said, "Well, go on then! Make my mum a cup of tea!" Jill scampered through to the kitchen.

"Did I come at an inconvenient time?" asked Ailie.

"As convenient as it ever is." Crawford turned his back to Ailie and rested his forehead on a little shelf above the main radiator, in place of the traditional mantlepiece.

Ailie wondered if he had been drinking. "How long were you in the police?"

"Four years."

"Did you like it?"

"'S aw'right."

"He still keeps up wi some o' the pals he made there." Jill entered with cups and saucers which she laid out on the glass coffee table. "There were a couple up in Edinburgh just a week or two ago, weren't there, Crawfie?"

No answer.

"Naw, ah tell a lie. It was about a month ago."

Only a grunt from Crawfie.

"Mind, they stayed the night wi us?"

"Mum's not interested in hearing about folk she doesn't know."

"But I am," protested Ailie. "I always feel I've got such a lot of catching up to do."

"Must be awful, that insomni . . . ah mean amnesia!" Jill tutted apologetically. "See me wi long words . . . ah always get them wrong. What I meant to say is, my memory's bad enough and I'm no amnesi . . . amnesi. . . "

"ACK," put in Crawford.

"Are you working just now?" asked Ailie.

"Aye. Civil Service."

"Which Department?"

"Internal security. Again, it's to do with the administration of the police."

"When he was down in England he was with the GCHQ folk," Jill revealed, as she sliced up a wholemeal loaf. "All very hush-hush, wasn't it?"

"So it was hush-hush!" Crawfie rounded on her. "So hush-hush means you don't megaphone it to the world!"

"I'm hardly the world," said Ailie. "Was it so secret you couldn't even tell your mother where you worked?"

"'Course it wasn't." Crawfie turned back to the wall. "Anyway, I didnae work there long. When they started splitting off the Scottish Civil Service I got a transfer back here."

When Jill went out again Ailie asked Crawfie what was wrong with him.

"Nothing! Should there be something?"

"Are you always this tetchy?"

"I don't waltz about like Pollyanna, kidding on weeds are orchids, if that's what you mean."

"How's Debbie?"

"She's in Canada."

"Permanently?"

"Aye."

"Do you miss her?"

"We get peace n' quiet to think, now. And the phone bill's taken a tumble."

Christmas Day Ailie spent at David's. Karen served goose with all the trimmings, and David told her they hoped to put a bid in for a new house.

"So we won't be in this dump much longer. It's a nice house – a six-apartment in Pollokshaws. There'll be plenty room there for any of the girls that want to stay – and of course, for you if you ever want to. . . "

"Lovely kitchen," put in Karen.

Ailie burst into song – the old Animals number *We Gotta Get Out Of This Place*. She growled it through word-perfectly, then shut up, worried at her own state of inebriation. Had she overdone it? She wanted so much to stay in this good period for a bit longer.

She stayed the night, her son giving up his half of the bed to her, while teenage acolytes littered the floor with sleeping bags or without. To her relief, she awoke in the same place, on the next morning. Ten people waved her onto her taxi. David was also invited to Sandy's, but would follow later.

Sandy greeted her at the door. "Welcome to our Feast of Stephen. You're not to refer to it again as Boxing Day, a term born of the English class system."

Ailie was sipping a cappucino when Jojo swept in like a new era. Long gipsy hair, chemically black, swirling red cape, scarlet nails and lips, ear-rings like gold bangles. From the look of her jowls her neck would have given her age away, save for the tastefully knotted silk Paisley scarf.

Tall, statuesque, the picture of health and well-being.

She kissed Sandy. "And how are the rich relations? Sandy, I saw your article in the *Herald* – never knew things were so tough for speculators! Jasmine, you're a regular Peter Pan. A carbon copy of yourself last time I saw you. And here's our banshee," she took Ailie's hands, "dropping into the mortal world if but for a day!"

"Jojo. A sicht for sair een." Sandy took her coat. "The nomadic life must suit you."

"Nomadic life! I've been retired for two years to a room and kitchen in Partick."

"Retired? Did you have a job to retire from?"

"Yes, you big Protestant-ethic-you, I did! An actual, nine-or-ten-to-five-or-six job!"

"What was it?"

"Would you listen to this! Hardly in the door after God-knows-how-long and he's trying to stratify me!"

Sandy smiled and moved to the drinks cabinet. "What are you all for?"

"A sweet sherry," said Ailie.

"Nothing for me," said Jasmine. "I'll have to see to the meal."

"Whisky and ice," said Jojo. "Well, don't worry, it's respectable enough. After the kibbutz episode I trained as an interior designer. Hmmmm, ye-e-es! Most acceptable, eh, Sandy? I got a job in a firm based in Ibrox specialising in hotels and worked for them for fourteen years. Not in Glasgow, though – I was all over Europe, even Saudi Arabia! Anyway, that gave me a wee pension to put alongside the State pittance. Hence the swishy clothes."

"You seem to have done well enough out of it," said Jasmine, bobbing in from the kitchen and just as quickly out into it again.

"Oh, and I forgot to mention – unlike most senior citizens I just treat getting into hock with the bank as part of life's rich tapestry, and that surely helps. Might as well enjoy it while you haven't got it!"

"What about your daughter?" asked Ailie. "I believe she's at college with my next-door neighbour's brother."

"Does she ever see her Dad?" asked Sandy. "That traveller fellow."

"Traveller!" Jojo giggled, nudged Ailie in the ribs with her elbow. "Must be my get-up. Sorry to disappoint you, Sandy! Lou wasn't a gypsy any more than I was a virgin! If he was anything, he was an middle-American Jew!"

"But you did stay in a caravan."

"Course we lived in a caravan – at the Faslane peace camp! We were protesters!"

"Jojo – always the rebel!" Sandy shook his head.

"Ailie looks disappointed," Jojo observed. "What's wrong – had you me marked down as a non-political?"

"Not at all." Ailie paused to gather her thoughts into words. "It's just . . . well, when I thought you'd moved in with the tink . . . travellers, I thought it was . . . well . . . a kicking-over-the-traces way to go. The sort of thing folk did in ballads, but not in real life. A real, individual, Jojo-type protest to make. Whereas, living for a while in an anti-nuclear camp – well, it's a very worthwhile thing to do, and I totally approve, although I wouldn't be brave enough to do it myself, but then you always were much stronger on courage than I was . . . " She heard herself rambling, and stopped in confusion. The others went on staring and waiting.

"What she means," explained Sandy, "is that living in a peace camp with a Yank is a typically bourgeois way to make your protest. Whereas living in a tinkers' camp would be rejecting middle-class values, as well as lifestyle."

"Always assuming the tinkers would have me. I must say, elderly rebel and all that I am, I'd think twice before inviting a crowd of me to share my wagon." Jojo sounded aggrieved. "Thank you, Sandy – you always did put things well. So my anti-authoritarian tendencies are all part of the Establishment, after all. You, of course, would be an expert on the art of protest."

"I've made my share of protests!" protested Sandy. "I was a founder member of the SNP '79 Group. . . "

". . . 'Til it foundered. . . "

". . . and of the Scottish Socialist Society afterwards."

"Gee, what credentials!"

"And I've had two convictions for fly-postering!"

"Sandy the fly-man!" cried Jojo. "Take a bow, Scotland's answer to Che Guevara!"

"And I was on the UCS march. . . "

". . . As a mere boy!"

". . . and countless demos against bombs, unemployment, for self-government. . . "

"Methinks you doth protest too much."

"It is strange, though," mused Sandy, "how the fight goes out of you as you get older. Have you noticed this, Jojo?"

"W-e-ll, your muscles get flabbier and your fists get weaker. . . "

"We saw it happening to the oldsters when we were students . . . and we despised them for it. The fear of change . . . we never thought we would fall heir to it."

"Speak for yourself!"

"I don't mean I've become a conservative in my old age. . . "

"Heaven forfend!"

" . . . But somehow I give less and less of a damn about it all. Things I felt strongly about. Politics, the rescue of Scottish culture . . . even the faces and accents of home."

"If this were true, I would experience great surges in my metabolism whenever I change to another age," said Ailie. "I can't say I've noticed. Emotionally I'm always about 25."

"Then the changes must be socially induced rather than biological," mused Sandy. "And yet. . . "

"You never were very hot-blooded anyway," pointed out Jojo. "Neither was Ailie. We're a cool lot. Comes of being reared by a cold, impersonal woman."

"Was she all that cold?"

"Och, we know she was proud of you, Sandy. You were her ego trip. That can't be the same thing as love. Not that I'd know, personally. But such a fuss is made about love, it can't be the same thing as vanity."

Jasmine chanted softly, as she laid out the cutlery, *"But as it grows older, the love grows colder, and fades away like the morning dew."*

Jojo went on, "Sex, now. Till you get it, you're led to

believe it's *the* experience of life. Then, when you get round to having it. . . "

"But you still feel sorry for anybody who dies without having had it."

"I feel sorry for people who die never having had other things. People who've never been abroad, folk without the education to appreciate art. . . "

Sandy put in, "Sex is more fundamental than these. Sex is basic to life."

"Sandy, that's a male point of view. Most women agree, sex gets far more significance than it would in a female-dominated society. It's the passport to adulthood, it's the proof of love, the mark of ownership of another human being, the basis of Sin. Women have been beaten, jailed, tortured, killed even, for doing it with the wrong people, or not doing it with the right people. Whereas, left to itself, it's a pleasant enough little activity with the right person, but lots of things are better."

"On the other hand. . . "

Jojo overrode him. "An orgasm is a reasonably enjoyable feeling. But on the physical plane it's no better and much shorter than a good curry. On the emotional plane it's no better and much shorter than an intimate conversation and a cuddle. On the mental and self-aggrandising level it's not to be compared with. . . "

"With having a baby!" cried Jasmine.

". . . Or with getting my designs accepted for a public building which people will be admiring long after the orgasm's lost in Dreamland."

"Or with going to bed old and rising young," murmured Ailie. She hesitated, then went on. "What happened to them, anyway?"

"To whom?"

"Mother and Stan. We were talking about them, a minute

ago." She tried to sound casual. "I suppose they're dead?"

"As dodos," nodded Jojo.

"Who went first?"

"They went together," Sandy smiled gently. "It's how they would have wanted it."

Jojo sang softly, "Dotty and Stan, they lived a lot together, and finally together . . . they died. Wah, wahwah wah."

"How did it happen?"

"Patch of black ice, up by the Devil's Elbow. Twelve years ago now."

"Was anybody else hurt?"

"Amazingly, no," said Jojo. "It would have been more in character for them to have taken a bus-tripful of deprived children with them."

Jasmine let out a nervous giggle, smothering it behind her hand.

Sandy stood up. "My mother gave you all the same chances as she gave me. I won't let you insult her in death."

"In death or in life," Jojo shrugged, "makes no odds to me."

"What have you got against my parents, Jojo? My mother looked after you from babyhood. . . "

"Rosita too," Jojo smiled slyly.

"Yes, Rosita too, until the accident!" snapped Sandy. "Can't have been fun, four young kids and two not even her own."

Jojo turned to Ailie. "Will I tell him?"

"Tell him . . . what?" Ailie felt cold.

"The other thing. What you told me, long ago. I almost believe I should."

"Tell us, then!" challenged Sandy.

"If I do, you'll regret it. What's said can't be unsaid." Jojo turned to Ailie. "It's not my secret to tell. I leave it up to you, Ailie. Should I?"

Ailie looked from Jojo to Sandy. "What. . . ?"

"Come on, then! If there's a family secret, I'll not be kept out!" stormed Sandy. "Ailie?"

Ailie stared at the floor, her mind racing in futile circles.

The fight went out of Jojo. Her shoulders slumped. "Maybe you're right, Ailie. What's the use of raking up old muck? Leads only to vendetta, and life's too short."

"The muck's raked already," said Sandy. "Finish what you started."

"Let's not quarrel," pleaded Ailie. "We haven't seen Jojo in so long."

"I agree." Jojo raised her glass. "To family ties!"

"But I've a right to know!" insisted Sandy, in the knowledge of his defeat.

"My lips are sealed." Jojo wagged her forefinger at Sandy. "Be thankful for the dilution of my Latin blood."

Nigel appeared, home for the festive season. In middle-age he had taken on a Roddy-like appearance – high, rosy cheekbones, mild blue eyes, the limp in place of Roddy's stoop. He was, however, different in important ways.

"Not for me, thanks. Never touch the stuff."

"For the glory of God?" smiled Jojo.

"Not this time. We've all of us seen the harm drink does."

"How is the religious world these days?"

"Still glorious," grinned Nigel. "But I'm back in Scotland for good."

"What about Blanche?"

"Soon as I find a place to stay, she and the kids'll follow over."

"Doesn't she mind?"

"Och, I think she's looking forward to the change. Scotland offers a good quality of life. Less materialistic."

"Poorer," put in Jojo.

"Not just. Canada's starting to get as lawless as the States.

Security guards in some of the schools. The kids'll get a better education here."

"You won't have your swimming-pool here," observed Jojo. "Not unless you plan to get as rich as your big brother."

"A good bit richer," protested Sandy.

"We didn't have one in Canada. Actually, we neither of us care too much for possessions."

"Well, you wouldn't, if you plan to squeeze through that needle's eye. But you'll need *some* bread. Do you even have a job?"

"Almost." Nigel drew himself up and tried to take a bow, but his leg scraped the floor and spoilt it. "You are looking at an ordained minister of the Congregational Church!"

"Never!"

"When did this happen?"

"Now all I have to do is find a church to take me."

"How desperate are they?"

Nigel shot Jojo a reproachful look. "I know how stood your relations with God. Running about over the world, defying moral codes. . . "

"Whose moral codes?" demanded Jojo. "Male possessiveness invented morality. Why make one man miserable when I can. . . "

Sandy cut in, "Dora used to talk of a Buchan auntie she had, whose advice to her nieces was, Aye coort, and never mairry, and aye gae rovin free!"

"True enough. Men are interesting, charming, intelligent and considerate – until you get to know them."

"What a misanthropist you are, Jojo," chided Jasmine with a sidelong glance at Sandy.

"No, I'm not. A misanthropist is somebody who's got it in for the human species. As usual the males have appropriated the one to cover both. I don't think there is a snappy Greco-Latin term for man-hater. Hey, one-time linguist!" she poked

Sandy. "You with the cerebral overhang – what's the female opposite to misogynist?"

"Eh . . . eh . . . misand . . ."

"Homophobe? Naw, that's something else again." She refilled her glass, and patted Ailie's hand.

"While we're on the subject of men and their ghastly ways, you haven't lived through your wedding yet, have you?"

"No-o-o."

"I was just wondering why you did it. Or do it, or whatever. Now you know exactly how neanderthal Boy Stephen is. Could you still get out of it?"

"I don't know. I've often wondered. . . " Ailie paused for reflection. "If I don't marry him, the set-up would be frighteningly different."

"Why should different mean frightening?" Jojo shook her head in despair. "Ailie, Ailie. Still wimpish after all these years!"

"It could have been worse. Steve never actually abused me – hit me, I mean. As far as I know."

"Let's award him the Nobel Prize for chivalry."

"No, and yet, he was okay at the start. As you said yourself, they're mostly okay – at the start. How do I know another would be an improvement?"

"You could take the plunge and try."

"And, without him, I wouldn't get Crawfie and David."

"You might get somebody better."

"I wouldn't want to miss out David. No, if I plan to try to alter the future, I would change something less significant than my man."

At this point there was another ring and David himself walked in.

"Talk of the Devil! And here we were just discussing ways your mother could gazump the future and avoid having you!"

David took his mother's hands in both of his and looked

into her eyes. "I don't think you should try to change anything. It's not to be recommended."

"Have you done it?" squealed Jojo. "Tell us about it!"

David plumped down on the couch and held out his hand. Sandy rushed to thrust a whisky glass into it. Antique crystal, old malt. David took a sip, cast a dramatic look around the room and announced, "My present wife, Karen, was not my first. At least, I don't think she was."

When everyone was suitably agog, he continued. "Seven years ago, when I was a student, I got involved with a girl in my class. Her name was Sylvia, and she was the same age as me, with the same interests." He shook his head sorrowfully. "A lovely, lovely girl."

"Different type from Karen," ventured Ailie.

"Och, chalk and cheese. Sylvia was quiet, you know, but extremely bright. She had an IQ of 160."

"Did she tell you that," put in Sandy drily, "or did you test her before you asked her out?"

"She was a member of MENSA. She was altruistic, too – she came from a well-to-do background, but spent a lot of time fund-raising for Yorkhill Hospital."

"We get the picture," said Sandy. "Mother Theresa, Einstein and Richard Branson all partying in Raquel Welch's body."

"You're showing your age," chipped in Jojo. "Who is it now . . . Paul Getty the 6th, Louisa Divina, and . . . Hey! There aren't any good or brilliant folk left in these corrupted times!"

"Please don't mock me." David stared into his glass, swirled it around. "I'm baring my soul to you."

"We're not mocking," soothed Sandy. "I know you take yourself very seriously. Maybe we should all do likewise."

"We really are genuinely agog," said Jojo. "Go on, tell us. What went wrong with this answer to all your prayers?"

"She told me she used to be much livelier, but there had been a disaster two years before. Her family – parents and one of her brothers – had been wiped out in a yachting accident. Since then she hadn't been interested in parties, or socialising – it all seemed so shallow. Anyway, with my secret problems, I also felt cut off from the others, and so we started going out together. She got pregnant that summer . . . "

". . . high IQ and all!" cut in Sandy.

". . . and we got married. We both managed to carry on our studies, we had a wee boy called Robbie, and . . . well, it was blue heaven for eighteen months. Then I slipped back into 1999. I managed to trace Sylvia and warned her and her family against going on the yacht trip." He took another gulp of whisky and wiped his eyes.

"And so?"

"So they eventually thought the better of it and never went on the trip. Then I carried on right through into 2002."

"You repeated the bit that went before?"

"With alterations. Sylvia was different. All vivacious and popular. She never gave me a second glance, and ended up marrying somebody else out of MENSA."

"Huh!" snorted Jojo. "So much for gratitude."

"David wouldn't be able to prove that a disaster would have taken place if they'd ignored his warnings," said Ailie gently.

"Exactly," said David. "As far as she was concerned, I was a crank who had once told her something unpleasant, probably out of envy."

Sandy frowned. "I don't see that it's possible, what you just told us. How could you live through the same bit twice, and differently?"

David held out his glass for more fuel. "There were no signs at all of the life I had led with Sylvia. No wedding photos, not even an entry in the Register of Births for wee

Robbie. I was forced to the conclusion that the whole two years from our first date on, had been a dream. Or had *become* a dream."

"You woke up into a nightmare," murmured Ailie.

"For me, it was as if Robbie and Sylvia had died." A tear rolled down David's cheek. Ailie rose and tenderly wiped it away. A pleasant tinkle, the theme of Sibelius' *Morning* on electronic bells, emanated from the kitchen.

"That's dinner ready," announced Jasmine. She disappeared for a moment, to reappear guiding a heated tea-trolley laden with covered plates.

Over the meal they discussed the way the media was pillorying Pandora.

The same English newspaper which had printed the Consorting With Terrorists pictures had last week dredged up an Irish grandmother, not to mention an old neighbour who bore witness to the Streams Of Men With Irish Accents who had come to call. It seemed Pandora had always been a closet member of Provisional Sinn Fein.

"That's nothing," said Jojo. "Have you seen today's banner headlines?"

"Tell us!"

". . . about Gerry McGlone, no less?"

"Go on! Go on!"

"Who's he?" piped up Ailie.

Sandy shot her a condescending look. "The Minister for Education."

". . . Caught with his pants down! In St Vincent Street Public Convenience!"

"A bit down-market for him, surely? It's usually mere councillors that get picked up there!"

"Isn't he supposed to have his pants down there?"

Jojo spread her hands to indicate headlines. "Rent Boy Tells All!"

Ailie asked, "Can anybody tell me what happened to that crowd that got put away for 25 years in 1971?"

"What crowd?"

"You remember, Jojo?" Ailie tugged at Jojo's sleeve. "Your brother Tony was involved with them. Remember, long years ago?"

"The People's Party of Scotland shower?" Jojo put another spoonful of curry into the middle of her rice. "They got out eventually, didn't they?"

"Decades ago," said Sandy."

"I was interested in them," murmured Ailie, "because I went to warn Jojo's brother Tony about them, once."

"I had a talk with Tony recently, too," said Jojo.

"How's he doing?" asked Ailie.

"Still with Senga, amazingly enough," sniffed Jojo. "Seems she mellowed a lot after old Agnes took her final bow."

Sandy chortled, "You mean the alter ego altered to become less ego?"

"You've said it. They're Darby and Joan, now. Pruning roses together, the lot. Anyway, what he told me would interest you, Sandy. That People's Party lot weren't the longest sentences ever given out in Scottish courts. There have been several since. All political. One guy's still serving a 100 year sentence he got under the Thatcher administration."

Sandy dropped his fork and his jaw. "A *what* kind of sentence?"

"A century. Must be a senior citizen by now. If a prisoner is a citizen."

"Was it all consecutive? What did he do, for Christ's sake?"

Jojo shrugged. "Bombed oil pipelines, etc. . . "

"It was never in the papers."

Jojo smiled. "Sandy. Wee soul. Don't know where you and Ailie take your naivity from. Certainly wasn't Dot."

Jasmine said, "It's awful how the papers leave out what's happened. . . "

". . . and put in what hasn't." Sandy shook his head. "I was living with Dora at the time they're talking about." He reached for the dahi. "The place was always full of chaps, it's true, but I'd have noticed if most had hailed from the Emerald Isle."

He turned to Ailie. "Incidentally, Jasmine says you were at one point in possession of the offending photos."

"Maybe I was," Ailie admitted, "but they're not in my album now."

"I think Crawfie has them," said David suddenly. "Last year I came round to pick out some of your old photos for my family trees, and you remarked that Crawfie had taken away all the ones with Pandora in them."

Sandy raised his eyebrows.

"We thought it funny at the time. Crawfie had never shown much interest in us or our friends, and it's not like he ever supported Pandora's party."

"No." Sandy looked down again thoughtfully at his meal. "Certainly Dora's keen to trace the leak."

"That's right," put in Jasmine. "She came round here late the other night, accusing Sandy and me of all sorts of things."

"Not of all sorts of things, Jasmine," Sandy corrected her. "Just of having sent the pictures and story to the paper."

"Are you still in touch with Pandora, then?" asked Ailie in surprise.

Jasmine cut in. "Talking of pictures, I want to take one of us all together." She fetched her camera and set it to automatic take, positioned herself with the others and pressed the remote control.

"Is it a hologramera?" asked David.

"You bet," said Sandy. "Jasmine's the one for the modern gimmickry."

"Nothing wrong with that," said David. "I would buy a hologramera if I could afford one."

"They're not all that dear."

"Not to you, maybe. But Karen and myself are trying to raise the deposit on a house."

He smiled at Ailie. "Then we could all live as an extended family."

"Not so fast!" protested Ailie. "I'm just getting to like this stage. The Independent Lady of Leisure."

"Forget independence," advised Jojo. "Think on the future. How do you want to spend your declining years – as a pensioner in a garret, or as the grand old hub of the household?"

Just before the party broke up Ailie asked to speak to Sandy on his own.

"What you once said about anything I wanted. . . "

"Say up," said Sandy. "Don't be shy."

"It's not for myself," murmured Ailie. "For David. It's so hard for him to get a foot on the housing ladder, with his low income and deposits as high. . . "

"Say no more. Your wish is my command."

"I promise I'll never ask anything more of you. . . "

"There's no need to make such an undertaking."

"Anything you choose to give David will pay back, when he's in funds."

"The deposit on the kind of house he's looking for," declared Sandy, "is not a lot to me. David needn't pay it back unless he wants to. But for my part, I've got a wee favour to ask of you."

"Say on!"

"Next time you visit Crawfie, mention Dora's picture."

"I will," promised Ailie. "I should be able to judge by his reaction."

Back and forth, in further stages, she was to recall with

disbelief her light assumption of the 'wee favour', and with nostalgia her buds of independence, early nipped.

A surprise visit from Pandora prevailed upon her to push forward her visit to Crawford, and December 30th saw her turn up at her son's door.

This time he was affable and full of what passed in him for social graces, such as offering her the last piece of quiche, or looking at her and uttering grunts while she related her own anxieties. This time it was Jill who scurried around like a shadow, head down, with never a word to say for herself.

Ailie mentioned the photographs. Crawfie stoutly denied ever having taken them. "I ask you, is she the stuff a fella'd want to stick on his walls? Her freckles must be somewhere in the millions, and that's only her eyelashes – eh?" He reached out towards Jill, who dodged him.

Although it was a bit early, Crawford persuaded her to celebrate Hogmanay. "Tomorrow night you'll be in 1820 Square. Let tonight be our own private mark for the passing of 2008."

On her guard, Ailie restricted herself to two small glasses of sherry. What sherry! She danced, sang and in the end wept 2009 in – as well she might. For she woke up in an altogether different old year.

# 12

PILLOW. FLOORBOARDS. SMELL. Ailie was back in Eric's and Linda's horrible hospital. For a few minutes she lay, sick, quelling the panic. If she wanted to make sense out of this she would have to approach the thing differently.

The bars were not in place. Cautiously she sat upright, and looked about. (Across the room the other beds are empty! I've avoided the dreaded nap-time!)

She swung her feet off the bed and edged out over the boards as if the place were mined. She reached the end of the corridor without mishap and keeked round the archway. To the left she spotted Eric, and so she moved to the right. Hurrying, she padded barefoot to the end of that corridor, turned right again and beheld . . . an outside door! The door had a glass panel in the top half, thick with dust and condensation. Ailie rubbed a space clear and looked through to open country, bleak, with ploughed fields stretching to a row of leafless trees at the horizon. The sky was the colour of watery milk, darker in the distance. No human habitation was to be seen, but in the foreground a crow perched on a fencepost.

The door was of the Push Bar to Open kind. Ailie grasped the bar with both hands and lifted, pressed, pushed, pulled.

She rested for a moment, then pushed and pulled again.

"And what do you think you're doing, Missus?"

Eric gripped her by the shoulder and manoeuvred her back from the door.

"I wanted a breath of fresh air," mumbled Ailie.

"Fresh air? It's freezing out there! And look at you! Bare feet."

"I don't know where my shoes are."

"You put that out your wee head. You don't need shoes in here. Come on and we'll find your slippers. They're probably under your bed."

Placidly, Ailie hirpled along behind him. "I don't even think these are my own clothes," she complained. "The trousers feel too baggy."

"They're hospital issue. Here, you silly old bat." He thrust at her a pair of down-at-heel slippers of doubtful colour. They were so big she had to cling with her toes and shuffle to keep from walking out of them. The gait lent her an extra decade.

"Why can't I wear my own clothes?" She hung back so that he had to look at her. "I want to see the doctor."

"There's no doctor here."

"No doctor? What kind of hospital is it with no doctor?"

"You've been seen by a doctor. You were seen by one when you were admitted, remember? Now, this is what you really want."

He pushed open the door of a large room, carpeted in puce. In one corner, high up so that no one could touch it to switch channels, a television blared out some quiz show. Around the perimeter of the room basket chairs were arranged at regular four foot intervals. Each of the chairs contained a person staring into the middle of the room. Only two were looking anywhere near the television. One younger man was walking around the room, rhythmically patting all those wallpaper roses which were on a level with his eyes. Faded roses. Faded people.

"You're wrong," cried Ailie. "I don't want this. I don't want this at all."

"Here you are." Eric pulled out a chair from behind the door. "Plank your bum on that and watch your programme."

The two hours until teatime were the longest Ailie had experienced in her life, although over the next few weeks she was to revise that opinion. No one spoke or moved at first, although two of the inhabitants of the room did turn their eyes towards her. She watched the youth with the obsession about roses do another two rounds, and then she turned to the lady in the next chair and asked, "What's the name of the person in charge of this joint?"

The other woman looked alarmed and frowned.

"The person in charge here. Who is it?"

The woman placed a finger on her lips, shook her head, and pointed to the television.

"But you weren't watching that anyway!" Ailie went to the centre of the room and called out, "What is this place? Is it a hospital, or an eventide home, or what? Somebody tell me, please!"

A few more pairs of eyes swivelled to regard the new stimulus. None showed interest, apart from one middle-aged woman who burst into fits of uncontrollable laughter. Marie, whom she recognised after a bit, was slumped in a faraway seat, possibly under the effects of something. The young man did not pause in his tracks around the room. If anything he speeded up, and walloped the flowers with extra vehemence.

Tea came as a welcome diversion. They were all led into a side room set with five brown formica tables and twenty grey plastic chairs of a kind Ailie recognised as institutional ware from thirty years before. The young man gave up walking around the room in favour of drumming out a rhythm with his plastic knife and fork – Rat-tat tatat-tat TAT TAT! Rat-tat tatat-tat TAT TAT! Over and over again. Ailie saw him take no food during the five minutes or so they were there. Small wonder he was so thin.

The meal consisted of half a tomato, a slice of spam and one cup of weak tea, so before Ailie had had time to absorb the new surroundings, little though there was to absorb, they were all herded back into the television room and the monotony began again. Bedtime released them at half-past seven. They were guided into their separate shallow recesses all in the one room and left to get into the grey anonymous pyjamas. At eight Linda came round with a cup of tea and two pink tablets.

"What are they?" asked Ailie.

"Medicine."

"What for?"

"To make you feel better."

"What's supposed to be wrong with me?"

"Just cut the crack and take the bloody pills," growled Linda.

"I think there's some serious mistake. These folk here seem to be – well, very, very insane. Worse than just neurotic. . . "

"They're psychotic, and so are you."

"But I'm not as bad as they are! I mean, I can hold a conversation. Look at us, now. . . "

"No, Ailie, you look at me. I've got twenty-two more folk to get round with thae pills, and I've no time to banter wi you. Ye've got a choice. Ye take the tablets, or Eric comes and administers them to you."

Ailie took the tablets. With a bit of luck they would provide her with an escape route, at least for a while. Still, if she had all these years to fill in in this hell-hole, she ought to take it in reasonable chunks, and not leave the whole lot to the end.

As it happened, the drugs were not strong enough to carry Ailie away except into a troubled slumber. She awoke twice during the hours of darkness. Official reveille did not happen until nine o'clock, when a small woman in a grubby green overall came around with a trolley-load of tea and individual plates each with one slice of bread and butter. These she laid on the central table. "Now, mind," she called up and down the ward, "none o' yese've tae touch the braikfast till yese're dressed!" She pulled out a magazine and sat down in front of the table, to guard the cups from onslaught by the indecently garbed.

The clothes draped on the plastic chair beside Ailie's bed were the same, apart from the washed-out-pulled-thread nylon pants – as she had taken off yesterday. Stained cotton bra, nylon vest, faded pink acrylic sweater, stretched at the bottom and with a look of having been at one point in its history washed alongside something grey or blue, brown nylon slacks, baggy at the knees and seat. The elastic in the waistband of the slacks had lost most of its stretch and had been pulled through a hole and knotted, to prevent the trousers falling over her hips. After breakfast came two hours in the dreaded television room again. Ailie watched her fellow-sufferers and realised that she was the best-dressed, as well as the most *compos mentis*, of the lot of them. (If the fashions have changed in the real world, I won't find out here!)

After television came lunch. A saucerful of scrambled egg and another cup of the weak tea. Some of the patients were unable to finish this feast. The room-runner did not start his, being taken up with the task of laying out individual grains of salt along the table edge. When he attempted the same with the pepper the woman beside him sneezed, undoing the fruits of his labour, but the young man uttered no words of reproach before starting again from scratch. Ailie wondered how they kept him alive. Did he get drip-fed at night? Before they left the table her question was answered when Linda came in with more pills, white capsules this time. Each person who had failed to clear his plate was given one. The room-runner was given three, and probably ended up the best nourished of the crew.

During the afternoon television Ailie made a systematic attempt to find someone with an ember of sense. Her fourth approachee looked the least promising, but appearances proved deceptive.

"It's a nursin-hame," declared Gerard, a blanched fellow rheumy of eye and nose, all toothless mumbles and soft white stubble. "Maist are auld, some are batty an a good batch o' us are baith!" He threw his head back and cackled until a long drool hung between his gums and his lap. He wiped it away with the back of his sleeve.

"But not, I think, you?" Ailie went and fetched her chair, planking it beside him. "You're sensible enough, are you not?"

"Don't know that ah wis ever that sensible. Ma wife used tae say ah hud a heid oan me like . . . like a . . . whit wis it she used tae cry it. . . "

He lapsed into silence. After a few moments Ailie ventured "But you're still 100 pence to the pound."

"Och, I got Alzheimer's." He raised his head and gazed absently into the middle distance. The stream from his nose reached his lips and he licked it away.

"Al . . . what?"

"Alzheimer's. Ye know. Senile dementia. Ah sterted huvin it six year ago. Didnae know wherr ah wis, didnae recognise visitors. Kept burnin pans. Flooded the place when ah took a bath."

"But. . . "

"But they treated it, like. Gied me tablets an it went away."

"How long have you been here?"

"Ah mind noo!" cried Gerard in triumph.

"Mind what?"

"Whit Margaret used tae call me. She said if ah hud a brain, ah wid be dangerous!" Again the snort of laughter, until phlegm shot out of his nose, to be wiped as before. He slapped his hand down on Ailie's lap, and squeezed her thigh suggestively. "That's a good one, eh? If ah hud a brain ah wid be dangerous!"

Ailie gently prised his hand away and returned it to his own lap. "How long have you been here?" she repeated.

Gerard lost his grin. "Mony a year."

"Then were you here when I. . . "

"Aye, it wis ma son-in-law pit me in here. Efter Margaret died ah steyed wi ma daughter. But then she wis killed in a car accident."

"That's a . . . shame." Ailie did not know what to say. She could not cope with the bereavement of others, never having been herself bereaved. (I'm certainly the only senior citizen present who hasn't gone through my mother's death.)

"Then ma son-in-law pit me in here, because he wanted tae take his ain mither in. Understandably enough."

Ailie waited a decent interval before pressing on. "You must remember the circumstances when I was admitted here?"

"Ye know, he's never paid me a wee visit?" Gerard turned his tearful cheeks to her. "No wance in aw thae years."

"Not once?" ('I'm sorry' is such a clichéd, insincere, pointless thing to say.)

"Ah never see ma grandweans! Three o' them. Graham must be . . . let me see now. . . "

"Time for tea!" Linda and Eric swept into the room, clearing away chairs, leaving the patients staggering, marooned in the centre.

"Och, I don't know. In his twenties, by noo. Fiona too.

Aye, an wee Scott . . . wee Scott . . . If ah ever see them agin ah'll no know them, they'll be that chinged!"

"I know the feeling well," murmured Ailie. "But to get back to what we were talking about. . . "

In mid-sentence she was dragged away. To her disappointment she was placed at the room-runner's table, out of earshot of Gerard.

After tea came visiting-time. A noisy, colourful gush into the monochromatic stillness. Red anoraks, royal blue coats. The black which had been fashionable amongst the young of the 1980s seemed to have swung back to a more 1960s ambience. Thatcherite yuppies – black. Liberalism – psychadelia. Bright spruce people in hard-backed chairs sitting in clusters talking animatedly at dingy wabbit people in easy-chairs.

The room-runner had parents, Marie a husband. Nobody for Gerard or Ailie. Did David know where she was?

Getting information from Gerard was a slow process. Most days when she tried to talk to him he would reply in monosyllables, or say he was tired and wanted left alone.

Late the following Wednesday Ailie learned that the Home was, despite its Spartan atmosphere, privately owned.

"If it wis State-run it might be better," lamented Gerard. "At least we wid get inspected noo an again. Here, we're the forgotten few." He snorted noisily in the back of his throat. "But, then, ye've tae wait years on a place in a State-run outfit."

"Where does the money come from?"

"Affa yer faimily, an they get a subsidy forby," said Gerard vaguely. "They take aw wur pensions, mind. Maybe yours n' mine urnae that great, but there ur folks in here that wis on private plans." He poked her in the chest. "See thon wee mingy dinners we get? Thon's their profit margin."

"So is everybody put in here by their own families?"

At this point, the conversation was interrupted by bedtime. Next day, when Ailie sought Gerard, she was told he had been moved in the night to the hospital, having suffered a mild stroke. For two weeks she chafed at the bit, unable to talk to anyone else.

Gerard returned late on a Friday. On the Saturday, fortunately, he looked more or less the same as ever. Ailie discussed with him the effects of the stroke, his experiences in hospital, the prognosis for the future, the fact that he had had one visit from his son-in-law while in hospital, what the son-in law had said, what Gerard had said, what the grandchildren were doing these days. At the end of the conversation Gerard was suddenly tired and took to his bed.

On the Monday he appeared again, looking much brighter, looking, for him, very alive. Ailie risked, at last, broaching the subject nearest to her heart.

"How do folk get admitted here? Is it just when their relatives put them in?"

Gerard gave her an appraising look. "Unless they're Sectioned."

"You mean, certified?" Ailie looked around the room to see who could come under that category. "I suppose they'd have to be considered dangerous for that to happen."

"Maybe."

"Is that how Marie got here?"

"Naw. Her hubby jist pit hur in when he couldnae cope ony mair."

"The room-ru . . . Gary?"

"Naw." He cleared his throat, and looked around in vain for somewhere to spit. "Naw, you're the only wan here in under the Section."

"What!"

"Aye." He snickered. "Ye musta been a bad lassie!"

"But . . . what did I do?"

"Well, if you cannae answer that yersel," he sniffed, "maybe it's right ye should be in here."

"There must be some mistake!" Ailie's voice rose to a wail, so that some of the other patients raised or lowered their eyes from carpet or television to see what the distraction was. "I never . . . " (Never . . . what?) She corrected herself, ". . . I'm not the kind who hurts people!"

"Ur ye sure?" Gerard grinned and squeezed her knee. "I think you could be a right wee handful if ye pit yer mind tae it!"

Again, the conversation was broken by tea, then visiting-time, and bed.

Next morning Ailie sought out Linda and Eric. She found them playing cards behind a door marked PRIVATE.

"I want to know the circumstances of my being admitted here in the first place. I want to know it now."

Linda screwed up her face. "Uch, Ailie, away back tae the telly room. This is no the time nor place."

"Well, when is?"

Eric scanned his cards, withdrew one, and threw it down with a flourish on the table. Linda squealed, "Uch, ye rotten swine, ye!" She tutted and looked in despair at her own hand. "What's left for me to do?"

"Please. . . "

Eric grinned at Linda. "Might as well pack it in, sweetheart. Ye're up against an expert, now."

"Tell me," shouted Ailie, "how I come to be here?"

Linda looked up at her in irritation. "You still about? Ah told ye tae get tae the telly room."

"Not till you tell me what I want to know!"

"There's no need to shout!"

"Yes there is!" yelled Ailie. "Nobody hears unless I shout!"

"Ailie, I don't know how you got here," said Eric. "It was before my time."

"If you don't tell me," said Ailie, "I'll stay here and scream." She opened her mouth.

"Okay, okay! What do you want to know?"

"Why I was committed. What I did, and who arranged it."

"Right you are." Eric looked back at the cards. He pulled out one from the back and put it to the front. He looked up again. "I said okay. We'll have a look in the records, soon as we've a minute."

For the next three days Ailie lost no chance to nag at Eric and Linda. Finally, when she brought the subject up one Monday as she was being settled for the non-existent visitors she got a response at last.

"I did look in your file," said Linda. "And it's right enough, you are here under the Act. I never realised that before."

"Why?" asked Ailie brusquely. (The last thing I want is for Linda and Eric to start treating me worse now they know.)

Linda shrugged. "It wis your son arranged it."

"What!" (*Et tu, Brute!*)

"You took a knife to his wife. And you gave his house a right going-over. Thousands worth of damage."

Ailie was stunned into silence.

"He said it wisnae the first time, but he wanted it to be the last time. The police and everybody was involved. Do ye not mind any of it?"

"No."

Linda shook her head. "There you are, then."

"But I can't believe. . . " (Which? . . . Surely Crawford. Even so. . . )

"It wis true enough. His wife wis hysterical. Hud tae get fifteen stitches in her arm. You went for him and all, but he took the knife off you."

"But why should I do such a thing? Which son was it, anyway?"

Linda screwed up her face. "Oh, that ah cannae tell ye . . . Ah didnae know ye hud more than one."

"If it's . . . David is . . . if I've alienated him. . . "

Linda laughed. "Alienated! I should say. Did you no wonder that he never visited you?"

"I thought maybe he didn't know where. . . "

"But ye wrote to him yourself, did you not?"

"I thought maybe I had the wrong address. . . "

"How? You were brought in from his house."

"Yes, but I still might have an old address. . . "

"And he said you had been very close at one time."

(Must have been David, then! Or. . . )

"In fact, he said in his statement jealousy was likely the cause of it. He said you'd had it in for his wife from the start . . . Och, hey, now, you don't huv to start bubblin. . . " Awkwardly she patted Ailie's shoulder. "You go for a lie down. Want a couple of tablets, to calm your nerves?"

Despite the pills, Ailie found it impossible to sleep all that evening and throughout the night. Every little irritation of institutional life returned to torment her, things she thought she had long grown used to – the narrow bed, the tight thin quilt, the ever-burning night-lights, the sound of thirteen different rhythms of breathing and of Isobel crying down the ward, "Oh, God, help me noo. Please, God, help me noo. For God's sake, help me noo."

Next morning, full of fresh determination, she sought out Linda and demanded she check the whereabouts of both sons.

"Ailie, hen. Ah asked Eric about it last night. You've only got one son."

Ailie's eyes widened. "I've got two. David and Crawford."

"One o' them's dead."

"I don't believe you!"

Linda sighed. "Your son said you found it hard to accept

his brother's death. . . "

"Which son?" screamed Ailie. "Who the hell are we talking about?"

Linda bit her finger. "Ah cannae mind the name," she said at last.

"Yet you recall so much detail?"

"Well, it wis an interesting wee story. Quite dramatic." Linda finished making the bed and stood up. "Here, do you not know yourself which wan o' your sons is dead?"

"How could you forget the name? For Christ's sake!" Ailie's voice reached a crescendo.

"Aw right, aw right. Keep your hair on. I'll have another gander at your file."

For the rest of the day Ailie sat numb with shock. When Gerard came to sit beside her she moved away. The one son dead, the other her enemy. Did it matter which was which?

When the weak equinoctial sun hung low on the scraggy horizon Linda came to tuck them up for bed. "I did look at it again," she told Ailie. "It was Crawford arranged the commitment."

No use in longing for the first of the month now. Ailie joined the others in waiting for reveille, waiting for breakfast, waiting for lunch, waiting for television, waiting for tea, waiting for bedtime. Waiting for days, waiting for weeks.

At first she ignored Gerard. Then, gradually, her resilience took over. She had not seen the last of David, nor of the outside world.

"Ah wis sayin," said Gerard one afternoon, "Gary's away."

"Where to?"

"The hospital. He's tae get an operation, or something."

Ailie said, "I once saw written on a toilet wall, I'D RATHER HAVE A FULL BOTTLE IN FRONT OF ME THAN A FULL FRONTAL LOBOTOMY."

"Eh?" Gerard wrinkled his brow. "Whit's at mean?"

"A lobotomy. You know, a brain operation."

"A brain operation."

"It was a joke."

"A joke!" Gerard cackled. "It's well seen the kinna piss-houses you go intae!" Conspiratorially he patted her on the shoulder, giving it a painful squeeze. "'Scuse the language, hen."

"That's all right," murmured Ailie.

"But ah mean tae say," Gerard laboured the point, "it's a bit different frae . . . SHUGGY LOVES BETTY, or . . . FUCK THE POPE, or . . . " he gave her a sidelong glance and squeezed her shoulder again, " . . . MALKY WANKS."

Ailie edged away from him slightly.

"Noo, that's the kinna writin ye get in the cludgies ah've been tae. But then, ah'm no educated like you."

"I'm not that well-educated," murmured Ailie. She turned and met his gaze. Poor soul, he looked a bit better than usual. His nose was clean and his chin shorn. "After all, I didn't write the thing."

Gerard laughed again. "Well, ah'm glad you're able tae joke. For a wee while therr, ah thought ye'd fallen oot wi me."

"I'm sorry. I was preoccupied. They'd told me one of my sons was dead."

"Jesus Christ! And here's me . . . when did it happen?"

"I don't know. . . "

"Whit age wis he, fur cryin out loud?"

"I . . . don't know that either. Please . . . I'd rather not talk about it."

Even as she spoke, a shred of doubt came into Ailie's mind. When had she seen David before? What year was it, at all?

"Terrible thing tae lose a son," Gerard went on. "Worst thing in the world."

"I said I didn't want to talk about it."

"Okay, well." Gerard glanced shyly at her. "I'm glad yer more yersel, noo, onywey. Yer a fine bit o' stuff, ye know." Again, the hand on the knee, or rather, the thigh.

Ailie blinked at him in surprise. Who had said that in jail King Kong looked like Marilyn Monroe?

"I'm a mess," she said, "like everybody else here. Is it of any consequence?"

"Ye're no a mess," Gerard contradicted her. "Come an ah'll show ye."

"What do you mean?"

"Ah know wherr therr's a mirror. Come an ah'll show ye."

"There's a mirror in the ward."

"Naw, but ah waant tae show ye. C'moan!" He rose.

A stroll, even within the building, would be nice, if they could avoid Eric and Linda. Ailie followed him past the zombies and out of the room.

"This way." Gerard padded down a corridor and Ailie shuffled after in her too-big slippers. "Through here." He opened a door, and Ailie went in. By the time she realised it was a broom cupboard, Gerard was on her.

"Ailie! Ailie!" His voice was hoarse, his face rough, his body heavy, his hands everywhere. Up her jumper, down her trousers, squeezing her hips, crushing her breasts.

"No!" she wailed. Then his mouth was on hers, bruising, drooling. She had forgotten how sour other folks' saliva tasted. A picture flashed into her mind of Gerard as he had looked before his last trip to hospital – runny-nosed and bleary-eyed – and revulsion washed over her.

"Mmmmmhhhh . . . Get off! Get away! No! no!"

To her horror she saw that he was not going to take No for an answer. Off with the washed-out cardigan. Off with the stained brassiere. For an elderly stroke victim he was incredibly strong. She wrestled long and hard, yelling all the while, to keep her trousers up, but in the end down they came, and somebody's cast-off pulled-thread once-white pants with them. He hooked his ankle around hers and suddenly she was on her back on top of hard brush heads and damp mop-heads. Again the slobbering mouth on hers, cutting off her cries, again the hands squeezing and scratching her breasts. Then the mouth was chewing horribly on her shoulder as the hands fumbled at his own waistband (he had no belt). Down with the trousers, down with the pants. At the moment she felt him thrusting towards her, she put down her own hand and dug her nails in hard.

"Yaroo!"

The door was flung open and light flooded in.

"What the hell is going on in here?"

Saved by Eric and Linda!

Pitifully she crawled out to new humiliation. She was naked, wet with sweat and saliva, and at the moment when they opened the door she had been clutching Gerard's. . .

"You randy wee buggers, you!" Eric sneered. "Crawling into cupboards. . . "

"There's no winchin allowed in the hospital," said Linda primly. "You must understand why we have this rule."

They stood impatiently by as she and Gerard fumbled into their clothes and then frog-marched them back to the television room. Gerard tried to meet her eye, tried to sit beside her, but she spurned him.

"Ah'm awfy sorry," he bleated. "Ah know ah wis oota step, therr."

Ailie looked the other way.

"An you such a lady!"

Ailie turned her back on him.

"Thanks for no lettin on tae them . . . ye know."

"If I thought they'd have believed me," flashed Ailie, "I would've."

"Aye. Well, it'll no happen again."

Ailie rose and carried her chair to the other side of the room, where she started up a conversation with poor demented Isobel. Gerard followed.

"Wonder what we'll have for tea today?" said Ailie desperately.

"Tea? Have we no had wur tea yet?"

"Do you know," whispered Gerard, "in State-run nursing homes couples get tae share bedrooms even if they're no mairried tae wan another?"

"No, not yet."

"Och, ah thought we'd hud wur tea."

"That was dinner we had. It all runs together, doesn't it?"

"Whit does?"

"Meals in here. Breakfast runs into lunch, which runs into dinner, which runs into supper. . . "

"An if wan o' the couple's ootside and the other's in, they get conjugal visits!" breathed Gerard.

"It's no time fur supper yet, is it?"

"No, no. It's teatime, now."

"Visits lastin aw night! In a double bed! Even if they're no mairried!"

"Bed?" Isobel turned her head towards Gerard. "It's no bedtime, is it?"

"No, no! Teatime."

"This crew only waant tae make us aw miserable. That's their wan aim in life! Perra shites!"

For the next few days Ailie found herself pursued by Gerard. Wherever she placed her chair he would follow, and talk and talk, about the lost minds of their fellow-patients, about the misery of their lives under Eric and Linda, ultimately, always, about the lack of privacy and the need for double beds. If she left the room alone he followed her out, and physically blocked her return so that she had to squeeze past him. If she snapped at him he told her he liked her spirit. If she attempted conversation with anyone else he intervened. Finally she sank into an introspective denial of his existence, of the room's existence, of the Home itself. She discovered a knack of keeping her eyes open to ward off his little sly grabs, while switching her mind to loftier things.

After a couple of months of this, Eric interviewed her.

"You don't look happy," he informed her. "You used to be one of the ones that spoke in here. Now you don't. What's up?"

Ailie was amazed and delighted at this interest in her state of mind. She said, "It's Gerard."

"Auld Gerard?" Eric smirked. "Aw, I get it. It's because we broke up your wee love nest thon time."

"Actually it's the opposite." Ailie took a deep breath. "It's sexual harassment."

"What!" Eric's jaw dropped. "How? What's he been doing?"

Ailie hesitated.

"Touching you up? Eh? Feeling your bum?" Eric was struggling to keep his face straight.

"If you don't mind," said Ailie, "I'd rather tell Linda about it."

"Look, Ailie," Eric leaned his elbows on the desk and pressed his finger tips together. It was a studied pose. "I know a bit about mental illness. . . "

"Forgive my asking," Ailie bent towards him, "but exactly how much training did you get for this job?"

Eric flushed. "Enough to know that it's common for women of your age and condition to suffer from delusions. . . "

"I want to speak to Linda. Now."

". . . No matter how unattractive they are, they imagine all the men are after them."

"I've never imagined anything of the kind. Not even,"

Ailie raised her voice as Eric cut in on her, "when I was young and fresh."

"It's a symptom of the Change."

"Can I speak to Linda? Yes or no?" (Not that Linda would be a likely improvement).

"The time we caught you two in the broom cupboard it looked more like you were harassing him."

Ailie closed her eyes for a moment. When she opened them, Eric was still there, and twice as horrible. So she turned to go.

Eric called after her, "I want to see an improvement, mind. If you don't cheer up a bit we'll have to do something about it."

Do something about it? she thought. Might be all right. Could hardly be worse than spending her life being ignored.

Thus it was that after two more weeks of staring serenely into space she found herself in Eric's car whizzing up the motorway. The route was monotonous enough, and the buildings mostly far away, but Ailie drank it in eagerly until, too soon, she was taken out and into a big hospital.

"Surely here I'll see a doctor," she told herself. Too late she realised their plan for her as they tied her down on a trolley and gave her something to grip between her teeth.

"I don't want electro-convulsive therapy!" she squealed as they fitted the electrodes.

"Let me up! Let me out!" as they held her down.

"You've got no right. . . " as they switched on the current.

There was a flash of exquisite pain. Then she found herself bounding up a mountain shaped like a perfect cone. Although she had never been there, she knew it was Schiehallion, epicentre of mainland Scotland.

With great seven-league strides she louped over the high heather, and then, ever more swiftly, over the boulders to the peak. When the mist which swirled about her cleared, the whole country sprawled out at her feet. Moorland, bog, rocks, sheep like aphids against the green. Farmlands and winding rivers. Glasgow – a mass of high flats, low flats, parks and bridges. Edinburgh – all funny Gothic turrets interspersed with elegant facades. Dundee, plain and brown at the end of the bridge. Aberdeen, sparkling silver, with the grey sea beyond.

She opened her rucksack. Although it had seemed so light she had been practically unaware of it, inside was a video recorder, on its own, plugged into neither mains nor TV set.

After a moment Ailie pressed the Rewind button. Her environment began to change. The flashing alternations of day and night dazzled her at first, like a strobe light, but soon they settled into a bright grey which illuminated the scene below.

Fields changed their boundaries, moorland reverted to pasture and then again to heath. Behind her the oil-rigs crumbled into the sea. Conifer forests in the distance shrank back to nothingness, leaving peat-bogs in their place. Glasgow, far-off, belched smoke into the sky and ships into the sea. Deciduous forests crept over the landscape, rowan, hazel, oak. Here and there small villages appeared, thick stone, with slate or thatch roofs. In Edinburgh, Princes Street Gardens filled with water. Castles patched themselves up. Glasgow lost its grime and dwindled into a few stone and wooden wynds and, at last, into a little wooden church.

"And now. . . " Ailie pressed the Fast Forward button. The church expanded to a village, a town, a dirty city and a clean city. The conifers and the oil rigs returned, and disappeared again. Ribbons of road unravelled across the country, instantly crawling with cars, and here and there clear plastic domes appeared, encasing the centres of population.

"How far ahead dare I go?"

The matter was decided for her by a growing pain in her

head. It started at the back of her neck and quickly took over her entire cranium. A screaming, doleful agony inside her skull, as if her brain were on fire. If this were part of her dream she must awaken now. She closed her eyes and willed the domes, the mountainside to go away.

Too late! She opened her eyes and realised she should have kept a hold on Schiehallion. The pain was part of reality. She was lying in bed, surrounded by the most dreadful Faces, and Pain had its strongest grip yet.

Was she back in the hospital? Or . . .

Hardly able to focus for pain, she looked and thrashed about. Her legs did not reach the foot of the bed. The eiderdown was pink satin of the old-fashioned kind. A basin stood at the side, near a particularly malevolent configuration, hollow of cheek and glittering of eye.

"Who are you?" whispered Ailie. "What do you want?"

The apparition grinned and stretched out a scraggy hand. Ailie shrank back as she saw the two fingers nip her. She felt nothing. It was the Hag of Barra, it was the witch of Endor!

The torture renewed its intensity. Piercing, burning. The faces round the foot of the bed dimmed to shadows, obliterated by flashing lights and colours. She knew her head was going to explode right away.

"Mummy!" She crawled out of bed, every movement of her head or neck a fresh agony. Stumbling on her pink winceyette nightie she reeled out onto the landing and was sick all over the top step. She could hear raised voices downstairs. Mummy and Daddy and Uncle Roddy too. Uncle Roddy sang in the same choir as Mummy and came round often to practise. If she could only make it to Mummy. Mummy would see her all right. Mummy would make the pain go away, if only Ailie could reach her and tell her how bad it had suddenly become.

Getting downstairs was difficult, with the whole house

jigging and dancing and tossing her about in such a fashion. She fell over the carpet into the living-room. Her face hit the ground. She pushed herself up to her hands and knees, and raised her head.

Mummy and Uncle Roddy had their backs to Ailie. They were standing over Daddy as he lay, as usual on the sofa. Mummy was pressing down at the top end, while Roddy held down his legs. Ailie could not see Daddy's face because there was a cushion over it. It was the pink cushion Mummy had embroidered when she was a girl. Daddy's arms were waving and feebly shoving at the cushion, but as Ailie watched they slackened. His left hand fell down and hit the floor. Still, Mummy pressed the cushion to his face.

Ailie's pain ebbed at the sight. The witch's head, disembodied now, but still leering, floated past her and came to rest behind Daddy. The witch opened her mouth to laugh. She had no teeth, no tongue, no throat. Ailie screamed and the agony returned in force.

Mummy turned at the sound. She kept the cushion over Daddy's face, but she called, "The child, Roddy, the child!"

Uncle Roddy left Daddy and came towards Ailie. She did not want Uncle Roddy. She wanted her mother. "Mummy!" she yelled. "I've a sore head! It's awfully, awfully sore!"

She tried to escape Uncle Roddy, but the witch developed long arms and caught her round the middle. She struggled and cried and the anguish built up inside her until her head exploded.

The time after that was a kaleidoscope of her mother thebed theFaces UncleRoddy theambulancemen thestretcher hermother theambulance thehospital hermother thenurses thebed hermother themedicines thedoctors thetubes thedrips thebed hermother thenight theFaces theday thenight theFaces theday hermother.

And, through it all, Pain.

There came a period of lucidity. (Why did I become a child again? I was no longer big in a small body, like now. I was five years old and wanted my mother. Does such pain make us all five years old? Or at least, if we can get away with it? What was true? Can I trust the testimony of a small child? As I lay on the floor, did I really see Daddy's angina tablets scattered on a level with my cheek? Too melodramatic – a product of my sickened imagination, a product of future decades of watching the Hammer House of Horror, or even Tales of the Unexpected. And the rest?)

Dorothy came and visited her, stroked her hand and told her that she was to have an operation to drain fluid away from inside her head. They would shave part of her hair, but Dorothy would style the rest so skilfully that, certainly by the time she was back at school, no one would ever know. And after this Ailie would feel much better, and wouldn't take the funny turns, and wouldn't see the Faces any more.

She also very gently told her that Daddy had gone to heaven and become a little angel, fluttering among the clouds. Ailie received both bits of history in silence. She knew what would happen when they put her under the general anaesthetic.

# 13

AILIE WAS AROUSED by the alarm clock ringing. Half-past three. Morning or afternoon? She wondered why she would have set the alarm for such a time.

Outside it was broad daylight. Unless it was midsummer, it must be p.m. . . She was in the house in Bellahouston, and when she went to the mirror she assessed her youth. No children in sight. Had she left herself a note? A search revealed nothing. Perhaps she should write a wee note to herself each time she fell asleep. But what to put in it? Her history for the past two weeks, months, years? What a bind.

Nothing for it but to get on with things. She was just putting the kettle on, when the phone rang.

"Mrs Carmichael? This is Garrowglen. Would you please come and uplift your son? You know the children should be collected by 4 o'clock. He's holding back two of the staff."

"Oh, I'm sorry. I . . . fell asleep. I'll come right away!"

"Thank you!"

"Just a minute. . . " CLICK!

The woman on the other end had hung up before Ailie could work up the courage to ask the address.

Must be a nursery. Public or private? Ailie opened the phone book and searched for Strathclyde Regional Council.

Nothing. Must be before regionalisation. She looked up Glasgow Corporation Social Work Department, then Glasgow Corporation Education Department and only then finally found the place. Not knowing which bus would take her there, she looked at the map and ran the whole way.

Red-faced at the nursery, she had to endure a lecture from the Head about the importance of uplifting her child punctually, along with a threat that she and Crawfie were on their last warning. Crawfie, for his part, greeted her in silence.

Thus, Crawford's unformed years gave way to his time of memory. He grew, taking for granted the air he breathed, the blankets which warmed him, the food in his plate, the gravity which supported him. For Crawfie, the world would be as expected, a gentle relentless eddy from plump youth to scraggy age. No breaks for Crawfie.

One night Ailie left Crawford with Dot while she and Steve attended a party at Sandy's and Pandora's house. It was to celebrate the recent General Election, where the Scottish National Party had ended up with seven MPs . . .

Minis were passé, which meant that only Ailie wore one. However, the air was still thick with flower-power, or was it joss-sticks? With her still long hair tied back and her figure collapsed back to its pre-pregnant position, she felt like a fourteen-year-old allowed for the first time to a grown-up party.

Pandora, in Arabian trousers the correct shade of green for her hair, showed them into the kitchen. She was bubbling over with euphoria and strong drink. "This is a question I'm asking all my guests. Where exactly were you when you heard about the first gain?"

"Do you mean for the first time, or on this occasion?"

"Aha! Clever, very clever! I'd forgotten for a moment . . . The point I wanted to make is that you can give people marks for enthusiastic participation. Were they rooting for Margo at the Kelvin Hall? Were they at one of our out of town hopes? Were they watching the count on the telly, or listening on the radio? Did they go to bed and only hear next day? Do they not even remember?"

Steve groaned and reached for the bottles.

"Steve. I have just the group of fellow-feelers for you. The Commiserating Opposition." She led him to a group of about five standing in a corner near the record-player which was belting out *The Scottish Breakaway*. "All these people voted Something Else. So you should have a lot in common with them. Hey, get off my sleeve!" She pulled a record cover out from under someone's feet. "This record sleeve was banned in its time! Not a lot of people have a copy."

Ailie she took into the other room where a small choir had formed seated on the couch and on the floor with copies of the *Rebel Ceilidh Song Book*. Over by the window, standing casually with a glass in his hand, deep in conversation with some strangers, was . . .

After that the night swept by. She seemed to have been only five minutes, there, on the couch with Don John, listening to his silver words, touching his lustrous hair, when Steve appeared. "I've had enough of this rubbish. Y' coming?"

From her dream world Ailie shook her head and didn't notice when he'd gone. In a short time Don John's head was in her lap. Pandora smiled slily, Sandy tutted, but the two were oblivious. "What about politics? Are you into all this?" murmured Don John.

"I find it hard," said Ailie, "not to get it in perspective. Not to take the longer-term view."

"I couldn't help overhearing that," remarked a chap in green corduroy. "So get it all in perspective, eh? You're one of those who is proud to put your country last? Big is beautiful – it's selfish to be small!"

"I meant chronologically, not geographically," Ailie flushed.

Sandy, passing, turned to put his part. "Once you've been abroad," he said, "you realise how little Scotland matters to the rest of the world. If Scotland disappeared tomorrow below the sea the Chinese would hardly notice. So why should we knock our pans out to save Scotland and the Scottish culture, just because it's ours?"

"The Jews have a saying," murmured a chap by the mantlepiece. "If I am not for myself, then who will be?"

"All the same," pressed Sandy, "you can't get away from the fact that nationalism is a selfish philosophy. It concentrates on one sector of humanity and tries to improve the situation there while ignoring similar or much worse problems elsewhere. And, by the way, I speak as a nationalist."

Pandora, seeing the debater in him surface, bounded across to haul him into line. "Sandy, every place in the world operates on this selfish basis. Big countries like England are more selfish than wee ones. At least we're not trying to take over other people's lands."

"But is it right to be selfish just because other people are too?" Sandy persisted.

"So whoever sets out to be saintly? Most people have no inhibitions about doing what's best for themselves and their children. Certainly as long as it doesn't hurt anyone else. It's only such as the Scots and . . . and women who feel guilty if they once in a while don't put themselves last – and that's because other more pushy people have always trained them that their needs don't matter. No, I think Ephraim's right. If you don't have enough self-confidence, other folk who have too much walk all over you and give you a miserable life."

"Aren't most philosophies selfish at the foundations?" murmured Ephraim.

"Socialism isn't," replied Sandy.

"Not if you're well-off," said Pandora. "Socialism can only be selfish if you're poor."

"Couldn't you be doing it just to feel good about yourself?" asked Ephraim.

"Socialism is never selfish," said Sandy. "How can it be selfish for the group to care for its weaker members? It's an unselfish creed whether the individual believer stands to gain or not. However, it can be taken on board for selfish reasons, that I grant you."

"Anyway, you can be for self-government and socialism too," protested the corduroy fellow. "They aren't mutually exclusive. Look at the African National Council. Look at Mugabe."

Teasingly, Ephraim began to sing, "The people's flag is blue and white, it flops by day and flops by night. . . "

"Well, to me," said Don John, "the colour of Scotland is not blue, and still less is it tartan. For me it'll always be black. Black Glasgow tenements, black Northern landscapes. Rocks against grey skies, sticking out of glassy seas. Sunday clothes and churches. Sombre Christmas under rain, winter solstice lasting days."

"When you're abroad it can seem like that in retrospect," said Pandora. "But I'm always glad to get back to the pastel shades of the North. Water-colours rather than oils."

"I never said I didn't love it," said Don John. "I'm a winter soul myself. Storms and mountain crags are what fire the blood. Any fool can make a verse about an English rose garden."

It was at that moment that Ailie knew what she had to do about David.

That night, while Steve snored, she worked back, with the help of a medical dictionary which she hoped was accurate, from 3rd of March 1975. She calculated it to sometime in the last week of May. That was the deadline, then, although she supposed she would have to have some kind of lead-in, some kind of warm-up. One day she would tell David. She knew that she would tell him. His remarks regarding Steve and the video all fell into place now. Whether she would tell Don John was something she would have to work out.

Meanwhile, the last three guests swayed happily out of Pandora's flat, waving cheerily, staggering down the stairs, lurching across Byres Road and down the back lanes. The University tower was a black goblin against the heavenly pink. From back-courts and quadrangles warbled the harbingers of spring, of dawn, of fresh beginning, and every shiftworker or reveller got a clenched fist and a *Saor Alba!*

"What's wrong?" Sandy asked Pandora as she bustled coldly amongst the ashtrays and abandoned cans.

"It's you."

"I thought it was. Which particular aspect of me?"

"You play the Devil's advocate as happily as God's."

"A skill possessed by any debater worth his salt. I thought you would know that."

"I didn't say, as easily. I said, as happily. Sometimes I think you've no sincere opinions at all."

"You and I – we both love an argument," soothed Sandy. "To me it's the intellectual challenge – a bit like chess. You just like a fight – you enjoy the passion of it, and the cruelty of demolishing the other side."

"I do it with the aim of permanently changing the other person's wrongful viewpoint."

"Just remember, A man convinced against his will – is of the same opinion still."

"If that was true we'd still be throwing Christians to the lions."

"I'm not saying your kind of preaching never achieves anything. There's room for both kinds of warriors in the verbal battlefield. The tactician and the berserker."

"But only the berserker risks getting hurt."

Sandy grinned. "That's why tactician is the smarter option."

Pandora slapped him lightly on the cheek. "But not invulnerable in all senses."

Sandy's face hardened. "That's the first and last time you resort to violence. Between civilised people it's not the way."

"Am I to be civilised now? You just called me a berserker."

As an apprentice liar, Ailie laid her plans carefully. She told Steve she would want to spend the odd evening at her mother's, and she told her mother she and Steve planned to go an odd evening without Crawfie to the pictures. Dorothy and Steve disliked each other enough that they would be unlikely to exchange notes. She felt uneasy at lying to her mother, a bit less so at lying to Steve. After all, if he wanted to take up his declared option, he would not have to lie, he would just vanish for a night, as he did so often. He never had to make arrangements.

She supposed she would have to deceive him once more, in the wake of the deed. Perhaps if she wrapped up in a bathtowel and called him, Domine? Perhaps a pretend palla and a bit of scent, with a little Latin gleaned from her old grammar would lure him into her plans one last time. Worth a try, anyway.

She waited until a film came on that she genuinely wanted to see, before phoning Don John.

It had been so long in her experience since she had attempted to dress up to seduce that she had little idea what to wear. Don John, she thought and hoped, went more for the mysterious than the tarty. She bought a flimsy – in a fairy-ballerina sense rather than see-through sexy – dress and jacket ensemble. When the day dawned however, into April or not, a freezing wind whistled round the corners, so that she had to wear her woolly jumper and anorak instead.

Nonetheless, the evening passed most pleasantly. Before the film they went for a curry together. The conversation took off without effort and marched through his work – he was in teaching but hoped to get into Gaelic broadcasting – his poetry, the Gaeltachd now, in the past, and in the future, her condition, the nature of Time and Space and of Life and Death, his mother and her mystic experiences, religion, spiritualism, the body physical, genetics and sex. Unfortunately, by the time Ailie had successfully wangled the topic around to where she wanted it, it was time to leave if they wanted to catch onto the story.

In the cinema they both felt a bit past necking in the back stalls. However, they held hands throughout, murmured sweet nothings, occasionally pecked each other on the cheek. The film itself was disappointing, all blood, gore and shock-horror. Telekinesis, Hollywood-style. Afterwards, at the stop where she would get the bus to Dorothy's house, they kissed until their hearts thudded, and made a promise for May.

This was a beautiful day, just right for the fairy-frock. Her mother gave her a second look when, all perfumed and rosy, she deposited Crawfie.

"You and Steve having a second honeymoon, or something?"

"You're half-right, Mummy."

"Can't you call me something else? It sounds so prissy, now you're grown-up."

"Mum, Ma, Mother, Maw, Dot, Dottie, or Dorothy. Whatever you like. Though I'll still think of you as Mummy."

No films tonight. They ate in a Greek restaurant, and then went back to his place. During the meal he had seemed morose, and in his living-room, over coffee and to the strains of the Incredible String Band, he explained why. "I'm leaving. I've got a job in Nova Scotia, working with the Gaelic community there."

Ailie tried to hide her disappointment. "It's what you want, isn't it?"

"The job is, yes. I'll get a chance to do some research into the state of the Canadian branch of the language."

"When do you leave?"

"The appointment starts in August."

"Good." Ailie snuggled up to him. "Then we have some time."

"I would like to take you with me, but I don't know if it's feasible."

Ailie made it easy for him. "It isn't. I've got Crawfie to think of. Anyway, I always knew we weren't long-term together. That's not the way it went. For you, I'm a temporary landing-stage. For me, you're an occasional soul-mate."

Making love with Don John was the way it was described in books, and the way she still hoped it might turn out to be in the beginning with Steve. In the first place, she flew to heaven; in the second place she tumbled through all the generations of lovemakers who had gone before; in the third place the two of them were surrounded by the Faces and Shades of her past, all playing atonal music on scores of different instruments. During the fourth, she slipped away to a completely fresh year.

# 14

*At seventeen,*
*he falls in love quite madly,*
*with eyes of shining blue . . .*

Strumming the ukelele, Sandy dropped to one knee beside Ailie who sat simpering into a hand mirror.

*At twenty-one,*
*he's got it rather badly,*
*for eyes of a different hue . . .*

Curse! He hit a false chord, which jarred in his ears, although the audience showed no sign of noticing. Now, in this Highers year, he had devoted less time to acquiring new accomplishments, such as the uke.

*But it's when he thinks he's past love,*
*it's then he meets his last love,*
*and he loves her like he's never loved before.*

Ukelele over to Ailie, who strummed for Sandy's tap dance, making mistakes all over the place.

Nigel saved the day. White shirt, tartan shorts and bow tie and *Doggie in the Window*. Darling bratlet. The audience loved him . . . and how he loved the audience! For encore he launched into *Robin in the Rain*. Still they applauded. *I Belong to Glasgow* got the audience – a pensioners' club – joining in, and *I Love a Lassie* got his mother worried. When he started *Coulter's Candy* she marched on stage to drag him off to cheers.

"They loved me, Mummy, didn't they?"

"They did indeed, honeybunch."

"Am I very good at singing for my age?"

"You certainly are, pet. There aren't many wee boys your age who can keep the tune so well."

"Could Ailie keep the tune at my age?"

"Not as well as you."

"Could Sandy?"

"Well, he was no better."

"But was he as good?"

"I don't remember, Nigel."

"What about Jojo?" Nigel loved this bit.

"Jojo can't sing as well as that now."

Sandy and Ailie stared out of the car window at the driving rain, saying nothing.

In No 46, Jojo sat hunched over a cup of coffee, the French Revolution on her lap and her eyes on the prostrate form on the couch. To avoid looking at her history notes (it was her second attempt at the Higher) she would look at anything.

He spoke. "Dottie, get me a cushion."

"You've got two already."

"Och, Dottie, pet, dear, c'm'ere."

"It's Jojo, Uncle Roddy."

"Dottie . . . " He half sat up, then fell back again. "We should never have done it, you know."

"Done what?" Jojo laid her books on the floor and was at his side in a moment.

"Dottie. . . "

"Here I am. Dottie here." Jojo stroked his hair.

"It was a crime."

"What was a crime?"

Damn. The key in the lock. In a trice Jojo was back at the fireplace, Robespierre on her knee, smile on her face.

"Well? How did it go?"

"Fine. Wee Nigel stole the show." Sandy flung his coat over the slumberous stepfather and himself into an armchair.

"Sandy! Surely you're not jealous?" Friction was her lifeblood. Without it, she would have withered in this stony place.

"Sandy's jealous! Sandy's jealous!"

Sandy rose. "I'm going next-door."

"Good luck with the Happy Families!"

"Don't you mock Sandy," chided Dorothy. "What he gets up to is honest and decent. I've given up trying to check your activities!"

"Last week it was purple hearts," sneered Jojo. "This week it's pot. Next week I'll try shoplifting. If I'm still bored after that I'll go down to the Holy Loch and get myself an American sailor."

In No 48, Jasmine put on a pile of singles and turned back to Sandy who was laying out the board.

> *Wild Thing*
> *You make my heart sing*
> *You make everything*
> *groovy . . .*

"I think we can do without the background accompaniment, Jasmine."

"Sorry. I just thought. . . " Hurriedly she switched off.

"It is a game which demands a bit of concentration." He smiled. "Maybe this time you'll catch me out."

"I don't think so. I can't seem to work out the moves far enough in advance."

"Natural intelligence – which you've got – and lots of practice. That's all it takes."

Jasmine moved her King's pawn forward a couple of places. At once Sandy did likewise. Jasmine thought for a minute and then moved one of her knights.

"That's the same opening as you always make," complained Sandy.

Mrs Patel came in with a tray. "Here's a wee bowl of Gobi each."

Sandy sniffed at it after she'd left. "Curried cauliflower?"

"It's very nice, Sandy. You'll like it. Maybe," Jasmine cast a timid glance in the direction of the bowl, "we should eat it up now, before it gets cold?"

Sandy heaved a sigh.

"It's nicer taken warm."

"All right, then." Sandy addressed himself to the bowl. "Just remember, Jasmine, man does not live by bread alone."

Neither spoke again until the dishes were empty. When they returned to the chess-board, Sandy found his concentration was gone. Instead of looking at the pieces, he studied Jasmine. Her eyes were lowered over the board and her chin rested on her hand. She wore an Indian shirt in the fashionable cheesecloth fabric with the top three buttons undone. Her breasts stretched the material so that through the space he could glimpse. . . He shifted restlessly and wondered what was in that Gobi? (Mrs Patel should start an export business. I'm sure it could be produced more cheaply than rhinoceros horn.)

"Sandy! You've gone bright red!"

Now, surely. He was sweet seventeen and never been . . . With an effort he raised his eyes from her cleavage to her face. "I was wondering if I could . . . if you would let me kiss you." There. It was said, after all this time.

Jasmine's smile deepened and broadened. "All right."

He cupped her face, smooth and flawless, in his hands and kissed her lips. Then, warming to his task, he wrapped his arms around her more tightly and kissed her again. She was as soft as he had imagined her many, many times at night in his single bed. He had half-pulled her onto his lap when a clatter of dishes from the kitchen reawakened his sense of propriety.

He pushed her away. "Back to the game."

Jasmine wound her arms more tightly round his neck. "I like this game better."

"Jasmine!" He broke her hold and placed her firmly back on her own seat. "Someone might come in." He smoothed down his hair and reapplied his mind to the board. "Your move, wasn't it?"

Sulkily Jasmine moved her Queen and Sandy took it. Disinterestedly she moved a bishop.

"You can't do that. You're putting your own king in check. You're not concentrating, Jasmine."

At ten Sandy's rook closed in on the hapless white King. "Checkmate." He loved chess. "I'll get along home now. I've got Latin to do."

"You're remembering about the *Maid of the Loch*?

"On Sunday. We can get the blue train out to Balloch at ten o'clock."

"What about Saturday? Are you doing anything then?"

Sandy frowned. "I'm going to a party."

"I didn't know you went to parties."

"I don't. I wish I wasn't going, or that I could take you with me. It'll be all older people there."

"Whose party is it?"

"Malcolm Urquhart from the Lit and Deb Society. Well, it's his sister's, really. She's in her first year at Uni."

"Couldn't you take me?"

"It's awkward. Christine – Malcolm's sister – only told him to invite six people, and they're accounted for."

"I see." At the door she lied, "Hope you have a nice time."

Sandy gazed anew at her bright eyes, her flushed cheeks, her full lips. After checking to either side for witnesses he squeezed her so hard that she gasped, and kissed her until her lips bruised. "See you on Sunday," he muttered hoarsely, and vaulted over the garden wall.

At home, he snibbed himself into the bathroom and relieved the pressure on his mind and body the only way he knew, fantasising all the while about the nakedness he had yet to see. With his customary efficiency he was finished in five minutes. Afterwards, brain cleared for serious work, he put the kettle on and went for his Latin books. To the sound of his stepfather's snoring, Sandy translated the Trojan War.

On the landing Sandy fingered the red neckerchief under his school shirt. Did he look Bohemian? . . . adult? . . . like the others? Through the glass dim shapes moved against the light, and beat music poured through the storm doors. Courage! He pulled the bell.

Christine opened the door. She wore a silver mini and golden tights. Her eyelids were also golden, her lips a whiter shade of pale. Malcolm pushed past her, drab in a polo-neck. "Come in, Sandy."

Such crowds in a house! Some walked to and fro, some sat on the floor, but most stood in groups, one talking, the others listening with occasional laughs. Everybody held a glass or a can.

"I'll get you a drink," said Malcolm grandly. "What are you for?"

(What am I for? What am I expected to drink?) He thought about drink, about Roddy. "I'll have a dram." What did normal, social drinkers mix with their whisky? "Straight."

Sandy surveyed his glass. He had tasted whisky only a couple of times before and found it oily. He sipped. Yeuch! "Think of it as medicine," he told himself, and took a bigger gulp, and then another. The whisky became gradually nicer, more warming. He finished it and took another.

Sandy surveyed the company.

Right, the grief of non-matriculation:

—"God, if *you* get a knock-back, what hope for the rest of us?"

—"I know a guy got in with lower grades than me. It's the bloody quota."

—"What quota?"

—"The Faculty of Medicine limits female entry to 40 percent."

—"Christ! Is that allowed?"

—"Sure. They argue it's a waste training women doctors, when they'll eventually leave to have babies. God! I haven't told my Dad, yet."

Left, the more light-hearted approach:

—". . . Then, would you believe, he yelled, Pretty People Rule OK! and jumped the parapet!"

—"Was he all right?"

—"When he waded out the Kelvin, the fuzz got him. Did him for breach!"

—"Poor old Harry! The staff and comfort of the Beer-bar! Is he putting a stunt together for the debate?"

—"So I hear. Gilmorehill will be the poorer for Harry's graduation."

—"I wouldn't worry about that for a long, long time!"

Laughter. One of them turned, addressed Sandy. "You wanting past?"

"Yes," lied Sandy. He wandered out, read the notice on the bathroom door.

LOLOAQIC; I82QB4IP

"You the end of the queue for the cludgie?"

"No." He was in everybody's road. He sought Malcolm, found him with the familiar little band of boys this side of adult status.

"Smoke, Sandy?"

"No thanks." He sipped his whisky and watched the others discuss school.

"Sandy? For next Friday's debate. That this House abhors the excesses of the Cultural Revolution in China."

"You want me to propose?"

"We thought oppose, Sandy. We can't find anyone else to do it."

"Wasn't it you," remarked Malcolm, "who said the wee Chinese kids looked sweet on TV recently, all waving their red books and chanting?"

"Not me," Sandy shrugged.

"Anyway, you're experienced enough to play devil's advocate."

"All right." Sandy liked to think he could propose a convincing flat-earth motion, if called on. Gradually his attention focussed on a chat-up scene to his right – a red-haired freckly girl, and a small Neanderthal-looking bauchle.

"You've a t'rrific figure, y'know. . . "

"I know. Shame about the face."

"Naw, naw, don't get me wrong, I mean it, I mean it. But you'd look better – hope you don't mind my sayin this. . . "

"Say on."

"You'd look a doll in mair casual gear, like. F'r instance, perra cords and a Grandpa nightshirt. . . "

"The stuff second-hand boutiques pick up at Paddy's market for 6d and resell for £6?"

"No . . . necessarily. . . "

". . . the resell price rising in direct proportion to the creases?"

"I like my burds tae look like they're livin off the land. A mini-skirt like yours. . . "

"I'm sorry if my sartorial taste doesn't meet with your requirements."

Sandy moved closer in disbelief. It was all wrong. This wee guy looked like he'd want his girls tarty, all tinsel and tight Bri-nylon. Here he was advocating back-to-the-earth dressing to a dolly-bird witch with a line in patter out of a nineteenth-century novel.

"Of course, pleasing you is my only desire. Perhaps you could send me a list every morning?"

"Sarcasm is the lowest form of wit," mumbled the wee one.

"And a cheque to go with it, of course. My grant doesn't stretch to pretend tatters."

"Okay, okay." The beetle-brow gave a lop-sided grin and clapped the object of his attentions on the shoulder. "What I'm meanin to say, is, how about a date, well? You'n me thegither, like?"

Sandy caught his breath at the boldness of it. He began to feel sorry for the swimmer, so obviously, so obliviously out of his depth.

"No. I don't think so." The girl put her freckled face close to Beetle-Brow's. "Can I give you a word of advice? Review your patter tactics. Otherwise you'll get nowhere with women."

Two feet away, Sandy began preparing patter-lines of his own, ready for when Beetle-brow got the inevitable heave-ho.

"Eh?"

"They particularly resent advice on dress sense."

"Don't take it like that. I find my girls. . . "

"Your girls? Are you a pimp? A patriarch? Jean Brodie in drag?"

"What are you doing tomorrow?"

"Washing my hair."

"The day after?"

"Washing my hair again."

"Okay, what day would suit you to come out for a drink?"

"14th February 1990. I'll maybe be lonely and desperate by then."

"Look, I'm no trying to insult you. . . "

"You haven't the imagination to insult me."

"Aw, piss off. Bloody blue-stocking." The chatter-up lurched off in the direction of the bar, and Sandy moved in.

"Hello."

"What, what is all this popularity? Maybe I should take to the veil, and give you all a break."

The prepared opening. "Only God and I could love you for yourself alone, and not your reddish hair."

"Who is this person who puts himself in a parenthesis with the Almighty?"

"Sandy. Sandy Lorimer."

"Sandy should be careful. Anne Shirley and I – we share sensitivity on the same subject."

"But she did marry Gilbert Blyth in the end."

"*You* read *Anne of Green Gables*? How liberated of you." She smiled. "I'm Pandora McAlpine."

"A very classical name." Pale eyes, wide mouth, freckles.

"My parents went in for mythological waifs. My sister they named after Deirdre of the Sorrows. At least that goes all right with a Celtic surname."

"Och, I think your name suits you."

"I don't. Males have always blamed their sins on imaginary females. I'm the Greek scapegoat."

Sandy smiled. "So you're a Women's Libber?"

"I hope your next remark will have nothing to do with bra-burning."

"What do you take me for?" (This is one for cerebral companionship. As well she isn't a looker. She won't be forever reminding me of my animal origins. With Pandora I can be pure Plato. With Jasmine there's always a bit of the satyr about it.)

Pandora took his hand. "You look like you could do with some grub."

(Is she meaning my state of inebriation? Is it showing already?)

"Why do party hosts always treat their guests like they have long ears?" She stripped a cocktail stick of its cube of cheddar, its pickled onion, its cube of pineapple. "Give me Gibson Street fare, any day."

(Gibson Street?)

Cardboard plates in hand, they drifted amongst the wisps of conversation.

". . . due to the landlady's monotonous insistence on the regularity of rent. . . "

". . . World's biggest balloon. Swore he'd manage three Munroes before the winter set in. Never got further than the Munro pub!"

". . . and in September, like the Sword of Damocles, the Logic resit. . . "

"AC/DC, I'd say. I've seen him with both."

From a side room came the thrum, thrum, thrum of a guitar.

> *Fare-weel, ye banks o' Sicily;*
> *fare-ye-weel, ye valley and shaw. . .*

They wandered in. Sandy seated himself at the piano, found the right key, and picked out a little of the tune – enough to make a good impression on Pandora, not enough that he would be expected to stay, for he was generally unacquainted with the repertoire.

"I wish I was musical," said Pandora. "My sister Deirdre landed all the genes for that."

"Does she play the piano?" asked Sandy.

"Very well. But just now she's interested in Celtic music. She's teaching herself the clarsach."

"I've always been interested in learning the Lowland pipes," volunteered Sandy. "You know, they take less maintenance than the Highland bagpipes, because it's dry air that goes through them." (No need to mention his inability to get more than a peep from the Highland drones on the occasions he'd tried.)

"Have you got a set?" asked Pandora eagerly.

"Not . . . yet. But I'm saving up for some." Then and there Sandy determined to screw a set out of his mother. She was always generous where the development of musical talent was concerned.

Back into the main living-room where the drink was laid out. Sandy discovered his plate was no longer in his hand. All the easier to carry his next refill.

A wreath of real roses balanced on the chipped black marble mantlepiece. One had become detached. Pandora stuck it in her hair and declared,

> *The rose of all the world is not for me.*
> *I want for my part*
> *Only the little white rose of Scotland*
> *That smells sharp and sweet*
> *And breaks the heart.*

Sandy swayed towards her, studied her lips, swayed back and murmured softly,

"You like poetry?"

"Hugh McDiarmid's, anyway."

Sandy composed his voice so that she could not possibly think him patronising – a hard job through the woolly whisky – and murmured, "You into Nationalism?"

"Doesn't necessarily follow. But yes, I am."

"Actively?"

"I bash on doors and try to convert people. What about you?"

Sandy hesitated. At the last two elections he had been mildly pleased when Labour had won, because it annoyed the Tories of the Lit and Deb, with their parentally-inspired gripes about council house subsidy. This would not be so interesting for Pandora as. . . "Last week at the Lit and Deb I pro-proposed the motion, The SNP deserved their recent near-win at Pollok."

"The Lit and Deb?"

"The school Literary and Debating Society."

"You're still at school?"

Sandy cursed his lack of discretion. "I'll be at Glasgow Uni in October."

"Are you in Sixth Year? So you've an unconditional acceptance."

Sandy shrugged. "Conditional, unconditional. To me it's all one."

"How modest of you."

"Just realistic."

The whisky on the table was finished and so he poured himself a vodka.

"Must be off," said Pandora, suddenly. "I'm staying the night with my friend Frances, and she's for offski."

"Hey, wait!" (Is this the brush-off? Am I too young for her? Have I not talked sense?) Sandy pulled himself straight and tried to focus.

"Unlike you," she smiled, "I don't go partying during my exam season. You know the Rubaiyat?"

The Rubaiyat. After all, he had read the work, although she could not mean that. "Yes."

"See you there June 5th? Half-past eight. We can carry on the conversation then."

(Must be a pub. Will I get served there?) "All right."

After she'd gone Sandy found his way to the room with the singing.

> *What would yer Mammy think,*
> *gin she heard the guineas clink*
> *And the hautboys standing around ye, O?*
> *What would yer Mammy think,*
> *gin she heard the guineas clink*
> *And she kent that ye'd married a sodger, O?*

Everyone seemed to know the words except Sandy. If he planned to attend more student parties he would have to gen up on Scottish folk-music. Dorothy's kind of Scots song, of the piano back-up and the full dress kilt, would be less than acceptable here.

Song followed song. Sandy felt tired and sat on the floor with his back to the wall.

He awoke to someone shaking him. The room whirled in a polka around and above his head. In the midst of the rosette he recognised someone. Malcolm!

"Are you all right? Can you make it home?"

Sandy struggled onto numb feet, falling against the wall and bouncing back again. This must be how Roddy felt every Friday night.

"Yes, I'm all right," he whispered with difficulty. Holding his head very high he walked carefully out of the front door. The second flight of stairs came up to meet him unexpectedly and he landed in a heap at the bottom. He picked himself up, in terror that Malcolm had heard his clatter and might witness his indignity. Ignoring a faint twinge in some limb or other he ventured into the clammy mists of the new day. Where . . . Byres Road? When . . . 3 o'clock? Christ, how was he to get home?

The pubs had been five hours shut and Byres Road was almost empty. Only a few stragglers wended a subdued way home from parties, well buttoned-up against the dew.

In Queen Margaret Drive he found a taxi and tumbled in. At the second attempt he got his tongue round his address and sank back on the seat.

"Pandora," he muttered. "A classical name."

And Bacchus slid off the scene, leaving Morpheus in full charge of Sandy.

Next moment, as it seemed, the taxi pulled up, spilling Sandy half onto the floor. An unreal driver held out an insubstantial hand. "One pound ten," said a voice, far away.

Sandy felt in his pocket, drew out three notes, scattered a few coins on the floor, scrabbled in vain to pick them up.

"Ye should get on intae the hoose, son," advised the driver. "Ye've fairly hud a night o' it. Sure ye can manage, noo?"

"'M a'right," slurred Sandy. He kept his eyes staring more and more widely in case he should lose control and they might close, never to open. After a struggle he got the car open and half-fell onto the pavement. As the taxi roared off, the night air hit Sandy. He lurched up the path, failed to make it, and threw up in the big hydrangea pot which his mother kept in the porch. In disgust he wiped his mouth and searched on his person for his keys. Eventually he gained entry and tiptoed inside, sliding along the wall to keep straight.

"Well, now! Just look what the wind blew in!"

Curses! What was she doing, still up? And so loud, too!

"What will darling Mummy say when she sees her lily-white boy?" Jojo smiled. "Little man has had a busy day!"

"Is that you back, dear?" floated from upstairs. "Was it a nice party?"

Somehow he stumbled to Roddy's store of Polomints on the sideboard and peeled one in front of Jojo's laughter. He tried to straighten his eyes out. "Hello, Mum."

"You're awfully late home." She peered at him. "Are you all right, son?"

"Sonny Boy's stocious!" announced Jojo. "Stocious, steaming Sandy."

"You've been drinking." Mum's face loomed large at him.

"Ten out of ten! Dot spots it again!"

Dorothy turned on her. "Is it not time you were in your bed? What are you doing, up this late?"

Jojo shook her head sadly at Sandy. "Like stepfathers," she stressed the plural, "like stepson."

Sandy screwed up his face. The world was so confusing, tonight, or tomorrow or whenever he was at.

Under her nightcream, Dorothy reddened. "Get to bed now."

"I'm going!" Jojo rose and dawdled towards the door. "Better leave the heart-to-heart till tomorrow. That great sodden brain can take no more!"

A drink of water.

Sandy opened his eyes and stared at the ceiling which birled like a tornado, sucking at his head. He reached out and knocked the alarm clock to the floor. Eight-thirty. Sunday. A drink of water. He licked parched lips, padded to the bathroom with pain shooting through his right leg. His ankle was stiff and swollen. As he groped for a glass he knocked down the toothbrush rack. He stooped to pick it up and pain bored through his head this time.

Never again! he thought. If this is what Roddy calls fun

he's welcome to it! Three glassfuls of water later, as he slid back between the sheets, he thought, some company I'll be for Jasmine today! And then, if it weren't for Jasmine I could have a long lie! Then he surrendered to the black tornado from whence dreams came at squint angles.

Two o'clock saw Sandy and Jasmine scrambling on all fours up a scrubby rock. In defiance of the climate she wore a short skirt and the hem bounced prettily against her thighs, fluttering in the breeze, flirting with her movements. When they reached a narrow plateau they spread their anoraks in a clearing in the heather and lay down.

"Look at how wee my bag is now!" They had unburdened themselves of Jasmine's raffia bag full of flasks, boiled eggs and raincoats, and now it was nothing but an orange spot on the bracken belt.

"You can still see the *Maid of the Loch*."

Sandy sat up and followed the white paddle steamer with his eyes. The sun beamed down on the old Scots pines below and from somewhere on the hillside a cuckoo persisted in calling for a mate. Jasmine was a golden profile against the sky. The sun found brown highlights in her hair. Sandy's leg and head had been throbbing all afternoon, and now there was a new ache. He took her hand, kissed it, looked profoundly into her eyes and said,

> *I'll kiss your lips and take your hand*
> *And walk among long dappled grass*
> *And pluck till time and times are done*
> *The silver apples of the moon,*
> *The golden apples of the sun.*

"That's nice. Did you make it up?"

Sandy sighed. Jasmine was so . . . artless. If she would even try sometimes to hide her simplicity! Still, he was unfair.

The lighter parts of English literature, such as Yeats, were reserved for the fun and games of Sixth Year. Jasmine probably thought all poetry was like *Paradise Lost*. Would Ailie recognise it as a quote? Probably not. He must test her when he got home.

"Did you?"

"Did I what?"

"Make it up."

"No."

"What's wrong?"

"Nothing."

From a branch above them a caterpillar descended on a silken thread, landing unfelt on Jasmine's hair. Sandy watched in silence as it pulled itself through the long black strands. When it reached her temple Jasmine touched and squealed. "Och, you . . . you're laughing! Could you not have let on there was a beast in my hair?"

"Beasties in your hair? Really!"

She was vibrant, like an exotic flower. Sandy thought, why fight it? Why try to make it something it's not?

He put his arms round her. She responded with pleasure, lay back and drew him down to her. Her hair, her neck . . . a fragrance filled his senses. He could feel her body, warm and alive, through the thin cotton blouse. His fingers traced the form of her, found the buttons, and nervously undid them. How soft, how . . . when was she going to draw the line? He unhooked her at the back and gently, unbelievingly, lifted . . . was she never going to put the hems on him at all? The touch of her breasts brought a red glaze to his eyes. He rolled away and sat up, looking down the slope, trying to control his breathing, his voice, his thoughts. "I guess we'd better call a halt."

"You don't have to."

"What?" Sandy turned to stare. "You can't mean that."

"I do. We can go all the way if you want to."

Sandy laughed with a terrible unease. "Jasmine! I'm shocked!"

"I thought you'd never get started. All these months . . . these years we've been going about together."

"But we were never going out *like that*. Why didn't *you* start it up if you wanted to?"

"It wasn't up to me."

Poor Jasmine, thought Sandy. It would have been up to a girl like Pandora.

"What would your Dad say?"

"What's he got to do with it?"

"Well, I know Indians have strong views about the virginity of their daughters. . . "

"So you're an expert on Indians too? Is there nothing you're not an authority on?"

"Jasmine. It isn't like you to pick fights!"

"If my Dad was a traditional Indian would I be up this hill with you? Anyway, what he doesn't know won't hurt him." Decisively she slipped off her blouse and bra and lay back with outstretched arms. "When in Rome do as the Romans."

Sandy dared to fondle her and again the flame leapt through him, shocking, blinding. For a moment the lust overcame his terror. Then a third party appeared. Pandora hovered over them, between them, silently mocking their pubescent fumblings. Sandy drew back.

"Must be the first time Scotland's been held up as an example of the permissive society!" To his annoyance his voice was shaking. "I suppose everything's relative!"

Jasmine sat up angrily. "I'm letting you make love to me and you theorise about society! Do you not want me?"

"Want you?" His fantasies, his dreams, half-heard sniggery jokes in the school cloakroom, the *Song of Solomon* Chapter Seven, Andrew Marvell's *To a Coy Mistress*, the *Playboy* Iain

Nicholson had brought and passed round the other boys (Sandy had taken his own private look at the thing in the toilets while Iain was having school dinners) . . . Jasmine's living, breathing person so close. "Oh, I want you with all my heart."

"Well, go on and do it, then. Just be gentle, try and not hurt me." Jasmine's face set bravely.

For an unworthy moment he thought, Pandora is probably a woman of experience. This is my chance to get even with her.

Then he thought of the importance of the thing. "I can't."

"What?" In Jasmine's book, apparently, boys never said No.

"You're only fifteen. It's against the law."

"Who's to know about it?"

"You might get pregnant."

"It's a safe time of the month."

"The Safe Period?" Sandy snorted nervously.

A tear glistened on Jasmine's long lashes. "You don't want me."

"Oh, but I do, I do, I do." He thrust her clothes at her. "Put them on. You'll get the cold."

Jasmine buried her face in her blouse and burst into tears. Sandy patted her shoulder. "It's just that I'm scared too."

Jasmine broke off in mid-sob and stared at him. "What of? It wouldn't be sore for you, would it?"

"It's the responsibility. The guilt." He laughed.

"And you said my Dad was a Puritan!"

"It's different. Indians are mostly uptight over sex for the woman. Scots are fairer – both genders are ridden with guilt!"

Jasmine pulled on her clothes. "I thought I was offering a great gift."

"You were. I'll never forget the honour you did me."

"You make it sound as if we're splitting up."

"Now, how can you think that?"

"We won't, not for years and years, will we?"

"Oh, Jasmine." He rubbed his cheek on her hair. "What am I to do with you?"

In the evening, when he returned, Ailie was practising her scales. Jojo laid down her book as he entered.

"Enter Love's Young Dream, Stage Left!"

"Cut it out, Jojo. I'm not in the mood."

"O, Sandy, Sandy, wherefore art thou Sandy. . . ? A Jasmine by any other name would smell as sweet."

"Leave him alone," said Ailie.

"Aw! Wee sister leaps to the defence!" Jojo crossed to the piano and closed the lid. "But I'm her sister too, though you'd never think it." She drew out one of Ailie's long pale plaits. "Hair like old rope. Who'd think she was as closely related to me as to you?"

"No she isn't."

"Think not?" Jojo ruffled Sandy's hair.

Ailie said, "Where's the *TV Times?* There's something coming on STV I thought might be worth a look."

"She knows," said Jojo. "Don't you, Ailie?"

"What the hell are you on about?"

"Ailie knows a lot of things. Don't know *how* she knows, but she does. She's not nearly as dim as she looks."

"Why are you such a troublemaker?" asked Sandy. "A disgrace to the Lorimers."

"You should establish your right to my father's name before you use it against me."

"Here it is. A documentary about Glasgow trams."

"You . . . toad of the first order!"

"And you're a bastard!" Jojo smiled. "I mean that most sincerely."

A long pause. Jojo stopped smiling. "Ask your mother.

Ask Ailie. Ask even Roddy. Bet you're the only one here who doesn't know."

Sandy swept out and down the hall. They heard the kitchen door opening. Voices. Sandy's then Dorothy's.

"You should have broken it more gently," said Ailie.

Jojo grinned, put her finger to her lips and crept out, to hover behind the kitchen door.

"How dare she talk to you like that!"

"You don't look surprised."

"I've long since given up being surprised by anything that little madam comes out with."

"Is it true?"

"Is what true, dear?"

"It is true, isn't it?"

"Sandy, I. . . "

"Why didn't you tell me, Mum? Leaving it to Jojo, of all people. . . "

A knot of excitement seized Jojo until she nearly burst in a gurgle of glee.

"If old Joe wasn't my father, who was?"

Somewhere the telephone rang and was answered.

"Sandy, you've always been a credit to me. I've . . . had children by three different men, and your father was the only one worth knowing."

"Knowing?" sneered Sandy. "In the Biblical sense?"

"Don't." Through the crack in the door Jojo saw Dot lay her hand on Sandy's arm and saw him shake it away. She swallowed a chortle.

"You should have told me, Mum."

Dorothy sighed. "Your father's name is Stanislaus Karpinski."

"A Pole?"

"He lives in Greenock and is married with three children."

"How do you know? Are you still in touch?"

Ailie came in. "That's Jasmine on the phone for you, Sandy."

"Tell her to get lost! I can't understand why you never told me! And you told Jojo?"

"I never told Jojo! Even Roddy doesn't. . . "

"Ailie knows! Jojo knows! Everybody. . . "

"I'm sure I don't know how Jojo found out. As for Ailie . . . well, sometimes I wonder. . . "

"Does my father know about me?"

"Not yet. . . "

"Why keep it such a secret? Are you ashamed of me?"

"You know you're the part of my life I'm most proud of. . . "

"Then why, for Christ's sake. . . "

"Sandy, when you were born attitudes weren't as free as they are now."

"Attitudes! God help you!" Sandy stormed out, throwing Jojo against the wall. She called, "Sandy, I never knew you cared!" after his disappearing back.

Dorothy came out, grim beneath her make-up. "Always ready to stick a knife in the first back turned, aren't you?"

"You laid yourself open," said Jojo. "You should have told him long ago."

Ailie was coming into her seventeenth summer. Old enough to see an X film, to stay alone without a baby-sitter, to marry with or without parental consent, to remember the Thatcher Government, her own grandchildren and into the next century. Dorothy marked the passage of time by making an appointment with the doctor to find out why her daughter was not "maturing" as she should.

While Ailie was hopelessly sitting an 'O' Grade Maths paper for which she had last studied a decade before, to the east and across the water, where the great yards still sucked in thousands of men every morning and poured them out again at dusk, Tony turned his job into the lathe. The water poured, the curls of metal rolled off as the sweat rolled off his forehead and the thoughts churned against the bang-bang-bangs of the caulker-burners to his left. He remembered his talk with Maw two days before, when he'd announced that Senga was coming to tea again.

"I don't know, Tony. It seems to me you could do a bit better than her."

"Ah'm no marryin the lassie yet! Gie's time!"

(A pang of guilt, here, as he recalled the date, when they'd made a trip round a back-court, and he'd spread his coat on the ground, and. . . )

"Just you watch yoursel, son." (If his mother ever found out. . . ) "Mind, I've nothing against her. She seems a nice enough wee girl, even if she isn't of the True Faith."

"Aw Ma! Don't drag that into it! Ye don't even go every Sunday yourself."

"I know it isnae supposed to matter much nowadays. . . "

"Anyhow, her folks urnae real Proddies. Her auld man supports the Jags."

"I said I wasnae holding religion against her. That's no the main thing."

"Whit is?"

"She's no our type. The way she talks. . . "

"The same wey ah talk!"

"Uch, but it's different for a girl. The things she says, the way she decks hersel out . . . I feel you could get a nicer type of girl."

"Ever since Jojo showed up you've had pretensions!"

"It's no that."

"Aye it is. Anyway, ye don't need tae gie it a thought. Ah'm no settlin doon fur a long time yet." (It'll be all right. I've been careful, and I'll go on being careful, each time. I know my responsibilities to a girl like Senga. Apart from anything else, to end up with an in-law like Agnes would be a fate worse than death.)

At half-past four the whistle blew, the big gates opened and the Govan streets swam with men again, Tony among them. Back in the west, Sandy took off his school uniform and dressed very carefully – new corduroy jacket, trousers of a different colour of corduroy, open-necked Paisley-patterned shirt – before taking the bus down to the Rubaiyat pub in Byres Road.

Roddy had to go to an overnight teachers' conference at the Seamill Centre. His own licence had been taken away for six months. To his amazement Dorothy volunteered to take the afternoon off work and drive him down.

They took the inland route, winding farmland roads, hitting the coast only at Ayr. Seamill was a bunch of solid, even stately bungalows, one of them belonging to Glasgow Corporation Education Department, who owned the school Roddy taught in (subsidised snobbery, it was called in some quarters). Dorothy braked at the foot of the winding drive. Good for his legs to make it up the brae on his own. She remained in the car as he got out and opened the boot for his case.

"Well, cheerio, then." Her foot was already feeling for the clutch.

"Thanks for the lift." Roddy smiled down at her. "It was good of you. I could have gone in the bus, but it was nicer like this."

"I'll pick you up again tomorrow night." Dorothy quelled a pang of guilt.

"And don't worry about me. They've got a bar, but I'll behave myself."

She roared away, watching his figure dwindle in her mirror

and in her mind. Out of bourgeois Seamill, and into raucous Largs.

"Awfy nice toma'a soup, this, Mrs Lorimer."

"It's just tinned."

"Aye, that's the kind ah like." Senga took a few more spoonfuls and sat back apologetically. "Is it okay if ah jist leave that wee bit?"

"Certainly, m'dear." Maria started to take the dishes away.

"Whit's the main thing?" beamed Tony.

"Your favourite. Lasagne." For the first time, Maria smiled on Senga. "A real Italian treat for you, dear."

"Ah don't usually take foreign food. Is it okay if ah gie it a bye?"

"You cannae dae without your tea!" cried Maria. "Have a wee bit to taste it. It's lovely lasagne, toasted over wi cheese."

"Jist leave her, Ma," advised Tony. "She'll be aw right."

"She's got to have something." Maria took a deep breath. "What else would you like? I've got eggs, tomatoes, bread. . . "

"Chips?" suggested Senga brightly. "Mebbe Tony could go oot fur chips fur me, eh Tony?"

"Aye, okay, well." After a brief ignoble moment Tony rose and went for his jacket.

"Just chips? What about fish? Pudding?"

"Don't like fish. Jist chips." When Tony had gone, Senga went on, "We're aw like this in ma hoose. Thurr aboot three things we like. Cracks ma mammy up, sometimes."

"Maybe if you *tried* some other kinds of food. . . "

"Naw, it widnae make nae difference. See Linda, ma big sister, well wan time ma mammy made hur take a haill big Chinese cerry-oot an she wis awfy awfy no weel efter it. She boked it aw ower the new 3-piece suite, so she did, an it wisnae even peyed fur yet. Ye shoulda saw ma mammy – she went sperr."

"Oh, well, I won't chance you with the lasagne, then," said Maria primly.

The restaurant at Nardini's was different from the café. Here was a vast hall of worn splendour, yellow endless walls from which old paintings regarded the diners. The first class saloon of a liner in the age of elegance.

Dorothy and Stan drank each other across the table. They were fifteen-year-olds on a first date, Romeo and Juliet, hearts entangled down the decades, Antony and Cleopatra. They tingled in anticipation, and sparkled with the wine.

To Dorothy, his face was young and smooth. The sea wind had tanned over the lines of the years, and with his modern thick hairstyle he seemed fresher than in days gone by. Infinitely fresher than yellow Roddy.

To Stan, she had matured like good whisky. Her mop of curls had ripened into a leonine harvest, and her face was alive with knowledge. He thought fleetingly of his short-legged wife, and reached for the mint sauce.

On the way to the guest house they stopped the car near the beach and went down to the black edge of the ocean. On a headland a lighthouse pulsated white. They were alone in the breeze.

After a few kisses they strolled back to Dot's car. No use in rushing. At their age they knew that the expectation was the best part.

The guest house was white-harled and crow-stepped, a piece of Scottish primness. Tea and shortbread fingers were served in the lounge in the company of a Dutch hitch-hiker, two elderly ladies and several scores of framed family photos on top of the piano. Dorothy rose and browsed amongst these ghosts, noting how the landlady's heavy eyebrows and big grey eyes cropped up again and again, backwards in sepia and forwards in colour. She rested her eyes on Stan and came to a decision.

Upstairs, the room was pink and unheated. Dorothy shivered slightly as she started to undo the neck of her blouse.

"I'll warm you, Mrs Schmidt," promised Stan, already in bed.

Dorothy laughed. "I had to explain your accent. Don't expect they know their Krauts from their Poles."

Without shyness, confident in her body, Dorothy stripped and slipped between the ice-cold sheets. Her feet found the hot water bottle, and in a moment, her arms found Stan.

Afterwards, she rose to put on her nightie. Sleeping nude was difficult in coastal bedrooms, even in May.

"Amazing," said Stan.

"What is?"

"Three children, and no stretch-marks!"

Dorothy laughed quickly. "You say the most romantic things. Just luck, I assure you. No merit of mine." She got back into bed and Stan put out the light.

"Stan."

"Yes?"

"Ask me about my children."

"Not now, dear. I'm tired."

"Ask me about my elder son."

"What do you mean?"

"Ask me his full name."

Stan sighed. "What's his name?"

"Alexander Stanley Lorimer."

"Stanley!" He chuckled. "Now, that's surely a compliment."

"Ask me," she cleared her throat, "when he was born."

For a full minute the two watches, on separate bedside tables, ticked away the silence of the night. Abruptly Stan switched on the lamp and faced Dorothy. "Why did you never tell me?"

"I don't know." Now it seemed incredible that she had not told him at once. "Over these two years we met so irregularly. The time was never right."

"What!"

"And before that I thought you were in Poland."

"What's he like?"

"Sandy? Och, you'd be proud of him, Stan. He's got your brains, all right. Top of his class – an all-rounder!"

"I was a late developer," grunted Stan. "A bit of a duffer at school." Suddenly he turned, put his arms around Dorothy and burst into tears.

All over the city, love was in the air. Except for Ailie.

"I don't want to go to the doctor," she told Dorothy after her mother returned from the business trip to Carlisle. "It'll be all right."

"I changed from a child into a woman at fourteen," Dorothy informed her, "and girls are at least a year forward of that nowadays."

"So I'll be seventeen. What's the big deal?"

Her mother was adamant. That night Ailie avoided the doctor's appointment the only way left to her . . . and woke up, still flowery, hippy, pop-arty but indeed a woman – in 1968.

# 15

THE ACTIVITIES of June 5th 1968 – Jojo left her West-end flat to attend a reunion at Langside College, where she had at last amassed the Highers necessary to save the family honour, and where over lunch she was persuaded to come along to an anti-Vietnam demonstration the following week. Sandy, fresh from France, trimmed his newly-fledged beard, dressed carefully in denim bomber jacket and jeans and blue peaked cap and set off to reach the Rubaiyat as soon as it opened. Nigel went to school, but stayed only until the interval as he and his friend Brian found better entertainment in the street. Ailie also went to school, where she told eight fellow-pupils and two teachers that Bobby Kennedy would be assassinated that day by a man called Sirhan Sirhan. When the news came over the radio, instead of being impressed, the others appeared to avoid her, as if she had done a conjuring trick in bad taste, or even had some involvement with the murder.

Not to worry. She had an appointment, an appointment of which she could remember the outcome. Was it worth keeping.? Could Fate ever be cheated?

Bang, bang, bang. Thank God he was a turner and not a

burner. He could never stand a racket like that. But soon, maybe, he'd be hearing a new racket. . . Oh, hell's bell's! The whistle went and for the first time (but not, alas, for the last time) Tony was reluctant to down tools.

Senga was at the gates to meet him, eyebrows pointing anxiously upwards, tight skirt four inches above her chubby knees.

Tony acknowledged her presence by the merest nod. He turned up his collar and hurried on. Senga scurried after.

"Well?"

"It's righ' enough. Positive, they said."

Tony closed his eyes momentarily. His pace barely slackened.

"Haud oan, Tony," puffed Senga. "Ah kin hardly keep up."

"Sorry." Tony faced her. "We need tae talk. C'moan tae the cafe."

Installed in one of the booths, over a cup of coffee for Tony and an iced Irn Bru for Senga, she looked at him searchingly. "Whit we gonnae dae?"

"Whit can we dae?" Tony stirred his coffee again and again, obsessively. "We'll jist huv tae get hitched." (There. It's out. What's said cannot be unsaid. The die is cast. But that it has to be Senga! To throw my lot forever in with her, to join her set, to tie myself to her and to . . . her mother . . . ) To get his mind off Agnes he looked up again at Senga. What had he seen in her? Why had he gone with her all these years? Was there anything special, anything to mark her out at all from the usual run of scruffs, of hairies, who hung about closemouths being slagged and slagging back at the boys? Except that she was crazy about him. . .

Senga was trying to conceal a sigh of relief. "That's okay then, I suppose. Ur ye . . . dae ye mind awfy much?"

"Course ah mind. Who waants tae be merried an a Dad

at my age?"

"Lotsa folk! Ah know boys that got merried at *sixteen*, an no jist because they hud tae!"

"Aye. Well, ah'm no like that."

"Uch, Tony, ah don't waant tae force ye intae nothin. . . " Senga began to cry, and fumbled in her bag for a hankie.

"Here." Tony gave her his. "C'moan, it's not as bad as all that." (To be a married man, a Dad, head of a household, sole support of three people, the very giver of life to at least one, maybe more . . . not that bad.)

"Dae ye mean it? Ye're no mad at me?"

"Course ah'm no mad at ye. It takes two tae tango!" Tony pulled her up and over to the counter. "Heh, Belle!" Isabella, one of Uncle Luigi's many daughters, came out of the back shop. "Belle, Senga an me's gonnae get hitched!"

Half-past four. A long, scrubbed shining corridor, with crisp nurses striding up and down, carrying their wholesome mystique, their professional enigma as an atmosphere.

"The Director will see you now."

A neat little office, brown desk topped with black leather. A mail tray, a vase of pink carnations, a good Parker pen. In the corner a grey filing cabinet.(Will I ever flick knowledgeably through these files, or is there no chance?) A bright window with a view over to the University.

A round woman, cheeks aglow as if she had lived all her life on country fare and sea breezes.

"Take a seat, Miss Lorimer." She smiled. "So you want to be a nurse?"

"Yes." (What's the use? What am I doing here?)

"What attracts you to the nursing profession?"

(Crisp uniform. Brisk authority. Healthy glows. Angel of Mercy. Reading about Koch and Pasteur in *The Microbe Hunters*.) "I want to help people."

"Indeed? Well, if you want to help people you could not find a better way than through a nursing career. Now, let me see. It's the Registered General Nurse training that interests you."

"The three year course, yes."

"It's much more than a three year course, you know. The RGN is the very backbone of the profession. You would have a great deal to learn on the academic side, as well as practical nursing."

"I don't mind that."

"Let me see. You stayed on for a sixth year at school, but still sat only five 'O' grades when you left."

"I'm a bit slow when sitting exams."

"There's no room for slowness in nursing."

"I know." (Should I just get up and go, now? What's the point?)

"What about your outside interests? We have quite a good social life here. Do you take part in sport?"

"I quite enjoy it," lied Ailie "but I'm not very good at it."

"What do you mean?"

"I'm a bit too slow."

The Director frowned slightly. "That's the second time you've mentioned being slow."

(Here we go!)

"Is there any reason for your being so slow?"

Sandy wandered along the banks of the Kelvin, guitar in hand. Now and then he stopped and stared gloomily down to where the trees dipped into the gurgling waters. This afternoon had been like all the others. He had gone to talk to Pandora, to demonstrate that he shared her opinions, shared her knowledge, shared her fervour. He had ended up sharing her company with five others, all apparently of more interest to her than he was.

At last the talk had turned to music, whereupon Pandora for once took a back seat, pleading tone-deafness. In despair Sandy had volunteered his own vaudeville experience, making it out to be altogether trendier than it was, allowing them to visualise the old folks' homes as folk-clubs, *The Banks of Loch Lomond* as *The Banks of Sicily*.

One particularly obnoxious fellow in an oh-so-arty long black coat and floppy hat, a fellow who had grinned into Dora's face all evening, turned his attention to Sandy. "You couldn't be a folk-singer," he informed him. "You're not intoxicated enough!"

"If that's all it takes," Sandy's reply was icy, "you should have your own show on TV by now."

To his horror Dora took sides. "No, but I see what Mike's getting at."

"You do?"

"A folk-singer should be a wild man, extrovert, boisterous, hard-drinking."

"And forget all the words after verse one."

"Well, part of the skill lies in exerting control over the songs even through a bucketful of pints. You must strike a balance between wild life and repertoire. You're too. . . "

". . . inhibited," supplied Mike.

"I was going to say, formal."

Shortly after this Sandy had upped and left. Dora had been the only one to raise her eyes and wave.

Now night was falling, and he had but one chance left, as he saw it, to redeem himself. It would take a bit of courage, but to a veteran of debates and music-hall, not much.

Sandy reached the close, went through to the back court and positioned himself under what he knew to be Pandora's window. He took a deep breath and started to strum.

*Au clair de la lune, mon amie Dora*

> *Prête-moi tes levres pour baisser un peu.*
> *Ma chandelle est vivante, j'ai beaucoup de feu*
> *Ouvre-moi ta porte, pour l'amour de Dieu.*

When there was no response, he began again, more slowly and clearly.

> *Au clair de la lune, mon amie Dora. . .*

She appeared at the window and flung up the sash. "Sandy!" Her face was pink.

Sandy laid down the guitar and dropped to one knee, clasping his hands over his heart. "Oh, Pandora. You are ill-named. You should be Pallas Athene, goddess with the clear grey eyes and sparkling mind. Hearken to your acolyte, O Deity beneath the moon. Break not his heart. Consent once more to rove with him through the mazes of Kelvingrove, to taste of the golden apples of the sun, to feast upon the harvests of Dionysus. . . "

Pandora's flatmate, Bernadette, appeared behind her. "Where did you pick him up?"

"Oh, I don't know. I don't know."

"Must be stoned out his mind."

"I don't think he is."

"What if Reilly hears?"

"I think he sleeps towards the front of his flat."

"How embarrassing anyway. Make him go away."

"How?" Pandora made no move to try.

"What about the plant sprayer? Full of water?"

"Maybe." Pandora had a wide grin on her face.

Sandy, his own face burning in the night air, lifted the guitar again. This time he adopted a more modern air, *Windmills of Your Mind.*

"For Christ's sake shut him up!" hissed Bernadette. "It's

11.30. We'll have old Reilly on our tops."

Pandora leaned out of the window. "Sorry to cut you off in your prime, but our landlord lives in the upstairs flat."

Sandy completed the first verse of his song, pleased with the melodic tone of his own voice. "Can I come in?"

Pandora disappeared for a moment, then reappeared. "All right. Just for a wee while."

Bernadette shook her head and went to bed muttering, "You're crazy!"

Pandora took Sandy into her own room, which had a heap of leaflets in the middle. "Here. You can help with the folding."

"What are they?"

"Monthly newsletter the Branch has started. The idea is to keep interest alive between elections."

"I was hoping to talk to you."

"So? You don't need your mouth to fold. Get those mitts going."


When Ailie saw the moon rise over the university tower she knew she had been wandering in Kelvingrove Park for hours. Coming up Kelvin Way, glad of the shadows which hid her sorrow, she was angry at the tower, looming down on its hill on those failures, those lesser beings barred from its Gothic portals. Lofty. Aloof. Sandy's kind of place.

Sandy. Her mother. Overflowing with success, health and good fortune. Taking it for granted and surprised that anyone could be different.

(Tonight is the night it all joins up. Tonight I go and cry on Jojo's shoulder and tomorrow I leave home forever to live with her. On Tuesday there will be another time-lapse.)

Slowly she slipped into the direction of Otago Street, of Jojo's close, Jojo's dunny.

# 16

THE CARPET was still pink, but there were more Busy Lizzies. Busy Lizzies always do tend to take over. So do spider plants. A big tinsel Christmas tree stood in the corner, bedecked with fairy lights and surveilled by a drunken looking fairy with slightly tarnished wand.

Ailie raised her head off the desk just as the Morning Roll came into the room.

"Have you been having a snooze? Good idea. I'm a believer myself in catnaps."

"Is that . . . have I . . . is this you just finished hypnotising me?" gasped Ailie.

"Hypnotising you? Goodness, no. We finished that course of treatment last year."

"So where are we now? When?"

The Morning Roll smiled gently. "The Year of Our Lord 1978. The hind end of it."

Ailie was deflated. "I thought for a minute the bits were starting to join up," she said. "Last time I recall being here was in 1977. You hypnotised me and I woke up in 1961."

"A lot of water has passed under bridges since then. You stopped treatment for a bit – but then you said the changes were coming too fast and so you came back to me."

"Did the hypnosis achieve anything?"

"You seemed to see a lot of strange people around. You talked to some of them. That was all."

"The Faces," said Ailie dully. "I suppose it was inevitable they would get in on the act."

Sandy usually avoided political arguments at work, preferring to keep the atmosphere harmonious. However, when Walter announced that he did not know which way to vote in the coming referendum, Sandy was honour bound to do his utmost unnoticeably to influence him.

His own opinion, he knew, would be contaminated with Scottish Nationalism. He had heard that the explanatory pamphlet issued by the Citizen's Advice Bureau was subtly biased towards the Yes side. Through driving rain up Bath Street he squelched, past an official billboard bearing a red triangle and the proclamation WARNING! THIS BILL IS DANGEROUS! VOTE NO! He procured the leaflet, found it to be indeed politically sound, passed it to Walter. Next day Walter confided in him, "I've read the pamphlet you got me and I've decided to vote No."

Sandy's school was not used for voting, and so he did not get a holiday out of Referendum Day. However, he used his every free moment in a masochistic listening to the earpiece of his transistor radio.

The last period of the day was a 'Please Take', and not in his own subject. The class he knew well, and in fact he spent three minutes in the toilet, examining his face for signs of weakness, before taking his place in wait. The door opened and two-thirds of 3P stormed in. The last third, he knew, would straggle in in twos and threes during the next ten minutes, doing their best to disrupt the lesson.

Two of the worst boys did not go to their seats at all, but crossed in front of him and perched on the low window-sill.

"Get down off there!" he growled. No response. Next, he tried barking the order. One of the boys, James Paterson, slowly turned.

"You talkin tae me?"

"You know I'm talking to you."

"Ah'm no the only wan. How dae ye no tell Stewpot tae get doon an a?"

It was all a game – to them. (God, what mountains 3P made out of every molehill, trials of strength out of trivia.)

"Stuart!" Sandy poked him with his finger.

"Heh, mind the material, huh?"

The class was marginally easier to handle than usual, probably because that awful boy MacPherson was still absent. Unfortunately MacPherson was the bearer of a Red Tab Card – the mark of the dogger – and so on Monday Sandy had been forced to send out his attendance card. Clearly his days of 3P minus MacPherson were numbered.

Sandy covered the back row, giving out one book between two and ignoring complaints. He wondered if the Orkney and Shetland result had declared yet. He had a feeling that Orkney and Shetland would not go for Yes, not after all the tale about Westminster caring for them more than a hypothetical Edinburgh Assembly would, and . . . THUMP!

He knew before he cast his eyes behind him what he would see. Sure enough, all the books were piled tapsalteerie on the floor and the back row had bland smirks on their faces.

Sandy glanced at the clock on the back wall. Twenty minutes gone. Another sixty minutes to get through. He considered whether to ask one of the culprits to pick up the books so that he could retrieve a small part of his dignity. ("Uch, ah'm no pickin them up! Ah'm no yer teaboy! It wisnae me that flung them!") He retraced his steps, redistributed the books, this time taking care, like a lion-tamer, never to turn his back on the known trouble-makers.

"Turn to page 23."

Five or six did so at once, about ten got around to it during a lull in their conversation, and the rest ignored the request.

The door flew open, so hard that it bounced off the side wall. Three members of 3P swaggered in, to cheers and applause. They swirled to their desks, sweeping two other desks clear of books and pens as they did so.

"Where have you been?" Sandy went through the ritual.

"Lavvy."

"Gettin ma jaiket aff a boy."

"Hud tae see the janny."

The poem Sandy had chosen was one that he thought might possibly capture some of their imaginations – *Black Friday* by James Copeland. He started to read aloud, and was interrupted at once by a chorus of "Whit page? Whit page?" Sandy repeated the page number in a loud voice and began again. This time he ignored all questions, merely raised his voice above them. He was about one third through the poem when the door opened and all nonsensical interventions ceased instantly, indicating the majestic entrance of Mr Gilmour, Principal of Guidance.

"Mr Lorimer, has Billy MacPherson put in an appearance today?"

"No, he hasn't." ( – trying to control the lightness in his voice.)

"Hm. I hope you've taken action."

"The card went out on Monday."

"And it hasn't come back yet? This is most unsatisfactory."

"Isn't it!" ( – hoping he'd stay longer, perhaps chat to the class; use up a bit more of the horribly long double period.)

"I don't expect he'll show up now, but if he does, be sure to send him straight to me!"

"I will, Mr Gilmour!" (If Billy did appear, sending him away again would be pure pleasure!)

Mr Gilmour walked out – and the noise level rose to meet him like a wave of energy. Sandy began reading again, but the fragile train of events in the poem was broken for good. It might have been the very kind of thing to appeal to them, written in their language, about folk they knew. Sandy's voice carried on reading the meaningless words to the end. Discussions were always abortive where 3P were concerned, and after a monologue from himself to the backs of their heads, and a barren pause for questions, he told them to select a stanza and draw a picture to illustrate it.

Four o'clock! The bell rang. 3P rose like a blanket, overturning two desks, and made for the door. Sandy began gathering up the books. Another copy was missing. He wondered if any more regions had declared yet. In his stomach he now knew that the Yes majority had tripped over the 40% hurdle. He took a Milk of Magnesia tablet.

In the corridor he met Lorraine Bell of 3P.

"Heh, Sur, thon wis a great poem ye gied us the day."

"*Black Friday*? What did you like about it?"

"Sur, ah liked the slang in it."

"It's not slang. It's Glasgow dialect."

"Aye. When Mrs Ross comes back ah'm gonnae ask hur tae gie us mair Scotch poems."

A shaft of gold in a Black Thursday.

Pandora had taken a day's annual leave for Referendum Day and spent most of it handing out leaflets in the street. At six o'clock she was relieved. On her way home she dropped in at the Blythswood Cottage and made her way pointedly to the public bar. Years ago another woman had thrown her out for being the wrong sex. Now, with the law on her side, she ignored custom and tradition to pour a whisky down her throat. She glared belligerently between sips at the men standing around the bar or seated at the tables, daring them to cast an improper look or thought in her direction, but it was early in the evening and no one was drunk enough. If she wanted an argument she would have to start it herself.

"Did you read recently," she announced to two fellows at the next table, "that the Scottish average IQ has gone down?"

The one in the beard turned on her a look of mild surprise. "Izzat a fact?"

"Uhuh. It used to be 105 and now it's 96. The best have left. Only those too apathetic or too unwanted to get anywhere else have stayed."

"And which lot dae ye include yersel in?" he responded.

"Neither, I'm here because I'm committed to Scotland."

"There ye are, then. Therr another group already. No that I believe in a thon IQ rubbish, masel."

"Neither did I, till today. Now I see the numbers that think the people of their own country are less capable than the most powerless local authority."

"Aw, it's the Referendum ye're on aboot, ur ye?"

"Is it not uppermost in your mind? It should be."

"It's the slippery slope to separatism," asserted the navy sweatshirt.

Pandora drained her glass. "What's wrong with independence, anyway? Plenty of other countries do it – have it."

"Aye, aye, now it's aw comin oot!" grinned Beardie. "That's whit she really wants. When she says devolution, she really means separatism."

"Another o' the same?" Sweatshirt rose and headed for the bar. Gloomily, Pandora surrendered herself to their hospitality and their dialectics.

It was considerably later that she put the key in the lock. Sandy looked up from the armchair, unsmiling. "Back at last? I was beginning to wonder if you'd decided to end it all, or something."

Pandora regarded him as she would a No voter. "You cold fish, how could get by without a drink on a day like this?"

"Look, Pandora, they're not worth it. They're cringing, apathetic, beggarly remnants."

"They have an inferiority complex," Pandora declared, "bred in by years of propaganda masquerading as education, colonialism dressed as culture."

"The question is, is it a complex, or are they just inferior?"

"They? What's this, They?" blazed Pandora. "It's our people. Everything we attribute to them we attribute to ourselves."

"For God's sake! Get it in perspective! Plenty countries are struggling against genocidal empires and nobody steps in. Who'd take an interest in a wee region that's too shy and backward to even vote itself in as a nation?"

"But we did vote ourselves a Parliament!" roared Pandora. "And we are a nation!"

Sandy shook his head. "It's no use arguing with you when you've had a skinful."

"What the hell do you suggest we do, Mr Cucumber?"

Sandy wiped his cheek where a speck of spittle had hit it. "I suggest we go for a curry."

Pandora's eyes stood out at him so that he could see rings of white around the blue. The thought crossed his mind that she had an over-active thyroid.

"Is that all you can think about," she breathed, "when we have a Yes majority to build on?"

"Dora, you're overwrought. And smashed."

"What I want to know is, why aren't *you* overwrought?"

"Would that help? Tears and gum-gnashing never solved anything yet."

"Sandy, you're an emotional illiterate." She slammed out of the flat again, and Sandy, who had agonised through the day with his moods tied to the numbers game, who had almost wept in public, who had looked forward to mutual comfort with Pandora, all to be called an emotional illiterate, watched her from the window as she disappeared round the corner.

He still could go a curry.

He lifted the phone and dialled. "Jasmine? It's me."

Ailie heard Roddy was in hospital. On Referendum Day, when the kids were off school, she took them round to see him. He was in a bed up the middle of the ward – no window, no flowers, no shelter.

"Uncle Roddy, it's Ailie." She patted his hand. "How you keeping?"

His eyes opened. Milky-blue eyes in an off-white face. An old, unloved man. Yet, not so old. Dorothy, scarcely younger, was surely in her prime.

"I'm sorry."

She bent low over him to catch his words. "Sorry? You've nothing to be sorry for. Look, I've brought the children."

His eyes flickered over them. "Fine wee boys." He stared down the ward a bit until she began to wonder if he had forgotten she was there.

Crawfie tugged her arm. "The sweeties."

"Look, Uncle." She fumbled in her bag. "I've brought you some Ferguzade. It's just like Lucozade. And a wee box of chocolates."

"Thanks." His voice was distant.

Crawfie said, "Is he going to open them?"

"That's up to Uncle Roddy," Ailie rebuked him.

Roddy murmured something she could not catch.

"Have they been gving you tablets or something, Uncle?

You seem a bit. . . "

"Drunk, eh? No such luck."

"Uncle Roddy, when are you going to open the sweeties?"

"Crawford! That's enough!"

"That's all right. Open the box for the wee ones. Let them take all they want. Least I can do."

"They can have *one* each." Ailie opened the box. "The rest are for you."

Roddy's eyes wandered back to her face. "Do you believe in the hereafter?"

"I don't know. I hope there's a good. . . "

"Do you believe in the Justice of the Almighty?"

"Uncle Roddy!" She tried to laugh. "Are you turning religious in your old age?"

"Ah, but there you're wrong. I always was. Nobody knew that. Nobody ever knew. I never . . . no. Can't apportion blame. I was a grown man. When I was a child I spake as a child. I was brought up Free Kirk, you know. Aye, the Auld Kirk, the Cauld Kirk . . . God, I wish my mother was here the day."

"My mother?"

"*My* mother." He gripped her hand. "You never answered the question."

"I don't think I do, Uncle Roddy. There's too much natural unfairness about."

His grip slackened and he turned his face away. His lips moved, but all Ailie caught was the word, father.

"You were a good father to us when we were children," she said. "I mind you once taking us all to see *Peter Pan* in the Alhambra. I asked you how Peter Pan was able to fly and you said it was magic dust. I believed you right up until the interval, when Sandy spoilt it by saying it was done with wires."

"But I wasn't your father."

"Of course you weren't. We knew that. But you were the biggest father in our lives, all the same."

"No, no. Never say that."

"But it's true. We all bore you affection."

"Undeserved."

"Maybe you took a drink. But in your own way you were a better parent to us than Mummy was . . . to Jojo."

Roddy's lip curled slightly.

"In fact, you were a better father, a more real father than. . . "

*"Don't say that ever again!"* He rose half out of the bed. "I mean it!" He broke off in a spasm of coughing. David began to cry and Crawfie to giggle.

"All right! Don't get het-up!"

Roddy sank back on the pillow. For a long time he said nothing. Ailie pacified David, gave Crawford his crayons to draw with, chattered to Roddy about Sandy, Pandora, the referendum. She wondered if she should take this last opportunity to tell him about her own strangeness, but he seemed too wrapped in his own world.

"That's why I'm here."

"What's that?"

He waved a contemptuous hand around the ward. "Hardly sixty and washed up in a shoal of geriatrics. Liver, kidneys gone, brain mostly there, eh?" He burst into a tremble, half coughing, half chortling. "I turned against my God."

"That's nonsense. I'll bet the hospital's as full of good church-goers as the streets are of healthy old atheists."

"Ah, but you don't know what I'm on about, do you? No. A secret to my grave. When's Nigel next coming, did you say?"

"Eh? Tomorrow evening, I think."

The nurse approached to say that time was up. Ailie remembered that would be the last time, and that she would have to reinforce her warnings to Nigel. When she got home she tried to phone him, but he was not at home.

On Good Friday Pandora planned to stay the week with her sister in Aberdeen. She told Sandy she would leave her car behind and would catch the 5.30 from Queen Street, straight after work. As the train was leaving the platform, Sandy, his suitcase and Dora's car were already at Jasmine's door. This time the cooking was just as good as last week, and the lovemaking even better. After the foreplay, each time he would tell Jasmine which position he would enjoy her in, and she would get herself into it without a murmur. It was Fantasyland. It was better than a hundred . . . Not that he had ever been with a . . . nor any woman except . . . But he would not think of *her*. Jasmine! Jasmine! Jasmine! Let him only dance on her body, drink in her fragrance, drown in her tresses.

On the Saturday Jasmine donned her only sari, turquoise lavishly trimmed in silver, put on a record and demonstrated Indian dancing for him.

"I took lessons for a while, when I was wee."

"So did my sister. Different kind of dancing, though." Sandy pictured Jasmine pas-de-basquing and reeling with Ailie on the stage. "Your kind of dancing is much more flowing."

"Every movement has a special meaning." She fluttered fingers in his direction. "Like classical ballet."

The singer on the record sounded to Sandy like a five-year-old, but he supposed her the equivalent of a prima donna. He thought he ought to ask more questions about it all, but from the depths of his ignorance did not know what to say. He wondered about Jasmine's Indian side, how strong it was, what caste her father had been. If he had been a Brahmin or something like that, she might be happy to talk about it, but what if he had been an Untouchable? In any case, maybe he'd left all that behind him in the old country. Better not to ask at all.

At the end of the dance Jasmine balanced motionless for an instant and then plumped down on the couch beside him, sari flapping, breath coming in gratifyingly amateurish pants. "There's a movement of the neck I never mastered . . . " she sat upright and tried to demonstrate ". . . a kind of apparent dislocation. . . "

Sandy pressed a finger to his lips. "Never point out your inadequacies to others," he advised. "Show them what you *can* do, and if you're lucky they'll expect no more."

Over dinner Sandy could not help mentioning the referendum. Jasmine said, "I'm not really into politics. I voted Yes in the referendum just because I don't approve of colonialism, I suppose."

"Well, now, that's a political statement in itself. How can you say you're not into politics?"

Jasmine smiled gently. "I mean I'm not into party politics. I think all these politicians are the same – in it for the power."

Sandy parted his lips to continue the discussion, but an image of Pandora superimposed itself over Jasmine's tranquil features, and he forked puff pastry into his mouth instead.

On Easter Sunday Sandy and Jasmine played Easter Bunnies, hiding each other's eggs. Jasmine's, for Sandy, were arty and numerous – red chocolate hearts, cotton-wool chicks and a sugar egg with a cellophane window revealing a pseudo-Victorian scrap. Sandy's, for Jasmine, were few (two) but costly – a big gift-wrapped chocolate effort full of hand-made sweets, a satin egg-shaped box containing a Luckenbooth brooch, two hearts entwined.

On Easter Monday they drove to a country park far off the beaten track of Pandora's West End friends. There Jasmine cooed over waddling ducklings, baby goats and Vietnamese pot-bellied pigs. They rode on a haycart, Jasmine dimpling like a sixteen-year-old. Sandy, feeling all of twenty, remarked on a resemblance between the anxious-looking haycart driver and the pot-bellied pigs, and he and Jasmine giggled over possible family connections for the rest of the ride.

On Tuesday, Jasmine let slip that she had started organ lessons. Sandy took until Wednesday evening to persuade her to display her new accomplishment. Finally she gave him a two-finger rendition of *Campdown Races* from her tutor. He then taught her *Chopsticks* and by the Thursday they had mastered a successful duet. For her homework he scribbled a simplified version of *Sweet and Low*, maximum of two notes at a time on the treble clef and one on the base. He promised that, if she practised, next time they would make a duet of it with himself performing a complex accompaniment.

On the Sunday night they lay as one for the last time. On the Monday, Sandy forced himself up and into his clothes, kissed Jasmine goodbye, drove the car to the flat, leaving it outside in the street for Dora when she arrived, and took the bus to the school. In the evening he returned to find the locks changed and no answer to his battering. Eventually the neighbour across the landing emerged and gave him a note.

> *Dear Sandy,*
> *If it's your things you're wanting, Mini-movals have already delivered them chez the new tootsy-wootsy. If it's your share of the house payments, I've opened up a bank account for the purpose, and you'll have the total in your cold little hand by the end of the year. Pardon me if I wish you bad luck: May the road fall away at your back, and the mouse in your empty meal poke drown herself in her tears.*
>
> *Yours never more, Dora.*
> *PS Deirdre phoned me at work to cancel the visit as she has shingles.*

Sandy hot-footed it to Jasmine's flat. Never did a No 59 bus crawl more painfully up University Avenue; never had Sandy louped so fast through Dowanhill to Partick.

> *I loupt the burn and I ran tae her,*
> *She met me wi goodwill. . .*
> *Oh, the broom, the bonny bonny broom. . .*

. . . rang in his head all the way down the hill. However, the broom was not yet in season, and he found Jasmine in tears, sitting in her living-room surrounded by his familiar objects. How out of place his musical instruments looked there – his Lowland pipes on the wickerwork chair from Oxfam, his guitar dropped amongst a pile of clothes. His books were in two cardboard cartons, his records in a third. The silver bowl he had won for debating had a label tied round one of its handles – TO GO UNDER THE BED. Dora's sense of humour. There was more evidence of it in Jasmine's hand.

"Look what she gave the removal men to pass on to me!" she wept. "It was in an unsealed envelope and they all read it before I got it. You should have heard their sniggery comments, and the way they looked at me! Why did I have to face them all alone?"

"I'm sorry . . . I didn't know till. . . "

"Read it!" She thrust the note at him. "Is this the way you've described me to Pandora?"

> *Dear Jazzy (or do you prefer Minnie?)*
> *I'm donating Sandy's rubbish to you as I*
> *know you'll feel privileged to scrub his*
> *underpants and won't leave the young god to*
> *do his own hard graft as I was wont to do.*
> *He tells me he prefers the dog-like devotion by*
> *day and sexual acrobatics by night which you*

*will provide and I won't, to the conversation
and opinions which I can provide and you
can't. I wonder if in years to come your
quality from the neck down will compensate for
the lack of it from the neck up. If he is the
type I once took him for it won't, but then, he
isn't; I know that now. Anyway, have fun in
the hay, and maybe later when the lust grows
colder you can take a crash course in brains.*

*Yours in haste, Dora
(Previous Owner)*

"Is this what you think of me?"

"Of course not. This is the fury of a woman scorned!"

"But the way she describes . . . It must have come from you! How would she get any sort of impression of me except through you? I'm sure I've never exchanged words with her in my life!"

"Don't you see, Jasmine – she's just throwing out insults at random!"

"But this reference to . . . what have you told her about . . . what we do?"

"Nothing at all! I swear it! Look, she has seen you before."

"Only in the distance. There was that time. . . "

"Then she knows you're a good-looking . . . you're a beautiful girl! The rest is pure conjecture!"

"Then you didn't tell her that?"

"Tell her what?"

"That you preferred me to her?"

Sandy regarded her searchingly. "Well, no, I didn't. How could I? The whole thing was a total secret from her until now! In fact, if . . . " he stopped.

"If she hadn't found out you'd never have told her! I'd

always be just your bit on the side!"

"You know you're much more to me than that. Goodness, I can still remember when I saw you that time in the supermarket . . . I knew then I'd been searching for you ever since we'd parted!"

He reached out for Jasmine and she pulled away from him.

"I don't know anything anymore! Except that all men are liars. You've got half an hour to clear your stuff out of here."

To lose both his women, and his home at once! Sandy gripped her arms and pulled her round to face him. "I don't know anything anymore either, except that now I've found you, I never want to let you go!" He gazed at her, tears brimming in his eyes.

"You mean that?"

Such effort, at his stage, to find a new girlfriend. Too old for discos, disinterested in sport, to have to force himself on the social rounds again. . . "I've never meant anything more in my life."

"Will we get married, then?"

Just for a second, Sandy froze. Then the tears brimmed over and coursed down his cheeks. Jasmine threw her arms around him, staggered to a chair with him, mopped his face, hugged him and rocked him. "Oh, Sandy, Sandy, you're all right now. I've got you. I love you. I've always loved you. It'll work out all right now. Don't cry, Sandy. I love you, Sandy, I adore you. Sandy, do you love me?"

He was 31 years old. To return to live at his mother's, or else to have to start out on the business of house-hunting again, this time all on his own. To case out a new batch of females, wheresoever he could find them, to start up again the superficial flirting, the checking out of common interests, the banter, the wooing, the winching, the heavy relationship theory, the introduction to each others' networks, the tiffs and sensitivities, in a market of shrunken availability, and all against a background of trying to make a real go of his consultancy business and to build on his recent fragile entry to the lecture tour circuit.

"I love you, Jasmine."

# 17

TO POUND YOUR FEET on nothing while the stinking waters of Clyde closed over your face and forced themselves into your mouth, nose and lungs. To jump off a chair forcing your frail neck to snap by the weight of your body. To settle into a steamy bath, slice your wrists and watch your heart pump out life to the last. To swallow a bottle of pills and slide into sleep while the paracetemol destroyed your organs one by one. To climb a pylon, a ladder to Hell.

These were the thoughts which surrounded Nigel as he lay clothed on his bed one forenoon, supposedly writing an essay on *Hamlet*. The play set him on refining ideas of self-slaughter, working out ways to make the pain more bearable, to shorten the transition between life and death, to avert the danger of permanently crippled survival. He pondered on suicide as Agatha Christie must have on homicide, theoretically but logically. One day he might write a book on the subject, although it had probably been tackled before.

He pulled on his shoes – platform soles, a bit dated, but okay for the boys, and his leather bomber jacket, a Christmas present a few years ago from his mother and new father.

His clogs scrunched on the chalky pebbles of the driveway dividing his mother's shaven lawn. He turned along suburban avenues, deserted on a bright Saturday. The children were at the tennis club, the Dads at the golf, the Mums at the coffee mornings. The Kamozans were laden with pink pompoms, weeping, upright or candelabra, the roses were just coming out. Here a garden wafted new-mown lawn, there the scent of early honeysuckle or dying hyacinth.

His path led away from the spacious bungalows and turreted sandstone villas, down a narrow passage between two walls. Here the houses were identical four-in-a-blocks with two doors to the front leading to the upstairs flats, and the ground floor flats leading in from the sides. Most of the buildings were still dingy grey, but aspired towards their turn of the pastel wash adorning the harling in the southern part of the scheme.

Nigel found Gary in his driveway, kneeling on the concrete flagstones, tightening up the works of his motor-bike. He slumped down beside his friend. Gary grinned up at him. "Cheer up! It might never happen!"

"It already has."

"What has?"

"My old man finally died off last Friday."

Gary dropped his wrench and wiped his hands on a greasy rag. "Christ, I'm sorry to hear that. Was it . . . he'd been ill, hadn't he?"

"Och, off and on for years. Guess you could say it was expected." Nigel turned his back on Gary.

"Jeez. Look, is there anything I can do to help you?"

"Naw, it's okay. Just a bit of a downer. I'll be a'right."

"When's the funeral?"

"Day after the morra. It's a cremation."

The garden gate creaked as two youths in black leathers and white crash helmets blundered up the path. One jerked his head towards the house door.

"Hi Gary. Yer old dear in?"

"Naw, she's went to some Church do."

"Magic." The lad raised a clanking carrier bag. "Fancy a wee one?"

Gary glanced towards Nigel. "What's the occasion?"

"His birthday." The one with the bag jabbed a thumb at the one without.

"Eh?" emanated from the declared birthday boy.

"Ah, ye clown, ye!" The boy with the bag scudded his pal affably on the back of his head. "If it's no his birthday it ought to be. Must be somebody's birthday, for fuck's sake."

"It's my Dad's death day," Nigel spoke for the first time, "practically."

The two newcomers stared at him for a moment, slightly agape. "Who's yer mate, Gary?"

"Nigel. Nigel, the one with the carryout is Alasdair. Big Al. The wee guy is Jimmy."

"Nigel." Big Al rolled the name around, savoured the bouquet. "Bit o' a poofy name thon, eh?"

"Not as pretentious as Big Al," Nigel defended his nomenclature, "and not as nothing as Jimmy. That's no a name at all. You might as well be called Mac or Mister."

There was a moment's silence, and then Big Al burst into raucous laughter. "Mac or Mister! I like it! And wi his kinna surname! How'd ye like to be plain Mac Donald? Like ye had only wan name, like Christian, or Lulu, or. . . "

"Aye, aye, helluva funny!" grumbled Jimmy Donald good-naturedly.

"Or if ye were a lassie, ye could be hen! Hen Donald! Heh, howzat fur a variation on Donald Duck, eh?" He pushed Jimmy playfully into the privet.

"Look, Al, I think we've about drained this joke now," advised Gary. He looked uncomfortably towards Nigel. "Totally wrung out it is."

Big Al stopped laughing. "Yer auld geezer really kick the bucket?"

"Good and hard."

"Aye. Well." Big Al looked down, and then up again. "Well, then you've the best reason o' any o' us to get guttered. Come oan an we'll gie yer auld feyther the best wake he's ever had." He put a kindly arm around Nigel's shoulder and guided him into the house.

Considerably later, Jimmy drained the last drop from the last can and rose unsteadily to his feet.

"Wait," muttered Gary, "I'll gather up the empties and put them out." He went right out the house, to leave all evidence in the skip at the corner of the street. When he returned, Big Al stretched and burped noisily.

"Ah, well, now for a wee spin to clear the auld heid. How about it, wee guys? Stockiemuir Road?"

"Aye. The Stockiemuir Road. The very thing. You fancy, Nigel? I'll gie ye a len o' my girl-friend's helmet."

Nigel looked doubtful. "Uch, I think I'll just be getting along back."

"What? What's wrong?" asked Gary.

"He's feart," declared Big Al.

"It's okay, Nigel. Really. Look, Alasdair and me – we've only had – whit – three cans between the two of us. I knew I'd be biking, so I didnae take a lot."

"Aye, it's you and wee Mister Mac here that done all the heavy bevvyin. Jist because you two feel pissed disnae mean Gary'n me dae."

"It's not that I feel pissed. It's not that at all. I feel okay."

"Well, whit we waiting for, then? Let's go!" Big Al rose, scrunched the plastic bag into a ball and kicked it playfully into the air. Gary caught it and crammed it deep into the wastepaper basket.

"No, really. I'm not in the mood the day, with one thing

and another."

"Let me handle this." Big Al again put a kindly arm around Nigel's shoulders. "Have you ever ridden pillion before?"

"No..."

"Listen to me. It's fantastic. It's just... the ultimate dream."

"Like Ursula Andress," quipped Jimmy.

"Shurrup, bubble-brain. As I say, it's utterly out of this world. You see your whole life pass before..."

"That," quipped the bubble-brain, "is what he's feart fae."

"Tell me, have you always been feart fae bikes?"

"It's not that I'm scared. Not exactly."

"Well, then, what is it, exactly?"

"Uch, don't force him," said Gary. "If he disnae want to come he disnae want to come."

"Naw, naw. Let the boay speak. He's said what it's no. Let's hear what it is."

Three pairs of ears listened expectantly.

"Well, you see, I've got this sister. She's a bit... weird. A bit..."

"Slate slidin?"

"Not... well, she's usually right, that's the thing."

"How d'ye mean?"

"Not that I see her very often. Pretty seldom, in fact. But she's always warned me off motor-bikes."

"And d'ye always dae what your sister tells ye?"

"Course not. But... well, she's always said that something awful's gonnae happen to me on a motor-bike."

"And just because she's feart fae bikes, you've to stay aff them?"

"No, you don't understand. It's not bikes in general." There was no help for it. "See, she seems to have this power."

"Oh aye."

"She can . . . well, she can sort of . . . see into the future."
It was out.

Big Al and Jimmy looked at each other, and at Gary.
Jimmy pursed his lips and softly began to whistle the theme-tune from the TV programme *Jackanory*.

"I know it sounds impossible. But the thing is, she's usually right. And she told me to steer clear of motor-bikes."

"Thought you said ye never saw her very much."

"Only occasionally."

"Then she cannae a made all that many predictions."

"She predicted I'd be a boy."

"What!"

"Before my mother had me."

"50% chance."

"She predicted my father would crash his car on the way to see my mother and me at the hospital."

"You told me your father used to take a drink," said Gary.

"So he did. But. . . "

"So she watched him celebrating the birth of his wee man and then tottering in behind the wheel. Wouldnae take the Brahan Seer to work that one out."

"The who?"

"Never mind," said Big Al. "Look, this is all stuff you must have got from your folks. Has she ever made any predictions to you, personally?"

Nigel considered. "Well, most of her prophecies huvnae come to pass, yet. . . "

"You see?"

"Wait. She did predict the first man on the moon."

"Well, everybody knew the Yanks were gonnae send somebody up there. They were spendin dollars on it like it was goin out o' fashion."

"But she foretold the name and the date."

"And was she right?"

Nigel furrowed his brow. "I was wee at the time . . . she certainly got the year right. I'm pretty sure she got that bit right."

"Nigel. Nigel." Big Al shook his head. "Why don't you put all this fortune-teller stuff out o' yer heid. I'm surprised at you, believing all this garbage. You come an have a wee spin wi us. Nothing like the Stockiemuir Road for making you feel at peace wi yerself!"

"Come on," urged Gary. "You need cheering up, don't you?"

"Sure do." Nigel thought back to the morning.

> *I do not set my life at a pin's fee.*
> *As for my soul, what can it do to that,*
> *being a thing immortal as itself?*

Was it set my life, or put my life?

"How about it, then?" wheedled Big Al. "We'll no go fast, we promise."

"Okay, you win. Lead the way."

Almost immediately, Nigel's anxiety was quenched in the exhilaration of the wind, the noise, the speed! Vroom! Vroom! Leaving the houses behind, they zoomed along a woody lane and veered right as they emerged. They surrendered to the freedom of the country road, yelling in joy as it wound round hills and hairpin bends, howling in laughter as it bucked over mounds, leaving their stomachs behind. On either side lay heathered hills, brackened braes. It was the season between the gorse and the broom, and patches of yellow died or were born before their eyes. For long stretches the road was empty, and the occasional approach of a car elicited growls of excitement as they had to swerve left off the crest of the road. To the right against the horizon rose the Campsies, a long brow of hill with Dumgoyne a beehive at the top end.

At the wayside inn they stopped for pints of heavy. Unusually for Scotland, there were tables out in the yard, several of them occupied by other bikers. Nigel breathed in the good air, sipped his beer, studied a couple of horses in the field across the way, thought about his father. As a young man before the War, Roddy had come this way regularly on a Saturday. With other members of his cycling club he would cycle to Loch Lomond, climb Ben Lomond, stay the night at Rowardennan Youth Hostel and be home in time for Church. Probably the road was the same now as then, apart from the replacement of the bicycles by cars and motor-bikes, and the erection of a few weekend huts in the field to the right.

On again, a mile or two up the road to the Queen's View car park. The gang left the two motor bikes behind and raced each other up the hill. As with all such hills, over the brow of the most obvious winning post there always loomed another.

"First to spot Loch Lomond gets to miss his round on the way back!" yelled Gary, in the lead.

On the way down they gambolled over rocks, uneven ground, high tufts of grass. Big Al kept his footing all the way to the bottom, only to slide on the wet planks and land up in the bog. "Aw, ya swine ye!" he hopped about shaking the lumps of glaur off his legs while the others doubled up with glee. Back on the road, they were more subdued. Big Al suggested a race, but Gary declined in view of the drink they had taken. Soon Big Al and Jimmy were well in the lead, with no chance for the others to pass them. They disappeared round a blind corner, a big bluff of rock forcing the road into yet another elbow. A cry floated back on the wind. Was it a warning? Then the others rounded the bend. Gary's last words on this earth were, "It's a fucking caravan!" He swung out wildly to avoid it. The bike hit the wall of rock, rose up in the air and bounced back against the corner of the caravan which sheered across them with a sickening scrape. Both parted company with the bike and Nigel with a lot more. As he flew through the air Nigel's last thought was that he must relax.

He landed, and pain and darkness came. Agonising pain, much worse than he had ever experienced. He tried to open his eyes to get rid of the darkness and realised that they were open. His cheek seemed to be resting on broken glass, possibly from the caravan. The pain, the pain!

Then a speck of light appeared in the distance. It seemed at the end of a brown whirling tunnel. He walked, and yet did not walk, towards the light, which grew brighter and brighter until he squeezed out into it.

The pain vanished. He was looking down on the scene from some unspecified vantage point, no longer part of it. There was his body, lying broken and covered in blood. "Well, thank God I'm out of that lot," he thought. He searched for Gary and spied him with his neck askew and the battered crash helmet at some distance. The people from the car and caravan were stooping over him. "He's dead," said the woman.

"There was a pillion passenger," cried the man, looking around. "I'm sure there were two of them."

"Over this way, Mister," Nigel willed him. "Over here in the ditch."

An approaching roar signalled the return of Big Al and Jimmy. They bounded off their bike leaving it on its side in the heather and rushed over to the scene of the accident.

"Gary's copped it," announced Jimmy. "Oh, my God, whit we gonnae dae?"

"Where's Nigel?" asked Big Al.

"I knew there was another person!" moaned the man.

"Calm down," soothed the woman. "It wasn't your fault."

"Look for him! He must be about!"

They found him at last. "He's deid an aw," stated Big Al. "Christ on a bike, would ye look at his leg."

The irony of his choice of expletive was lost on all present except Nigel who smiled broadly.

"Don't want to look at it," Jimmy turned his head away. "Whit should we dae?"

The news that he was dead came as a surprise to Nigel. He had assumed that, as he was conscious, he must be alive. He looked around on his own level for clues to the conundrum.

To his left, before where the Campsies ought to be, there was a pleasant meadow, yellow with buttercups. He suddenly realised that he was moving across this meadow. The trees were fresh, green and alive with birdsong, and there was a sheen to the very air. At the far end a burn in spate gurgled down the slight slope, almost skimming the bottom of a little rustic bridge. Across the bridge was a figure, silhouetted by the sun behind. As he came closer Nigel recognised his father.

"Dad!"

Roddy smiled in recognition, but made no active move to beckon his son. However, as Nigel neared him, he looked down at the burn and then up again, just enough to draw Nigel's attention to its significance.

Should he cross the bridge? Did he still have a choice?

He was in no hurry to return to that painful, mangled body. He had not himself examined the thing, but Al's reference to the leg certainly discouraged him from reclaiming it.

Who would mourn him? He supposed it would be a major blow only to his mother. The others would get over it in time, some in a very short time indeed. Could he do this to Dorothy? It would be easier to do it to her than to a softer, less abrasive kind of mother, the sort who was kind to everyone and who did not see warmth as weakness, encouragement as flattery.

On the other hand, he was not yet eighteen, and his prime was yet to come. It would be a bit pointless for him to be put together just for the bit of childhood and disgruntled puberty he'd had so far. Anyway, if there was a life after death, as now seemed clear, maybe the rest was true too, the all-seeing God, the lot. If so, Nigel had nothing much to trot out on the day of reckoning. He had never had a job, never done any good works, never had any children, never even had sex. He had never done anything with his chance at all. And it was, after all, an opportunity in countless trillions, an opportunity denied to all the eggs and spermatazoa that failed to meet up, not to mention all the ones which never even got to form because their would-be parents died too young. And what about those poor souls who had to play out their only chance at life as lice, or even germs? He had had a conversation with Ailie on this very subject last spring. She was the only one who would talk to him about such things – all the others dismissed it as adolescent introspection.

Ailie! She had warned him about this very accident. She had said he would be seriously, even permanently maimed. She had not, however, said that he would die. He must, therefore, be designed to live.

He looked again at Roddy for guidance. Would Roddy be terribly disappointed if he turned back? He smiled at Roddy, and waved. Roddy waved back, a friendly wave, the sort of wave you give a friend who passes you in a car, without necessarily expecting the friend to pull up and offer you a lift. Nigel turned around, and began walking back across the meadow. He glanced back once. Roddy was still smiling after him. He did not look as if he bore a grudge. They would meet again later.

Nigel gathered speed over the buttercups, and soon was hovering again above the scene of the accident. He looked anxiously up and down the street. No sign of an ambulance. He would prefer to wait until morphine was available before reentering the shell. Then it struck him that they had written him and Gary off. Perhaps no one would call an ambulance until he showed a spark. The end of the tunnel was before him and heavily he squeezed into it.

Whoosh! He was back with his cheek on the glass. This time none of his senses were dulled. He saw the slivers glinting towards his eyelashes, felt his arm jammed the wrong way round underneath him, all in pitiless reality. The pain surged up through him, impossible to control, too much to bear. He groaned.

"Hey! This one's alive after all!" At once he was surrounded by faces. Someone tenderly brushed the glass away from his face. Someone else gently eased out his arm, until a fresh pain made him yell out again. No one dared move him too much. Then he heard the welcome sound of a siren. Big Al had fetched the ambulance after all.

"Look, Frankie, it wasn't your fault." His mother stroked his head at the bit she thought of as his tonsure, where an unusual birthmark stood out in relief on the skin. She had watched the progress of this birthmark from the earliest time when it was covered with down and friends remarked on it, through the years when it was covered in thick red hair so that only Frankie or herself or anyone who washed or tended his thatch was aware of it. Now it was on display to the world again.

"I told you, Mother, that's not the point. A boy is dead, and I'm the cause of it!"

"Nonsense! He was the cause of it himself. That other pair that were with him, his pals, you could smell the breath a mile off."

"They certainly came across as sober. I mean, they weren't falling about."

"There's a world of difference between being able to keep your feet and being able to steer a motor-vehicle. That's what the breathalyser's for. You don't suppose most folk that fail the breathalyser are too drunk to walk?"

"I don't know what I suppose."

"Drink up your tea, Frankie. It'll do you good."

As Frankie drained the cup she went on. "For sure I don't see what else you could have done. The speed they came round that blind corner. . . "

"Mother, what's in this tea?" Frankie had come to the end and was peering into the dregs.

"Only a couple of codeine to settle your nerves."

"I am 28 years old, Mother. If I think I need codeine I'll take codeine."

"Your nerves are so bad tonight! I just thought. . . "

"Of course they're bad! Today was the death of my innocence."

"Don't let the insurance companies hear you saying that. Or the police. You drove as well as you always do."

"Bugger the insurance companies! I've never done harm to anybody before. Now, because I exist, a young man is dead and the other . . . " He stopped for a moment and went on more heavily. "Because I exist. If I had never been born, if you had never had me, these lads would still be all right. That's the difference I've made to their lives and to the lives of their families. That's what I'll mean to their families from now on. That's the burden I have to carry for the rest of my days."

"Frankie, Frankie," his mother shook her head wistfully. "You would have made a great priest. What a shame. . . "

Frankie rose and made for the telephone. "I'll see if there's any more news."

"Don't think about it just now," said Big Al. "You concentrate on getting better."

"But I have to think about it! It's the most important thing that's ever happened to me!"

"Did you tell your Maw about it?"

"Och yes." Nigel wriggled about restlessly. "I told her the morning after it happened. She didn't listen much, but I guess I wasn't all that coherent. I told her that evening again, but she was only interested in the medical facts. The third day was my Dad's funeral and she only saw me for a short time and *he* was there, so I didnae mention it. Then yesterday I told her in more detail. First she said, like you did, it was my imagination, a dream. Then she told me these things have happened to people in the past. She said mystics even have a word for them – OBEs. Short for Out of the Body Experiences. She said she didnae think it was anything to do with Life after Death – more likely some function of the brain that we haven't found out about yet."

"Well, I don't see how that kin be," said Big Al. "I mean how could yer brain get right outside yer body, like? I mean to say, it's impossible, intit?"

"So what's *your* explanation?"

Alistair shrugged. "Like I said, a dream."

"Look," snapped Nigel, "I'll prove it to you. Yon bloke out the caravan, I only saw him from below, right?"

Big Al considered. "Right."

"Well, he had red hair. Right?"

"Right. But you could have seen that from the ground."

"Hold on, hold on! I'm not finished! Now, on the very crown of his head he had a round baldy bit. And right in the middle was a big black mole."

"A mole?"

"A mole. I remember it well. When I first looked down on him it gave me a fright. It looked like a big single eye staring back up at me. A big beady eye with orange lashes. Now, am I right or am I wrong?"

Big Al considered. "I don't honestly know."

"But you saw him!"

"I wisnae looking at the tap o' his heid! I wis lookin at you, to see if you were alive or deid!"

Nigel growled in frustration. "That's another thing. You pronounced me dead. So I did die and come back."

"Aw come on!" Big Al shifted uneasily. "How could ah pronounce you dead or alive? Ah'm no a doctor! Aw ah wis gaun by wis, your eyes wis a wee bit open, and ye didnae seem tae be breathin. Ah didnae feel for a heartbeat or nothin. Ah doubt if I widda felt one ablow your jaiket." He rose. "I'll be getting along now, for ah think that's time about up. You see an get better fast, and before you know where you are we'll be skiting all over the. . . " He cleared his throat. "Well, anyway, aw the best." He left.

When the nurse came in with the tea-trolley, Nigel told her he wanted to see the minister on his next rounds on Sunday.

"I can't help but blame myself." Ailie gazed sorrowfully at the floor and shook her head.

"I'm sorry, Ailie, I can't be annoyed with all your angst just now. You say you sensed that this accident would happen."

"I didn't sense. I knew."

"And you say you did warn Nigel, several times."

"But not in detail! I just told him he'd be severely, permanently injured."

"Surely that's clear enough."

"But I never spelt it out for him! I didn't say he would . . . I didn't tell him exactly what would happen. Maybe if I had . . . but when he was younger I didn't want to depress him. Then when I did try to reach him. . . "

"So you had an idea when it was likely to happen?"

"I didn't know the date. I just knew it would be shortly after Uncle Roddy died."

"Well, dear, if I were you I wouldn't bring all this up when you see him. He's a bit strange at the moment anyway."

"What way?"

"I just wouldn't start him up again thinking about . . . unnatural occurrences," said Dorothy decisively. "Talk to him about cheerful matters, about when he's coming home, and plans for the future. Really, there are more important things at stake just now than your conscience, dear."

"Of course."

Nigel was sitting up in bed, leaning a book against the cage over the lower half of the bed. He was quite absorbed. Dorothy peered over.

"Nigel! Is that the Bible you're reading?"

Nigel flashed a grin. "Book of Revelations. It's quite astounding. Have you ever read it?"

"I don't know. Probably, once upon a time."

Nigel nodded in Ailie's direction. "You'd find it interesting. It's full of predictions."

Ailie glanced from him to Dorothy and back again at him. "How are you feeling today?"

Nigel shrugged. "The stock answer is as-well-as-can-be-expected. I'm doing a bit better than that, I guess. They're going to try out the peg tomorrow."

"You shouldn't call it that," Dorothy remonstrated. "Nowadays they're very sophisticated with these things. I was talking to the prosthetist yesterday and she was telling me the advances they'd made in recent years. . . "

Nigel interrupted her. "Ailie, did you used to go to spiritualist meetings?"

Again, Ailie looked at Dorothy and then back at Nigel. "I went to a few at one time. It was when I felt all mixed up about my own situation. . . "

"What happened?"

"Nothing much. At the third one I got a sort of message,

but it didn't make much sense. After that I stopped going."

"What message?"

"The medium said it was an elderly man. I thought it might be my father. The message was I should open my windows at night to let the fresh air in."

"Open your windows?" exclaimed Dorothy.

". . . and let the fresh air in. Or words to that effect. Might have been, not let it get too stuffy. Anyway. . . "

"Whatever it was, it didn't signify," put in Dorothy. "And that's what I've always heard myself about such nonsense. If these folk were really in touch with the dead, surely to goodness the dead would tell us something useful. Maybe what it's like over the other side. But, no! If anyone tries to pin them down on that they seek refuge in platitudes such as, Beautiful or Very Happy. Otherwise it's advice about remembering to keep taking the medicine, or to keep studying hard at school."

"And yet," mused Nigel, "sometimes they come up with something they couldn't have just guessed about you."

"Very seldom."

"But occasionally."

"Well, who knows," Dorothy shrugged. "I've always been a believer in the uncharted regions of the brain. Ailie's a prime example. Hypnotism's another. Now, if there's such a thing as telepathy, as there may well be. . . "

"Ailie," he grasped her hand. "Tell me about the ghosts you've seen."

"Well," again the apologetic glance at Dorothy, "I don't know that they were . . . are ghosts. I call them the Faces."

"What else could they be?"

"They hardly ever speak. That's why I wonder if they might just be Time-lapses . . . symptoms of my other condition. For example, one of the Faces, one I saw regularly as a child . . . I later met in real life."

"Oh?" asked Dorothy sharply. "Who was that?"

"Her name was Catriona MacKinnon. Just an ordinary woman. But I saw her by night, in childhood. Yet she obviously wasn't dead then, because I later met her."

"When did you meet her?"

"Much later."

"How much later?"

Ailie wriggled uneasily, looked her mother up and down. "I got to know her in 2008."

"We're getting off the point here," fretted Nigel." What I really wanted to ask you about, Ailie, was out-of-the-body-experiences."

"I've heard of them," said Ailie. "I've never had one, and so. . . "

"So she can't help you. As I say, all these things, if they're not dreams. . . "

"It wasn't a dream!" cried Nigel. "How often do I have to spell it out? I saw things from above I couldn't possibly have seen from the ground. I saw. . . "

"If they're not dreams," his mother overrode him, "then they're yet another manifestation of the powers of the unknown part of the mind. Now, can we get off this subject? We have to discuss your future, Nigel. I don't think you should attempt to return to school this session. You could maybe do a bit of private study over the holidays, and then go back for a sixth year and sit your Highers then."

"I'm never going back to school, Mum."

"Not this session, of course. But next session we would hope to have you fit and well again. . . "

"Not this session, not next session. Never."

"But what about University?"

"I'm not going to University, Mum. As soon as I'm fit to hirple about, I'm going to apply for Bible College."

"You're going to *what*. . . ?"

"Bible College. I reckon God must have had good reason

for letting me come back to the world, back there. He must have meant me to make good use of the rest of my life. That's why. . . "

"But what is this Bible College? One of these funny American places?"

"Not so far away. It's just at the corner of Byres Road and Great Western Road."

"And what sort of diplomas do they give out? Would they be recognised?"

"Recognised by whom? Other people? I don't know and I care less. But I'd get there the training I need."

"Need for what?"

"To give my life in the service of God."

"Och for heaven's sake! Don't be so melodramatic. What does any God possibly want that you could give him?"

"Myself."

"That's a cliché! If any God wants you then he can have you for the taking! Anyway, why do people always think they're so important? If there's a God then to him the Earth can only be a speck of dust. And take that look off your face!"

"He's looking at you as if you were the Devil sent to test him!" observed Ailie.

"Nigel, dear, I don't want to argue with you. Not when you're hurt."

"That's all right," grinned Nigel. "I can take it."

"If you really want a career in the Church, then I suppose you could train as a minister. . . "

"No." Nigel shook his head. "Takes too long. The minister here told me. You have to do your Highers, then a degree, and then a post-graduate degree." He flopped back on his pillow, looking suddenly tired. "Anyway, a career is the last thing I want. I want to get out there and make myself useful to the Lord."

"I can't believe it's my son saying this! Where's your sense?"

Ailie said, "You're arguing in different fields. There's no point in bringing reason into play against blind faith."

"To think a son of mine would choose wishful thinking over logic. Nigel, you're the very opposite to your brother Sandy."

Nigel closed his eyes and turned his face to the wall.

On the following Monday Ailie, with Dorothy, went up to Roddy's bedsit to clear out his stuff. The room looked even smaller and dingier than it had last time. One double bed, sagging in the middle; one 1930s vintage wooden wardrobe with an inclination to tip forward and kill you whenever you opened the door; one basket chair, peeling brown paint, with an old blanket folded in place of a cushion; a heavy chest of drawers; one ancient imitation leather bed-settee. All these the landlord would lay claim to. The relics of Roddy's 23,204 days spent on Earth were even more insignificant. A few excessively shabby suits, one good suit, some old grey shirts and underwear. Dorothy picked out the good grey suit. She sniffed it. "Mothballs!" she proclaimed. "Who uses mothballs nowadays?"

"I don't recall Roddy ever wearing that suit," said Ailie.

"He wore it to our wedding," sniffed Dorothy. She laid it on the settee. "That can go to Oxfam. The brown shoes and blue trousers can go to Paddy's Market. All the rest is fit only for the bin."

"What about the books?"

Roddy had a bookshelf groaning with books, and an overspill area of two square metres where they were piled in two foot stacks.

"If there's any you want, dear, just take them. The rest," Dorothy shrugged, "Oxfam again."

"Shouldn't Nigel look through everything in case he wants

souvenirs of his Dad?"

"What, clutter up his room even more? I don't think boys of Nigel's age are prone to that kind of sentimentality."

"You didn't think they were prone to religion until now," Ailie pointed out. Suddenly she cried, "Look at this!"

Amongst the old literature textbooks was a dusty little hardback entitled *The Celtic Knot – A novel by Roderick M Macleod*. The publication date was 1952.

"Did Roddy write this?"

Dorothy glanced over. "Right enough, he did say he used to try a bit of writing. Not that he ever made much out of it."

"He got a book published!"

"Yes, well, it wasn't a best-seller. Didn't exactly change his way of life."

"Did you ever read it?"

Dorothy shook her head. "You know I don't bother with novels. Anyway, he'd given most of that up by the time we met. Just did an odd poem now and again."

Back home, Steve asked no questions about the sweeping over of Roddy's traces. The boys needed their baths and to be put to bed, and then there was ironing to be done. Altogether it was after midnight before Ailie curled up with Roddy's novel. It was his great-grandmother's tale. Ailie fell asleep at the part where the great-grandmother was showing her niece how to twist heather into ropes. She stirred, poured herself a whisky and lemonade to keep alert by, and next awoke in another era.

# 18

SHE AWOKE to the bars again. Polythene, this time, painted jolly colours, every one different. Scarlet, blue, green, butterfly yellow . . . no, not butterfly yellow . . . butter . . . butter . . . could it just be butter yellow? No, there was another comparison, another . . . what was the word again . . . another . . . likeness . . . another . . .

"She's awake!" remarked a woman in a purple boilersuit with silver stripes. "Are you coming up, Ailie? Ready for breakfast?"

The bars were quickly lowered, and Ailie was helped to put her feet to the ground. She herself wore a fluffy pyjama-suit. The woman helped Ailie through a doorway to a room where six elderly people sat, plumped on top of brightly coloured beanbags. The walls were covered in garish murals, transparencies stuck to the window panes and mobiles dangled from the ceiling. Was it a nursery school?

To her surprise her skinny legs held out and carried her shakily to an orange beanbag with flames printed all over it.

"Is it safe? she asked. "I don't want my backside singed."

The woman laughed more heartily than was warranted. "Now, you're one for the jokes, all right! As long as you can raise a laugh, things can't be too bad, neither they can!"

Ailie was too polite to say she thought the sentiment was rubbish. The woman's accent was . . . not Scottish . . . it was . . . no, not English either . . . it was . . . what was that other place again. . .

The bean-bag moulded itself exactly to her contours, soft, but just firm enough, low, but just high enough.

"Very comfy!" she nodded approvingly.

"So I should hope! It's ergonomically designed by clever people who know every centimetre of your back and bottom . . . better even than you know them yourself!"

For some reason an old rhyme popped into Ailie's head, and she gave the woman the benefit of it.

> *Of beauty I am not a star*
> *There are others more elegant far,*

*But that I don't mind . . . but that I don't mind . . . but . . .* How does it go on again?"

"Sorry, that's a new one on me." The woman went to the table and fetched a tray with porridge, salad and coffee on it. The tray was on legs, and when she pulled out the legs it came to just the right height for Ailie.

"The plate's too heavy!"

"Now, these are electriplates, to keep the porridge and coffee warm!"

Ailie wondered if she should ask what year it was, but she feared to hear. "Are you a nurse?"

"Sure! Don't you remember me? You must remember Bernadette!"

"Och yes!" lied Ailie. "You don't look like a nurse, though."

"Well, we don't dress in uniform now, you know! All the old starchy whites . . . that went out with the Ark! And a good thing too, don't you think!"

"It certainly looks nice!" said Ailie carefully, looking around.

(Must be later than the last gerrymandering . . . geri . . . old folks' ward I was in – much more modern.) "You've still got us in cots, though."

"Ah, yes, well, that's just for those inclined to fall out of bed. You know you don't have to lie in bed if you don't want to. We'd rather see you up and about!"

Ailie munched automatically at her food while Bernadette attended to the other six people in the ward, helping those still in bed to rise, bringing breakfasts, clearing breakfasts away. She noticed that her teeth felt different, as if they were not quite of her, but almost. She tried in vain to shoogle them with her tongue. Clapped fast, they were. If they were dentures, they were certainly well-fitting. Not like poor . . . who was it now? A picture flashed into her mind, an old man, blotchy face and Granny's tartan . . . was it . . . could it have been her father? Yet . . . *Of beauty I am not a star, there are others more elegant far* . . . How did it go on, again?

". . . for today?" Bridie was speaking to her. No, not Bridie, Br . . . Brr . . .

"Pardon? Did you say something?"

"I'm asking you what your plans are for today."

"Plans? What's the choice?"

"The chart's up on the wall where it always is." Brenda pointed. "Have you filled in for tomorrow yet?"

"Filled in for . . . I don't think so . . . Roddy. That's who it was. Uncle Roddy. Poor old man."

"You'd be as well to do it now. It's best to fill in your plans at least a day in advance. For the numbers. All right, have you got everything you need? You're on the Zimmer again, this week, aren't you?" she indicated a walking frame on wheels, "and there's a new batch of books in the ward library there. Right folks, I'm off now! See you later, alligators!"

"In a while, crocodile!" chorused six old voices, and Betsy skipped jauntily out.

Nervously Ailie grasped the walking frame and eased herself up. She had no pain. To her surprise the frame seemed to brake firmly when she leaned her weight on it, but glided smoothly over the carpet when she pointed it in the direction she wanted to go. It took her weight easily, surely, like a . . . maid in a heavenly dream . . . what was that song again? *The graceful white swan goes gliding along, like a maid in a* . . . but that wasn't how it started. How did it go? Surely . . . did she not used to sing it, once upon a time, dressed up like a cowgirl, with . . . who was it now, who used to sing along with her, not David, no, it was . . . it was another boy, now, she had him pictured, fairish hair, fine features, slim build, quite good-looking . . . Sandy! Of course, it was Sandy! How could she forget Sandy? Where was Sandy now? Not in this place, that was for sure.

The chart had seven names down the left-hand side, and various activities marked along the top. Ailie found her name, and discovered that she was down for a discussion group in the forenoon, and choral singing from four to five. A pen hung from the chart, and she marked herself down for the morrow for Drawing Class and Trip into Town. Might as well take everything going.

The Zimmer felt such fun that she spent the next half hour exploring, floating about the room, and then out along the corridor, where, every three metres, there was a recess with four or five people seated watching a screen on the wall. All the screens showed different programmes, and Ailie lost count after ten. One of the most popular recesses boasted a couple of amusement machines and a computer games console. As ever, elderly people gravitated towards the pleasures of their youth. At the far end of the corridor she entered the common room, where old ladies and gentlemen in day clothes sat and read books, played draughts, dominoes, chess and scrabble, wrote letters or diaries, pushed buttons on hand-held machines, calculators perhaps, or video games. There were two tea-and-coffee machines against the wall, and a biscuit dispenser.

Ailie crossed to the French windows. There was a balcony out there, which she noted for future use, being afraid to venture out at her age in night clothes. For the moment she contented herself with drinking in the view, the sunny lawn which swept down to an ornamental pool, overgrown with tiger-lilies and surrounded by willows, with a richly vegetated islet in the middle. As she rested on her Zimmer, dreaming, a family of swans appeared from behind the island, two parents, four grown grey cygnets.

She knew it now.

> *O, give me a home,*
> *where the buffalo roam,*
> *where the deer and the antelope play,*
> *where seldom is heard, a discouraging word,*
> *and the skies are not cloudy all day!*
> *Home, home on the range! . . .*

At this point her trembling, cracked alto was joined by a strong baritone which accompanied her through the refrain.

"Yon's an auld ane!" smiled the spruce-looking old gent at her side. "Lang afore my time!"

"Before my time too!" smiled Ailie. "I used to . . . I learnt it from my mother."

"Ma granny, God rest her soul, hud a record o' it. She'd a grand collection o' discs, ma Granny. Aul' 78s, 'ee ken. John McCormick. Harry Lauder. Funny anes too, ken. *Spaniard that blighted my life.*"

"Do you know how this goes on? *Of beauty I am not a star, there are others more elegant far. . .* "

" *. . . But that I don't mind, for my face I'm behind; it's the* *people in front get the jar!*" the fellow finished it for her. "You shouldnae be chantin that kinna limerick, fine-lookin dame like you!"

"Och, come on!" Ailie found herself simpering. "I must be about a hundred years old!" She hesitated. "I'm so ancient, I don't even know what age I am!"

"We're nane o' us chickens in here. Do you know, I'm of an age to mind the auld money! No the stuff we hud afore this Ecu dirt. The real auld money. Pre-decimal. Ah hud a paper-run, ken, up in Findochty, and I got my wages in the pounds shillings and pence."

"I was at the stage of getting housekeeping money when they decimalised," revealed Ailie. "So I think I've the edge on you there. Not that I remember a thing about it."

"Well, ye don't look it at a'. Ye don't look a day ower . . . seventy. Here, let me introduce masel. Iain. Big Iain Cowie."

A boy-friend, already! Ailie chuckled in glee.

In another hospital, across the city and miles of country, David awoke. A young girl, in jeans and T-shirt emblazoned with FREE HEALTH CARE – A BASIC HUMAN RIGHT asked him how he felt after his operation.

"A bit disoriented," said David carefully. "What has been done?"

"It's all gone now. Don't worry any more about it."

". . . What's all gone?"

The nurse looked anxious. "You can't remember?"

"Don't worry about it. This happens all the time. Just tell me what disease I have, or had."

"But it shouldn't happen any more. I'll get the neurologist to have a special look at you when she comes on her rounds."

"I don't want a special look. I tell you there's nothing out of the ordinary wrong with my memory."

"If you can't recall what you're in here for, that's out of the ordinary, and should be investigated."

David lost patience. "Who are you? You're not old enough to be a nurse."

"I'm a Nursing Assistant."

"A what?"

"I'm on Junior Job Training."

"Well, go and fetch a real nurse. Somebody who knows the background to my case."

The bloke who approached wore a dark brown poloneck jumper, above which his face shone with that wholesome luminosity often seen in nuns, and occasionally in female nurses. He reached over and shook David's hand vigorously. "Hi. I'm Chris Waterford, Nurse Officer. Loss of memory? Nothing to worry about. Just a tiny touch of post-operative shock."

"I tell you all, I'm not worried. I just want somebody to tell me what's wrong with me."

"You were in to get the bulge on your head removed. Purely cosmetic. Once your hair grows in again it'll cover the tiny scar. Geraldine, go and bring David two mirrors."

"What caused the bulge?"

"Your brain tumour."

David drank this in in silence.

"Ah, good girl, Geraldine. Here, you see, at the nape of your neck? Hardly anything to be seen."

"Was it malignant?"

"We don't use these terms nowadays, David. We did tell you all about it at the time. But a wee jag soon puts paid to that nasty group of rampant cells, eh?"

"How soon will I know if I'm clear?"

"David, you were told, after we injected you last March, that that was the end of the matter."

"What about secondary cancers?"

"That was what the course of tablets was for. We don't reckon with secondary cancers nowadays. In fact, it's a long time since I heard the term." Chris frowned. "Maybe the neurologist should take a look at you. . . "

"Never mind all that. What date is it?"

"First of May."

"What year?"

The Nurse Officer shook his head slightly. "What do you recall. David? Do you still know your full name?"

"David Joseph Carmichael. We're wasting time."

"Your wife's name?" Chris was checking the records as he spoke.

"Karen. What I want to do is get in touch with my mother. Can any of you tell me where she is?"

"What is your address?"

"42 Gilshoch Street."

Chris exchanged a look with Geraldine. "Does 18 Waverley Gardens mean anything to you?"

"Och yes, of course. That's it. I'd forgotten I'd flitted." (18 Waverley Gardens, 18 Waverley Gardens, 18 Waverley Gardens, 18 Waverley. . . )

"Who is the present Prime Minister of Scotland?"

David considered. His own hands were gnarled with age. Ewan McEvoy would certainly be retired by now, if not dead. He tried to think of the up-and-coming politicians of the old days. He stabbed in the dark. "Jenny Johnston?"

Three times a week, the option was available of a stroll around the Park. Although the grounds were small, they were intensively gardened, with strange miniature caverns and rock-pools hidden amongst the bushes. For the benefit of the elderly patients these had been fitted with ramps and bridges broad and gentle enough to accommodate any Zimmer or wheelchair.

"It's very well laid out," remarked Ailie. Her magic Zimmer could adjust itself to any slope and to most ground irregularities. Iain did not use a Zimmer at all.

"It's been like this a long time," Iain told her. "Used to be a private hospital, ken. But with the Edinburgh Government runnin down private medicine, they made it into a Palace of the Third Age."

"Palace of the Third Age! Is that the eu . . . the eu . . . the phrase they use now?"

"Well, is it no like a wee palace? They're affa nice, the queans in there. Affa good tae us. They tak a lot o' bother. Us senior citizens, we're the Kings o' the world, ev noo."

A nurse came tripping down the path. "Mrs Lorimer? Time for your injection!"

"Great!" enthused Iain. "You'll have that walking frame thrown away by tea-time!"

Ailie went obediently with the nurse. When they were out of earshot of Iain she asked quietly, "What injection am I having?"

"The bone jag, of course!"

"What does it do?"

The nurse was used to senile dementia. "You get it every month, Mrs Lorimer. I'm sure you'll remember once you find you can walk without the frame."

"Why did I need the frame before?"

"Your April one had worn off. The effects only last three weeks, unfortunately. The last week it's back to the Zimmer!"

"So why don't I get the jag every three weeks, then?"

"My, you're full of questions today! It has been explained to you before, there are side effects if the drug hasn't completely cleared out of your system by the time you get the next dose. So, to be sure. . . "

One day, when she had forgotten to book any activities the

night before and was at a loose end, Ailie decided to put the liberal philosophy of the place to the test. Was there anywhere she was not allowed to go?

She took the lift to the top floor and started at the little gallery of pictures produced by the art class, all displayed for best effect under the glass of the roof conservatory. She visited all six common rooms, the billiards room, the darts room, the computer room, the tiny theatre-cum-cinema. She peered in the glass doors of the handicraft room, the four different classrooms with the activities of the day. She looked in at the sequence dancing in the hall, and knew a moment's longing – but her time would come again. She slid her way into the empty dining hall, plucked up her courage, and pushed on behind the serving-hatch into the kitchen. No one challenged her.

Here, all was clean and sparkling – smooth plastic surfaces, germ-free machinery. There were only two cooks, apparently. A young man took a raw frozen turkey out of a plastic crate, held it momentarily to a crackling machine, then pushed it into the doorway of a second machine. This whirred for a moment, spat out bones and gristle into a waste dispenser on the floor, and passed neatly sliced turkey steaks into a giant micro-wave oven.

Meantime a middle-aged woman mixed up a sauce, a little of this, that, and the next thing, holding each ingredient in turn against the crackling machine before adding it to the mixture. She flashed a beam at Ailie as she poured the lot into a funnel on the microwave, there to join the turkey steaks. Ailie smiled back, reassured that no one was going to throw her out.

"What a lot of modern ... modern ... mod cons they have now!" she grinned. "What's that, now?" She pointed at the masticating machine.

"Electronic carver," the youth replied.

"And that?" (Why did she suddenly feel like Red Riding Hood?)

"Geiger counter."

The older woman approached Ailie. "Do you mind returning to the patients' quarters? We can get on with it all easier if we're on our own."

"That's all right." Ailie let herself be shepherded onto the lift. Back in her room she watched television until dinnertime.

In the dining-room, faced with her plate, she realised what she had seen.

"Did you know," she whispered to Iain, "they go over all our food with a. . . "

(What was the word now? It's slipped my mind. And it was a word I used to know, even in the old days. What was the thing for, again?) ". . . with one of these . . . thingmys . . . machines . . . for . . . for telling if . . . "

"Iain," Jenny Mackintosh leaned over interrupting, "we were wondering if you'd be doing a number for the Independence Day concert."

"What's this?" asked Ailie.

Iain beamed at her. "We always put on a wee show for the Independence Day holiday."

"Scottish Independence Day?"

"Aye. Last time we were very ambitious, were we no?"

"We put on *Carousel*," boasted Jenny.

"And very successful it was an a, if ye suspended yer disbelief tae include coortin pairs 'at wadnae see eighty again, an a hardman chibbin fowk wi a blade at seventy-nine!"

"We made Gracie the daughter, since she's younger than the rest o' us."

"Aye. Seventy-three. Onywey, this year it's a plain concert. I'll be daein a wee turn as usual. Whit aboot you?"

"I don't know. I'll think about it." Ailie scooped a forkful of turkey into her mouth and thought about it for the rest of the evening.

Next day, however, a new worry put thoughts of the concert right out of her head.

"Have ye cast eyes on the new manager?" Iain asked her, when he found her alone in the common-room. "A grimmer lookin chiel I never saw." He turned towards the door. "Speak o' the Devil!"

Into middle age, now, but unmistakeable. Icy eyes, mouthful of cruel teeth. His rusty hair had tinges of steel, oxidisation in reverse. In his juvenility his mouth had often opened to let out mocking laughter. Now it was settled, shut, as it seemed to Ailie, into a sardonic sneer.

"I know him!" Ailie gripped Iain's arm in agitation. "His name's Eric Faulkner. He was a member of staff in the last place I was in . . . that awful place!"

"Wis he now?" Iain looked Eric up and down appraisingly.

"I want out!" Ailie stared around in wild panic. "I'm not staying here if he's in charge!"

"Haud yer horses, noo! Steady on!" Iain put his arms around her to calm her down. "We've got a new regime up top, 'ee ken. They're no permitted tae treat senior citizens like auld daen carthorses ony mair."

"But still, but still," Ailie trembled, "you don't know that one. He'll get round the rules somehow. He'll find a way to make our lives torment!"

"Hey," Eric called sternly across the room. "What's going on there?"

Iain opened his eyes wide. "Nane o' your concern!"

Eric's eyes lit on Ailie. He stared for a long moment, then smiled. "Ailie! Fancy that. It's true what they say about bad pennies!"

Tremulously, Ailie tried to respond, "Which one of us is . . . "

Eric overrode her. He moved towards her, as she shrank

back. "Come with me, Ailie. I'll take you back to your bed."

"Would you credit it!" exploded Iain. "This young loon is trying to guard yer morals for ye!" He laughed loudly. "Teachin his granny tae suck eggs!"

"Come on, now. I'm in charge here. That lady with you is incapable of fully comprehending. . . "

"That lady," roared Iain, "is over eighteen, as mature as she'll ever be, twice as mature as you." He turned to Ailie and asked "May I?"

Ailie, not knowing what he meant, said nothing. Iain bent over and kissed her lips. Ailie, thinking briefly of Don John, felt her body respond.

Iain turned back to Eric. "If ever it's you I want to kiss, then I'll ask your permission."

Eric flushed angrily. "I have a responsibility. . . "

"We're aw responsible here, ee ken!" Iain grinned. He pointed to his arm. "Aids vaccinations richt up to date. How about yours?"

"Filthy-mouthed old twig!" snarled Eric.

Iain shrugged. He turned to Ailie. "What do you expect of the Thatcher generation? Prudes, ane an aw!"

Eric pointed a finger. "There's going to be trouble between us. You watch it!" He wheeled and left.

"See? That's how to treat thon kind!" Iain grinned at Ailie in triumph.

"I don't know!" Shakily Ailie made for an armchair, to brood over the kiss, her new feelings, and the fact that she could not, would not, stay at Eric's mercy for long.

That night she began collecting pills. She would regret cutting short her relationship with Iain, but then, she could pick it up again later. She asked for pills the first night, and kept them. The second night the nurse in charge looked at her askance. "Tablets again? You don't usually take them."

"I've not been sleeping too well."

"We don't like issuing sleeping pills on a regular basis, Ailie. Not unless you're in real pain. It can be counter-productive."

"I just can't sleep."

"In that case there are other ways we can try. Here, I'll give you them for tonight, but tomorrow you must make an appointment with the doctor."

She handed out the pills and Ailie looked at them. Two little pink capsules, to go with the two she already had.

She decided to wait until the next day, when she could mix them with something from the pub across the road, to strengthen them. Accordingly, next day she put on her coat and, with Iain, strolled down the driveway, across the street and into the hostelry.

The pub was upmarket, claret and old vineyards rather than cointreau and lemonade. The inside walls were rough sandstone (possibly reproduction) and hung here and there with blown-up designs from the *Book of Kells*. The name of the pub was The Illuminated Capital.

"It's a pun on the nickname Edinburgh developed last year when they floodlighted another dozen of their prime facades," explained Iain. "What are ye for?"

While he ordered at the bar Ailie found she could see into the kitchen through an open door. On a table lay the instrument she had met with in the Home kitchen.

When Iain returned, carefully wobbling the drinks on a tray, Ailie asked vaguely, "Is there a nuclear . . . what do you call them . . . nuclear factory near here?"

"There are nae nuclear plants anymore anywhere," Iain informed her. "They were aw daen awa wi after yon big meltdown at . . . aw curse it!"

As he laid down his burden his hand wobbled and his own whisky glass spilled all over the tray. "Haud oan – ah'll get a cloth."

After he had mopped it up he had to return to the bar to order a replacement drink for himself. By the time he settled in again Ailie was ready for a refill.

"My God, woman, you'll have me under the table," he muttered.

Several brandies and whiskies later the pair of them rolled back to base singing *You'll Never Walk Alone* at the top of their voices. They did not run into Eric.

Ailie returned to her room and eyed up the tablets. How strong were they? She certainly had no desire to make her exit from the stage permanent. Perhaps she should have refrained from the fourth brandy. Then, was there any risk, as long as periods of her life remained unlived?

In the event she took only three of the pills, and curled up in her bed.

"*Twenty, thirty, forty, fifty, a hundred years ago,*" she chanted . . . (What next? How does that poem go? We got it in school, primary school, even. Must have been Robert Louis Stevenson, or could it have been Walter de la Mare?)

In the night the Faces returned for the first time in ages. Desperate, cadaverous vultures in a circle around her bed. However, after she had struggled up, vomited on her way to the bathroom (Bernadette came and cleared it up with hardly a moan) and returned to bed the Faces took on a kindlier mien. There was Daddy, old faithful, and the pleasant-looking young lady with slightly slanting eyes.

Some time later a voice disturbed her sleep. A voice, far away, but . . . still here and now, she realised as her feet struck the bars at the end of the bed.

"You've got a visitor, Ailie."

She looked up, over the bars, through the fuzzy lens of myopia and pills. A knight was standing there, shining in his armour, all haloed in the sunlight streaming through the window. He raised his visor in respect for her great age. He himself was not a young man, but he looked kindly, and he lowered her bars and gently delivered her from her cell. Perhaps it was the anaesthetising effect of the drugs, but his armour was soft and yielding against her body as he bore her on strong arms out of the turret. In an anteroom two handmaidens dressed her in her robes and brushed her burnished locks before wafting her out again to meet her chevalier. He smiled the old familiar smile, and although his colouring was unknown she began to place his bone structure, but then he was behind her again on the charger and . . . Wheee! Faster and faster they galloped over the flowered meadows through the corridors by rivers winding past the reception desk over the hills and far away to Camelot.

"I thought I would never find you," explained the saviour. "I've been in hospital myself, and of course, I slipped a few years under the anaesthetic. I'd expected to, and I'd made arrangements but, well, the best-laid plans!"

" . . . *o' mice and men, gang aft awry!*" finished Ailie. (No, not awry . . . what was it? Something similar. . . )

"I came to under the clutches of some enthusiast who mis-diagnosed amnesia, and tried to cure me by his own patent method! Would you believe, he refused to let me see my family for two weeks, while he tried to jog my memory with silly quiz games!"

"Agley!" sang out Ailie.

"What was that?"

"Agley. It was agley." Ailie frowned. "Was it you put me in that place?"

David turned to face her. "I . . . understand that I gave you the choice. I knew I was going in for a week or so, and so there would have been nobody in for the Wednesday or the Friday."

"Just for two days?"

"Well, yes. Nobody works a five day week nowadays. But

these two days are only covered by me . . . the others all happen to be out at work or school then."

"The others?"

David waved his arm vaguely. "Descendants, mainly, and their boyfriends, girlfriends, spouses. . . "

"Watch!"

David whirled to look at the road again and swerved just in time to avoid an oncoming lorry. In a moment or two he recovered his breath.

"I asked you if you wanted to stay. You could have stayed but then, you'd been in the Palace before, when we'd all gone on holiday, and you'd liked it then. I knew the quality of care was good. . . "

"Och, it was not too bad at all."

David said plaintively, "You could get wee cups of tea all day long there. Wee attentions you'd miss if you were on your tod with us."

"It was fine!" Ailie reassured him. "Much better than that terrible place I was in before. . . " She stopped uncertainly. (Was I really in there? How long for? Could it have been a dream?)

"The Golden Years Nursing Home? Oh, well, of course! That was a terrible time you had in there." He sniffed. "You'll be glad to know that just after you left, it was the subject of a TV investigative documentary, and they closed it down."

"How long was I in there?"

"Three and a half years. I wonder it didn't knock you off for good. Crawford should have been jailed for what he did."

"How did it happen? I never found out."

"Crawfie-boy set you up," said David grimly. "He knew you were about to expose his dirty doings with the Special Branch, his involvement with the destabilising campaign and so on. So he got you drunk, let you stay the night, and then arranged it so it looked like you smashed up the place. He even took a knife to his own wife, who backed up his story. He still had pals in the police force and . . . well, he supposed you wouldn't be in a position to deny anything, since you wouldn't even know what you had or hadn't done."

"I will know, though. You just told me."

David laughed. "True. Though it seems you won't – weren't able to make your word stand against his. Friends in high places he's got."

"Funny-farm background I've got."

"No contest. The only chance would be if you avoided the trap in the first place. Don't go, and if you do, watch what you eat and drink."

"It's too late. I've already . . . I got in the trap."

"Then the die is cast."

Ailie rested her head on his shoulder. "I can hardly believe he did all this to his own mother. I knew we didn't have much of a relationship, but. . . "

"He put you in a wee obscure Home in Ayrshire where he knew I wouldn't find you. There's so many of these places now – Ayrshire in particular's full of them. He told the folk in the Home I was dead, so they wouldn't try to track me down, and he told me you'd disappeared on the way back from his home to your own. Plausible enough, in view of all the circumstances."

"How do I get out in the end?"

"Crawford's wife got a conscience about it after they split up. She came to me, all contrite, and blurted it out. God! When I found you you were skin and bone, depressed as hell. "

"Don't tell me any more. I've still got most of it to get through, remember?"

"Well, anyway, I think you'll agree the Palace of the Third Age is a different ball game. Particularly if you're only there on a temporary basis."

"Still, if it's all right by you, I'll just stay at home next time."

Camelot was a large detached mansion, stone-built, set in mature gardens. David helped his mother up the steps and rang the doorbell.

"This is Clan HQ. We've got four floors here. Fifteen apartments. It was relatively cheap because it's the East End . . . and of course we all chipped in."

A young woman opened the door and they crossed a noisy hall, with children shrieking from upstairs. They entered a large room full of people of all ages. David helped her to a chair by the fireside, sweeping away two pre-pubescent boys who had occupied it before. Ailie fumbled in her handbag for her glasses, put them on, and drank in the scene.

A young pair on the threshold of adult status embraced in the novelty of mutual desire, pitying the old dame with, as they thought, it all behind her. A toddler with the lot to go through grinned up at the worshipful ancestor, fat cheeks and ringlets, soft wilting scrags. The two boys sat on the floor, sharing some electronic game with a flat, portable, forty-centimetre screen.

Her head cleared and she was glad, after all, that she had thrown the dose up. She would linger awhile yet, at least until she had savoured the Age of Respect.

She sought out David again. "Come and tell me what's been happening. What about Jojo? Sandy?"

David shook his head. "You're the last of them. That is, I don't know about Jasmine. After she left Sandy she went to visit her relatives in India. We lost track of her there."

"She split up with Sandy?"

"He took it badly. Went into a bit of depression at the time. But that's another story. There is somebody here though, from your generation. He doesn't stay with us but he dropped in to honour your return." He beckoned across the room. An old man, snowy-haired, with a grandpa moustache, caught David's eye, rose and crossed to see them. For a moment Ailie thought it was Iain. Then she thought it was – her eyes flitted to his legs. Wrong again.

"I'm sorry. I don't. . . " What was it people said? "You've got the advancement of me." No, that wasn't quite right. Never mind. He was old too.

"You don't know me! And here we had tea together only a few weeks ago!"

"I wouldn't know about that."

"I'm your wee brother."

"Nigel?" She looked again at his leg. No trace of a limp. For his age, he had been positively lithe in his passage across the room. "Is this a latter-day miracle? Has all that praying paid off after all?"

Nigel laughed. "I reckon it did. Though it got a bit of help from modern science." Creakily he bent forward and eased off his shoe. A nearby youngster jumped forward and peeled off his sock for him. In place of the pale prosthesis was a pink, perfect foot!

"That's astounding!" cried Ailie.

"It's genetic engineering." With the help of the child he undressed his other foot for comparison. Where his left was white, shiny, with two visible corns, a bad bunion and horn-like nails, his right was slim, pink, with straight toes. "That there," he slapped his right knee, "is one youthful foot. That foot isn't of an age to step out of secondary school!"

"Seems impossible!"

"Why? Reptiles do it. Mind you, I was nearly born too soon. I've had to do without it most of my life. I got this wee fellow for my sixty-sixth birthday, but even with speeded-up growth I couldn't walk on him for two years. If by the Grace of God I'm spared for another twelve months I'll have had him as long as the original!" Tenderly he massaged the toes on both feet. "Too bad it can't get its full allotted span, eh? Too bad it'll have to go when I do!"

Ailie leaned back on her cushions and regarded her descendants. To grow up in an era when youth was in vogue and grow old in a household where age won respect – she had had her cake and eaten it.

The shadows grew long. Lamps illuminated, gradually, automatically.

"I think I'd like to have a wee lie-down, now."

A young woman showed her to the stair, sat her in the chairlift. She looked familiar. Slightly slanting eyes, a small mole on her left cheek.

"Who are you?" asked Ailie in wonder. "I've seen you in my dreams. Only, it wasn't dreams. It was. . . "

"I'm Eilidh. Spelt the Gaelic way, not like yours." The young lady smiled. "I'm David's youngest."

She pushed the button. Zoom! went Ailie to the top, where a second magic Zimmer awaited her. Her room had her name on the door. Ailie Lorimer.

A pleasant room, with a big bed (big enough for Iain too, if he came to stay? The thought made her chuckle) and her own armchair, table, and piano. A TV screen was built into the wall. She sank down in the armchair, which moulded itself to her contours.

And is there no one left of my level? No one to identify with? No one to remember with? No one who shared my childhood? No one, apart from Nigel, who recalls my youth? I was the weakly one, the Banshee. Skinny, pale, fits, blanks and all, yet I'm destined to outlive them.

She glided to the window, where Venus alone penetrated the Scottish clouds.

Other planets might have their specialities, electro-magnetic patterns, miracles of light, communication amongst the spheres. Earth has its living soup. The formula that groups and regroups into individuals, nations, races, species, melting again and at once into broth. Some suspected, but she and David knew all was here and now, the soup, the clumps and the soup, without beginning or end, which gave the whole some permanence and at the same time made it not matter a whit.

And as she lay that night in the bed where, after many experiences yet to come, she would breathe her last, she was comforted by the knowledge that there was here and then now. Universes spreading, universes shrinking, stars forming, supernovas dying, spaceships soaring, coracles cruising, microbes splitting, dinosaurs lumbering, blastocysts forming, corpses decomposing, computer buffs calculating, Beaker People pottering, chimney boys climbing, Covenanters praying, legionnaires marching, women spinning, proletariats revolting and aristocrats dining, Druids sacrificing, Indian scouts running, Roddy's drinking, Dorothy's singing, David's proselytising, Steve's womanising, Pandora's politicising, Don John's poeticising, Jojo's wandering, Crawford's girning, Gerard's groping, the Morning Roll's analysing, Tony's pamphleteering, Catriona's cooking, Old Joe's brooding, Sandy's speculating, Jasmine's meditating, Nigel's out-of-the-body experience and her own dancing, dreaming, learning, prophesying, hirpling and toddling, it had all happened, was all happening and would all happen in converging globes of Time. Before, in and after the soup, she would see her friends again.

For a full list of
Argyll Publishing titles,
send S.A.E. to

Argyll Publishing
Glendaruel
Argyll
Scotland
PA23 3AE